## Praise for Jackie Ashenden

"With a distinct voice and fresh, complex characters, *Mine To Take* is a sexy, emotional read that gripped me from page one. I can't wait to see what Ashenden brings us next."
—Laurelin Paige, *New York Times* bestselling author

"A scintillating, heart-pounding love story. A dark, sinfully sexy hero with a tortured past. I loved it!"
—Opal Carew, *New York Times* bestselling author

"The sex is dirty-sweet, with a dark lick of dominance and the tantalizing potential of redemption, and an explosive ending provides the perfect closure to Gabe and Honor's story while setting up the next installment."
—*Publishers Weekly* (starred review) on *Mine To Take*

"Intriguingly dark and intensely compelling . . . explosive."
—*RT Book Reviews* on *Mine To Take* (Top Pick!)

"A perfect mix of heat and humor."   —*RT Book Reviews*

"Ms. Ashenden is an incredible storyteller."
—*Harlequin Junkies*

"Sexy and fun."                       —*RT Book Reviews*

"Truly a roller coaster of a ride . . . well worth it."
—*Harlequin Junkies*

"Engaging characters, a crazy plot, and some steamy sex."
—*Guilty Pleasures Book Reviews*

# YOU ARE MINE

### JACKIE ASHENDEN

St. Martin's Paperbacks

This is a work of fiction. All of the characters, organizations, and events protrayed in this novel are either products of the author's imagination or are used fictitiously.

YOU ARE MINE

Copyright © 2015 by Jackie Ashenden.
Excerpt from *Kidnapped by the Billionaire* copyright © 2015 by Jackie Ashenden.

For information address St. Martin's Press, 175 Fifth Avenue, New York, NY 10010.

ISBN: 978-1-250-05178-3

Printed in the United States of America

St. Martin's Paperbacks edition / October 2015

St. Martin's Paperbacks are published by St. Martin's Press, 175 Fifth Avenue, New York, NY 10010.

10  9  8  7  6  5  4  3  2  1

To Maisey, excellent CP and awesome friend. Here's to having glassware!

# ACKNOWLEDGMENTS

Once more thanks to Monique Patterson for her fabulous editing, my agent Helen Breitweiser for her wonderful agenting, and to my family for bearing with me.

Also to the most excellent Megan Crane for giving me Zac pointers. Doms, indeed, do not hold back.

# CHAPTER ONE

"Can I buy you a drink?"

Zac Rutherford turned his attention from the heaving dance floor packed with scantily clad bodies.

There was a woman leaning on the bar next to him. A brunette with a full, red mouth and pale skin. She looked like Snow White. Except Snow White wouldn't be wearing a red leather dress with cut outs on the sides to emphasize the curve of her hips, the hem so short if she bent over he'd be able to see her panties. If she was wearing panties that was, and he was pretty sure she wasn't.

No, she definitely wasn't Snow White. And he was no Prince Charming. He wasn't even the Huntsman.

He was the dragon in the cave that ate virgins for breakfast.

The woman smiled at him then looked down. A submissive looking for a Dom for the evening. Limbo, New York's finest and most exclusive BDSM club, was full of them.

Perhaps a couple of months ago he would have been tempted. Hell, perhaps even a year ago he would have taken her up on the offer and not even thought twice.

But not now.

"I'm sorry, love," he said, regretfully. "Not tonight."

Her face fell. He had a reputation in BDSM circles—

the Gentleman Dom they called him—for being exceptional when it came to psychological mind-fuckery, and some subs loved that more than a good beating. It was also an added turn-on for them that he hadn't been seen in the club for months, and they all wanted to be the one to lure him back.

Sadly for them it wasn't going to work. He'd been here only an hour and already he wanted to leave.

"Oh," she said. "You sure I can't change your mind?"

*Perhaps if she had long white blonde hair and silver gray eyes. Wore black and liked to call him an asshole. Perhaps then . . .*

No. Not even then.

Zac shook his head. "I'm afraid not. But thank you for the charming offer. I'm sure there are many Masters here tonight who'd jump at the chance for a drink with you."

She blushed, pouting prettily. "Thanks. But I was kind of hoping . . ."

He reached out, took her chin in his hand and gave it a gentle pinch. "No, love. And we'll leave it at that. Understand?"

She responded instantly to the undercurrent of iron in his voice, her gaze lowering. "Yes, sir."

"Good girl." Zac released her then gestured to the barman to fill up her glass. The least he could do was buy her another drink. Manners were important, and he wanted to show her that he was flattered by the offer. No more than that though.

Turning away from the bar, he began to make his way to the exit of the club. Scantily clad people all moved out of his way, responding instinctively to his authority.

On a stage near the dance floor a scene was in progress, a sub tied to a post in the process of being whipped. The Dom supervising the scene, a guy he knew vaguely, paused and raised an eyebrow at him, gesturing with the whip. Obviously an invitation. Zac shook his head and continued on toward the club's exit.

Christ, this visit had been futile. He hadn't been even remotely interested in either the pretty sub or the whipping scene. What the hell was wrong with him? He'd hoped to be tempted back into renewing his Limbo membership, but far from being tempted, he couldn't wait to leave.

Nodding to the club's doorman, he stepped out into New York's early March chill, with snow heaped on the sidewalks and a cold bite in the air. Pulling his overcoat tightly around him, he headed across the street to where his car and driver waited.

So much for that. Perhaps he should give up on the idea of finding out just where the bloody hell his libido had gone.

*You know where it's gone.*

And that was the problem, wasn't it? He knew *exactly* where it had gone. It was worshipping at the temple of Eva King. His angel. Which meant that sooner or later, if it didn't get any sustenance, it was bound to die of hunger.

Something stirred in his gut. Probably anger. Zac ruthlessly crushed the emotion as he pulled open the car door and got in. Anger was never advisable and certainly not when it came to Eva.

"Where to, Mr. Rutherford?" Angus, his driver, asked.

"Home I think, Angus."

As the car pulled away from the curb, his phone vibrated in his overcoat. He took it out and checked the screen.

*Second Circle. Now. You're late.*

It was from Gabriel Woolf, his friend and fellow member of the small group of misfits and loners who'd banded together years ago and who now called themselves the Nine Circles club. After Dante's *Inferno*, naturally.

He frowned. A meeting? Now? No one had informed

him about it. A strange time for it too, at eleven at night. Then again, maybe they'd had a breakthrough with unraveling the mystery of who was behind one of the most notorious underground casinos in New York. Who'd had a man shot and a boy brutalized. Who'd torn the St. James family apart. And who, perhaps, had tried to get a particular piece of videotape destroyed.

A piece of tape that still hadn't given up its secrets no matter how many times he'd watched it.

Zac stared at Gabriel's text for a moment then typed a reply. *I wasn't aware there was a meeting.*

Another couple of seconds and a response came back. *Eva didn't tell you?*

Once again anger stirred, this time not so easily dealt with. So Eva had called the meeting, had she? And hadn't told him. Eva, who almost never did anything or went anywhere without him.

Eva, who was apparently hiding something from him.

Zac sent back a curt reply. *I'll be ten minutes.* Then he put his phone into his pocket and settled back in his seat. "I've changed my mind, Angus. Second Circle. Immediately. And don't spare the horses."

Angus didn't. And precisely ten minutes later, they were drawing up outside Alex St. James's club, the Second Circle, where the Nine Circles members held their regular meetings.

The doorman inclined his head as Zac approached, pulling open the doors with alacrity.

Zac nodded an acknowledgment then stepped inside, heading straight for the stairs that led to the club's private rooms.

He ignored the slow burn in his gut, the one he usually associated with anger. Clearly Eva hadn't informed him about this meeting for a reason, but by God it had better be a good one. She always told him first whenever she had something to share with the others. At least, she always had.

Until now.

He didn't want to think about what that might mean.

Zac pushed open the door that led to the Nine's favorite room and walked straight in, kicking it shut behind him.

The room had a warm, luxurious feel to it, with wood-panel walls, tall library bookshelves, and subdued lighting. A couch stood before a roaring fire, flanked on either side by two leather armchairs, one currently occupied.

There was a silence.

Zac didn't speak, nor did he look at anyone but Eva.

She stood by the fire, her small, fragile figure dressed in her usual uniform of black skinny jeans and black Doc Martens, Iron Maiden T-shirt, and leather biker jacket. Her hair, the color of pure white snow, was pulled back in a messy ponytail, strands of it hanging around her face. Her eyes were a pure, crystalline charcoal gray and met his, full of her usual prickly defiance.

He could feel his body already beginning to gather into yearning, like she was a compass point he turned to no matter where he was. A feeling he was starting to hate since it would never, ever go anywhere.

Eva, his beautiful angel, the girl he'd rescued nearly naked and broken and bleeding from the side of the road one night seven years ago, had never given him one sign, not a single one, that she felt anything for him beyond a twisted kind of friendship. And that rendered her untouchable.

He wouldn't push himself where he wasn't wanted. Ever. Especially not with her. Her past had damaged her beyond repair, or at least beyond his ability to help. A fact that ached like a piece of broken glass lodged deep in his soul.

Pity his body didn't seem to be taking any notice. It wanted her with a single-mindedness that bordered on obsession.

Luckily he'd gotten very good at ignoring it.

"Sorry I'm late," Zac said, directing this to Eva as he put his gloves down on a nearby table and shrugged out of his overcoat. "I was unavoidably detained."

She lifted her chin. The look in her eyes told him she knew he was angry she hadn't told him about the meeting and that she didn't care. But then she never did. And the way she constantly challenged him was part of her charm, part of his fascination with her.

"You haven't missed anything," Gabriel said. "At least not yet." He was sitting in a chair near the fire, his long legs extended. A pale, exquisite woman sat in his lap, black hair and blue eyes, perfectly dressed in a pencil skirt and blouse. Honor, Alex St. James's sister and Gabriel's lover, a new member of the Nine Circles.

On the couch sat her brother, one shoulder heavily bandaged from the gunshot wound he'd taken the previous week. Alex had only just come out of the hospital and looked like it too—shadows under his blue eyes, a pallor to his skin. Beside him, her hand on his thigh, sat his Russian bodyguard, Katya Ivanova. Another new member.

Really, it was getting far too crowded in here.

Zac nodded a wordless thanks to Gabriel for informing him of the meeting then walked over to the couch, slung his overcoat over the arm, then leaned his hands on the back of it, staring at the fine-boned woman standing in front of the hearth, the fire leaping at her back.

"Do go on, angel," he said levelly. "Don't let me interrupt you." *But if you think I'm not pissed off about this you're mistaken.*

The shrug she gave him was almost imperceptible to anyone but him. *I don't give a shit whether you're pissed off or not.* Aloud she said, "Okay, so where was I? I think I mentioned I've got a team at Void Angel dedicated to investigating this apparent human trafficking link Alex and Katya discovered at Conrad's Four Horsemen casino? Well, I've also been reviewing the security footage we got from him." She jammed her hands into the back pockets of her jeans. "And I think I may have some information."

Tension crawled along Zac's shoulders, stiffening his spine.

"Nothing," she'd said to him as they'd sat there, going over and over the tape Alex had gotten from Conrad South—casino owner; erstwhile member of Alex's father's mysterious Seven Devils club; rapist; and, as they'd lately found out, murderer. Footage taken at the Lucky Seven casino nineteen years ago, when Alex had been assaulted by the man.

It was their only lead to solving the mystery of who was behind the Lucky Seven and who had given the order for Alex and Honor's father to be killed and made to look like suicide. Why Honor's stepfather, still in a coma, had been shot. And why Alex had been warned off digging too deeply into the doings of the Seven Devils by a mercenary he'd met in Conrad's own casino.

So, Eva had lied to him. It would have surprised him if he hadn't guessed that already. If he didn't know her the way he did, every expression, every inflection in her voice. He always knew when she was holding back or when something scared her, and that day, watching the tape, something *had* scared her. And he'd hoped, he'd really hoped like he always did, that she would come to him with it.

*You always hope that and yet you are always disappointed.*

Story of his whole bloody life.

"What kind of information?" Alex asked, leaning back

against the couch, his hand covering Katya's where it rested on his lap.

Eva rocked on her heels. She was nervous, Zac could immediately tell. No, more than nervous. He recognized the tilt of her chin, the rigid cast to her shoulders, the cynical amusement in her eyes. Eva wasn't nervous, she was scared.

Instantly he straightened. "Sit down, Eva, and I'll get you some tea."

"I don't want any fucking tea."

Oh yes, she was scared all right. Was that why she didn't want him here? Christ, what had she seen on that tape? Unease shifted inside him.

"Say what you have to say then," he ordered. "Now." The quicker she said it, the quicker they could get on to sorting what it was that had scared her.

The quicker he could get on to finding out who'd brutalized her all those years ago.

The quicker he could shoot that fucker in the head.

Eva's gaze remained on his. "Last time I checked, you weren't my boss. Which means I'll tell you whenever I'm goddamned ready, okay?"

He didn't react to the aggression in her voice—she always got belligerent and pissy when she was afraid. Merely held her sharp, silver stare. Waiting.

"I recognized the guy who was guarding the bathroom door," she said flatly. "I've seen him before."

Eva's fingers curled in the back pockets of her jeans. They were cold no matter the fire burning at her back, but then again, her hands were always cold. She could never get warm, no matter where she was.

And now she felt colder still.

None of the others would know the significance of her confession—she'd never told anyone about her past and she never would—but Zac would know. Which was why she'd wanted to tell the others without him here. She didn't want to see the flare of knowledge in his familiar golden eyes. Or the glitter of anger on her behalf. The anger that made her so fucking tired. That made leaving behind what had happened to her impossible.

But someone had told him to come, and so here he was. She would just have to deal with it.

So she braced herself and stared at him, and sure enough, there it was, the understanding. And close on its heels, the rage. It burned like a banked volcano in his eyes, a heat he never let out because Zac never let anything out. She'd never met a man so completely in control of himself, which was why he was her one and only friend.

He was the only person she ever felt utterly safe with, a fact that both annoyed her in the extreme and yet formed the entire foundation of her present life.

Oh yeah, there was a reason she was in the fucked-up billionaire's club. She was probably the most fucked up out of all of them.

"What do you mean you've seen that guy before?" Alex sat forward, frowning. His blue eyes were so sharp. Too sharp. "Where? How?"

Eva's jaw tightened. "I'm not telling you where or how. Don't ask, don't tell, remember? All you need to know is that I recognize him. He's hired muscle. And the last time I saw him was around seven years ago."

Alex's frown deepened. "Well, what the fuck does that mean? We need context, Eva."

Beside him, Katya gave Eva a narrow look that Eva returned unflinching. She respected the hell out of the Russian woman, but no one was going to make her say anything she didn't want to, ex-military or otherwise.

"No you don't." Her fingers curled tighter in her back pockets. "All that matters is that he's hired muscle and if we can track him down, we might be able to find out who he was working for back then."

"We don't need to track him down for that. He was working for fucking Conrad, obviously."

"But do you know that for certain? Everything we've discovered so far points to involvement that goes deeper than Conrad South, Alex. Perhaps this guy wasn't working for him at all."

Alex's gaze was sharp as a sword. "Yeah, which is why we need context."

A silence fell in the room, the fire at her back crackling in the hearth the only sound.

"He's right, Eva," Gabriel said at last. "Context would be extremely fucking valuable here."

She shifted her attention to the other man in the armchair, Honor St. James sitting in his lap like a queen on a throne. His arm was around her waist, his hand resting loosely on her stomach, and there was something proprietary about the hold that Eva found deeply unsettling.

She ignored the feeling. Honor clearly welcomed the attention and seemed to enjoy having such an obvious claim stamped on her. It made Eva shudder, but if the other woman was happy, then that was her business. "I'm afraid you're not getting any context, so if you're expecting more you're shit out of luck."

Gabriel's dark eyes glinted. "Tremain is still in the hospital and Honor's life is possibly still under threat. Daniel St. James was murdered. Whoever is behind this is in all likelihood involved in drugs and human trafficking, and yet all you're worried about is your fucking privacy?"

If she'd had any nails left that hadn't been bitten to the quick, they would have been digging into her palms by now. But she didn't, so they weren't. Instead she fought down the thick, hot rage that welled up inside her.

All of those things were true, yet it wasn't just about her

privacy. None of them knew what she'd been through, none of them. Alex might have understood if she'd ever talked to him about it, but she hadn't and she wouldn't. The only person who knew the truth was Zac, and not even he knew all of it.

*Gabriel's kind of right though, isn't he? This is bigger than just you.*

Her jaw was so tight it felt like it would crack. Like she herself would crack.

Ever since she'd seen that tape, seen the strangely familiar man standing outside the bathroom and realized who he was, she'd felt as thin and fragile as a pane of glass. As if the slightest vibration would shatter her.

A vibration such as telling them all about what had happened to her seven years ago.

Christ, she would break, and she didn't want to break. She couldn't afford to. Because if she did, she wasn't at all sure she'd be able to fix herself again.

Don't ask, don't tell. One of the club's most important rules. That was all that was holding her together.

"You don't need to know," she repeated, as if by saying it enough times she could make it so. "And it has sweet fuck all to do with privacy." *More like survival.* "The only thing that matters is tracking him down and getting information from him."

"Eva—"

"No," Honor cut Gabriel off unexpectedly, her cool voice calm. "If Eva doesn't want to tell then she doesn't want to tell. If we can get a name, then that's all that matters."

The room fell silent again, everyone's attention shifting to the one person who hadn't said anything at all since Eva's confession.

The person standing behind the couch, still staring at her, the expression on his dark, compelling face unreadable.

Eva put her shoulders back, met his gaze.

He wouldn't ask for explanations. He never did. He always took her at face value and that was part of the reason she valued his friendship. Zac Rutherford was her safe haven and she would do anything, anything at all, to make sure that didn't change.

"Everyone out," Zac said softly, not taking his eyes from Eva's.

"Zac," Alex began.

"I need to talk to Eva alone." His voice was quiet and very, very certain. As if it was already a done deal that everyone would do what he said.

She didn't answer or flinch away from the look in his eyes. Of course, she knew there'd be payback for not telling him about the meeting. For doing this without him. He was pissed and no doubt she was going to get it in the neck.

It didn't worry her. He scared the shit out of everyone else but he didn't scare her. He never had.

There was quiet movement in the room as Honor slid off Gabriel's knee and the pair of them went out, closely followed by Katya and Alex.

Zac didn't watch them go nor did he turn his head to make sure he and Eva were alone when the door closed behind them.

He stood there, a massive, dark presence in his perfectly tailored Hart Brothers charcoal gray suit. His deep-set golden eyes betrayed nothing, the impressive line of his strong jaw set. His hands were still on the back of the couch, the ink of his tattoos swirling over them. Crosses and dots and swirling spirals. Cyrillic letters. The legacy of time spent in a Russian prison years ago, or so he'd told her once.

There were other tattoos too, hidden by the thin veneer of civilization he wore in the form of that suit. There was a dragon on his back, a Chinese sleeve down one arm, and some religious iconography on his chest. She'd seen them when they'd had a Circles meeting on his Caribbean island and he'd gone swimming in the ocean. She thought they were beautiful, but she'd never asked him where they'd all come from.

Just as he'd never asked her what had happened the night he'd rescued her from the side of the road in the middle of nowhere. There were some things even friendship couldn't bear.

Eva took a soundless breath.

Zac remained silent. He did that a lot when he wanted something, using silence to get people to talk. Or he used quiet, polite words, backed up with an undertone of iron that had a way of making most people obey him whether they meant to or not.

But she was not most people. "Yeah, I get it," she said at last. "You're pissed I didn't tell you about this meeting. But I had my reasons."

"I'm slightly annoyed you didn't tell me about the meeting." Again, his voice was mild. Deceptively so. "But what I am *fucking* pissed about is that you didn't tell me you recognized the man in that tape."

Again, not shocking. She'd lied to him so of course he'd be angry with her. Well, it wasn't the first time. She lifted her chin. "If you remember, we were warned off investigating this further. I was trying to protect you."

Surprise crossed his face. "Protect me? Are you serious?"

Okay, perhaps not entirely, since the idea of anything being a threat to a man as dangerous as Zac was lunacy. Then again, there were other dangerous men out there as she had good reason to know.

"Yeah, I'm serious."

He didn't smile and the banked heat of anger in his gaze didn't lessen. "I know why you recognized him, Eva."

The quiet words stood in the space between them like a black hole, sucking away all the light and warmth of the universe.

They'd never spoken about it. Not once.

All Zac knew was that she was a hacker he'd caught breaking into his computer system and who he'd wanted to come and work for him. So via email she'd agreed, in exchange for one thing: that he would pick her up at a time and place she specified, no questions asked.

She didn't tell him she'd been taken by force off the streets of New York when she'd been sixteen. And then sold into sexual slavery. Kept imprisoned alone in an innocuous suburban house in upstate New York for two years and used by a man she never saw because she'd always been brought to him blindfolded. That her only means of communication was the stolen hours in the middle of the night when she'd been able to escape her room and use the computer in the study. Her captors had no idea that she'd grown up with a natural ability for code and that she could hack her way into virtually any system.

They only saw her as a sex object. And that's all she'd been until she'd managed to escape. Until Zac had picked her up.

She did not want to talk about that. She wanted to never think of it again.

"Sure you do," she said easily. "But I'm not going to go into that. Not now. Not ever, understand?"

"The others have a point, don't you think?"

She ignored that. "Can you find him? I mean, you have databases you can search. Shit, I could probably find him myself. In fact, why don't you leave this with me? I'll find him. The past has got nothing to do with this."

"And yet you saw how well that worked out for Alex."

An uncontrollable shiver crept through her and she had to turn away from him, face the fire, to hide it.

But he knew. Oh yes, he did. He always knew.

"Angel."

"Fuck off, Zac."

"You won't even trust me with this?"

"Have I ever asked you about your past? No, I don't freaking think so."

There was a long silence.

The fire in front of her was hot and yet she didn't feel it. The cold had set in her bones, icing her marrow. Nothing was going to heat her up.

"Very well." Zac's deep, husky voice was expressionless, his upper-class Brit accent polished like fine silver. "Have it your way. But you can't run from this forever."

The flames burned bright gold, the color of Zac's eyes and just as hot. She put her hands out to try to feel the warmth. "Yeah, actually I can. Just watch me."

"I have never asked you about that night, Eva. Not once in seven years. Remember that."

Oh yes, she remembered. He'd never pushed her for answers about that night or anything else to do with her past. Just like she never asked him about his.

Don't ask, don't tell.

They were friends and yet perfect strangers. Which was the way she liked it.

She didn't turn around when the door opened.

Or when he closed it carefully behind him.

# CHAPTER TWO

"We need that information," Alex said.

Zac stood by the windows in Gabriel's Meatpacking District apartment, his hands behind his back, looking at the snow falling steadily outside.

Alex was sprawled out on the massive leather couch behind him, Gabriel standing off to the side, his hands in the pockets of his jeans.

It felt wrong to be having this meeting without Eva, but since it was about her, she hadn't been invited.

*She didn't bloody invite you to the meeting she was giving either.*

He ignored that thought. It was childish and this wasn't about tit for tat. He'd agreed to the meeting because the others had a point—they needed information and Eva was withholding it. That she may have good reason didn't make any difference. Lives were at stake, the lives of his friends and their loved ones.

"I know," Zac said, keeping his gaze on the falling snow.

"You have any idea why she might not want to tell us?" Gabriel asked.

"I do, but it's not my secret to tell." It was Eva's and he would never betray her trust. Besides, he only had supposition in any case. He knew nothing about what had happened to her the night he'd picked her up.

Eva had first come into his life in the form of code. A gremlin in the Black Star Security systems. A hacker, exploiting loopholes no one had even known were there. He'd been incensed, since his tech people had assured him that Black Star's systems were impregnable, and so the hunt had been on. He'd spent weeks trying to catch the mysterious hacker known only by the handle Void Angel, but she'd escaped every trap he'd laid.

One night, as he'd logged into his personal account, the screen of his laptop had gone dead and then lit up with a pair of white angel wings on a black screen. Then a chat window opened up and what started as Void Angel taunting him, ended with him offering her a job.

She'd agreed, on one condition: he come to a location she specified and take her away, no questions asked.

So he had, opening the door of his car on an innocuous suburban street, shocked to find a very young woman with silver hair, bloodied and bruised, and dressed only in a man's black overcoat.

His Void Angel. Eva.

He didn't know for certain what she'd escaped from, but not for want of trying. He kept his promise by not asking her any questions, however, he'd privately decided then and there that he'd track down what had happened to her. Find out who had brutalized her. And it had become an obsession. Like the woman herself was an obsession.

*Not a healthy one either. She's got her hand around your cock good and proper.*

Jesus, he didn't like that thought. Not one bit. The previous night in the club and his general lack of interest in doing a scene with anyone was a fucking worry. A Dominant being led around by his dick. Wasn't it supposed to be the other way around?

"I have an idea," Alex said slowly.

Zac shook off the uncomfortable thoughts and turned to face him. "You do?"

Alex, his shoulder still heavily bandaged, shifted uncomfortably. "Yeah. Just from a couple of things she's said I get the impression that we share . . . a common experience, shall we say."

"What kind of experience?" Gabriel took a couple of steps closer to the couch.

"I think Eva has her own personal Conrad walking around somewhere, if you get my drift."

It wasn't far from the truth, Zac was sure of it. Women didn't usually turn up bloody and bruised and naked in the middle of the night for innocent reasons.

Women didn't hate to be touched and didn't like going anywhere unfamiliar alone because nothing at all had happened to them.

"Then perhaps you should talk to her," Zac said. He hated the thought that she might confide in Alex over him, but if that's what she needed, he'd give it to her.

"Me?" Alex gave a wry laugh. "Because I'm so open about all my shit? No, I'm not sure I'm the person she should be speaking to. Eva's never trusted me anyway. In fact there's only one person she does trust, and that's you."

Tension slowly tightened through his shoulders. Ah, typical Alex to hit on the fundamental problem, the sharp piece of glass embedded in his soul. They didn't know and why would they? That even after seven years of being her protector, her friend, her confidante, her fucking family, Eva still didn't trust him. "She's never told me about her past," Zac said flatly. "And I promised her I would never ask."

"But you must know it anyway," Gabriel commented. "I mean, you have had her investigated haven't you?"

He looked at the other man. "No, of course I haven't. A gentleman keeps his word, Gabe. You know that."

"A gentleman. Yeah, right." Gabriel took a few steps over to where Zac stood then stopped, hands in his pockets. "I gotta ask this. What the hell kind of relationship do you have with Eva anyway?"

It was a question that had never come up before. Don't ask, don't tell. That was the only Nine Circles rule. And yet things had changed since Gabriel's quest to find his father had uncovered the complicated puzzle of the Lucky Seven casino and the people who ran it. A puzzle that had tendrils reaching into all of their lives.

*Except yours.*

Yes. Except his.

Well, the others had come to terms with their pasts and may be happy to share it with all and sundry, but he fucking wasn't. And he wasn't going to start now.

"That's none of your concern," he said coldly. "I seem to recall a rule we all agreed on. Or do I need to remind you?"

"My stepfather is in the hospital, my sister is in danger, my father was apparently murdered, and we have a goddamned mercenary throwing around threats if we follow up on any of this," Alex objected from the couch. "Which makes it very much our fucking concern. As I pointed out last night. Or does a rule take precedence over people's lives?"

An instinctive anger turned over inside Zac, the beast in him wanting to protect Eva. Keep her safe.

But no, he couldn't give into it. He'd known these men for nearly ten years, they were friends, and more than that, they were family and they wanted to protect the people they cared about just as he did.

Alex was right. This wasn't only about the three of them and Eva. This went wider, deeper than that.

"I'm Eva's friend," Zac said. "Nothing more."

The look Alex gave him was plainly disbelieving. "You're not sleeping with her? And please don't tell me it's because you're a fucking gentleman again, Zac. You might wear a nice suit, but you're no more of a gentleman than I am."

That was true. Oh, he'd been born one. To Sir Andrew Rutherford and his lovely wife Emma. But he hadn't learned anything from them except how to find a good vein when the ones in your arms were fucked. So you could inject your fix before cold turkey set in. Oh yes, and how to find food when there was nothing but champagne and weeks-old milk in the fridge and no money to buy any because your parents were high and had given all their cash to their dealer.

No, he'd learned how to be a gentleman from the movies he'd gone to see in the Kensington cinema just down the road from his parents' multimillion pound London townhouse. The one that played the old movies, with Clarke Gable and Cary Grant and Alec Guinness. Where men dressed beautifully and drank scotch and held the door open for ladies.

Everything looked happier in the movies. The days were brighter and the nights brighter still. Everything was clean, and people smiled and their stories all ended happily.

He'd learned so much from the movies. How to treat people with respect. How to romance a woman. How to tie a tie. How to be a man.

But Alex was correct yet again. That didn't make him a gentleman. Not when underneath his suit beat the heart of a beast.

"I'm not sleeping with her, no," he said, keeping his voice mild. "I would have thought any fool could see that."

Alex lifted his shoulder then winced. "Yeah, well, you're so damn secretive, the pair of you, who knows?"

"You've got a pretty fucking weird friendship if I may say so," Gabriel commented.

Zac let the remark roll over him. He didn't care what the others thought of his relationship with Eva. "The issue is not about the friendship I have with Eva. It's about tracking down this man she says she knows."

"Which she won't tell us about, if you remember." Gabriel's dark eyes were uncompromising. "You're protecting her, I get that. And fuck, so does Alex. Whatever happened to her isn't going to be easy to talk about, and we get that too. But we need to know this. Whatever information she has, whatever connections that man in the video has to any of this, we need it. You know we do."

Yes, he knew. Just like he knew that this meeting would consist of Gabriel and Alex putting pressure on him to get Eva to spill her guts.

He knew that had to happen too.

But the need to protect Eva had been the basis of his life for the past seven years, and the instinct didn't go away just like that. What they wanted would hurt her, and she'd been hurt too much for him to feel comfortable making her say what she didn't want to say.

She'd had things taken from her, and if Alex was right, he knew what those things were. And what they meant. And how long that took to recover from—if you ever recovered from it.

*Maybe you've been protecting her too much. Maybe that's not what she needs anymore.*

Zac turned away once more to contemplate the snow. His Dominant instincts whispering to him, telling him what he knew deep in his bones. What he'd been deliberately ignoring for the past several years because he didn't trust those instincts around her.

They'd whispered to him that night he'd found her too, the moment he'd laid eyes on her. *Mine. You're mine.*

He hadn't listened then—she'd been only eighteen and clearly marked by male violence—and he hadn't listened later either, after she'd recovered and become Eva King, software magnate. She didn't want to be touched or crowded. She was like a wild creature that went mad at the sight of a cage.

He didn't want to be her cage. He only wanted to set her free.

*But you haven't set her free. And now you're chained just like she is.*

Lazy and slow, anger stirred again like a bear waking from hibernation.

Fuck, it was true. He *was* chained. By his obsession with her. By his desire for her. He'd created the cage, locked himself inside, then thrown away the key. And all because he'd hoped something would change. That she'd recover and yes, he was a selfish bastard after all, that she'd grow to see him as more than a friend.

But nothing had changed for her and nothing would. She didn't trust him.

*You know what you need to do.*

He had to gain that trust. Let him take the fear and the pain he knew she still carried with her, a burden she wouldn't let anyone else near. Let him help her find her strength.

But in order to do that, he had to be ruthless. He had to listen to the instincts he'd been ignoring for so long. He had to break her.

A shard of longing pierced him, so intense he couldn't breathe for a long moment. He couldn't say he didn't want this. Couldn't say it didn't make him hard.

He wanted her at his mercy. He wanted everything.

"Very well," he said, watching the snow. "But we do this my way. I won't have her forced or pushed. If pressure needs to be applied, I'll be the one to do it, understood?"

"Of course." Gabriel's voice was cool. "Eva is your territory. We know that."

Perhaps they did. What they wouldn't know is how literally he wanted that to be true. He didn't hide his sexual nature, but he didn't make an issue of it either. Not that he thought the other men would have a problem with it even if they did.

*They might if they knew what you wanted to do with her.*

Then it would be best if they didn't know.

He turned from the window again, glancing at Alex then Gabriel. "We may not have to take action anyway. She's already investigating this man, and if she manages to identify him and locate him, that may be all we need."

*But not what you need.*

No, it wasn't. In fact, he hadn't thought of his own needs for a very long time. Eva had become his mission, his cause, and everything else had come second.

The lazy, long-suppressed anger stirred again and this time he didn't try to force it away. He let it smolder like an ember pressed against dry wood.

He was tired of putting his needs second. Tired of wanting something he couldn't have. Tired of giving everything he was to a woman for whom it seemed to make no difference at all. Both of them were caught in a holding pattern and he needed to change it.

Gabriel gave him a dark look. "No, fuck that. Like I said, we need everything, *all* the info we can get our hands on, not just a name."

The tension in the room tightened a notch.

He didn't like the way Gabriel was pushing, even though the other man was right and Zac knew it. "I said

I'll get it." He met Gabriel's dark eyes, letting his friend see his anger. "Or do you not trust me?"

A silence fell.

"Yes, of course we trust you." Alex sounded bored as he shifted on the couch, another flash of pain crossing his face. "Don't get your panties in a twist. Anyway, I hope she's being careful. That fucking mercenary Elijah wasn't kidding when he said he wanted you two to drop the investigation."

Zac let his anger die down a little. "This is Eva, remember? If she doesn't want to be found, she won't be." And she wouldn't. She was the equivalent of a digital ghost.

Alex frowned. "So we don't know what resources they have. Whoever the fuck 'they' are. If they're involved in human trafficking, then they're bound to have some pretty sophisticated systems in place, especially if they've managed to go so long without being caught. And shit, if they can shoot Tremain in the middle of Central Park in broad daylight, they could catch Eva too. We can't underestimate them."

"And we won't. But if there's one thing Eva knows, it's code."

The other man's blue gaze narrowed. "Speaking of Elijah, did you ever turn up any info on him?"

His friend hadn't given him much to go on, but Zac had sent out extensive feelers trying to find any information he could about the mercenary that Alex had met in Monaco. Yet his contacts had all come up empty. It didn't surprise him. If a man didn't want to be found, there were ways and means of going about it.

"No," he said. "Not a thing. I would have told you if I had."

"Shit. Well there goes that avenue." Alex leaned back against the couch cushions. "What about that girl I sent back to you?"

The young woman Alex and Katya had rescued from the casino a week ago. Zac had got her sorted with new documents and money and a safe place to live while she went about trying to find her family. It had been distressing, especially because she'd had very similar mannerisms to Eva, which only made the suspicions he already had about his friend worse.

"She's okay. At least as well as can be expected."

Alex nodded. "Good.

Zac reached into the pockets of his overcoat and brought out his gloves. "We won't mention this meeting to Eva, are we clear?"

"Zac." Gabriel's voice was flat.

"What?" He met the other man's dark eyes.

"Settle the fuck down."

And he realized, with a kind of shock, how tense he was. That his hands were in fists. That he was ready to fight, to impress his authority and his dominance on the other two.

He'd never done that before. He was normally the one who calmed the situation, who got others back on track, not himself.

Bloody Christ. This was worse than he thought.

It took a supreme effort of will to not stare Gabriel down like he would a sub questioning his authority. To relax the tension in his shoulders and neck.

"What about the other Devils?" he asked the other man curtly in a graceless change of subject. He wouldn't apologize. That was one concession too far. "Any leads on them?"

Gabriel shook his head. "With Elliot and Jordan dead, there's only Mantel and Fitzgerald left. And nothing major's come up so far. Inherited wealth in both cases; Mantel took on his daddy's manufacturing empire, while Fitzgerald expanded the family real-estate portfolio."

So pretty much what Zac had already discovered for himself. Powerful men from powerful families, aristocrats in a country with apparently no class system. What a joke.

Money *was* a class system. And the Seven Devils had apparently been at the top of it, just like his parents. And given what he knew about his parents, that made the surviving Devils dodgy as fuck, no matter that Gabriel hadn't been able to find anything on them.

"Keep looking," he said, putting his gloves on. "Men like that don't get to be where they are without some kind of casualties."

"Apparently." Gabriel's voice was expressionless, but Zac heard the undertone anyway. *Don't tell me what to fucking do.*

"I should go," Zac said curtly, before he could make the situation any worse. "There are some leads with the players in that game I need to follow up on."

Dear God. It was clear he had to do something about this obsession. Maybe he should just overcome his fucking scruples and accept the offer from that little sub in Limbo.

*Or maybe you should just collect what you're owed from Eva. After seven years, don't you think you deserve it?*

Ah, but he couldn't think like that. That was the mercenary in him doing the talking. The man who wanted payment for his services, whose only loyalty was to the dollar. Yes, he'd been that man for years after the army had let him down. But then he'd met Eva and he'd found himself a new loyalty.

He couldn't selfishly take from her like all the rest. What kind of gentleman did that to a woman?

*How long are you going to persist with that nonsense? You know what you are at heart. What you need. You need to break her.*

*And then, perhaps finally, you can both move on.*

\* \* \*

Eva let herself into her apartment—the top-floor penthouse of a building she leased with a view over the Brooklyn Bridge—but she didn't bother with the lights. She never did. It made her feel too much on display, and this way she had the sense of looking out while being able to stay hidden, a far better feeling.

She dumped the battered satchel that doubled as her purse on the floor of her lounge and went over to the only piece of furniture in the vast space. A massive desk with a bank of computer monitors set up on it, all showing different things. Newsfeeds and stock tickers. Camera feeds and YouTube videos. Email programs. And one monitor entirely devoted to a computer game she was currently playing—an online role-playing game.

Her window onto the world.

*Because you can't go through the door anymore, right?*

Eva ignored the thought. Her head often said the most ridiculous things.

Dropping into her chair, she let out a sigh as the constant tension she always felt when she was out of her apartment fell away. Like hands that had been squeezing her tight had suddenly let go, allowing her to breathe normally.

Thank God for this place. It was her sanctuary. Her haven. Her refuge. She never invited anyone here, never had guests of any kind. Not even Zac. This place was hers and hers alone. And since she'd never had anything that was hers alone, it was precious.

She leaned back in the chair and reflexively checked her feeds. Nothing of note had happened since she'd been out having drinks with Honor at the Second Circle. Alex's sister was making an effort to befriend her for no good reason that Eva could see. Honor was a nice woman but Eva preferred Katya's approach. Which was a brisk nod of greeting then silence.

Eva had never been one for girly chats. Then again, she'd never had a girl as a friend to have girly chats with so she was kind of out of practice.

Reaching for her mouse, she checked the search she'd plugged into one of the computers earlier that day, the one running the still taken from the security video. She'd put it through some of Void Angel's specialized facial recognition software—programs she'd designed herself—and was now in the process of checking it against various classified databases.

Still nothing.

She nibbled on a nail, staring at one of the monitors. Really, she should be checking her email and her schedule since she had a teleconference with some of the research team in LA, Void Angel's Silicon Valley offices. Problem was, she was finding it difficult to concentrate.

Had been finding it difficult to concentrate ever since she'd recognized the man in Alex's video—one of the guards in the house she'd been imprisoned in for two years.

Zac's response to the meeting yesterday hadn't helped.

She'd let him down, she knew that. And he had every right to be pissed with her for withholding the information he wanted.

*The last piece of your soul.*

Eva pushed her chair back and walked soundlessly over the thick dark-charcoal carpet to the massive floor-to-ceiling windows.

It was night and yet the sky was full of light. Manhattan in all its glory.

Man, she loved this view. At this height, with the dark apartment behind her, it was like she was hovering in the blackness, floating in the void. Able to see everything and yet remaining unseen. Hidden. Safe.

The rest of the world was a busy abstraction of light, a

galaxy, and she could see the connections between the stars like the connections between chips on a motherboard. Binary. Pure code. So much better than being on the ground among the noise and sweaty masses of people.

She'd once lived on those streets, a runaway, a lost girl, fighting every day for just the right to exist. Yet now she couldn't even remember what that had felt like.

*And you'd swap that existence for the one you have now in a second.*

Eva gritted her teeth. No, she wouldn't. She had money, she had her haven, and she had Zac. What else did she even need?

*A proper life?*

Yeah, well, no point in wishing for that. Any chance she'd had of a normal life had been taken from her the moment those men had pulled her kicking and screaming from the streets. What she had now was her best approximation.

*And that's so well adjusted and normal.*

"Shut up," Eva said into the darkness, to the city outside her window. To herself and her stupid fucking thoughts.

That was part of the problem of being alone sometimes. Her brain would get on a mouse wheel, thoughts going around and around in her head, a spiral she couldn't escape from or break. And when it got bad, there was only one person who could help her.

She tugged her phone out of her pocket and looked down at the screen, her finger hovering above the button that would call his number.

He always answered, no matter where he was, what he was doing, or what time it was. His dark, deep voice a reassurance that steadied her. That broke the thought spiral.

*"You won't even trust me with this?"*

She knew that voice. In seven years she'd come to learn its many textures and timbres: smooth velvet when he was calm, shot through with steel when he was angry, a deep, lazy thickness when he was amused. But she hadn't heard that edge in it before. An edge she thought was probably pain.

*Are you surprised? Seven years and you can't even trust him with this.*

Her throat tightened. She'd hurt him and she knew it, and yet she couldn't bring herself to say the words that would fix it. She'd been guarding herself, protecting herself for far too long to give in so easily now.

She had very little left of herself. She couldn't give those last few pieces away just like that. Not even to the man who'd been at her side for the past seven years. Giving her everything she asked for and yet asking for nothing in return. Not once.

*Ever wonder why that is?*

Eva stuffed her phone back in her pocket. No, she didn't. And maybe she could handle the night and all the thoughts that came along with it without him. She'd done it before. She could do it again.

At that point a soft chiming noise came from the bank of computers on her desk. Turning from the window, she crossed back to it and bent down, hitting one of the keys on her keyboard.

An email flashed up on one of her screens and her whole body went cold.

*You think you're invisible but you're not. I know where you live, Eva King. Stop hunting. Otherwise those angel wings of yours are going to get clipped.*

Fear gripped her, so tight it was like her chest had suddenly been encased in concrete.

Somehow she'd been discovered. How the *fuck* had that happened? How had they found her?

She stared at the screen, trying to get a handle on the

fear racing through her, trying to think clearly and logically.

There was no name on the email, the address something meaningless, probably run through an email router somewhere to hide the identity of the person sending it. But she knew where it had come from anyway: the mercenary who'd threatened her and Zac through Alex. Or at least the people behind him. The people who didn't want her and Zac digging into Conrad's poker game. The people who'd wanted to destroy copies of that security tape.

The fear began to spread inside her as another thought took hold.

If they'd wanted to destroy that tape, it was because there was something incriminating on it.

*Not something. Someone.*

Her brain sparked, making connections in the way it sometimes did, a wild leap in the dark.

Was it because of the guard she'd recognized? The same guard from the house. Who'd blindfolded her and taken her to The Man. Was it him?

Holy shit. Were they connected?

She tried to breathe normally, tried to think beyond the shakes that were taking hold of her.

Because if they were connected . . . Did that mean that the email had come from . . . him? The man who'd taken her and forced her into sexual slavery?

*You know it did.*

Shock coiled inside her as her brain made another leap. If it *was* him, it meant he was somehow connected with the Lucky Seven casino. With Conrad South's poker game. With Alex's family.

The Seven Devils.

Oh Christ.

Her phone rang, and she flinched at the sound. Jesus,

she had to get it together. Grabbing it from her pocket she glanced down at the screen. Zac.

Getting her breathing under control with only marginal success, she hit the answer button. "What?"

"Have you checked your email?" Zac's smooth, dark voice held an unusual note of urgency.

Eva closed her eyes. "Yeah," she said thickly.

And clearly he must have heard her fear in the word because he said, "They sent it to me as well."

She swallowed, her throat tight. "It doesn't mean anything. I don't even know—"

"There are some things we need to discuss, angel." The note in his voice now was unyielding.

No. Please God, she didn't want to discuss anything right now. It felt like her safe little world had been pried apart and someone was looking in. Someone dangerous. She needed some time to think about this, hell, to at least check her system to see if it had been compromised somehow. "No," she hoarsely. "I can't do it tonight."

"I'm going to have to insist."

She knew his voice. It could be hard as iron, dark and smooth as black velvet, thick and deep as mink fur. Now, though, it contained nothing but utter certainty, as if arguing with him was inconceivable.

To hell with that.

"No." She tried to make herself sound even more certain than he did, but she knew she only came across as afraid. "Not tonight. Not tomorrow. Or the day after, or the day after that. Not next week or next month or even next fucking year." Her voice had risen, the hard plastic of her phone digging into her palm. "We will not be discussing 'things' ever!"

And before he could respond, she hit the end button, cutting the call.

*Great. That wasn't hysterical at all.*

Eva swallowed. She put the phone back on her desk, stilling the tremble in her hand. For a long moment she stared at the computer monitor with the email on it. Then she shoved back her chair and got up, pacing restlessly over to the windows, pushing her shaking hands into the pockets of her jeans.

Of course she knew what things he wanted to discuss. The night he'd rescued her. What had happened to her. Everything she'd kept hidden for the past seven years.

Everything she couldn't tell another living soul. At least not without killing the last part of her, the part that had remained untouched.

The part that lived in the void, safe from the rest of the world.

Yeah, she had secrets. But they were hers. And she'd kept them protected for a long time. She didn't want to give them up. She didn't want to have anything else taken from her.

*You have to tell them. You have to tell him.*

No. No, she fucking well didn't.

To hell with that warning email. She'd continue with her investigations anyway, find the identity of that guy, track him down, and get Zac to protect her while she did so. He'd do it. He did pretty much whatever she told him to.

The thought calmed her. She remained in front of the windows, staring at her view of the city and its beautiful lights, waiting for her heartbeat to normalize and the fear to seep away. She knew she should probably go to bed, but sleep had always been difficult since she'd escaped the house, and it was going to be impossible now.

Perhaps she'd stay up, check over her system, then work on the information her Angel team had sent her, the small, private group that was part of Void Angel Technology and dedicated to investigating white slave trafficking. They'd sent her a file with some information about what was starting to look like a major international ring, specializing in the trafficking of women in particular.

The ever-present anger licked up inside her and she grabbed it, held onto it because anger had always been far easier to deal with than fear.

Fuckers. She couldn't wait to take them down. She'd break that ring apart, then crush the pieces under the heel of her Docs.

They wouldn't know what hit them.

And then something changed.

She didn't know quite what it was. It was like the quality of the air in her apartment was different, a subtle shift in density or texture, she wasn't sure which. And she could smell something familiar. A woody, warm scent, like cedar or sandalwood. Vaguely exotic and expensive. It was only faint, barely there, but it made her feel safe because she recognized it: the scent of Zac's aftershave.

Weird. Why would she be smelling Zac's aftershave in her apartment? She didn't have anything of his lying around and she hadn't noticed it when she first came in.

She blinked, staring at the massive window in front of her.

And in the black glass she saw something reflected back.

Zac. Standing behind her.

For the second time that night, shock froze her solid, forcing all the air from her lungs, and for a long, countless moment she stood rooted to the spot, staring at the man reflected in the glass.

It couldn't be him, not here. Not in her personal, private space where no one—*no one*—had ever been.

She whirled around as fear choked her. The wild, reflexive fear of a cornered animal.

Because he *was* here, standing in the middle of her lounge, a massive, dark figure that seemed to tower over everything. A tidal wave, smashing away her safety, her refuge.

A small, terrified sound escaped her and when icy cold hit her back, she knew she'd pressed herself against the windows as if she could push herself through them in an effort to get away.

*You fucking idiot. This is Zac. Why are you so afraid?*

The thought lingered in the back of her mind, but she could barely hear it over the noise of her own terror. The primitive warning that her home had been compromised and she was in danger.

He said nothing, merely stared at her, the look on his face utterly expressionless. Except for his eyes. They burned with that fierce, banked anger. An anger she'd never had turned on her.

Until now.

"What the fuck are you doing here?" she managed to force out, her voice thin and high.

"I told you we had things to discuss," he said, unutterably calm. "And I'm here to discuss them."

"I told you no." Her palms were flat against the window, icy cold seeping into them. She could feel herself begin to tremble. "I told you I didn't want to discuss anything!"

He moved at last, reaching out to grab her chair, pulling it away from the desk and turning it to face her. Then he sat down in it with the smooth, predatory grace of a tiger.

She flinched at the movement, her heart beating like a desperate bird against the cage of her ribs.

"For seven years we've done what you want, angel." He leaned back in the chair, put his elbows on the arms and steepled his fingers. "Tonight, we're going to do what *I* want."

# CHAPTER THREE

He'd expected she'd be terrified when he turned up, and he was right.

That only served as more fuel to the fire of his anger.

Yes, he'd never turned up in her private space before—he knew she fiercely guarded it and had never invited anyone, including himself, into it.

And yes, not giving her any warning he was coming was shitty.

But her fear was a small price to pay for the information she was withholding. Information he had to get out of her one way or another. Besides, fear wasn't a bad thing. It didn't hurt you. It could be an aphrodisiac in certain situations, a test of strength in others. And he knew for goddamned certain that Eva was nothing if not strong.

Zac regarded her small, slight figure pressed against the window, the New York skyline in all its glory at her back.

For seven years he'd been putting her needs above everyone else, everything else. Including himself. And that had to stop.

More important things were at stake now. The lives of their friends. Her life too.

If someone could get through her insane firewalls and discover what she'd been investigating, then they could get to her. They could hurt her. And that he would not allow.

So if it meant him scaring her, then Jesus, he'd scare the shit out of her if need be.

Slowly, Zac stretched out his legs, crossing them at the ankles and studying her over his steepled fingers. "Sit down," he said, allowing the hard edge of authority to creep into his voice.

She ignored him, her palms pale and spread out like starfish on the window, her long, straight silver hair falling over her shoulders. Her gray eyes were wide, fear and anger glittering in the depths. "How the fuck did you get in here?"

"I have a key."

Her eyes widened ever further. "You have a key? To my freaking apartment? How dare you—"

"A key that I've had since I leased this apartment for you five years ago," he interrupted in the same calm tone. "A key I've never used until tonight."

Her mouth closed in a hard line. Her finely carved face was pale, yet there was an obstinate jut to her chin. And beneath her silvery bangs, her eyes—almost the same color—were full of sparks.

Christ, the woman was a bloody turn-on. A delicious combination of delicate fragility and iron strength, possessing such deep passions yet armoring herself with a tough shell that dared the world to crack it.

No wonder she'd always fascinated him. He'd found all other women boring in comparison. No one else had her will or her strength. Or her secrets. She was a challenge he'd been resisting for too long—to both their detriment probably.

"This is my private apartment, Zac," she said shakily. "You've got no right to waltz right in here unannounced and just—"

"I don't care about your fucking apartment. What I care about is the information you've been withholding."

"I don't know what you're talking about."

"Oh yes you do. It's time for that discussion now, Eva."

She said nothing, staring at him.

"Answer me." This time he didn't bother hiding the order, injecting all his will into it.

"No." The word burst from her as if she'd forced it out. Her chest heaved, the curve of her small, beautifully shaped breasts outlined against the tight cotton of her black T-shirt. As usual, she wore jeans and heavy boots in addition to the t-shirt.

All part of her armor. Nothing pretty or feminine allowed.

Yet she didn't need pretty or feminine. There was a reason he called her angel, and it wasn't only because that had been her hacker handle.

She reminded him of an angel. Beautiful and fragile. Ethereal and otherworldly. Untouchable. A fallen angel in black boots and skinny jeans.

"Do you think I'll hurt you? Is that what you think?"

She didn't move. "Get the hell out of my place, Zac."

"Not happening. Like I told you, I have some things I want to discuss."

"Oh, fuck, you can't expect to come in here and—"

"Seven years, Eva. Seven years I've done everything you wanted. I've kept my distance. Respected your boundaries. Been your friend and asked for nothing in return." He met her gaze. "But now I've come to collect."

Her jaw was tight and it was obvious she was struggling to contain her breathing. "Collect what? Jesus, since when did our friendship become a damn transaction to you?"

"Since the lives of our friends were put in danger."

Color crept into her cheeks. "Yeah, okay. Look, I can find the identity of that guy no sweat. It won't take long." Her throat moved as she swallowed. "In fact, why don't you take me out to the island? You can protect me there while I investigate."

Of course she'd go for that option. Of course she'd expect him to fall in line, like he always did. "What do you think I am? Your tame housecat? Do you think you can order me around to suit yourself?" He held her gaze, letting the mask of the gentleman slip a little. Letting her see the beast he was inside. "I'm not your fucking pet. And the sooner you understand that the better."

Anger flared in her eyes. "I'm not stupid, Zac. I know what you are."

He watched her, studying the delicate architecture of her face. He'd been learning Eva King for years, and he knew all her expressions, all her moods, all her little gestures. "I'm not sure you do. You only see what I let you see. And I've been protecting you for a very long time." He leaned forward, noting the almost imperceptible flinch she gave at the movement. "And I know you're not stupid. What you are is scared."

"Bullshit." That anger burned bright, as if he'd personally insulted her. Her fingers flexed on the glass as she pushed herself away from the windows. "I'm not scared."

It was a low move because he knew she hated being told she was afraid. That she'd react to it. Nevertheless, it was true.

He put his elbows of his knees, linking his fingers loosely. '"Then if you're not scared, tell me what happened. Tell me how you know the man in that video. And why you'd get a personal email warning you off. We need the background, angel. We need to know those connections." He paused. "Or are your friends' lives less important to you than your fear?" Another low blow, but he'd push her, stoke her anger. That was preferable to her being afraid.

The color in her cheeks deepened. "No, of course not."

"So tell me. I won't ask again."

"Oh Christ. You're not my damn father, Zac, so quit telling me what to do."

She was stalling, that much was obvious. Which meant he was going to have to push her again and this time go further.

The time had come for him to stop protecting her from himself.

Slowly, he got up from the chair and rose to his full height.

Her head tipped back as she tracked the movement, and he caught the fleeting apprehension that crossed her face. Then as quickly as it had appeared, the expression vanished, her usual sarcastic, prickly mask firmly back in place.

"I think," he said gently, "that it's time someone told you what to do more often. And that you should listen."

"Or what?" She was operating on sheer bravado now, he could see it. "Are you trying to intimidate me? Is that what you're trying to do?" She took a step toward him, then another. "Nice way to treat your friends, asshole."

All the color had leached away from her face now, her cheeks pale as ashes. Her eyes glittered, fear bright in them despite her tough words.

That was the problem with his angel. She was a fighter; it was her greatest strength. Yet it was also her greatest flaw. Because she didn't know when to stop. That sometimes there was more strength in surrendering than in fighting.

*You can teach her how to do that.*

Oh, yes. He could. There were so many things he could teach her if she'd only let him. But of course, she was never going to let him.

Zac took the last step, closing the distance between them, getting right into her personal space. He wasn't touching her, but they were only inches apart. It was a tactic he used to intimidate and overwhelm. To assert his authority, his dominance.

Because if there was one thing Eva King had to learn it was that he was the one in charge now. Yes, her anger was preferable but her fear was also a useful tool, and use it he would. To break her.

It wasn't something he relished doing; it was necessary in order to protect her and the lives of their friends.

*Bullshit. You do get off on it. The Dom in you wants the challenge, it always has.*

He ignored that thought, crushed the reflexive surge of desire as her eyes widened at his nearness, as she held her ground in front of him. Good Christ, she was nothing if not brave.

He'd never been this close to her before since she didn't like to be touched. So close he could feel the warmth of her slight body, see the quickened beat of her pulse at her throat, smell the sweet, subtle scent of the jasmine and vanilla body lotion he knew she favored.

Desire rolled and stretched out inside him, lazy and hot. Fuck, she smelled delicious. It woke all the urges that should have been awakened by the sub in Limbo days ago but hadn't.

Not a good sign. Because as much has he wanted to, he wasn't here to dominate her. She wasn't ready even if she'd shown an interest in him. And she'd never shown an interest. Not once.

No, he couldn't satisfy those urges. Information any way he could get it, that's all he was here for.

"Are you challenging me?" Zac murmured softly, looking down into Eva's white face. "Because if you are, you're making a mistake. I'm not a man you want to challenge."

Her chin came up, courageous to the last. "Yeah and

why is that? What are you going to do? You can't force me, Zac."

He smiled and deliberately let the mask of the gentleman drop. "Oh I won't have to force you, angel. There are ways and means, and believe me, I know all the ways. I can make you want to give it to me." He let his smile turn savage. "I can make you want to give me everything."

Eva couldn't move. She could barely breathe. Her fear battered against the walls of her control, demanding she run, screaming at her to back away, throw herself out of the windows, something. Anything to get away from the man standing right in front of her.

Towering over her. Tall and dark and intimidating as a mountain. A demon. It was all she could do not to whimper.

But she wouldn't give into the terror. She never had, not while she was on the streets, not while she was in the house, not when He had had her over and over again, and certainly not now.

Even so, she couldn't quite process the fact that the man she'd always thought of as safe wasn't quite so safe any longer.

On the surface he was the same Zac she knew, wearing a beautifully cut suit even in the middle of the night, every button done up, the collar of his black shirt perfectly pressed, his dull gold silk tie knotted just so.

But something had changed. Like a blade drawn from the scabbard, he was all razor sharp edges and bright, glittering danger. A danger she'd never really understood.

*I'm not your fucking pet . . .*

The smile on his face held no amusement, only a savage intent that made her heart race even faster, panic burning in her blood bright as magnesium. It was the smile of a predator, pure and simple. And the look in his amber eyes . . . wolf's eyes.

She'd always thought the heat in them was anger. But this wasn't anger. This was something else, something far more intense and far more complicated.

The world spun as she became aware of other things, other aspects of him she'd never noticed.

*Because you've never let yourself notice.*

His height in comparison to hers had always added to that feeling of safety but now . . . she didn't feel safe. She felt something she couldn't quite pinpoint. It was fear yet there was another element in there like . . . excitement. The breadth of his shoulders too and the hard strength she knew went right down through muscle and bone to the core of him. The kind of strength you could dash yourself against and never make a mark. The kind of strength you could rest on, that could hold you up. Then there was the absolute authority in his voice. God. As if he knew all the answers to every question she'd ever thought to ask. And the answers would take away all the doubt, all the fear . . .

Her breath caught, a tight sensation in her chest, a pulse somewhere down low inside her.

Jesus Christ. What the hell was happening to her?

These weren't feelings she'd ever associated with Zac, at least not the Zac Rutherford she knew. But then this man *wasn't* the Zac Rutherford she knew. He was someone different. And he . . .

*Terrifies you?*

No, of course *he* didn't terrify her. What a ridiculous thought. Okay, so he wasn't acting like the friend she'd come to know and rely on for the past seven years, but he was still the same guy underneath that. Wasn't he?

"Give you everything, huh?" Ignoring the tremble inside her, the dread that dried her mouth and made her breath catch, Eva forced herself to lift her hands and touch him, smoothing the lapels of his suit in a casual movement. "That sounds ominous."

She only wanted to prove to herself that these feelings didn't matter. That she wasn't afraid and that he didn't intimidate her.

She'd never touched him before, not once in all the years she'd known him. Yet as soon as her fingertips met the fine wool of his suit, she understood that she'd made a mistake.

Even through the fabric she could feel the heat of his body and the hard, tensile strength that was part of him. Like a wall between herself and a raging fire. And if that wall were to collapse, she would be consumed.

She looked up, unable to stop herself, and as she met his intent, golden gaze, realized she'd only compounded her mistake by looking at him. Because the fire she'd sensed was in his eyes. Burning her to ashes.

"I wouldn't do that if I were you," he said softly. And before she could move, before she could even take a breath, his fingers closed around her wrists.

She had no more breath to lose. No smart-ass comebacks or sarcastic put-downs. No more tough-girl veneer. Nothing to put between her and the sensation of his bare skin touching hers.

The first touch in seven years, and she froze on the spot with blind panic.

He didn't hold her tightly but that didn't matter. She hadn't been able to bear anyone's touch after what the shithead in that house had done to her, and the sensation of those strong, scarred and tattooed fingers around her wrists was completely overwhelming.

Before she could even think properly she was wrenching her hands away, stumbling back, falling against the windows and sliding down on her ass, her heart beating so fast she thought she was going to die.

A helpless sound escaped, that whimper of fear she'd

been holding back, and she had to close her teeth against the rest that threatened to spill out.

How fucking humiliating.

Zac looked down at where she sat trembling on the floor, neither making a move toward her nor backing away. The expression on his face was neutral, as if she hadn't just collapsed in a heap. "Are you ready to tell me now, Eva?"

She swallowed, every part of her trembling. God, she didn't know if she was angry at how humiliated she felt or relieved that he hadn't said anything about her failure of nerve. Why the hell had she touched him? What on earth had possessed her? And then he'd . . . touched her in return. Which never, ever happened. It just wasn't what their friendship was about.

After a moment Eva slowly pushed herself back up on her feet, the windows behind her, trying to calm her racing heartbeat. If she pretended the last minute hadn't happened, then it wouldn't have. "Okay, okay," she said thickly. "I'll tell you." She couldn't keep denying him, no matter how awful it was to talk about it. He was right, there were other people to consider and those people were important to her. They were her friends, the only family she had. And if there was one thing she'd always wanted, it was a family.

Anyway, if she kept to the facts, then it would be fine. She could keep the details to herself.

Zac folded his arms, waiting.

"When I was sixteen, I was taken by some men. I don't know who they were. I was taken to this nondescript suburban house in upstate New York and . . . kept there. At first, I kind of liked it because I'd been living on the streets and now I had a proper bed and a roof over my head." She shoved her hands into the back pockets of her jeans because they'd gotten cold again. Stick to the facts. Only the facts mattered. "I was a prisoner though. I wasn't allowed outside and I didn't understand why they were keeping me until . . ." She stopped. No, she didn't need to elaborate on that. " Anyway, that guy on the video tape was one of my guards. He—"

"Wait." Zac's voice was flat and uninflected. "Let's go back to the beginning. What do you mean you were taken by some men?"

They'd never talked about their past. Not once in all the years they'd known each other. *Don't ask, don't tell.* God, so many cans of worms were going to be opened . . .

She didn't want to go into her shitty family life—what little she'd had. Her crack-head father and the mother who'd left when Eva had been seven. Ostensibly she'd gone to visit relatives in California, but then she'd never come back, so who knew? All that mattered was that Eva had had eight years of dealing with a drug addict dad, finally leaving when she was fifteen because the streets weren't any worse than the crappy apartment full of his drug-addict friends, dealers, and hangers-on. Men who didn't care she was only fifteen, groping her and generally making her feel unsafe. Better to look after herself than to trust someone else who didn't give a shit.

"My dad liked crack," she said baldly. "And I didn't like him or his friends. So I left."

Zac's dark brows pulled down. "Left for where?"

He was not going to like this. Not one bit. Ah, well, too bad. He'd have to cope.

Eva met his stare belligerently. "My fucking mansion in the Hamptons. Where do you think? Manhattan's got some nice alleyways in the summer, and there's a few homeless shelters in the winter."

"So you were on the streets." His tone was mild but the look on his face was iron.

"Yes I was on the streets. That's where they took me from."

"You don't know why?"

Now they were getting down to brass tacks. "I was a sixteen-year-old girl. Why do you think?"

A muscle ticked in his jaw. "You were eighteen when I found you. Which means you were kept in that house for two years."

"Yeah." She had to swallow again, her throat tight. "I'm not going to tell you specifics of what went on in there, okay? The only thing you need to know is that a man used to come and visit every couple of weekends. I was . . ."—*say it*—"kept for his use."

Zac may as well have been carved out of granite for all the movement he made. "Who was he, this man?" His voice was full of gravel and rough edges, the flames in his eyes leaping higher, his anger a living thing, straining at the leash.

"I don't know. I never saw him." She made herself hold his gaze. Would he think less of her that it had taken her two years to escape? Would he think she'd enjoyed it somehow? "I was blindfolded each time."

He didn't speak, only stared at her. There was no accusation in his expression, no judgment. But she could feel the weight of his anger like a heavy stone pressing down, crushing her.

"It's not your burden to bear, Zac," she said tautly. It was too much to have to deal with his anger, let alone her own. "So don't you get any stupid ideas about revenge in your head. Anyway, it's over now. It's history. What matters is that the guy who guarded me is the same guy as on that tape."

"That's the connection." It sounded as if he'd forced himself to speak. "The man who held you was related to the Lucky Seven in some way."

The glass at her back was cold and she could feel that cold seeping through her, into her blood and her bones. It was nothing new. Even in that house she'd felt cold, no matter how high they'd turned up the heat.

"Yeah, it seems that way."

Zac took a short, almost involuntary-looking step toward her. "It's one of the Devils. It has to be. Either Mantel or Fitzgerald." The expression on his face was suddenly blazing. "We'll find out which, I promise you."

There were ice crystals in her blood and her mouth was far, far too dry. Because if anyone could find out the identity of the Man, it would be Zac.

*And you don't want to know.*

That fear turned over inside her again, the fear she'd told herself for seven years she didn't feel. Because no, she didn't want to know. All she wanted to do was forget.

*But you can't forget. You'll never, ever forget.*

"No, we won't," Eva said flatly. "We'll find out who's behind this casino, who's threatening us, and we'll take them out. And that's all."

Zac searched her face, and she met the intensity in his gaze head-on, daring him to disagree with her. This was her fight. Her choice. And she would not have it taken from her. Not again.

As if he knew exactly what she was thinking, his expression changed, that iron look back again. The one that brooked no argument. No dissension. "Oh no," he said softly, clearly. "That's not all. Whether you like it or not, I will find the man who took you. And then I will kill him."

"And if I don't want you to do that?"

"Then things will have to change."

There was no warmth in his eyes now, amber freezing into a pure, icy gold, making foreboding turn over inside her. "What do you mean? What things?"

"Like I told you before, I've had seven years of doing

only what you want, Eva. And I'm done. I want something for me."

The foreboding sunk claws deep into her soul and held on tight. "What something?"

The expression on his face was impossible to misinterpret. "You, angel. I want you."

# CHAPTER FOUR

Eva's eyes went wide, and much to his satisfaction the pale skin of her cheeks suddenly flushed with color.

Good. Embarrassment was better than the fear that had been there before. The fear that had caused her to rear back from his touch and fall against the windows.

He hadn't intended to scare her, but putting her hands on him had been a mistake and he'd had to do something.

He could still feel the slight touch of her fingers as she'd smoothed the lapels of his jacket, as if there hadn't been layers of wool and cotton between her fingertips and his skin. And then, even more than that, the warmth of her actual skin against his as he'd taken her wrists in his hands. A brutal punch to the gut. A shot of pure alcohol to an alcoholic. A needle to the vein of a drug addict.

A mistake.

He shouldn't have done it and yet he didn't regret it, not for a second. Because now he knew exactly how bad her fear had gotten. And how desperate his hunger for her had become.

He was hard. From one touch of her skin.

Something had to give. Something had to break. And it looked like that something was him. Ridiculous for a man of his control, yet he'd let those words come out all the same, no matter that he shouldn't have said them.

And now that they were out, he wasn't taking them back.

Eva was staring at him as if she'd never seen him before. As if he were a stranger. "Me?" she asked, the edge of uncertainty in her voice. "What do you mean me?"

He studied her face, but the question seemed genuine, like she didn't understand what he meant. And maybe she didn't. From what she'd told him, her experience with men would have been extremely limited.

But then he didn't want to think about that. It made a red haze descend over his eyes, and for a man who prided himself on his self-control, that was unacceptable. Especially when he'd already had it compromised once already this evening.

"What do you think? I want you in my bed, Eva." He may as well be completely clear on that front, make sure there were no misunderstandings. Being straight up with her was the only way.

He watched her vivid, expressive face. Saw shock and fear cross it. And possibly disgust too, though he didn't know whether that was him or whether it was due to the thought of sex itself. He couldn't blame her either way. Her experiences must have been horrendous.

"No." The word was a soft, breathless denial. "No."

"Yes." He didn't bother to hide it, to dress it up as something it wasn't. "I've wanted you for years."

She was breathing fast, he could see the quick rise and fall of her breasts beneath her T-shirt. "Oh, so is that why you've stuck around all—"

"It is not," he cut across her, cold and sharp. "I've 'stuck around' because you needed someone. Because I respect you and because I like you." He held her shocked gaze. "The fact that I've always wanted you is almost incidental."

He could almost see the way she rallied herself, pulling

herself together again. Her courage was one of her great strengths and one of the many things he admired about her.

"And yet not so incidental that you're not going to use it against me."

"I'm not using it against you. I'm just telling you what I want."

She was still plastered against the glass, trying to keep as much distance between them as possible. God, the courage she must have had to approach him, to put her hands on him. That first touch in so many years . . .

He curled his fingers into his palm almost absently, as if to keep the warmth of her skin from fading.

If she noted the movement, she gave no sign. "Don't be so fucking coy, Zac. You said you wanted something for you. So what's that? A screw? Is that what you want?"

He could. Oh yes, he could definitely demand that. But tonight he was after something far more important. Something far more valuable.

Something that would break the holding pattern they'd gotten into.

"If it was just a quick fuck I was after, angel, believe me, there would be nothing coy about it. No. Tonight what I want is your trust."

She blinked. "What? But I do—"

"No," he cut her off before she could feed him yet another lie. "You don't. Because if you did, you would have told me what happened to you in that house long ago."

Anger sparked to life in her face. "Are you kidding me? That's not about trust, Zac. I didn't tell you because I didn't want to have to talk about it. With anyone."

"Deny it all you want. But one thing's for sure. We can't continue doing this anymore. Or at least I can't. Watching your life get smaller and smaller while your fear gets bigger and bigger. I thought after all these years you'd eventually start to trust me at some point, let me help you, but you haven't. And now my patience is at an end."

Her jaw went tight. "So, what? You think you can waltz in here, uninvited, telling me you want me, demanding my trust, and expecting me to just give it to you?" The sarcasm in her voice was razor sharp. "Typical alpha-male shit in other words."

He ignored that. "I've spent years doing things your way, Eva. Never pushing you, never crowding you. Respecting your boundaries. And look at you. You're absolutely terrified of me, even now."

"Only because you showed up without any fucking warning!"

At least she didn't deny it this time. "You wouldn't have let me in otherwise. Deny it if you can."

Her mouth opened. Shut again. "That's no reason for you to go—"

"I'm not arguing with you." It was time to bring this little discussion to a close. Give her something to think about and some time in which to think it. "I'm laying out the facts. If you want my help with this situation, you accept a few rules to demonstrate your trust in me."

"Rules? What freaking rules?"

"You don't hide things from me. You do exactly what I say, when I say it. No argument, no protest."

"And why the fucking hell would I do that?"

"Because you trust me." He held her gaze. "Because, Eva, if you don't, then you're on your own."

The long, pale expanse of her throat moved, the fury in her eyes making them burn as bright as stars. "Fine. I guess I'll be doing this without you then."

He hadn't expected her to give in—he already knew she was a fighter right down to her bones. But still, the fact that she didn't want to hurt more than he thought it would.

Good thing he wasn't bluffing.

He kept his gaze locked with hers, so she could be in no doubt. "Good-bye then, Eva King. It's been an honor and a privilege to have known you."

Then he turned on his heel and walked out the door.

Eva had a more-sleepless-than-normal night and woke up the next morning feeling like absolute shit. Business as usual in other words.

She didn't think about Zac as she painstakingly made herself coffee with the notorious and temperamental espresso machine she liked to use. She'd pushed what had happened the night before to the far reaches of her mind, and that's where it was going to stay for as long as she could manage it.

Wrapping her fingers around the vast, white china mug she liked to drink her coffee out of, she headed back into the lounge, intending to check on the results of her search.

Only to stop dead in the doorway. Her heart beating so fast she thought it might explode out of her chest.

There was no one there, her lounge empty of anything but her computer desk. But every nerve ending she had insisted that there was danger. That her sanctuary had been breached again.

Stupid. This was stupid.

She tried to calm her racing heartbeat with a few deep breaths. Only to catch a faint, spicy scent, familiar and warm. It was so faint it was barely there, but she could smell it nonetheless. Zac's aftershave.

A shiver whispered over her skin.

*You. I want you.*

The prick. *That* had never been part of their friendship and how dare he introduce it. How *dare* he change things. She'd never given him any reason to think there could be something between them, none at all. So why the hell he thought he could share that with her, she had no freaking idea. Because it wasn't as if she was suddenly going to fall into his arms, God no.

And as for demanding her trust like she could give it just like that . . . Well, he was shit out of luck there too.

*Don't you think he's earned it?*

Clearly *he* thought he had. And sure, after seven years, perhaps a normal person would have trusted him. But she wasn't a normal person. Trust wasn't something she gave lightly, if at all. In fact, after what had happened in that house and on the streets, it was highly unlikely that she'd trust anyone ever again.

Forcing herself to move, she walked over to her desk, coffee clutched in her icy fingers.

*It's been an honor and a privilege to have known you.*

She sat down in her chair, the weight of her anger heavy as lead. Fucking men. They were all the same. They demanded things from you, and if you didn't give in to them, then they acted like bastards. Who'd have thought Zac Rutherford would be the same as all the rest?

The weight shifted inside her, growing sharp edges. Disappointment. Hurt. Betrayal. Seven years he'd been her friend and now, because she wouldn't give him what he wanted, he'd left. Jesus, like he was any better. He'd never told her anything about himself, never trusted her with any piece of who he was. Why should she do the same for him?

Screw him. She didn't need him. She didn't need anyone.

Putting down her coffee and ignoring the painful feeling in her chest, Eva quickly ran through her searches again.

This was more important anyway. She needed to find out the identity of this guy, figure out if there was a connection between what had happened to Alex and the threats to her. Whether that was related to the human trafficking ring they'd discovered in Conrad's club.

And she didn't need Zac for that.

Eva scowled at the monitor in front of her. The searches hadn't thrown up anything overnight, but on the other hand, they hadn't led to her being discovered yet either. Always a good thing.

Gulping at her coffee, she went through her normal vast amount of emails then dealt with a number of issues that had cropped up during the night with Void Angel. The usual run-of-the-mill stuff. She'd set her special human trafficking team on the trail of linking any known trafficking rings with Conrad South's casino. So far they hadn't found anything, but it was only a matter of time, she was sure.

She'd met the girl Alex had rescued and had recognized the signs of trauma in her face. The same as in her own. Which had only made her even more determined to find out who was behind this.

*I will find the man who took you. And then I will kill him.*

Ice water slid down her spine.

This was not *his* problem to solve. And it wasn't *his* revenge to take. It was hers. The choice was hers. And it was up to her how she was going to deal with it.

Of course, what they really needed to do was get the FBI involved. But she didn't want to get the Feds in when they didn't have any concrete evidence. They had to find more.

*They?*

Eva snarled at the monitor. Well, Alex and Gabriel naturally, since they were now personally involved. But Zac? He'd told her she was on her own, and he wasn't a man to issue idle threats.

*I can make you want to give me everything . . .*

"Get out of my head, motherfucker," she growled, stabbing at a button on her keyboard.

All at once a chiming sound came from her computer.

Holy hell, was that one of her searches?

She quickly flicked through to the search that had been running in the background. And God, she was right. The complicated search program had turned up a match.

Her hand was shaking as she reached for the mouse, nervous fear coiling through her gut like a small, cold snake. No, not fear. It would never be that. But she'd admit to apprehension. Whomever this search had found would either be familiar to her or not. And if they weren't, then there went any connection to the Lucky Seven and Conrad South.

She really didn't know which one she was hoping for.

She clicked the mouse, and a file opened up.

And this time the shiver gripped her whole body.

She recognized the guy. He'd been at the house. Every time The Man had arrived, a bodyguard or some other henchman would come get her, make sure her blindfold was properly tied and that she couldn't see.

His face . . . she'd never forgotten it since it was always the last face she saw before the blindfold was put on. And everything else began.

Something lodged in her throat, the familiar ice sitting in a cold, hard lump in her stomach.

Abruptly she pushed back her chair and got up, walking restlessly over to the windows, pacing to the door, to the desk, then back to the windows. She shoved her hands into her pockets as she walked, biting her lip, her brain starting to do its mouse-wheel thing again.

Reflexively she pulled her phone out of her pocket, keying in a quick text to Zac. *I've found him. We need to move on it.*

There was no response.

She scowled at the phone. He always responded pretty much straightaway. Always.

Okay, so maybe he was out doing something. Or in the

shower. Or something else. There were probably good reasons for his nonresponse.

She did another circuit of the room, nibbling on her already chewed fingernails, the cold in her stomach not budging an inch. Memory began to creep up on her, of the sinking feeling in her gut and the crawling sensation over her skin that she always got the moment the big black car drew up outside the house.

Jesus, where was Zac? He would have texted her by now, surely?

But her phone remained resolutely silent, the screen blank. Goddammit.

Her fingers moved across the keypad. *Where are you? This is important.*

Once again, no response.

Impatient and feeling a little bit sick, Eva hit the call button. Bastard, he'd better pick up, otherwise she'd be seriously pissed with him. Not that she wasn't pissed already.

There was a click in her ear. "Hey," she said immediately. "What's up? Why didn't you answer?"

A long silence followed. Then a sigh. "I told you that you were on your own, angel. If you remember."

Eva came to a stop in front of the windows and blinked at the gray day outside. "Yeah, but—"

"You think I didn't mean it?"

*Weren't you only just thinking he wasn't a man to make idle threats?*

"No," she said curtly, starting to get angry now. At herself and her reflexive need to tell him everything. And at him for the ultimatum he'd given her. "But I thought you'd want to know."

"So now I know."

She looked down at her nails, at the short, bitten ends. "I need to go and talk to him."

"Excellent plan."

"And you're not going to help me because I wouldn't obey some stupid commands?"

He said nothing.

She tried again. "I thought friendship didn't have a price."

"I'm a mercenary, Eva. Everything has a price."

"But you're not a mercenary anymore."

"I'm a businessman. It's the same thing, only I'm not carrying a gun."

Frustration and anger curdled inside her, betrayal adding spice to the mix. "Prick."

"So you've already said."

"It's emotional blackmail. You're using our friendship to get me to do what you want."

"But we don't have a friendship, angel. What we have is codependency."

The words caught her unexpectedly, a sharp ache in her side. "That's not true!"

"Friendships are based on trust. And trust is the one thing we don't have."

She didn't know what to say to that since he was, of course, right. "Yeah, well, it's not like I'm the only one with trust issues. You're hardly an open book yourself."

He ignored that. "You know the price for my help, Eva," he said calmly, in that impeccable British accent of his. "If you want it, you'll have to pay."

Oh, but he didn't understand. She couldn't pay because there was no more trust to give. It had shattered the day her mother left, the pieces systematically crushed by her father and his junkie friends, the last remains of it burned to ashes while she'd been in the house.

She had none left. Not for anyone.

Eva swallowed, the heavy, thick thing in her throat

making it difficult to breathe. "So that's it. You're not going to help at all?"

"The others perhaps. Not you."

No, she refused to be upset about it. *Refused.*

"Fine. I don't need your help anyway," she said recklessly.

"I'm glad to hear it. Good luck."

She gritted her teeth. "So . . . when do you want to catch up again then?"

A long silence.

"Never," Zac said, his tone completely expressionless. "We will never catch up again."

The statement was a punch to the chest, all the air rushing out of her. "What? What do you mean 'never'?"

"I told you I can't go on like this." His voice was insufferably, maddeningly gentle. "Being at your beck and call, and getting nothing back. I've already put up with it longer from you than I'd put up with it from anyone else. I'm not helping you and I'm not helping myself. I need to cut loose, angel. And that means for good."

There were fingers squeezing around her middle, an inexorable pressure. If they squeezed too hard, she would shatter. "So you're . . . leaving? Just like that? What about Alex and Gabe? What about the club?"

"I feel sure they'll understand."

Bastard. Asshole. Prick.

If he wanted to fucking leave, then let him fucking leave. She was getting sick of him and his protective bullshit anyway. She didn't need it, didn't want it.

Yet a small, frightened part of her, the part she never acknowledged, shivered in distress.

*You can't let him go. You can't let him leave you.*

Eva crushed the thought flat. It was his choice. If he wanted to go, then she'd let him. And that was his damn fault if he didn't end up liking it.

An insidious grief wound through her, but she ignored that too.

Right now she had to be strong, not give in to any weaker feelings.

"Fantastic," she said, hoping she sounded bright and unaffected. "Well, I guess I'll see you around. I'll let you know if we catch the murderer and smash the human trafficking ring, huh? Or maybe I won't since you don't seem to give a shit."

"Eva —"

She hit the disconnect button. Probably with more force than strictly necessary but what the hell. Her hand was shaking. Fuck it.

Furious, she dialed Alex. "Hey," she said when he answered. "I've got our guy. The one in your video. Want to come along and help me interrogate him?"

There was a silence—clearly Alex needed time to process this. Then at last he said, "Well, obviously. But don't you usually take Zac with you?"

She didn't want to talk about Zac and his stupid ultimatum. Or about the fact that he'd up and left. In fact, let him be the one to tell Alex and Gabe he'd left them all high and dry. She wasn't going to do his dirty work for him.

"He's busy," she said shortly. "I thought you might like to come along as backup."

There was another pause. No, she was not going to say, I *need*. She didn't need him. But talking to this guy by herself would be a dumb move, especially with all the threats that had been pointed her way recently. The smart thing to do would be to not go alone. Which meant Alex, because he was a known quantity.

"Count me in then." Alex's voice held a steel edge to it. "We'll bring Katya too. She might be useful when it comes to . . . interrogating."

"Great." Eva tried to sound bright. "I'll send you the

guy's address. We should probably move on this now, so what say I meet you outside his apartment building in an hour."

Five minutes later, the address sent to Alex and her limo ordered, Eva pulled on a black beanie and shrugged on her leather jacket, stuffing some soft woolen fingerless gloves into her pocket as she took the elevator down to her front door.

Where she halted, the familiar, crawling sensation that she always got just before she opened the door inching down her spine. Sometimes, if she was very lucky, it wouldn't be there at all. But lately it seemed that every time she went outside, she'd feel it. As if the crosshairs of a gun were targeted at her back. Normally she'd just grit her teeth and ignore the feeling, forcing herself to pretend it wasn't there.

Yet today, now, it felt like the sensation was prickling over her entire body, chilling her skin, sitting coldly in her gut like all her insides had frozen solid.

*You're scared to go outside.*

No, fuck that, she wasn't scared. She didn't know where this feeling had come from or why it was significantly worse today, but she'd do what she always did. Open the damn door and get on with her damn day.

She put out her hand and quickly keyed in the code that would open the door. Her security system was probably a little over the top for what she needed but Zac had installed it himself and . . .

*"Never. We will never catch up again."*

Eva made a growling noise in her throat as the cold inside her solidified a little more. She stabbed at the buttons, gritting her teeth as the door unlocked and she was able to pull it open.

The cold March air flooded in, finding the gaps in her

clothing, whispering over her skin. It was a beautiful day. A plane traced a white trail through the sky like icing over a pristine blue cake, and she was conscious of the buildings on either side of her own, reaching like hands to snatch that plane out of the sky.

She didn't look at them, keeping her gaze fixed on the long, black limo that waited at the curb. And like it always did, that gnawing, desperate tension wound around her chest like a rope pulling tight, making it difficult to breathe.

Stuffing her hands into the pockets of her jacket, Eva stamped down the stairs that led to the sidewalk, the door to her building closing and locking automatically behind her. She was conscious of the sound, conscious too of the tension pulling even tighter as it did so. A primitive part of her wailed in terror as her retreat, her place of safety, was cut off.

But she walked on regardless, heading straight toward the limo, looking neither right nor left.

It wasn't far. Only a few feet. Some days it felt like a journey of a hundred miles.

*I can't do this . . . Watching your life get smaller and smaller while your fear gets bigger and bigger . . .*

She bared her teeth at the sound of Zac's voice in her head. Stupid bastard. What did he know? She wasn't scared. She wasn't.

Her driver, a woman hired by Zac who answered only to the name of Temple, got out and pulled open her door. Eva gave her a short, sharp nod, heading straight for the interior of the car.

Only once she was inside, once Temple had closed the door with that reassuring, heavy "thunk," did Eva feel the gripping tension begin to relax, the rope around her chest begin to ease, allowing her to breathe.

She settled back, reaching for the blanket she kept

folded on the warm leather of the seat and pulling it over her. Temple got in and immediately adjusted the heating the way Eva liked it, which was like a sauna.

She gave Temple the address and waited a few moments for the heat to penetrate her chilled flesh.

The car pulled away from the curb and into the flow of heavy New York traffic.

Eva let out a breath. She liked her limo. It was a little bubble of safety and yet allowed her to see out at the same time, making her feel as if she was part of things. Sometimes she went out with no destination in mind, getting Temple to drive her around the city streets purely for the pleasure of watching everyone around her with things to do and lives to live.

Zac had a car, but he often took the subway. Apparently to "gauge the mood of the city" or some such crap. She couldn't imagine doing so herself, all those people pressing against her. It made her shudder to think about it.

Which meant it was probably better she *not* think about it. Or him for that matter.

*Never catch up . . .*

Just like that, the tension was back, wrapping around her so tightly she felt suffocated. She tried to breathe through it, tried to calm herself with the techniques Zac had taught her over the years, but nothing seemed to work.

*He's not here. You're going to see someone who was at the house and Zac's not going to be there with you.*

She stared out the window, at the buildings on either side, windows glittering in the sunlight, and concentrated on the roar of the traffic.

It would be fine. She would have Alex and Katya.

*But they don't know. They won't understand. Not like he does . . .*

Her fingers twisted in the thick, dark blue cashmere

blanket on her knees as she tried to keep her thoughts from careering out of control, tried to think logically.

It was true that Alex was impatient like her, and his tendency was to enflame a situation, which wasn't exactly helpful. Zac, on the other hand, was calm, measured. And his authority was so absolute people tended to do what he told them even before they realized they were doing it. He was polite, friendly when he wanted to be, and his approach complimented her own, more impatient and fiery style. They worked well together in other words. Something she wasn't so sure would work with Alex.

*It's not that. It just doesn't "feel" right without him.*

She looked down at her hands, at the blanket scrunched up between her fingers.

It didn't seem to matter how logical her thoughts, how measured her thinking, she couldn't shake the terrible pressure in her chest, making her aware of how hollow she was. How awfully, awfully hollow . . .

No. She could do this without him. She *had* to do this without him. Because it was clear to her now that Zac thought she was some weak, frightened kind of woman. Someone he needed to protect, to coddle.

A fucking victim.

Eva lifted her gaze back to the cars passing outside, the cabs and trucks and other traffic clogging the streets. Right next to her was an RV with a couple of shell-shocked-looking tourists inside. Idiots. Did they really thing bringing something like that into Manhattan was a good idea?

As she turned away, she caught a glimpse of her own reflection in the window and her heart missed a beat. The expression on her face was exactly the same as the one on the faces of those tourists: shell shock.

*You're going to meet someone from the house without Zac. Your safety. Your refuge. Who's always,* always *there.*

Despite the warmth of the car and the blanket across

her knees, the cold seeped into her, stealing her anger and her determination, sapping her will.

No, this was ridiculous. She wouldn't be alone. Alex would be with her. True, Alex didn't have Zac's calm. He was more quicksilver to Zac's immovable granite. And he didn't—

*Keep you safe.*

The tension had crept back into her muscles again, squeezing around her heart. She couldn't breathe, her fingers knotted tight into her blanket. When it got this bad, she had difficulty even getting out of the car.

Shit. It wasn't going to work. Thinking she could take Alex and Katya, and expecting to be able to operate normally. Because she couldn't. Because Alex wasn't Zac. He hadn't spent years at her side, and she didn't know him like she knew the tattooed mercenary who'd rescued her from that house. He didn't represent the same things to her that Zac represented.

And if she went to pieces when she was supposed to be questioning this guy, then that wouldn't help anyone. This was about more than herself and her stupid feelings. And it was too important to fuck up, especially given there were other people involved with this. People she cared about. Gabe and Alex. Honor.

Zac had been right. She couldn't allow her own stubbornness to get in the way.

Of course, it was going to mean she'd have to give him what he wanted. The trust she no longer had a supply of. Tricky.

*"You do exactly what I say, when I say it. No argument, no protest."*

Could she really give someone power over her like that again? Everything The Man had done to her at that house had shown her how powerless she was, how insignificant, and she never wanted to feel so vulnerable and helpless ever again. Yet now Zac was asking her to do exactly that. Put herself in his power.

Well, she couldn't. Even after seven years, he was an unknown quantity and she had no idea what he might ask of her. That alone was reason enough to refuse.

But there was something else she could offer him. Something else he wanted.

Herself.

A small, primitive part of her screamed in denial but she ignored it. After all, it was only sex and it wasn't like she hadn't had it before. No big deal. What she'd done with The Man in that house had nothing to do with anything. It didn't affect her. It didn't matter. She was strong. She moved on.

*Hell, all you did was lie there and spread your legs and . . .*

"Think of England," she said ironically to the empty car.

Though it didn't mean she wasn't still pissed at him for changing the rules on her. For wanting something he shouldn't and using it against her.

*Wanting you . . .*

She swallowed as a sensation she couldn't quite identify whispered down her spine. Like heat or . . . no. It was nothing. Nothing at all.

Grabbing her phone, she quickly sent off a text to Alex. *I think we're going to need Zac for this. Wait until I've managed to get hold of him.*

Then she leaned forward and pressed the intercom. "Temple? I've changed my mind. We're going to Zac's office instead."

He wanted things to change? Well, they were about to.

# CHAPTER FIVE

On the desk beside him, Zac's phone buzzed. He picked it up instantly, glancing down at the screen. Alex. *She's just canceled*, the text read. *Says she needs you after all. WTF is going on with you two?*

Zac put the phone down without replying, his heart beating slightly faster than normal. Alex had sent him a text earlier with the name and address of the man Eva had identified. And a comment saying *Apparently you're too "busy"?*

He'd expected Eva would choose to follow up this lead, but he couldn't deny the bitter disappointment of her choosing to do it without him.

*You don't give a shit.*

Her words rankled. Because that was the entire problem, wasn't it? He *did* give a shit. He gave too much of one and yet she would only ever see it as betrayal. She wouldn't see just how their peculiar kind of friendship was twisting their lives into shapes they weren't supposed to be in. Stunting both of them.

He'd had to do something. Take some kind of action. Sure, telling her he'd never see her again the night before had been a calculated risk and leaving her one of the more difficult things he'd ever done. Yet one of the most necessary. He didn't regret it. Nor did he regret the ultimatum he'd given her. Emotional blackmail, she'd called it and maybe it was. Then again, she'd been using the same technique on him for years She just didn't see that herself yet.

Maybe she never would.

Still. Looked like his actions had had some effect.

*She needs you after all . . .*

He pushed back his elegant, leather chair and stood up, moving around the massive oak desk and over to the expensive wooden bookshelves that stood along the wall of his office. Pausing there, staring sightlessly at the spines of his beautifully ordered library. He had many more in his apartment, this was just the overspill. Kept because he liked knowledge. And beautiful things. And . . .

Jesus Christ, why was he thinking of books? Eva was coming. Which meant she was going to give him what he wanted. What she should have given him a long time ago. Her trust.

*About fucking time.*

Something stirred in him. Something hungry, but he quelled it. Took a long, silent breath, composing himself. Naturally the Dom in him liked the idea of Eva's trust, of her obeying him, and naturally it made his cock hard. Christ, how he'd love to test that trust, test her. Show her what her body was capable of, the pleasure it could give her.

But that wasn't going to happen. Sex wasn't his objective, and most especially not when she didn't want him the way he wanted her. What was more important than that was the fact that she had a lead. The first one they'd had since Alex had returned from Monte Carlo with the videotape.

He was pleased about that since regardless of what he'd told Eva, he hadn't actually wanted to leave Alex and Gabe in the lurch. They were important to him. Hell, they were more family to him than his own ever were and that meant something. Plus there was also the fact that the deepening mystery around the Lucky Seven was a fascinating puzzle he didn't want to give up. And now it looked like he wouldn't have to.

Zac straightened his tie, flicked a bit of lint off the lapel of his suit jacket, then strode back over to his desk and sat down behind it again.

So. She apparently needed him. Which meant she was either going to call or he would be blessed with a personal visit. He was hoping for the latter.

And indeed, fifteen minutes later, the door to his office banged open without ceremony and Eva came in, slamming the door shut behind her.

He couldn't take his eyes off her. Not that she looked any different—black jeans with a Nine Inch Nails T-shirt this time. Black leather jacket. Beanie. Silver hair caught at the nape of her neck in a ponytail. The same clothing she'd worn all the years he'd known her. And the same expression on her face—stubborn determination and fierce, angry pride.

Yet he drank her in because despite the fact that he'd told himself the risk was a calculated one, that she'd probably come to him eventually, he hadn't been sure.

And now she *was* here. She'd made her choice. And her choice was him, whether she knew that consciously or not.

"Good morning, Eva," he said calmly.

Her gaze narrowed, her sharp gray eyes moving over him. "So. I've been thinking. This obeying-your-commands / trust bullshit is just a front, right? For what you really want."

What the hell? He frowned. "What do you mean 'what I really want'?"

"You told me you wanted me. So I'm prepared to do that, give you what you want." Without any preamble at all, she shrugged off her leather jacket and threw it down on the plush armchair near his desk. One hand moved to the buttons of her jeans, beginning to undo them. "Where do you want it then? On the desk? Or the floor, I don't care."

He went still, his calm beginning to drain away. "What are you doing?"

"Taking my clothes off. What does it look like?"

Shock crawled down his spine as he struggled to understand. "Why?"

Her fingers undid another button. "You said you wouldn't help unless I gave you what you wanted. And since I figured trust was just a metaphor, I thought I'd cut out the crap and go straight for what you meant. May as well get it over and done with, right?" Yet another button undone, the denim coming apart.

"Stop." His voice sounded strange. This was not what he'd asked for and definitely not, in any of his dirtiest fantasies, how he'd expected it to go with Eva.

"Oh, come on. Please don't tell me you're embarrassed. You were the one who broached the topic after all." She undid the last button on her jeans, revealing the plain black waistband of what surely had to be plain black cotton panties.

His breath caught and the strange paralysis that had him in its grip broke. He surged to his feet, palms flat on the top of his desk. "*Stop, Eva.*"

Her fingers stilled. There was a stubborn cast to her chin, a defiant look in her eyes. And satisfaction, oh yes, that was there too.

It made him furious. "You think I said that about trust because I wanted to get into your pants? A quick fuck to get it 'over and done with'?"

Her shoulder lifted. "Wasn't that what you told me?"

"No. That's not what I said." He stared at her, at the expression on her face. And beneath the defiance and the satisfaction, he saw anger and fear. This would have cost her, he knew it. A blow to her pride to have to come to him. Not that she was here exactly for him anyway. She was here because she needed a fucking security blanket and he was it.

Fury sharpened its claws against muscle and tendon, tensing him up. He pressed his hands harder on the wood of his desk, directing all that energy down and away from him. "Why are you *really* here, Eva?" He wanted her to say it, admit it. "Did your nerve fail?"

Her chin came up at that. "No, of course not. You're better at interrogation than I am. I asked Alex to come along, but he's too impatient for this kind of thing. He doesn't have the finesse that you do." She paused, making no move to do up the buttons on her jeans, the way she was standing revealing a strip of soft white skin just above that tantalizing black waistband. "And hey, you were the one that told me this was too important to let my personal issues get in the way. So here I am. If sex is your price for your help, then I'll pay it. No big deal."

She made it sound like nothing. Like it was, indeed, no big deal. And yet at the same time sleazy and cheap.

Slowly, Zac took his hands off the desk and straightened, let the fury burn its way through his body. Let it show in his eyes. Because he'd be fucked if she thought she could come in here, waving her assumptions around like they were truth. Reducing his wants to sex because she was the one who was afraid. And she was afraid, of that he was certain.

She'd give him her body—no matter her past—but not the real prize. Her trust. Apparently even after seven years he still hadn't earned it.

"You think, after all this time, that all I want from you is a quick fuck on my desk?" He said the words clearly, enunciating every one. "If that's all I wanted, I would have taken it years ago. I would have had you so many times by now you wouldn't be able to walk straight."

Color swept through her pale face. "Like I would have let you."

Holy Christ, she had no idea. No clue at all. He held her gaze, letting her see all the savage rage burning its way through him. "You would have begged me, angel. I could have made you. But I didn't. Just remember that. Not once did I touch you, not fucking once."

Her lips pressed together, soft pink compressing into white. "So, what? I guess that's a no then?"

More bravado. More pretense. Did she really and honestly believe that's all he wanted? Or was that just a lie she told herself so she didn't have to give any part of herself away? To keep him at arm's length?

God, it made him so angry. The Dom wanted to punish her, teach her a lesson as if she was an insubordinate sub. And hell, why not? She deserved it for even thinking a quick fuck was what he wanted. Was *all* he wanted. For reducing seven years of care into a meaningless physical connection.

She stood on the other side of the desk, her chin tipped up, defiance and challenge written all over her face. A red rag to a bull. A virgin to a dragon.

Well, this dragon was hungry and furious, and that virgin needed to be taught a fucking lesson. He wasn't going to be kept at arm's length any longer.

"My price has just changed," he said, putting the edge of steel into his voice. "Since you seem to assume that all I want from you is sex, I've decided I'll take both. Your trust *and* your body."

For the first time since she'd come into his office, open fear flickered in her gaze. Clearly she hadn't actually expected him to take her up on her offer. And no wonder. Despite her tough looks, foul mouth, and the moments when she seemed old beyond her years, she was in many ways an innocent. She'd seen a lot of evil, a lot of pain and misery. And she'd known intimately the cruelty that could be between men and women.

But he'd bet his soul that she wouldn't know the pleasure.

He could give her that. And then he could deny it. That was what punishment was, after all. The denial of pleasure.

Abruptly, her fear vanished and she rolled her eyes, back to her usual bravado. "For fuck's sake, Zac. Make up your mind." She reached for the hem of her T-shirt. "We can deal with the sex part right—"

"No," he interrupted with hard authority. "This is not the time. You have a name, or so you told me. Which means we need to pay this person a visit first."

Eva scowled and folded her arms. "But you said you wanted me. That you wouldn't help unless I had sex with you. Are you changing your mind now or what?"

Goose bumps had risen over her skin and reflexively he glanced at the controls that determined the heating in his office. He preferred it cool so no wonder she was cold.

Zac came around the desk, noting the way she tensed up as he came close, eyeing him as if he was dangerous. Good. She should be wary. She'd been regarding him as safe for far too long and that was part of the problem.

He wasn't safe and he never had been.

"I'm not changing my mind." He bent and picked her jacket up from the armchair. Normally he would throw it at her for her to catch. Or hand it to her. They wouldn't touch, not even accidentally.

Now he held it in front of him with both hands, making it clear that if she wanted it, he was going to help her into it. "And what I actually said was that I wouldn't help you unless I had your trust first. So here we are. Your first demonstration of trust. Come and get your jacket from me, Eva."

Her gaze flickered. She glanced at the black leather then up at him again, making no move toward it. "So I'm just supposed to do whatever you say like a good little girl?" She made it sound like that was the worst thing in the world. He didn't move. He would have this from her, he fucking would. "Yes that's exactly what you're supposed to do. Or else I'm not going anywhere."

"Oh, Christ. You're treating me like—"

"Come. Here." He made each word hard and flat with authority.

Her mouth tightened. She glanced at the jacket in his hands, an almost imperceptible shiver shaking her. She was obviously cold and yet she didn't want to give in. Fighting, naturally.

"Prick," she muttered at last, walking toward him, holding his gaze as if daring him to find any sign she was scared or nervous.

But he knew she was, because the pulse at the base of her throat was beating fast.

About fucking time. He was sick of having no effect on her whatsoever. Of being the crutch she picked up whenever she needed support, only to be ignored when she didn't.

Eva turned around, shoving her arm into one of the sleeves he held for her. Then the other. He didn't release his hold on her jacket, inhaling the unexpectedly feminine scent of her. Jasmine and vanilla. And underlying that, the edge of soft musk, a unique smell that was all Eva.

It made him hard, that scent. Made him want all kinds of things. Things he'd spent years denying himself because of the scars he knew she carried. Once, he'd hoped to heal those scars, but no matter what he did, no matter how gentle or careful or respectful he was, nothing seemed to help. She'd resolutely kept him at a distance.

Well, not anymore.

Keeping one hand on her jacket, Zac reached around her with the other and slid his fingers around her throat.

She went rigid, her pulse racing against his palm, the warmth of her skin burning like an ember. She made no sound at all.

He bent his head so his mouth was near her ear. "How dare you," he said with quiet emphasis, allowing his fury to bleed through. "How dare you come in here and reduce the past seven years to sex. How dare you make everything I've done for you about *fucking*."

She swallowed, her throat moving under his hand, her body beginning to tremble. "I . . . I d-didn't mean—" Her voice was hoarse, her fear so intense he could smell it.

But he didn't let her go. "I don't give a shit what you meant. I know you're scared. I know this is difficult. But being afraid is no excuse. You don't fuck with me, angel. You don't fuck with what I've done for you. Seven years I've done everything you wanted and now it's your turn. You *will* give me what I want."

Her breath was coming in short, hard pants and even though his grip on her was light and she could have pulled away from him at any moment, she didn't. "W-what?"

He leaned down a little further, brushing his mouth against her ear, relishing the soft, frightened sound that escaped her. "Your promise, angel. That while we're dealing with this situation, you won't argue or protest. That you'll give me all the information we might need, that you won't hide anything from me. That you'll trust me."

"S-Says the man with his hand around my throat."

Christ, even now, shit-scared and trembling, she couldn't drop that brave front for him, not even for a second. "You just can't help yourself, can you?" He let his hold tighten a little further. "Your promise, Eva. Now."

"I-I-I promise. Now let me go, you fucker."

He didn't want to. He wanted to keep pushing, have the other thing she'd offered him. Strip her naked, push her down on her knees and take her body too. But with this man they had to find, they didn't have time.

Yet.

Zac.

Zac released his hold on her, watching as she took a quick couple of steps toward the door as soon as he let go. As if she couldn't wait to put some distance between them. "Come on then," she said, the slightest edge in her voice. "What are you waiting for?" She didn't turn around.

The anger in him had calmed, that hoarse promise of hers soothing the savage beast. Still, if she thought he wasn't going to put it to the test, she was wrong.

For the first time ever, Eva felt uncomfortable with Zac in the backseat of her limo.

He sat beside her in his usual place, several inches of space between them. And yet it felt like he was taking up all the room. All the air even.

She couldn't seem to stop shaking. That *asshole*. He'd put . . . his hand around her throat. God, she could still feel the touch of his fingers on her bare skin, like being seared by a naked flame. Then there had been the warmth of his breath against her ear and his voice, taut with fury. *"How dare you . . ."*

That made her feel ashamed of herself. Okay, so she shouldn't have used his confession that he wanted her against him like that. Made it about sex instead of trust. But, well, she'd been . . . nervous. No matter how many times she told herself on the way to his house that sex didn't mean anything to her, it didn't stop the nervousness from clenching tight in her gut or the insidious cold from working its way through her.

*How dare you come in here and reduce the past seven years to sex . . . to fucking.*

Her throat tightened. He'd been so angry with her, though she didn't know what she'd expected. She'd just been . . .

*Admit it. Say it. You were afraid.*

Eva bit her lip, shying away from the thought. Instead, she shot him a glance, unable to help herself. He was looking out the window, the lines of his dark face hard. There was no anger there now, no flash of what she'd thought was hurt. Both were gone as if they'd never been.

She shifted in her seat, bitterly conscious of his scent, the warmth of cedar and old, well-loved leather. A familiar, warm smell that she'd only been vaguely aware of before. And of the looming, massive presence of him.

A strange unease twisted through her. Dragging her gaze from his face, she looked down at her hands clasped tightly in her lap instead.

The way he'd held out her jacket for her, ostensibly ever the gentleman, and yet the expression in his amber eyes had been far from gentlemanly. Fury had lurked there and something else. Something . . . dominant. Calling weirdly to a part of her she'd never been conscious of before. A part of her that wanted to do whatever he said and have him take away all that nervousness and fear. Roll over and let him take the burden of it.

She'd seen him give that look to other people before and had often watched as they'd hurried to obey him. She'd always been scornful of such behavior.

But now . . . she could almost understand it.

Not that his command alone had made her cross the room to him, Christ no, despite the weak part of her that wanted to obey him and have him take everything away.

She wasn't that weak. But she did need his help and he clearly wasn't going to give it to her until she capitulated.

*Your trust* and *your body, don't forget.*

Yeah, like she'd forget that. The sex thing she'd handle, no problem. It was the trust thing she had difficulties with. Then again, all she'd had to promise was obey a couple of commands and not hide things from him. That wasn't so much of a big deal, was it?

She shifted again in her seat, keeping her hands clasped together, fighting not to brush her neck, touch the place where his palm had rested against her throat. Fuck, she could still feel the imprint of his fingers there like a burn.

Maybe she should have just snatched her jacket out of his hands, but then that would have given away the fact that he affected her. That he scared her. So she'd had no choice but to thrust her arms into the sleeves and stand there as his hand slid around her throat. Making her want to scream with terror. And yet . . .

There had been something else behind that mindless terror. A lingering memory of safety. Of the softness of the cashmere coat he'd wrapped her the day he'd come to take her away from the house. No questions, she'd told him. And he didn't ask any. Only given her his coat, making her feel warm for the first time in her life.

Eva swallowed, trying to untwist her fingers from the blanket.

The silence in the car was deafening, but she didn't want to speak. Didn't know what to say anyway. Perhaps an apology, but then that would mean admitting she'd been driven by fear and there was no way she'd admit that to him.

She should be thinking about the man she was going to face. Get herself used to the idea of seeing someone she recognized from that time. Perhaps finally knowing the identity of who had taken her.

The memory of safety and warmth faded abruptly, and she shivered.

No. Perhaps thinking of that was a stupid idea after all.

Beside her Zac shifted, and despite herself, every muscle in her body tensed as if acknowledging a threat.

But he was only leaning forward as the limo slowed, coming to a stop outside a disreputable-looking apartment building. In fact the entire neighborhood was disreputable-looking, now that she got a good view through the window. Graffiti on the buildings and trash in the gutters. Men hanging around in little knots; one group sat on the steps of a nearby apartment building while another stood in front of a liquor store. A crowd of young women wearing far too much makeup and far too little clothes passed, and there was catcalling and shouting going on.

God. It was too close to home for her comfort. These were the kinds of streets she had grown up on. In fact, her father could have been one of those catcalling men, with nothing better to do than drink and sell a little meth to get by. And those men could have been his friends, the ones who drank, took the meth her father sold, and grabbed her in the dark when they thought she was sleeping . . .

"Angel." Zac's voice was full of its usual calm and authority. "We're here."

Temple had gotten out and opened the car door for them, the cold air and the stink of the city suddenly permeating the interior.

She didn't want to get out. She didn't want to see the man they'd come for. She wanted to stay in the safety of her car and get Temple to take her straight back to her apartment, where she could stay in the warmth and never, ever leave.

But she couldn't. Zac was here and she had to prove to him there was nothing wrong. That she wasn't scared. That her fear was *not* getting bigger and bigger the way he seemed to think.

"I'm ready," she said, sounding hollow and as far from ready as it was possible to be.

She could feel his gaze on her, amber eyes searching. But he said nothing, getting out of the car to stand on the sidewalk, waiting for her.

Jesus, her reaction was ridiculous. Completely and utterly.

Forcing herself out of the car, she kept her gaze trained on the buttons of Zac's elegantly tailored black overcoat and not on the sudden, yawning sense of space as she stepped onto the broken concrete of the sidewalk.

"We should have taken my car," he murmured, glancing at a group of sullen youths who'd drifted closer to where they stood, eyeing them with guarded, wary eyes. "The limo is too ostentatious."

He wasn't wrong. But right then, Eva was extremely glad she'd taken it. In fact, she couldn't wait to get back inside it.

"Come on." She stuffed her hands into her pockets. "The quicker we do this, the quicker we can get out of here."

"If anything happens, let me know," Zac said to Temple, giving her a meaningful look. "We won't be long."

Temple seemed to understand. "Don't worry, Mr. Rutherford." Her hand drifted to her hip, where the weapon she carried was secreted. "I'll make sure the car remains in one piece."

For some reason, the exchange annoyed Eva. Yes, Zac had recommended Temple, but Eva was the one who paid her salary. And Eva was the one who gave the orders.

Yet here was Zac, assuming command the way he always did, while she . . . let him.

*I've been protecting you for a very long time . . .*

Had he always done this? She had a horrible feeling he had and she'd never noticed.

He'd found her a building to live in. Loaned her money to start her business. Installed the security. Recommended employees to her. Provided company whenever she went anywhere because she didn't like being outside on her own. Been the calming voice on the end of the phone when her thoughts wouldn't shut the hell up.

She swallowed, momentarily forgetting the yawning sensation in the pit of her stomach as another feeling took up residence. A kind of acute, sharp realization.

He'd done so many things for her. Why? What did he get out of it? Was it really because he'd been hoping she'd sleep with him in the end? Seven years was a long time to wait if so.

*I respect you . . . I like you. The fact that I have always wanted you is almost incidental.*

For some reason she found herself looking up at him, at the strong, distinct lines of his face. The angular edge of his jaw, darkened with a hint of stubble. High cheekbones that gave him a hawkish, predatory look in some lights. Slightly winged black brows that he arched to devastating effect when he wanted to. A long, hard mouth.

A familiar face and yet a harsh, uncompromising one.

There was no softness in him anywhere.

*Would he be that hard all over?*

A shiver went through her and it didn't have anything to do with the cold. It was like fear and yet not. A kind of twist deep inside her. An emptiness. A hollow sensation that reminded her of . . . hunger.

Zac turned his head abruptly and those golden eyes met hers. And she found herself transfixed by them, like a deer in the headlights. As if watching her doom come rushing to meet her.

"Come, angel," he said. Then he turned toward the building. Waiting for her.

And she shook off the strange feeling, the shivering sensation in the pit of her stomach, ignoring it as she focused on the door to the building. Forcing her footsteps toward it with him moving beside her.

As soon as she was inside, she felt better, though not by much.

The foyer seemed to breathe old cigarette smoke, the wood floor pitted and stained. The elevators weren't working so they made their way up the stairs, sour smells of old cooking filtering through the stairwells. As they came out onto a long hallway, Eva heard a baby cry, thin and thready.

The familiarity of it all was suffocating, the walls closing in.

This was like home. The place she came from. The place she'd run from. Only to run into the arms of the men who took her.

*At least the house was safe . . .*

The traitorous thought paralyzed her. And for a moment it was all she could think about. No freedom, but a roof over her head. Warmth. Food. A safe place to sleep at night. Things she'd never had before in her whole life.

"Eva."

She blinked, realizing she was standing in the middle of the dim, dingy hallway, breathing hard. Completely still.

Zac was standing in front of her, a dark, massive presence. He was frowning, his amber eyes sharp, searching her face.

*Don't say it. Don't say a fucking word.*

"I'm fine," she said aloud before he could ask. "Which number is his?"

His penetrating gaze lingered on her for a second. Then he turned away, looking down the hallway. "Two twenty-six. Down here."

She followed his tall figure as he moved along the hall, her palms damp, her heart feeling like it was going to explode out of her chest.

*Ignore it. Ignore it. Ignore it.*

Zac stopped in front of one of the nondescript doors, raising one black-gloved hand and knocking. There was no response. He knocked again, more insistently.

The thready cry of the baby echoed. In an apartment down the hall, someone was shouting.

Eventually there came the sound of heavy footsteps, locks being undone, the rattle of a chain. The door opened a crack. Eva, standing a bit behind Zac, couldn't see their face.

"Whaddya want?" a distinctly unfriendly voice rasped.

"Mr. Bryson?" Zac asked, ignoring this.

"Who's asking?"

"My name is Mr. Black." It was what Zac normally called himself when he didn't necessarily want people knowing his real name. "I need to speak with you. I assure you it won't take longer than five minutes."

There was a pause. Eva could hear her heartbeat now, loud and fast in her ears. The voice didn't sound familiar to her but then would she have remembered it? She'd pretty much ignored that part of her life so completely that her brain may have erased the memory of it for her. At least, that had been the plan. Perhaps it had been successful.

Clearly Mr. Bryson didn't like Zac's look because he said curtly, "I ain't talking to nobody," and slammed the door shut.

Zac turned and glanced down at her. Raised one black

brow. And she knew exactly what he was asking. She gave a curt nod. They had no choice but to follow up this lead. It was the only one they had after all.

With a smooth economy of motion that spoke of complete and utter physical confidence, Zac took a step back. Then he kicked the door in.

It exploded back with a crash, and there was a shout from Bryson. But Zac was already stepping into the apartment without hesitation, making straight for the man standing there staring at him in shock. One black-gloved hand closed around Bryson's throat as Zac continued moving forward, stopping only when Bryson was shoved against the wall, cutting off his shouts.

"As I said"—Zac's voice was as calm and level as if he was carrying on a polite conversation that had been rudely interrupted.—"I only need five minutes of your time, Mr. Bryson."

That hand had been on her throat not fifteen minutes ago and now it was holding someone against a wall . . .

What little breath Eva had left vanished.

She'd never seen Zac use force on a person before. Usually he got what he wanted through polite requests, his natural authority and sheer presence doing all the work for him. Oh, she knew his past as a mercenary, that he'd certainly killed people on the various missions and jobs he'd once done. But that had always been an abstract kind of thing. Something that had happened in the past, that certainly wasn't part of the present.

*I'm not a tame house cat . . .*

A small, tight knot of some emotion she didn't want to name gathered in her throat as she watched him hold Bryson against the wall with no apparent visible effort. Not fear. Definitely *not* fear.

She forced herself to take a step inside the apartment

closing the ruined door behind her. In a place like this, no one would be alarmed at the sound of a door being broken in.

It was a tiny apartment, with only a couple of windows. Worn, nondescript furniture and dank carpet. It smelled of cigarettes and spilled alcohol.

Bryson was choking in Zac's grip, his round, beefy face going red. He clawed futilely at the hand on his throat, and Zac shifted it a little to allow the man some breathing room.

And abruptly Eva forgot all about Zac choking the other man, her attention focused on Bryson's face.

Holy Jesus.

A wave of cold air passed over her skin, the icy press of memory.

*The blindfold being tied and then fingers making sure it covered her eyes completely. Then the material slipped, a bright stab of light hitting her, allowing her a glimpse of the face of the man adjusting it. A curse, darkness covering her once more.*

"He's ready for you," he'd said. "Go on now."

But she'd seen the man tying her blindfold. An older guy. Round face. Bald. The same man she'd seen guarding the bathroom door in Alex's video.

"Seven years ago you were employed as a bodyguard, were you not?" Zac's accent was clipped, his voice diamond hard.

Bryson pulled at Zac's hand, struggling to get free. "Fuck off! I'm not telling you shit!"

"Take a look at the woman behind me. Do you recognize her?"

Eva struggled not to shiver, her whole body tensing with the effort. Her mouth had gone dry. No, she wouldn't look away. This was important. More important than fucking memories, that was for goddamn certain. Anyway, memories couldn't hurt her, couldn't touch her, so why she was getting so worked up about it was anyone's guess.

Bryson's gaze found her. And widened.

*He's ready for you . . .*

She had no nails to dig into her palms, nothing to stop the flood of memory that crashed through her whether she wanted it to or not. Of the darkness of the blindfold, the tie around her wrists. Of being lead through what felt like a maze of corridors until she was brought to the room where The Man would be. Her owner. And then a softer, deeper voice. Hands touching her. Sometimes gentle, sometimes not. A mouth . . .

"I want the name of your employer," Zac ordered, the words tinged with the dark ruthlessness that had always been part of him. "Give it to me now and I'll let you go uninjured."

Eva found herself focusing on that dark, terrifying voice, leaning against the arm of a worn brown couch struggling to breathe, a blind kind of panic slowly rising up inside her. She didn't want to close her eyes, didn't want the blackness. She'd retreated there once before, to the void she'd created for herself every time she was led to The Man. And at the time, it had been an escape from the reality of what was happening to her.

But she didn't want that now. It was associated with too many bad things. She needed to see.

*Focus . . .*

She stared down at the dirty wood floor. At the stained rug near the tip of one boot. Focused on that and on Zac's hard, deep voice.

"Motherfucker!" Bryson was panting. "You think I'd tell you anything?"

"You think I'd let you live if you didn't?" Zac sounded so calm and matter of fact, which only made his words even more frightening. "We can do this the easy way, or the hard way Mr. Bryson. The easy way involves you giving me the name of the man who employed you seven years ago. And then my compatriot and I will leave you with your life, such as it is. The hard way involves me choking the shit out of you. Which I assure you, I have no compunction about doing." There was a significant pause, broken only by the sound of Bryson's frantic breathing. "I've killed men before," Zac added, almost conversationally. "I don't like it, but I do what I have to do. I'm sure you understand."

*I will find the man who took you. And then I will kill him.*

The darkness in his voice ran like an icy current beneath the polite words and polished accent.

She lifted her head, stared at Zac's powerful back. A shiver crept down her spine.

He never made threats he didn't mean.

"Tell him," she ordered Bryson hoarsely. "He will kill you if you don't and I won't be able to stop him." Whether she would even try was another thing altogether.

Bryson had been part of what had happened to her. Had colluded in it. And there was a part of her that was violently, furiously angry about it. But not listening to that part, not thinking about what had happened in that house, was the only way she'd managed to stay sane so far. Listening to it now would be pointless.

Besides, it was easier to look at Zac. To focus on him. To observe the casual way he held the other man against the wall with seemingly little effort, indicating a massive, brutal strength she'd never consciously thought about before.

Dangerous. So dangerous. How had she not seen it? Or perhaps it was more that she hadn't wanted to see it. Hadn't wanted to know.

*He scares you.*

She pushed herself away from the couch with a certain amount of force. Okay, so she'd never seen him get physical with someone like this and even though she knew of his brutal past, she also knew he'd never do anything to hurt her. So there was no reason to be scared of him even if she had been. And she definitely wasn't.

*Oh, sure. Like you weren't scared when he invaded your apartment. When you offered him sex in his study. When he had that hand around* your *throat.*

Eva swallowed, her thoughts starting to spin out of control. How many men had he killed? Had he wanted to do it? Did he *really* take pleasure in it? Why had he taken on those mercenary jobs in the first place? Why did he never talk about himself?

*No wonder you're scared of him. No wonder you don't want to give him your trust. He's essentially a stranger.*

With a violent effort, Eva got a grip on her flailing brain, stopping the thoughts dead in their tracks. This was not the time to be thinking about that stuff.

They were here to get the name of Bryson's employer. The man who'd taken her and kept her prisoner for two years.

Which Devil was it?

"Now, please, Mr. Bryson," Zac said coolly. "I suggest you do as the lady says."

Bryson sucked in a desperate breath, and Eva could see the fear in his eyes. "I can't tell you." His voice was hoarse. "He'll kill me."

"I'll kill you if you don't. At least you get to choose which kind of death you prefer."

The man panted, his eyes darting from Zac's face to hers. Zac moved a leather-clad thumb over the man's trachea. Pressed down.

"F-Fitzgerald!" Bryson gasped out. "It was Evelyn Fitzgerald."

Instantly Zac took his hand away and Bryson collapsed against the wall, sliding down it to land on his butt, his hands at his throat as if Zac's were still there.

Evelyn Fitzgerald. It *was* a Devil after all.

Eva stared at the man on the ground, the ever-present cold beginning to work its way through her again. She should go over there, demand that Bryson give her absolute confirmation that this was the name of the man who'd taken her. Who'd held her prisoner. Who'd made her his sexual slave.

Yet she couldn't bring herself to move.

A part of her didn't want to know. Just . . . didn't.

*Because then you'd have to remember. You'd have to remember everything.*

Without another word, Eva turned on her heel and walked out of the apartment.

# CHAPTER SIX

Zac heard Eva's footsteps, felt the empty space at his back that told him she was gone. But he didn't turn around to follow. Not yet at any rate. He'd never actually wanted to kill anyone as badly as he wanted to kill this man. A man who'd hurt Eva. And right in this particular moment, he wasn't quite sure whether he'd let him go or not.

He bent, jerked Bryson up onto his feet again then moved his thumb, black leather against the flushed skin of Bryson's throat. All it would take was a certain amount of pressure, right there.

He'd done it before and no doubt he'd do it again.

"Let me go," Bryson hissed, his voice scraped raw.

Zac studied the man's red face and watering eyes, not moving a muscle. Anger was a caged beast inside him but he kept it under tight control. "Tell me what you did to her."

"I already gave you that name!" Bryson struggled. Futilely. "You said you'd let me go!"

"Answer the question." Oh, he could let this piece of shit go certainly. But he needed information. He wanted to know exactly what had happened to Eva in that house. Who had hurt her. What they'd done to her and how.

And once he knew, he'd take them apart. Piece by piece.

"I didn't do a fucking thing," Bryson panted.

"Liar." Zac applied a little pressure. "Tell me the truth."

The other man made choking sound, his face flushing an even deeper red.

Zac had never killed unnecessarily or in the heat of anger. But the beast was rattling the bars of its cage. It wouldn't mind killing this man, not in the slightest. Because it wasn't only Eva who'd suffered, but Alex. This was the man who'd guarded the door while Conrad raped him.

*Better not kill him. Not when you need information. Besides, Eva probably won't like it.*

Well, that was certainly true. Eva knew his background, but he'd never allowed the dragon out while she was around. At least, he never had before. Though perhaps it was a good thing she knew what he was capable of. It would be one of the many things they'd need to discuss.

Bryson made another grab at the hand that was choking him, pulling at Zac's fingers. Unfortunately he wasn't strong enough to loosen Zac's hold.

"Come now," Zac said softly. "I haven't got all day, Mr. Bryson. I suggest you tell me before I lose my patience." He took his thumb away, allowing the man some breathing room to speak.

Bryson's face was brick red, sweat beading his greasy forehead. "Why the fuck should I tell you?" he gasped. "I'm a dead man either way."

Zac considered him for a long second. He didn't want to have to make any kind of concessions for this bastard, yet information was important. Certainly more important than his anger or the need for revenge. "I can make certain . . . arrangements," he conceded. "In return for every bit of information you have."

The man's bulging blue eyes were wary. "What arrangements?"

"I can help you disappear. If that's what you want."

Bryson's Adam's apple bobbed. "How do I know you'll keep your word?"

"I'm a gentleman, Mr. Bryson. I always keep my word. Even to bastards like you." He allowed his fingers to close just a little, adding more pressure. "But I'm tired of this conversation. You have ten seconds to decide."

"All right, all right!" The man's chest heaved. "I don't know much, but I'll tell you what I can."

"Excellent." Zac did not remove his hand. He smiled, watching fear bloom in Bryson's eyes. Even better. "You can start with what you know about the woman who was with me." No reason to give him Eva's name. "You recognized her, I saw it."

"Yeah, okay. But all I know is that she was at this house that Fitzgerald owned. He used to visit once a month, sometimes more. I wasn't allowed to talk to her or ask questions or anything. All I had to do was blindfold her each time and take her to him. That's it."

Zac searched the man's face, looking for any sign that he might be lying. But there were none. It wasn't likely anyhow. A man wouldn't put at risk his only avenue of escape for a few lies. At least, an intelligent man wouldn't.

"Did you hurt her?" Zac asked. "Did you touch her in any way?"

"No." The word was emphatic. "Mr. Fitzgerald was particular about that and it wasn't worth my job to disobey him." A small bead of sweat trickled down the side of Bryson's face.

"Where did she come from? Where did Fitzgerald get her?"

"I don't know. She was just at this house and that was it. Then one day . . . she escaped. We tried to find her but . . . She was gone."

Briefly Zac debated applying more pressure, just to be sure Bryson was telling him everything. Then discarded the idea. As a bodyguard, Bryson probably wouldn't know much. Certainly if Zac had been in Fitzgerald's place, he wouldn't have told a lowly guard anything he didn't absolutely need to know.

"Tell me about the Lucky Seven," Zac said after a moment. "And don't pretend you don't know what I'm talking about."

"T-The casino?"

"Yes, the casino."

Any thoughts of holding out had quite clearly vanished from Bryson's head. "I went with Mr. Fitzgerald. He liked to watch the gambling but he never took part."

"He had connections there, didn't he? With the owner."

Bryson gave a jerk of his head. "Not sure. I think so. It was a long time ago."

Nineteen years to be exact. "Something went on there. Something you were a part of, Mr. Bryson. In fact, you stood guard . . ." Zac let the sentence hang, watching the other man's face.

But there was no disguising or hiding the puzzlement in the man's face. "What 'something'? Stand guard over what?"

"I have security tape evidence of you standing outside the men's bathroom, stopping people from coming into it. In fact, the footage consists of you having an altercation with the owner of the casino itself."

Bryson's brow furrowed. "Yeah, okay, I recall that. But I don't know what went on in there. All I was told was to keep people out."

"By a man called Conrad South?"

"No. I took all my orders from Mr. Fitzgerald."

A sliver of ice slid beneath Zac's skin. An unexpected and unfamiliar sliver. It had been a long time since he'd felt trepidation, at least not when it didn't involve Eva.

So Fitzgerald had ordered his bodyguard to guard a bathroom while Alex was raped. By one of Fitzgerald's friends. Which meant that obviously he'd known about it. And had colluded in it.

The same man who'd kept Eva in a house as his personal sexual slave.

The fucking bastard.

Anger spiked, escaping its cage and piercing him, sharp and heavy as a bolt from a crossbow. It lodged in the center of his chest, radiating outward, filling him. Making his skin feel tight with the pressure of it.

"Tell me about the Seven Devils. What do you know about them?" Zac demanded.

Bryson shook his head violently, terror filling his eyes, and Zac realized he was snarling. Then Bryson began choking and when Zac looked down, he saw his hand pressing hard around the man's throat.

Fuck his word. This bastard deserved death for what he'd done.

And yet . . . A body would alert Fitzgerald to the fact that someone was onto him and that wouldn't do. Not when they needed definitive proof as to what his role was in all of this. And definitely not considering the threat against Eva and her investigations, not when logic would suggest that the threat was Fitzgerald's work too.

Jesus. He was bloody going to have to let Bryson live.

"If you breathe a word of this to anyone, anyone at all," Zac said calmly, "I will tear your throat out. Understood?"

Bryson gave a jerky nod, the red in his face draining away like the tide going out, leaving nothing but pallid, wet sand in its wake.

It took a certain effort of will to release the prick, but Zac managed it, taking his hand off Bryson's throat and leaving him to slide down the wall in a choking, spluttering heap for the second time that day.

Then he stepped back and turned to follow Eva.

"What about my arrangement?" Bryson croaked out as Zac left the apartment. "You fucking promised me!"

"All in good time." Zac adjusted his leather gloves, noting with distaste the evidence of the other man's sweat. "Try not to get murdered in the meantime."

Curses followed him out the door, but he ignored them, Bryson already forgotten.

What mattered was Eva and the information she'd just had handed to her. The name of her faceless captor.

He increased his pace down the shitty apartment stairs and out of the building. The limo was still sitting by the curb, a couple of groups of people standing around surreptitiously eyeing it.

It didn't take much more than a glance to send them off, but that was enough, especially considering he was already as pissed as fuck, his anger boiling like lava inside a volcano.

Christ, he'd love the excuse to take someone down right now. Let off some of that steam. But that was a release he never allowed himself, unless it was in the context of a gym and a punching bag. Or the boxing matches he sometimes took part in.

Or a little bit of carefully controlled domination followed by some rough, raw and dirty sex.

He knew which option he'd go for. Except for the small problem he had in finding a partner he actually wanted.

*You have a partner already.*

The knowledge hit him like a punch to the gut and he had to pause beside the limo, the heady mix of violence and anger and desire seeping into his bloodstream like opium.

Of course he had a partner. Eva. Who was no longer off-limits. He took a silent breath, not wanting to get into the car just yet. He had to be in control of himself, be the absolute master of his emotions and his desires before he got anywhere near her. She wouldn't be able to handle the dragon, the hunger that lived inside him. The kind of hunger that had turned his parents into aristocratic junkies. That need for something more, something that had no name. Though his parents had found a name for it—heroin. He wouldn't fall into that trap. He had control over his desires, unlike them. Control was all there was.

He would have her, take what she offered, but she didn't feel that way about him yet and he wanted her to before he made any kind of move. Wanted her desperate for him the way he was desperate for her. Wanted her aching and empty and wet for him. Only then would he take her.

Or maybe he wouldn't. Maybe that could be a punishment. To want and not have. Like he'd been wanting for so damn long . . .

A couple of youths who'd been creeping back toward the limo took one look at him, turned tail and ran. Fuck. He'd been snarling again.

Zac composed himself with an effort. The sex would have to wait anyway. Right now he needed as much information as he could get about Evelyn Fitzgerald, and since Bryson knew nothing more, the only other person he could get it from was sitting in the limo right now.

Time to put her promise to the test.

Pulling open the door, Zac finally got in.

Eva was sitting on the seat opposite, her hands still in the pockets of her jacket. She looked even paler than normal. Like a woman made of snow come to life. White skin, silver hair, eyes glittering like quartz.

"Did you kill him?" she asked point blank, her voice brittle, fragile.

Perhaps he should have been offended by her assumption, then again she knew what kind of man he was. "No. I'm not sure we need to advertise the fact we're hunting for information. Not when it's probable that Fitzgerald is behind those threats to you. "

Her expression hardened. "If you're expecting a discussion about what went on in that apartment, you're shit out of luck. I don't want to talk about it."

He kept his hands clasped together, hanging between his knees. "We need to let the others know."

"We'll give them the name. That's fine. But I'm not talking about anything else, understand?"

Oh, he did understand. All too well. Pity he wasn't going to let it pass. "You promised, angel," he said gently.

She ignored him. "About the second part of this ultimatum of yours . . ." She kicked up her feet onto the seat next to him, her heavy black Docs crossed at the ankles. "You want to do this tonight? Tomorrow? When?"

The car pulled away from the curb, leaving the scummy neighborhood and Bryson behind, the purr of the engine the only sound.

So, she wasn't going to honor her promise. She wasn't going to trust him.

Disappointment bit deep. Yes, she was probably shocked and scared, and in pain. But that didn't matter. It felt like a betrayal. A denial.

*And you've been denied before.*

He ignored that thought. This wasn't about the past, this was about the present. About Eva. About the promise she'd given him.

He always kept his word, but it seemed she wouldn't.

She had to learn.

Slowly, he unclasped his hands and sat up. "Do you think you can promise me something, angel, then break it? Just like that? With no consequences?"

His tone must have clued her into the fact that she was in deep shit, because she tensed, the look on her face belligerent, her whole body radiating defiance. "Well, excuse me for not wanting to talk about what it was like to be raped, asshole."

He stared at her, held her still with the force of his gaze. "Do you think," he said softly, "that I don't know what it's like to have your choice ripped away from you? Do you think I don't know what it means to feel powerless? To be afraid? To be hurt? Because I do, angel. I've been there. I know the darkness as well as you do. But sometimes we have to go back whether we want to or not, and not for ourselves. There are other people at stake here besides yourself. How many more times do I have to remind you?"

Anger leapt in her eyes, the kind of bright, wild anger that often accompanied fear. "I know there are others! You don't have to keep telling me! But I don't see how reliving something like that is going to help anyone."

He moved then, lightning fast, reaching out to grab her small, stubborn chin holding it tight.

She froze, her eyes going wide, watching him like a mouse watches a cat about to pounce. Her breath came in short, frightened bursts and he could see her pulse beating frantically at the base of her throat.

His touch would scare her, but he was starting to think that was the only way he could get past that prickly, belligerent front of hers. The one that blinded her to how much the fear had taken over her life to the extent that she couldn't go anywhere without him. It drove her like a devil on her back, dictating her every reaction, her every move.

She had to see past it, she had to. But in order to do that, she first had to acknowledge it existed.

"You made me a promise, angel," he said forcefully. "And we need information. So tell me, what do you remember from that house? What do you remember about the man who took you?"

"I don't . . . I don't want to." Her voice sounded raw, and he could feel the tension in her jaw. Could see the denial burning in her eyes. Could see the pain. It hurt him like it was hurting her. But he wasn't going to let her go and he wasn't going to stop. This was necessary.

"I know you don't." He moved his thumb in a minute caress that was supposed to reassure, wishing that he didn't have his gloves on, that he could feel her skin beneath his. "But I'm here, angel. I'm with you." He put iron in his voice. "Don't be afraid."

Pale lashes fluttered. "I'm not fucking afraid."

But that was reflex. He let it pass, remaining silent yet not relaxing his grip on her one iota or looking away.

She swallowed, her throat moving against his fingers, and her lashes fell, veiling her gaze. "I . . . I don't remember much. I was blindfolded, like I told you. I only remember . . . his voice. And his body. Tall and big. I think . . . he was older too, his skin felt rough in places. I . . ." She stopped and her eyes closed, her voice thickening. "I don't know anything else about him. I was blindfolded every single time and he was careful to make sure it stayed in place."

Zac ignored the tightness in his chest, the sharp edge of pain in her words. "And the guards, they never spoke his name while you were around? Never gave any hints as to his identity."

Slowly, Eva opened her eyes. Fury burned in them. "No," she said tightly. "I've given you everything I know. Now if you could let go of me, I'd be pretty fucking grateful."

Of course she'd be angry with him for forcing this from her. And yes, he was a bastard for making her relive this.

*How can she trust you if you force it from her?*

Good question. But she'd left him with no other choice. Any information was vital, no matter how small, and she was the only other person they knew who'd had any kind of contact with Fitzgerald. And, Christ, gentleness and care hadn't worked. Respecting her boundaries hadn't either.

It was time for different tactics.

He released her chin, sitting back in his seat, clasping his hands in his lap. He pressed his fingers together as if he could force the warmth of her skin through the leather of his gloves and into his own.

"Thank you," he said. "I know that wasn't easy."

She turned her head away, folding her arms tightly across her chest and looking out the window. "You don't know shit." Her voice was low, fierce. "So are you going to force me to sleep with you too?"

He knew what she was doing. She was covering the fear and the hurt, drowning them in anger and defiance. Fighting to the last. Keeping him at a distance to protect herself.

Well, after all these years, getting her trust was never going to be simple. Getting her desire, even less so.

Nevertheless, that's what he wanted.

"No," he said levelly. "I won't force you. I'm going to make you want to."

She gave a mirthless laugh, her head whipping around, eyes the color of polished silver meeting his. "Are you fucking kidding me? After what you just did?"

"After I made you keep your promise to me you mean," he corrected mildly.

"A promise you blackmailed me into, asshole!"

Of course she was angry. He decided she could keep it for a little while, hide behind it and lick her wounds. Let her have that bit of distance to recover herself. But after that? No more.

"A promise I wouldn't have had to demand if you'd only trusted me in the first place," he pointed out.

"Why should I trust you?" She sat forward all of a sudden, her anger a living thing between them. "Give me one goddamned reason, Zac!"

"If you have to ask me that question after seven fucking years, angel, then you're even blinder than I thought."

Her cheeks had gone pink, her eyes glittering. She stared at him for a moment longer then eased back against her seat, turning away again. "Blind? Blind to what?"

"To the fact you're afraid."

"Ha! As if."

A silence fell, heavy as lead.

On the seat beside him, one Doc-clad foot jerked back and forth in a display of nervous tension.

He'd let her have that too.

Reaching into his jacket pocket, he drew out his phone and texted Alex and Gabe. Time they told the others what was going on. *We have a name. Second Circle. 30 minutes.*

"So you've told the others then?"

"Yes." He didn't look at her. Sure enough, a couple of seconds later, Gabe's reply appeared on the screen.

*Who?*

"And are you going to force me to stand up in front of them and tell them all about what happened to me too?"

"If it'll help the situation." Quickly he texted back a response. *Fitzgerald.*

"No." The word was flat with negation.

Carefully Zac tucked his phone away and glanced at her.

She looked even more fragile now, her skin almost glowing in the light through the windows of the limo. But her eyes were full of sparks and lightning.

"Alex did," he pointed out quietly.

She flushed. "That doesn't mean I have to. I don't see you getting up and spilling your guts to all and sundry either."

"But I'm not connected to any of this. You are."

"So you *would* force me."

There was no point denying it. He was through protecting her from what he was. "If it would save the lives of our friends then yes, I would."

"Which makes you just like *him*." She virtually spat the word. "You don't care what I want at all. I don't matter."

His anger simmered, but he kept a tight grasp on it. She was only attacking him because she was hurt, like a wounded animal. "If you didn't matter, I wouldn't be here," he said mildly. "Now stop sharpening your claws on me, angel. We have more important things to worry about."

She didn't know what to do with her anger. Or the shock. Or the fear she told herself she didn't feel. The betrayal at what Zac had forced her to do.

He'd made her give up her secrets because of that stupid promise. Because of that stupid ultimatum he'd insisted on giving her. Trust? Fuck, what bullshit. If he'd really wanted that, he wouldn't have made her tell him what had happened to her. Forced her to revisit old memories that should have stayed dead and buried.

Bastard. Bastard. Bastard.

The emotions twisted and knotted in her gut. There was an atmosphere in the car she didn't understand. A growing tension, dense as the snow clouds in the sky outside.

It made her want to open the door and flee into the city. Get away from him.

Or maybe it wasn't him. Maybe it was the knowledge that sat inside her, burning like an ember from a fire she thought she'd long put out.

Evelyn Fitzgerald. The man who'd taken her. A name that meant nothing to her and yet it was now the name of what had happened to her. The Man was now no longer some nameless, faceless person. He wasn't even The Man.

She couldn't bear to think about that. Easier to focus on the prick sitting opposite her than think about what that name meant.

Zac was sitting casually, his elbows on his knees, his gloved hands linked between them. An unthreatening pose and yet she didn't find it any less threatening than when he'd held Bryson pinned to the wall with one hand. Any less dangerous.

With his golden eyes on her, it felt like his presence filled the entire car. She seemed to be so incredibly conscious of it. Of him. In a way she hadn't been before.

So they had more important things to worry about. Apparently.

Patronizing asshole.

"Okay," she said, channeling anger since that was easier than anything else. "So what about this screwing business then? I presume you're going to get that out of me too at some stage?" May as well talk about this as anything else. They couldn't do a thing until they got to the Second Circle and now seemed as good a time as any.

Zac was silent a long moment, his gaze on her measuring. She couldn't tell what was going through his head.

"Screwing?" he said finally, his fingers loosening in his lap as he eased back against his seat. "Who said anything about screwing?"

"You said you wanted—"

"What I said was that I wanted your body." He paused, and she could sense something lingering in that pause. A hard, insistent meaning. "To own."

At first she didn't quite understand. "What the hell do you mean by that?"

He'd gone quite still, his gaze fixed on hers. His body was loose and relaxed but his eyes . . . were not. "I want some very specific things when it comes to you, angel.

Things that you will not want. Yet that's what I'll demand anyway."

No, she still didn't understand. Sex was fairly simple wasn't it? "Things? What kinds of things?"

He said nothing, only looked at her.

Holy hell. Realization dawned, along with a slow kind of shock stealing through her. "Jesus," she said on a long breath. "Are you into kinky shit?"

One corner of his long mouth twitched in what looked like amusement. " 'Kinky shit'?" he echoed. "Do you even know what you're talking about?"

She could feel her cheeks going red. Okay, so her experience of sex had been extremely limited, but she wasn't stupid. "Of course I do. Leather and whips and stuff."

That amusement lingered on his mouth. She found she couldn't look away from it. His top lip was firm and hard, like his will. But that bottom lip was fuller, softer. A mouth made for seduction . . .

"I'm a sexual Dominant," he said with that mouth she'd suddenly found so fascinating. "So I guess if that's what you mean by kinky then yes, I am into 'kinky shit.' "

She swallowed. A sexual Dominant. Well, that came as no surprise considering Zac was a man who liked to get his way and who prided himself on his control.

Whips and chains and leather. Gags. Ropes. Being tied up. Pain . . .

Her hands felt icy, her toes numb. She wanted to shiver. And she knew she had to acknowledge the gut-deep feeling that wouldn't be denied this time.

She was afraid. Of him and what he'd just told her. Of what he wanted.

Which of course meant she had to fight her fear. Deny it.

"You like to tie women up?" She tried to sound blasé.

"Whip them? Make them crawl around on their knees and crap like that?"

He didn't reply, studying her, the look in his eyes completely opaque. And for a second she hated how he could be such a closed book and yet could read her so easily. It didn't seem fair.

"Will you do that to me?" she demanded when it was clear he wouldn't say anything. "Tie me up? Flog me? Because I've got news for you, asshole. That's a big fucking no. Been there, done that, got the goddamned T-shirt."

Zac folded his arms, still studying her. "Is that what he did to you? Did he beat you?"

"We've already had this discussion. Not talking about it again." He hadn't actually done that to her. In fact, the sex had been fairly straightforward. However she'd felt like a piece of property long enough to know that being tied up and at the mercy of anyone else would be intolerable.

"Everything I do," Zac said levelly, "is for the pleasure of the submissive. Everything. That's my job. To give a sub freedom to experience as much physical pleasure as she can. And if being tied up and flogged was what you needed then yes, I'd do that to you."

As if his words had conjured it, an image sprang abruptly into her brain. Of herself tied naked to a bed. Of Zac, stripped to the waist, a whip in his hand . . .

Her mouth went dry, a pulse of something hot going through her. Oh, *shit*. She made a grab for the blanket, spreading it over her knees like armor, a barrier between herself and him. "Did you not hear me say 'big fucking no'?"

Again that twist of amusement on his mouth. "Angel," he said, as if she were a child, an innocent. "I can make you desperate for me to flog you. I can make you unable to think of anything else you'd want more."

*He could too.*

"No." Her voice was unsteady. "No, you couldn't."

His head tilted, amber eyes holding hers. "Are you sure about that?"

"Yeah, pretty damn sure." Her heart had begun to race for some completely inexplicable reason. "In fact, I'm pretty fucking positive."

Slowly, like a big cat stretching out in front of a prey animal it didn't want to frighten just yet, Zac leaned forward, his elbows on his knees, his gloved fingers laced together. "But see, here's the thing," he said quietly. "You will want me Eva King. I'm going to make sure of it."

It was a promise—of that she had no doubt. It had the certainty of a vow, making ice run in her veins, along with a strange heat she didn't understand.

Which in turn made her angry. "You think so?" she said, staring belligerently at him. "Prove it then."

A bright gold spark flickered in Zac's eyes. He didn't move, his hands still clasped between his knees, a loose, easy posture. But the look on his face was anything but.

"Are you sure challenging me is a good idea, angel?"

She'd never given it much thought. He'd always been her faithful guard dog. Her tame house cat.

Yet looking into that hot, amber gaze, she sensed a will as hard as an iron bar, as inexorable as the pull of the moon on the tides. Titanic. Implacable. A will she'd never had to deal with before because she'd never crossed him, not in any real way.

*He let you win. He's always let you win . . .*

This man in the perfectly pressed suit and leather gloves, the calm, controlled, soft-spoken gentleman, this wasn't Zac. This man was a front. A mask.

She couldn't breathe all of a sudden. Who the hell *was* Zac Rutherford? The man behind that front? And, more to the point, did she want to know?

Fear, comfortable and familiar, nestled her heart.

"Of course I'm sure," she forced out, her voice thin and reedy. "Why shouldn't I be?"

He tilted his head, the cold light from the outside sheening his glossy black hair. "Do you even know what I'm talking about?"

Blind temper coiled inside her. "Jesus, I'm not some innocent virgin. I've been screwed in pretty much every way you could imagine, so yeah, I know exactly what you're talking about."

*Do you? Do you really?*

He leaned forward, the movement almost imperceptible but she noticed it nonetheless. And it made all her muscles seize. "Sexual desire, angel," he said, as if she hadn't spoken. "That's what I'm talking about."

*You don't know. You've never felt it.*

She tried not to listen to those insidious thoughts. Tried not to acknowledge the truth of them. She'd been only sixteen when she was taken, and had never had a boyfriend. Didn't even want one, not given the shitty life she'd led with her father. It was enough just staying alive, let alone struggling with romance too.

And then afterwards, after she'd escaped, the thought of letting anyone touch her . . .

She found she was breathing fast, hard.

*You have no idea.*

"It's when you're aware of the person you want," Zac went on, his voice quiet, rough-edged. "Physically aware of them in every way. And you're desperate to touch them, to be touched in return. To have their hands on your body. On your breasts, between your thighs. To have their mouth on yours. It's an ache, angel. A hunger you feel deep inside."

She tried to keep her gaze on his. Tried hard. But for some reason she couldn't do it. His words seemed to grab onto something inside of her and tug, pulling at whatever it was as if trying to drag it from her.

Eva turned away, looking sightlessly out the window. It had begun to snow, white flakes drifting in the air, so clean and perfect. Before they settled on the dirty street, turning gray and slushy.

No, she hadn't ever wanted someone like that. Hadn't ever felt . . . hungry for someone in the way Zac was describing. She'd been given physical pleasure, not at first, it was true, but later. Sometimes she'd even had an orgasm.

*That he forced on you.*

Her eyes felt dry and sore. As if she might cry.

There had been boys at school that she'd thought were cute, but she'd never gone beyond that. Never imagined kisses or touches. And then she'd been taken, and . . .

"That's what I want from you." Zac's voice had deepened, become even softer, like mink fur. She could sink into it, close her eyes, let the warmth of it lull her. "That's what I want you to feel. I want you to be hungry for me. I want you to ache for my touch. I want you to be desperate." There was a slow heat to the words now. A heat that curled around her like a hand gripping on to that thing inside her, pulling harder. "I want you to beg, angel. And when you finally surrender everything you are to me, I want to hear you scream my name."

Eva kept her gaze out the window. But she didn't see anything. Wasn't conscious of the snow falling or of the traffic outside, or of the sounds of horns or sirens.

It felt like every sense she had was focused on the man opposite her. On his voice.

And it came as a shock to realize that for the first time since she could remember, she wasn't cold.

That heat in those words had done something to her, settled over her skin like a blanket. And it didn't feel like it was pulling on whatever it was inside her now, but thawing it. Melting that ever-present kernel of ice that sat in her gut. Warming her right through.

She took a breath, forcing out a hard, brittle laugh. Breaking the spell. "Wow, that's some ego you've got there. I never imagined."

"Look at me, Eva."

She didn't want to. Because if she did, he would know she was pretending. That she was denying the strange warmth inside her. He would see what a liar she was. But then if she didn't, that would give something away too. Damned if she did. Damned if she didn't.

Eva braced herself and met his gaze, because in the end she wasn't a fucking coward.

Tiger's eyes. Wolf's eyes. They burned right through her, molten gold.

"You will come to me," he said with such certainty it was as if he'd already seen the future and knew exactly what it contained. "I can show you everything you've been missing. Everything you're curious about." That gaze of his was like the sun, she could barely look at it. "And everything you're afraid of."

She swallowed, unable to speak. It was taking everything in her to not look away.

"I can take your fear from you, Eva. You only have to give it to me."

*You could. You could let him take it from you. Give you freedom.*

Ah, Jesus, no. He just didn't understand. That was the one thing she could never do. Because in order to give him her fear, she first had to admit that she was afraid, that she'd been afraid all her life. And she couldn't do that.

Denial was all she had, a wall between her and her past and all the pain there. Denial was survival. And she couldn't give that up, not for him, not for anyone.

It kept her strong, kept her fighting. And without the fight, she'd be destroyed.

Eva finally broke his gaze and turned away, pulling up her blanket higher. She didn't need his voice or his words to keep her warm, not when she had cashmere.

"Well thanks," she said, knowing it sounded inane. "I'll be sure to keep that in mind."

# CHAPTER SEVEN

There was no fire in the grate of their usual meeting room at the Second Circle, but the central heating had taken the chill off the room so it wasn't exactly cold.

Eva paced restlessly in front of the fireplace, her hands in the pockets of her jacket.

She hadn't spoken a word to him since they'd arrived, and he supposed he couldn't blame her. He'd been very clear about what his needs were, and she wouldn't be ready to hear that. Then again, she had to know.

He'd told her he wanted to own her. He hadn't lied.

He wanted her submission. Her surrender. Nothing else was going to do, not with her, not after seven years. But she had to be willing. He wasn't going to compromise on that either.

He just hadn't realized that desire was a foreign concept to her.

*You should have known that, given her experiences.*

Yes, he really should have. She'd been so young when she'd been taken, barely old enough to know what sexual desire was all about, let alone having experienced it for herself. At least not in an adult way and certainly not in the way he wanted.

Then she'd been taken to that house and . . . used. No wonder she didn't have the first idea what he was talking about in the car, despite what she'd said. Jesus, even though she technically wasn't a virgin, she was such an innocent.

Eva wasn't looking at him as she paced, her head down, her silver ponytail falling over one shoulder.

She didn't know desire. Probably didn't know pleasure either.

He stood behind the couch, his fingers digging into the material almost hard enough to rip it.

All those things she should have had. Desire. Pleasure. Safety. Laughter. Love. They'd all been taken from her, torn from her. Left her this prickly, frightened, shell of the woman she should have been. So wrong on so many levels.

Evelyn Fitzgerald was going to pay for what he'd taken from her. With his life.

The door opened suddenly and Alex came in, Katya at his heels. His eyes were bright, glittering with anger, determination. He didn't sit down, coming to stand next to Zac, looking first at him then at Eva.

Eva stopped pacing, standing to face Zac and Alex, her features carved from ice.

"I'm going to kill Evelyn Fitzgerald," Alex said with relish. "Very fucking slowly."

So. Gabriel must have shared the name with Alex.

A pale, long-fingered hand crept up to rest on Alex's shoulder: Katya standing behind him. "What do we know about him?" she asked.

Zac kept his gaze on Eva. On her pale, set features. As he watched, she turned away and began pacing again.

"The Fitzgeralds are one of New York's oldest families," Zac said, when neither Alex nor Eva seemed about to explain. "Rich. Powerful. They have connections right across the country. In the White House. Everywhere. Evelyn is the current patriarch, with all sorts of fingers in all sorts of different pies. Mainly real estate from what I've managed to discover."

Alex pushed himself away from the couch and walked over to one of the armchairs, throwing himself down into it without a word. The expression on his face was impenetrable.

Katya went over and stood by the chair, looking down at him. As Zac watched, Alex tipped his head back and met her gaze. Something wordless and intensely private passed between them.

Discomforted in ways he couldn't quite pinpoint, he looked back at the woman pacing in front of the empty, cold fireplace.

Silence sat like a black hole in the room, dense and heavy, sucking away all sound.

Behind him, Zac heard the door open again then close with a thunk.

Gabriel.

" 'Fitz'," Gabriel murmured cryptically as he went to stand next to Zac. "I always wondered what Tremain meant."

Zac turned his head, met the other man's dark eyes. "What are you talking about?"

Gabriel leaned a hip against the back of the couch, folding his arms. He glanced first at Eva, still pacing, then at Alex, who'd pulled Katya down in his lap and was now holding her as if afraid she might be torn from his grasp at any second.

Zac found the pair vaguely disturbing so he kept his gaze on Gabriel instead.

"The night I went to the Lucky Seven," Gabriel said after a moment. "When Tremain turned up. He thought I was someone else. He said, 'Fitz. Is that you?' He must have thought I was Fitzgerald."

"Tell me what else you found out, Zac," Alex demanded suddenly. "I want to know."

Zac didn't much like being ordered to do anything, but

he'd give Alex a pass on this. It had taken the other man a
long time to confront what had happened to him in the
bathroom of the Lucky Seven casino, but he'd done it in
the end. And that deserved respect.

Gabriel said nothing, eyeing him.

"Where's Honor?" Zac asked. "We have to be careful
with this information. I don't want to have to go through
it all again."

"She's coming. She had a meeting she couldn't resched-
ule on such short notice, so she'll be a little late." Gabriel
shifted against the couch. "Don't worry, I'll fill her in."

Zac was aware that Eva had stopped pacing and was
watching him. No doubt she was concerned about her secret.

*Are you going to force me to stand up in front of them
and tell them all about what happened to me too?*

He'd told her he would and he'd meant it. And if that
made him as bad as the man who'd taken her, then too bad.
He was ruthless. About time she learned that. The lives of
their friends were too important for either secrets or scruples.

"Bryson told me that Fitzgerald used to take him to the
Lucky Seven," Zac said, keeping his voice level, calm.
"And as far as what happened with Alex, Bryson said he
was ordered to stand outside that bathroom." Zac shifted
his gaze to meet Alex's intense, blue eyes. "But not by
South. By Fitzgerald."

"Bastard," Alex said softly. "That fucking bastard."

Katya shifted in his lap, lacing her fingers through his
where they rested on the arm of the chair.

Gabriel was silent, the look on his face hard. Then at
last he said, "He's part of this. He and Conrad, working
together from the looks of things. Jesus, were the rest of
them in on it too?"

"Dad knew," Alex murmured. "He tried to stop Conrad.

And then he was killed." He paused, one hand twining in Katya's hair, his thumb stroking one golden strand over and over. "On Fitzgerald's orders?"

Gabriel's head turned toward him. "The Apocalypse game. That mercenary, Elijah. He told you to stop investigating, threatened Zac and Eva. Could he be working for Fitzgerald?" He turned sharply to meet Zac's gaze. "Fuck, maybe this prick is the one pulling all the strings? Maybe he's the one dabbling in a little bit of human trafficking?"

Zac could feel Eva's tension like a physical force.

What had happened to her *was* important. It was a link to what had been going on in Conrad's casino. Because if Gabriel was right, if Fitzgerald was behind all of this, then it looked like the Seven Devils had been more than a rich boys' club running an underground casino. They'd been building an empire. Or at least Fitzgerald was the one building the empire. Since of course, that's what rich men like him did. They weren't content with what they had. They had to have more. Wealth was an addiction all its own, and Zac knew all about addiction. He'd had a grandstand view.

"We don't know that for certain," he said. "All we have is the testimony of this bodyguard."

"Is he telling the truth do you think?" Gabriel asked.

"Yes," Eva said unexpectedly, her voice sounding thin. "He was."

"Ah." Gabriel gave Zac a shrewd look. "You offered him some incentive."

Zac lifted a shoulder. "I did. He also mentioned that his life would be in danger if he told anyone."

"What a pity," Gabriel observed without sympathy. "Did you end up killing him anyway?"

A natural question. Gabriel, at least, knew what kind of man Zac was.

"No," Zac answered calmly. "We don't need any bodies lying around that might alert Fitzgerald to the fact that someone is investigating him. Besides, the body-guard might be useful when the time comes for making a move."

"What move?" Eva asked sharply.

Zac glanced at her, noting the lines of tension bracket-ing her pale mouth. The conversation was obviously get-ting to her and despite himself, his heart twisted, dark filaments of anger beginning to wind around him again. "To take him down, angel," he said flatly. So there would be no misunderstandings. "I've told you this."

An expression he didn't recognize flickered in her eyes. "I don't want you to kill him."

"Fuck that," Alex said from the armchair. "If you don't kill him, I will."

Eva's head turned sharply to where Alex sat. "No." The word sounded almost desperate. "I don't want anyone do-ing anything until we have more information."

"We don't need more information." Alex's voice was hard. "That prick's bodyguard stood watch over the door while I was fucking raped, Eva. It's all right there on that damn tape. What more do you need?"

The words echoed around the room, harsh and cold.

Eva shivered.

"The fire, Alex," Zac snapped, his patience suddenly on a knife-edge. "For fuck's sake. It's cold in here." He pushed away from the couch, picking up the overcoat he'd been wearing that he'd flung over the back of it. Stalking over to the fireplace where Eva stood, he lifted the coat, ready to drape it around her, but she moved away, putting her-self out his reach.

He frowned, staring after her, the overcoat still held awkwardly in his hands.

She'd never done that before.

Clearly she was still pissed off with him.

*Can you blame her? Would you feel comfortable telling all your secrets to everyone?*

Zac ignored the thought. It wasn't relevant.

Slowly, he lowered the coat to find both Gabriel and Alex watching him speculatively.

Zac stared back. They could think what they like about the relationship between Eva and himself. He'd guarantee it wasn't what either of them thought it was.

*But you wish it was.*

"Eva's right," he said coldly, tossing the overcoat back over to the couch. "We need more information. We need proof."

Alex made a disgusted sound, but Katya was nodding. "I agree," she said in her cool Russian accent. "I'm not sure Fitzgerald's bodyguard would have been able to tell you much in any case. You're going to need more than that if you want to take this to the relevant authorities."

Gabriel shifted, put his hands on the back of the couch, leaning against it. "Who said anything about taking this to the fucking authorities?"

Katya was in no way intimidated. "If this man has links with what was going on in Conrad South's casino, with that girl Alex and I freed, then Interpol need to be involved."

"Oh Christ," Alex muttered. "Katya mine, the fucked-up billionaires club is not much interested in bullshit operations like Interpol."

Katya tilted her head to look up into her lover's eyes. "Perhaps you're not. But if a human trafficking ring is going on then the authorities are the only ones who can help the people involved in it. In which case I think they might care about such 'bullshit operations.' "

Alex let out a long breath, the corner of his mouth turning up. "Why the hell do you have to be so damn intelligent?"

Gabriel snorted. "Fuck, get a room."

"You're talking sense at long last, brother." Alex didn't even look at him.

The bickering did nothing for Zac's patience or his temper, not with Eva standing on the other side of the fireplace, keeping the distance between them, her gaze turned inward. She'd taken one hand out of her pocket, fingers at her mouth. Biting her nails. Making him want to close the distance, take her hand in his hand, just hold it. Maybe turn it over in his own, kiss her palm. Soothe her.

The urge was so strong that for a second it was all he could do just to remain where he was.

*What are you waiting for? Isn't that what you always do? You wait for her to be ready. But she'll never be ready . . .*

No, she never would. Not to tell her secrets. Not to trust. Not to want him.

Which meant that if he wanted things to keep changing, he was going to have to be the one to change them.

Zac moved, closing the distance between himself and Eva. Slowly but surely stalking toward her. And like the wild creature she was, her head came up, her eyes going wide as she saw what he was doing.

Shock flared bright over her face like a jag of lightning and he saw her take an instinctive step back. But there was nowhere for her to go. The mantelpiece was at her back, an armchair blocking her route to the side. She was trapped.

The shock turned to panic, her hand dropping from her mouth. But by then it was too late. He reached for her, closing his fingers around her wrist.

Eva made a soft, gasping sound, what little color she had in her checks leeching away. Her whole body had gone rigid, her panicked gaze locked with his. Her skin was shockingly warm beneath his fingertips and so unbelievably soft, like heated silk. He could feel the rapid drumbeat of her pulse, see the frantic rise and fall of her chest, sense the panic clawing at her.

But he didn't let go.

The air seemed to go thick around them, time moving slow and sluggish as an animal caught in a tar pit.

She was shaking now.

He held on, locking her silver eyes with his. "Tell them, Eva."

And for one long, timeless second, he thought he saw something leap in her gaze. The kind of response he'd spent seven years longing for.

Then Eva jerked her hand from his grip.

And slapped him hard across the face.

Shock crashed through the room like a ship hitting an iceberg and shuddering with the impact.

The feel of Zac's skin against Eva's palm burned, the hard contours of his cheek, the roughness of stubble, the sheer, stinging heat . . .

She was shaking.

Jesus. She'd hit him. She'd actually hit him.

The skin around her other wrist burned too, like she'd been handcuffed with hot metal, a bracelet of fire that stung and stung and stung.

She could hardly breathe she was shaking so much.

He'd touched her. Again. In front everyone else.

Her heartbeat was out of control, fear a wild thing clawing in her chest. *Tell them, Eva.* But she didn't want to tell them. Not a single damn thing. And he was going to make her, force her. Use that stupid damn promise against her . . .

*That's not why you hit him.*

She could feel the places where he'd held her wrist, where she'd slapped him. Like matches to touch paper, they were still burning. The reflections of that fire leapt in his eyes, bright amber flames.

Then he smiled, a feral kind of smile. As if he knew something she didn't.

*You didn't hit him because you were scared of having to tell your secrets.*

"Well," Alex murmured into the tense silence. "I guess it's not a Circles meeting if someone isn't getting hit in the face."

"Christ," Gabriel said. "What the hell is wrong with you two?"

Eva blinked, the rest of the room abruptly coming into sharp focus.

Alex and Katya staring at her in surprise. Gabriel's dark eyes narrowed in puzzlement.

And Zac . . . He wasn't looking anywhere else except at her.

*Your physical reaction to him scared you. That's why you hit him.*

Behind the fear, under the panic, heat unfurling inside her like a flag. A strangely familiar heat . . .

The door opened suddenly and Honor came in, the sharp tension in the room snapping like a twig.

Everyone turned to look at her and she stopped, raising one dark brow. "Did I miss something?"

From somewhere Eva found her voice. "No, nothing. Or at least, the only thing you missed was the name of the man we think had something to do with what happened to Alex."

Honor's cool blue gaze met her brother's briefly. "It's okay. Gabe's already told me."

"You okay about it, baby?" Gabriel asked.

Honor frowned, coming slowly over to where Gabriel stood. "Not especially. He's Violet's father."

"Tall," Alex murmured. "Blond. Arrogant. Entitled. At least that's what I remember about him."

Eva didn't move, her heard still beating too fast, too

hard. Her wrist still burned, her palm still stung. And Zac was still standing far, far too close. He'd turned to look at Honor like the rest of them, but she was so intensely conscious of him she couldn't concentrate on anything else.

Why had he touched her? What the *fuck* did he think he was doing?

*"It's when you're aware of the person you want . . . Physically aware of them in every way . . ."*

God. Oh, holy fucking hell.

He was wearing another of his dark suits, this time in black wool, and he'd taken off his gloves. His fingers were long and blunt, and quite elegant. The dark ink of the tattoos that covered them and the backs of his hands were beautiful. Crowns and stars and religious iconography. That hand had touched her, those fingers had been against her skin.

Her wrist throbbed.

Honor was speaking, but Eva couldn't seem to focus on her voice.

He was so tall. If she closed her eyes, remembered the last meeting on his island, where he'd gone swimming, she'd be able to see his body without those suits. Broad and heavily muscled. Flat stomach. Lean waist. Powerful thighs and long calves. There had been Chinese koi carp up the bronze skin of one arm. A dragon on his back.

She swallowed, her gaze helplessly drawn to his face, turned away from her. A stunningly perfect profile, the straight angle of his nose meeting his elegantly sculpted mouth. High forehead. Strong jawline.

*Beautiful. He's beautiful.*

How had she not seen? How had she not realized?

It felt like she'd been leaning for years against what she thought was an ordinary brick wall, only to turn around and find out she'd been leaning against beautifully carved marble instead. That was attached to an exquisite palace.

Her heart thumped behind her breastbone, a fast, frantic beat.

She didn't understand what was happening to her, why here, now, she should suddenly be seeing Zac Rutherford in a way she'd never seen him before. Even after he'd forced that promise from her, told her he'd take her body as well as her trust, made her give him her secrets, deliberately frightening her . . . Even after all of that, she was aware of him in a way that was quite frankly —

*Terrifying?*

She blinked, stuffing her burning hands back into her jacket. Trying to drag her consciousness back into the present.

"What do you think, Eva?"

Eva blinked again, realizing that Alex was staring at her. That everyone was staring at her. "Excuse me?" she said hoarsely. "What?"

"You can hack into his computer system."

Zac was looking at her now, she could feel it, and a rush of heat washed over her, like a warm current in an icy sea. This was madness.

*I can make you want me.*

"Hack into his system," she echoed stupidly. "Yes."

"You'll have to be careful." Zac's deep voice was a shock, strange when she knew it as well as her own. Yet now it seemed to hold timbres she'd never heard before, a soft roughness, sensual as the caress of velvet. "Especially if, as we suspect, he's the one behind those threats."

The word "threats" pierced the fog surrounding her. Threats such as the email that had stolen past her firewalls and gotten into her own system.

Not that there was any doubt in her mind that Fitzgerald was behind that.

The heat began to dissipate as she realized something else.

Fitzgerald had targeted her. Which meant he knew her name. He knew she was Eva King. He knew what she looked like. He knew *her.*

Terror surged inside her, a blind, primitive panic, and it was only sheer force of will, of habit, that enabled her to swallow it down and not let it show.

But, of course, Zac knew. Because when she met his disturbing amber gaze, she could see the knowledge of it in the depths of his eyes. The recognition.

Evelyn Fitzgerald wasn't the only man who knew her.

Another emotion blazed through her, swallowing the fear, so intense she didn't know how to deal with it. Christ, where were all these feelings coming from? It was like finding out the name of The Man had unlocked Pandora's box, letting all the curses loose on the world. Or rather, letting them loose on her world.

She had to shut the box, keep the hope. The hope that she could survive this.

Eva curled her hands into fists, dug her bitten nails into her palms. They were too short to cause real pain but long enough to cause a bit of discomfort. Which helped settle her.

"You want me to hack into Fitzgerald's system?" she asked, pleased that her voice was sounding more or less normal now.

"That's the idea," Gabriel said. "We need proof. And you're good enough to be able to do it without anyone noticing."

"Or," Honor murmured, "we could just attend a party."

Gabriel frowned and turned to her. "What?"

Honor lifted the phone she'd been bent over. "There's a party on in a couple of days, organized by a charity funded through one of Fitzgerald's companies. It's a fundraiser for the homeless. Looks like Fitzgerald is going to be attending." She looked around the room. "Who wants an invite?"

"Why wait? We could pay Fitzgerald a little visit right now." Zac's voice was dark, the rough, sensual sound she'd noticed earlier vanishing completely from it. "I have certain . . . contacts who could arrange a more personal meeting."

But Honor shook her head, glancing down at her phone again. "Looks like he's out of the country at the moment, at least according to this particular news report. He's coming back in time for this fundraiser."

"A party." Alex smiled. It wasn't a pleasant smile. "Oh, I do like a party."

"So what's your plan once you get there?" Katya asked. "Corner him and ask him your questions?"

"Why not?" Gabriel lifted a shoulder. "I'm sure between us we could persuade him to answer."

"Or," Zac said softly. "You could go, angel. And save us all this trouble."

Oh, damn him. Damn him to hell.

She was conscious of everyone's attention on her.

"Why would Eva going save us the trouble?" Katya asked, sounding puzzled.

Eva didn't look at anyone else. Only at the man staring at her. The man who'd brought the past she'd been desperate to leave behind her crashing back into the present.

The man she'd thought she was safe with and now knew that there was no such thing as safe with Zac Rutherford.

No. He wouldn't get this from her, he goddamn wouldn't.

"This meeting is fucking over," she said.

There was a silence. Everyone stared at her, and suddenly she wanted to scream at them all to leave. To get out, to stop looking at her. Stop asking her for things she didn't want to give.

But it was Alex of all people who moved. He murmured something in Katya's ear and she got off him, rising to stand beside his chair while he got to his feet, only wincing a little as he took a couple of steps toward the fireplace.

Unable to help herself, her nerves frayed beyond endurance, Eva backed heavily into the mantelpiece as Alex came closer.

Only to come to an abrupt halt as Zac moved smoothly to put himself in front of her, a tall, muscled barrier.

Her heart thumped. She couldn't even find it in herself to protest at Zac's obvious protective behavior. Because she knew what Alex was going to say. Knew it with certainty.

Alex gave Zac one intense, piercing look. Then he turned his blue gaze on Eva.

There was a terrible understanding in his eyes and she found herself shaking her head, wanting to deny it.

"Eva," Alex said in a voice full of gentleness. "Remember what you told me? Put a bullet in his head. That's what you said."

She remembered. Before Alex had gone to Monte Carlo, when he'd been trying not to involve himself in the deepening mystery of the Seven Devils. When she'd thought all this wasn't so personal. When the past hadn't returned from the grave she'd buried it in to slap her across the face.

Even back then she'd recognized the trauma in Alex, mainly because she'd always felt it herself, deep down. But she didn't want to be reminded, not now. Not with the prospect of her past being laid out for everyone to see.

*For you to remember.*

"Leave her alone," Zac said, iron in his voice.

Alex ignored him. "You know I'm right, Eva. Running doesn't solve anything. Believe me, I know.

"This is not your fight." Violence simmered beneath Zac's cultured British vowels. "Go and sit down."

Alex's focus switched to Zac. He stared at him for a long moment. Then he said, "You two need to sort your shit out. And do it quickly. The rest of us need you."

*Tell them, Eva.*

She turned around sharply, staring down into the empty black grate of the fireplace. Focusing on that and not on the wild beating of her heart or the fear that curled like an animal inside her chest. An animal with sharp teeth and claws.

Please don't let him make her do this. Please.

Behind her Zac was saying something while Alex replied, but she tuned them out.

Everything in her howled in protest at the thought of going to this stupid function. Apart from anything else, she hadn't been around large groups of people in years, which meant that in itself was going to be difficult. But the thought of confronting *him* . . . In the flesh . . .

*You have to do it. They need you.*

How? How the hell was she doing to do it? Because for once she knew that denial wasn't going to work, not with Zac pushing and pushing and pushing.

Zac, who as it turned out, was beautiful.

The voices behind her had grown silent, and she could feel the tension in the room like another presence.

They were arguing about her. God, what a terrible time for them to be arguing among themselves, especially when they were so close to finding out what was going on.

*All because you can't deal.*

Eva swallowed and turned. The room she'd once felt so comfortable in, so safe, didn't feel so safe any longer. And everyone was looking at her, waiting for her to say something.

But it felt like the walls were closing in, her throat tight, the fear in her chest starting to claw at her. And she couldn't stay here any longer. She had to get out.

Without a word, she brushed past Zac and headed for the door.

"Eva," he called, and the iron in his voice only made her fear turn choking. "Don't you dare run."

But she didn't reply or turn around.

"Eva, stop!"

She didn't do that either.

# CHAPTER EIGHT

Zac cursed viciously and without a word strode after Eva. The door slammed shut after him, leaving a heavy, uncomfortable silence.

Honor's heart caught painfully. Something had scared Eva, that much was obvious, and it was difficult seeing that fear and hurt flare in her delicate, pale face. She was normally so tough and yet it seemed that toughness hid a desperate vulnerability.

It was especially difficult having some inkling into what might have caused such fear and pain.

Alex and Eva had a shared experience from the looks of things, and though Alex might have come to terms with what had happened to him, it was clear Eva had not.

And it had something to do with Evelyn Fitzgerald.

Honor caught her brother's gaze.

Though it had been a rewarding couple of weeks, each of them painfully rebuilding the bridge that Alex had burned behind him, it hadn't exactly been easy either. There was still much that hadn't been spoken of. That would come in time, she had no doubt, but until then, some things were going to be painful.

Such as finding out the real reason Alex had left and not spoken to either her or her mother for nineteen years.

Such as finding out her father hadn't committed suicide after all. She hadn't told her mother that yet, was still trying to figure out when she actually would, since Elizabeth St. James had enough to deal with already with her husband in the hospital in a coma.

Except not for much longer.

Beside her Gabriel shifted as if sensing her tension, sliding an arm around her waist to draw her in close to his big, muscular body. She let herself lean against him for a moment, enjoying his warmth and wordless support.

"Violet, huh?" he said quietly.

Honor's ex-roommate and friend. And Evelyn Fitzgerald's daughter.

"Yes." Honor sighed. "I can't quite believe he might have something to do with it."

Alex stuck his hands in the pockets of his suit pants. "I thought she was in France?"

"No," Honor said. "She came back and was staying in my apartment for a while. I've just shifted into Gabriel's place so Vi took over my lease. God, if it's true, if her father is involved with this . . ." She stopped. Violet was restless, a rebel. Constantly trying to throw off the shackles of her blue-blooded family's expectations. But she had a good heart, was a good person, and Honor thought she loved her dad deep down.

Finding out he perhaps wasn't what he seemed would be devastating, as Honor herself knew from her own experience.

"But we don't know anything for certain yet." A faint, wry smile turned the end of Alex's mouth. "Jesus, listen to me. Who'd have thought I'd be the fucking voice of reason?"

The unexpected thread of humor loosened the tension in the room.

"Someone needs to be," Gabriel said. "Might as well

be you." He released Honor, putting his hands on the back of the couch and leaning on them. "So we have a name. Anything else? I didn't turn up shit about Mantel or any of the other Devils. Whatever they've been up to, they covered their tracks pretty thoroughly."

"I might be able to help with that," Honor offered.

Gabriel glanced at her. "You got something, baby?"

Honor nodded, turning her attention back to Alex. "The reason I was late was that the hospital called. They're going to bring Dad out of his coma tonight."

Alex had gone very still, as had Gabe.

"Shit," Gabriel muttered. "That could be extremely fucking helpful."

"Mom wanted you to be there," Honor said, keeping her gaze on her brother.

Alex had seen his mother a couple of times since he'd recovered from his bullet wound. Initially their meetings had been awkward and painful, mostly on Alex's part since Elizabeth had been so glad about her son's return that she hadn't cared about his reasons for leaving. It only mattered that he was home.

Neither Alex nor Honor had told Elizabeth about Conrad South. Just as they hadn't told her that her first husband had been murdered.

"Then I'll be there," Alex said.

Honor glanced at the woman standing beside Alex's abandoned armchair, her golden hair in a braid down her back, her black suit only slightly rumpled from sitting in Alex's arms only five minutes earlier. "She wants you there too, Katya."

The Russian woman looked startled. "Well, of course."

Honor let out a breath. "I don't want to get anyone's hopes up. The doctor mentioned that there might be some brain damage, so I wouldn't count on Dad remembering anything. He might not even be able to speak."

Beside her, Gabriel shifted again. "Then we carry on with our plans. I'll see if I can get an invite to this fund-raising thing. Hell, maybe Woolf Construction already got one since we do build fucking houses after all."

"I'll see if I can get one too," Alex said. He'd begun to pace in front of the fireplace. "Jesus, we need Zac and Eva. I want to know whether Zac made any progress finding out about the Apocalypse players. And what kind of stuff Eva's managed to turn up about trafficking."

"Yeah, but they looked like they had other stuff on their plate to deal with." Gabriel straightened. "Now we have a name, we can do this without Eva."

Alex shook his head. "Running away won't help. And yeah, I know, that's ironic coming from me."

Gabriel held up a hand. "Hey, I didn't say a word."

"So the plan," Katya said impatiently. "You are going to interrogate him? That could be dangerous if he knows you are all going to be there. What if he's connected to Elijah? To whoever issued those threats in the first place?"

Worry twisted in Honor's gut. "Katya has a point. You all going in there guns blazing is probably not a good idea. My father was murdered, and they shot Guy. They're dangerous. If Fitzgerald is actually connected in any way to all of this, then lives could be at risk." She paused, staring at both her brother and Gabriel. "I've only just found you both. I couldn't bear to lose either of you."

Katya moved, going over to where Alex stood. She put a hand on his arm. "Alexei . . . Honor has a point. I will protect you, you know that. But what if it gets out of hand? We need more—"

"Information?" Alex lifted a hand, cupping her cheek. "Don't fret, Katya mine. I agree that we need to take this slowly."

The tenderness in her brother's face caught at Honor's heart. Despite the awkwardness between them, it had been wonderful to see all these unexpected sides to Alex that she hadn't known were there. Or maybe she had. He'd been a protective, loving big brother once and it was lovely to see that those aspects of him hadn't been completely buried by his experiences.

"Good point." Gabriel's arm once more slid around her waist, pulling her close. "But we can look after ourselves, baby. You know that. We've gotten very good at it over the years."

Honor turned to look up at the man she loved. "I know. But this is turning out to be far more dangerous than any of us could have predicted. And we don't know what else is going to come out of the woodwork. I just . . . we need to keep our risks as small as we can make them."

A rare smile flickered over Gabriel's face. "Typical financial advisor." The warmth in his voice made her want to arch her back like a cat being stroked.

She raised a brow at him. "You're investing your lives, Gabe. And I would be severely unhappy with you if you were to lose your investment."

He bent and kissed her, a swift, hard kiss that promised all kinds of exciting things. "Katya's right. And you do have a point," he said as he straightened up. "We're going to have to rethink this. Perhaps only one of us needs to attend then?"

"It has to be Eva," Alex said. "At least, from what Zac said it sounded like she might have more information about this than the rest of us do."

"Yes, but it doesn't look like she wanted to go." Honor let herself lean into the man holding her. "What about me? I could—"

"No," Gabriel interrupted flatly. "Not you. Not after Tremain ended up in the hospital."

It wasn't a battle she was going to win, so Honor only shrugged. "Okay, not me. Alex?"

But it was Katya who answered. "If Fitzgerald is involved with this, Alex's attendance will possibly do the same thing."

"Yes," Alex slowly agreed. "He knows I was at the Lucky Seven, and it's looking like he was in with Conrad when it came to what happened to me. Perhaps me turning up at this party isn't such a good idea if we want the element of surprise."

"Zac then," Honor said. "It's either him or Eva. We don't know for sure if Fitzgerald has been the one issuing threats or not, and I guess if he is, he'll know who Zac and Eva are. But . . . they're the only ones otherwise who aren't directly involved."

Alex's blue eyes met hers. "That we know of."

"Yes," she echoed, remembering Eva's white face. "That we know of."

"Eva won't like that," Katya murmured, with supreme understatement.

"I think," Gabriel said, "that's going to be Zac's problem."

Eva was already halfway down the hallway by the time Zac managed to get out of the room, walking quickly, her head down, hands still stuffed in the pockets of her jacket.

She wasn't going to stop for him, that much he already knew. Which left him with only two options: let her go or stop her in another way.

Letting her go wasn't an option, especially not when it wouldn't solve anything for them or for the people in the room they'd just left. And besides, he'd be damned if she'd slap him in the face in front of everyone else, then walk away like it was nothing.

He was angry. No, scratch angry. He was fucking furious.

Zac didn't call her name or shout at her to stop this time. He just moved. Fast.

A few long-legged steps took him right to her, then he reached out, took her by her upper arms, spun her around, and pushed her firmly up against the wall.

Her mouth opened in shock, her delicate features about as white as her hair.

He didn't keep hold of her, releasing her almost immediately. But to prevent her from escaping again, he put his palms flat on the wall on either side of her, caging her against it with his body.

There was terror in her gaze, a blind, unthinking terror. And yet she bared her teeth at him like a cornered thing, wild with fear and ready to attack.

"Do. Not. Run. From. Me," he said, enunciating each word with absolute, complete authority.

"Fuck. Off," Eva spat. She lifted her hands and shoved against his chest with surprising strength. The move was a shock since he wasn't expecting her to touch him, and it almost unbalanced him. But he managed to remain on his feet, and when she gave him another shove, he didn't move.

With a small cry of frustration, Eva raised a hand as if to hit him again.

Christ, he'd had enough of that.

Zac grabbed her wrist before she could get in another slap, pinning it to the wall beside her head. Then he did the same to her other hand for good measure.

"You're panicking." He kept his voice clear and cold, aiming it with the precision of a scalpel to cut through her unthinking fear. "Take a breath and calm down."

"No! Let me go, asshole!" Eva pulled at his restraining hands, trying to get free.

"I won't allow you to run away or hit me again. Now do as I say. Calm the fuck down."

Her chest heaved, small round breasts pushing against her black T-shirt, her skin flushed pink. Giving him a taste of what it would be like to have her submitting to him.

He'd always tried not to think about it since there was no point fantasizing about something that may not ever happen, but now, holding her against the wall like this, he could imagine it vividly.

Eva, naked. Her skin glowing in the light, like alabaster lit from within. Her pale hair over her shoulders, covering her breasts. Her silver eyes would find his and stay there as he whispered dirty things to her, playing with her mind to get her as wet as he possibly could without even touching her. Only once she was panting, willing to do whatever he wanted, would he allow himself a touch. His fingers trailing down her throat, between those beautiful little tits, over her stomach, down to the pale curls between her thighs.

More than a touch. A claim of ownership. Making her his in every way that counted.

His blood pulsed, thumping loudly in his head. His cock getting hard.

He wanted, oh Jesus, how he wanted. Her heat, her sweetness, her sensuality, because he was sure they were all there, just waiting to be unlocked. And also her courage, her fight, her spark. All of it given to him.

But most of all, the most precious, the most vital: her trust.

Which she still hadn't handed to him, despite her promise.

Eva had stopped pulling, twin spots of color now blazing on her cheekbones. She was staring at him as if she'd never seen him before in her life.

And he knew, he goddamned *knew,* that it wasn't with fear this time. There was something different in her eyes. Something that looked, whether she realized it herself or not, a hell of a lot like heat.

He caught his breath, the dragon inside him hungry, roaring to get out. But he ignored it. He wanted her begging for him, desperate for him. And that spark of heat in her eyes was too new, too small. If he took what he wanted now he would crush it.

She looked away from him. "Let me go," she said, her voice breathless yet less panic-stricken.

"Not if you're going to hit me again."

She was silent a moment, her mouth tight. "I won't. I promise."

He didn't want to let her go. The rapid beat of her pulse against his thumb, the soft, vulnerable skin of her wrist, the scent of her . . . all intoxicating sensations that he wanted to keep hold of. Savor them as he savored all the things he enjoyed.

*Patience.*

Zac forced himself to release her. But he didn't move away, placing his palms back on the wall on either side of her, keeping her caged.

She dropped her hands, rubbing absently at her wrists. "Give me some room, asshole. I can't breathe with you looming over me."

"No."

"Oh Christ, Zac, what the—"

"You slapped my face in a room full of people, Eva. Then you ran. Why?"

"Because you were being a prick."

Hell no. He wasn't going to let her get away with that. "Don't lie to me. It was because I touched you and you couldn't handle it. Just like you couldn't handle the thought of confronting Fitzgerald."

Her jaw had gotten hard, defiance in her eyes. "I was fine—"

"You were scared," he cut her off. "Acknowledge it. Accept it. Because until you do, afraid is all you'll ever be."

That spark of defiance glowed hot in her eyes for a moment. Then she turned her head again, looking away. She didn't speak, her fingers still rubbing at her wrists.

"I know this is hard," he said. "I know you don't want to go to this function and confront Fitzgerald. But the people in that room need you. They need your strength and your determination, and you have so much of both, angel."

Her throat moved in a convulsive swallow. "I . . . just want the past to be over. I don't want to have it dragged up again. And I certainly don't want to fucking talk about it."

It wasn't an admission, not quite. But it was step in the right direction. "Ignoring it won't make it go away. You know this."

She looked down at her hands. "I want to go home."

"No, what you want is to hide."

"What's so damn wrong with that?"

"One touch, angel. I took your hand and it terrified you. That's why you hit me, wasn't it?"

She said nothing, still looking down.

"You don't want anyone getting close to you. You don't want anyone touching you. You can't even go outside without me, yet you still won't trust me. And you insist you're fine." He paused, watching her face, her features set. "You're letting your fear do your thinking for you, Eva. And that could put every person in that room at risk."

Again silence.

And he let it sit there for a long moment, trying to read her expression. Pale lashes shielded her eyes, but her mouth was tight. She was struggling.

"You have to trust someone, sometime, Eva," he said, keeping his voice hard, because he couldn't be gentle anymore. "Otherwise your fear will swallow you whole."

He hoped she knew he took no pleasure from having to do this, from forcing her to see what was happening to her.

He didn't want to undermine her very real strength, but the fact was, she was fighting the wrong enemy and she had to understand that.

This was a strong woman. Who'd overcome a difficult past, whose sharp intelligence and energy had built a company from the ground up and turned it into one of America's biggest in a very short space of time.

And it was wrong that she should be trapped like this in a cage of her own making.

"You want me to go to this fundraiser," she said after a moment. "You want me to face him."

"You have to. We need confirmation of who he is, and you're the only one who can do it." He paused. "You told me you remembered his voice."

She looked away, her lashes falling, veiling her gaze. "I'm not ready."

"You'll never be ready."

"I can't . . ."

"You can. You will." He pushed himself away from the wall, allowing her some space. "Right now, you're coming home with me so we can sort this out once and for all."

Her head came up sharply. "Why? I just want to go home."

"You mean you want to run away and hide." He couldn't allow her to keep following this pattern of running when she was scared. Because a day would come when she ran home and stayed there. "The time for running is over, angel. Besides, you promised me. No more arguments."

She muttered something filthy under her breath. Then shrugged. "Okay, fine. Whatever."

More bravado. And yet he noticed that her breathing had normalized, that the tightness around her mouth was gone. She was still touching her wrists and not quite looking at him, but she wasn't shaking. Almost as if she'd forgotten how close he was standing.

Almost as if she was getting used to it.

He didn't want to count it a victory yet, but it was definitely progress of a sort.

That little spark would become flame, would burn hot, he'd make sure of it.

# CHAPTER NINE

Zac's place was a five-storied brownstone on the Upper West Side that he had all to himself. Built around 1910, it had been beautifully restored and radiated old world glamour. Yet behind its beautiful façade was a high-tech, state-of-the-art security system and computer network that Eva had installed.

The place was very much like Zac himself, at least on the outside. Polished, civilized, and very, very upper-class Brit.

Her favorite place to be, though, was his library. Probably because it reminded her of the Nine Circles clubroom at the Second Circle.

The walls were covered from ceiling to floor with expensive library bookshelves, all filled with books. There were Persian rugs on the floor in muted golds and blues, soft dark brown leather wingback chairs, a dark brown leather sofa in front of the old fashioned fire, low tables here and there with lamps on them, stacks of books, and other knickknacks.

It was in the front, overlooking the street, long dark blue velvet curtains drawn back from the windows, letting in the afternoon sun.

A peaceful, restful room.

She used to feel safe here. Yet right now . . . not so much.

Not after Zac had held her up against the wall in the corridor of the Second Circle, his fingers around her wrists. Not after she'd felt that hot pulse go through her when his eyes met hers, and she'd become so conscious of him. Of where his fingers touched her skin, of his big body inches from hers, of being surrounded by him. Overwhelmed by him.

Yes his closeness had overloaded her already screaming nerves and okay, she'd admit it, she'd panicked. Shoving him, trying to hit him again. Going totally off the rails until his cool, calm voice had penetrated her fog of terror.

And that's when that awareness had struck. That strange heat. A heat she'd seen reflected in his golden eyes.

For a second she hadn't been afraid. In fact, she'd wanted . . . more.

*You want him.*

Eva ignored the thought, moving to the fireplace as Zac went over to a large, beautifully carved oak cabinet and pulled out a bottle of wine and a glass, pouring himself some of the deep red liquid. Then, as he always did when she was here, he switched on the electric kettle he kept there too, boiling water for her tea.

She shoved her hands in her jeans pockets, watching him, an odd restlessness churning inside her.

She should have argued more. Should have insisted she went home. That stupid damn promise he'd made her give him . . .

The careful movements he made as he began organizing her tea infuriated her. Christ, no matter where they were, no matter what they were doing, he was always doing things for her. Making sure the room was warm. Making sure she had her favorite drink. Making sure she was comfortable. Caring for her needs. And she'd never questioned it, taking it for granted, barely even aware of what he was doing.

Well, she was bitterly aware right now. And it only added fuel to the burning mix of emotions inside her, an anger she didn't quite understand.

"You don't have to make my tea for me," she snapped gracelessly. "I'm not a child."

"Too late. It's done now." He turned around, coming over to where she stood by the fire and placing her china cup and saucer on the table near the sofa. Then he turned to put his wine down on another small table beside his usual armchair before sitting down in it.

"Why?" she demanded. "Why do you do all of these things for me? The tea. The fire. The blankets and shit. Do I look like a kid to you?"

Zac said nothing, stretching out his long legs in front of him, crossing them at the ankles. He picked up his wine, sipped at it meditatively as his amber gaze studied her.

She felt uncomfortable and antsy. She couldn't seem to stop noticing things about him. The way his tattooed fingers curled around the glass. The pull of the material of his suit pants around his powerful thighs. How thick and soft his black hair looked.

These things were wrong. She didn't want to notice them. She wanted to go back to the way it was before when he was just a wall she leaned against.

*Where you were safe.*

"You don't look like a kid, angel," he said in a measured voice. "Because that would make me a pervert and while I am kinky, I'm definitely no pervert."

That look in his eyes . . . There was no mistaking it.

She turned away, going over to the table where her tea rested, picking up the cup and taking a sip to cover her reaction. "Okay, fine. But I still don't know why you do all these things for me."

"I do them because I'm your friend. Because I'm not sure you've ever had anyone who's ever looked after you before."

Eva stared down at the hot liquid in her cup. He was wrong. She'd been looked after before.

*In the house she'd always had food. TV dinners she'd had to cook herself mainly, or takeout when her guards hadn't been bothered to go to the supermarket. It had been amazing for a kid who'd been living on the streets for months. And she'd always been warm. Even had her own bathroom . . .*

She took a sip of the hot liquid, feeling it burn her throat, the pain burning away the memories.

"What do you get out of it?" she asked, flicking a glance at him. "Or is it more a case of money in the bank?"

Zac placed his wine down on the table at his elbow. "Money in the bank meaning I'm doing all of that just to make you more likely to sleep with me presumably?" There was an edge to his voice.

She stared at him, her heart thumping. Remembering the burning gold of his eyes as he'd held her against the wall and the look on his face, a hungry, yearning look.

He was always so in control of himself, so contained, but in that moment he hadn't been. Just like he hadn't been the night he'd come to her apartment, when he'd told her what he wanted.

She got to him. She tested that seemingly perfect control of his. Even now, that simple question had gotten a reaction from him that wasn't his usual patient, measured response.

*This isn't new. You're always doing that. You're always pushing him, fighting him. Testing his boundaries. Testing the limits of your friendship.*

She stilled, pierced by sudden realization. She *was* always fighting him, snarking at him. Pushing him. Because she could, because he was safe.

Because she had power over him and she knew it. And liked it. Especially since she'd had too many years of not having any power whatsoever.

Satisfaction sank down inside of her, heady and exhilarating. Unfamiliar and yet familiar at the same time. It made her want to keep pushing him. Keep fighting him. Test this new power, see how far she could go.

"Well, isn't it?" she couldn't resist saying. "I mean, you do want to sleep with me. At least, that's what you keep saying. Not forgetting the fact that you also want me to want you." She paused for effect. "And hey, you did say you were a mercenary after all and that everything had a price."

Zac steepled his fingers, his gaze absolutely enigmatic.

Eva took another sip of her scalding tea. Ginger and lemon, her favorite. "You can't have it both ways, Zac. You can't accept sex as the price for our friendship and then get annoyed when I question your motives."

There was a long silence. Too long.

"Yes," he said quietly. "You're right." Reaching for his wine glass, he drained it in one swallow, his golden eyes never leaving hers. "I can't." He put it back down on the table with a sharp click before getting slowly to his feet. One hand reached for the knot of his tie, undoing it as he began to walk slowly toward her.

Eva stared at him, a deep trepidation turning over inside. "What are you doing?"

"What I should have done a long time ago." He was coming closer, his tie undone now, his fingers going for the top button of his shirt. There was something intent in his gaze, like he'd made a decision.

*He's coming for you.*

A pulse of unthinking fear went through her and she dropped her cup, tea splashing all over the expensive silk of hand-knotted Persian rug on the floor.

Zac didn't even look at it. Instead, those intense, incredible eyes of his looked only at her. "Sit down, angel," he said softly.

"What?"

"I said. *Sit. Down*." His voice smashed across her like an iron bar laid heavily across a pane of glass. There was no arguing with it, no avoiding it, no pretending she didn't hear.

Something inside her screamed "yes." Like she'd been waiting to hear those words for a long time now, maybe years. Desperately hoping that voice of his, that will of his, could take away her fear, free her from the pain she'd been trapped in for so long.

Yet, there was another part of her that only wanted to fight, to keep protecting herself against the threat he presented. That part had been battling for too long to give up so easily, and it won now, her chin lifting, meeting him as he closed the distance between them.

"Hell no. You think you can—"

Then there was no distance at all, Zac's warm hands on her hips, propelling her back until she found herself sitting in the other wingback chair, with him crouched at her feet, his hands on the arms of the chair.

She couldn't breathe, her heart pounding in her ears, fear igniting small fires everywhere.

*But not only fear.*

There was intensity in Zac's face, his indomitable will she'd seen turned on others before yet never on herself. A will she'd been longing all this time to test herself against yet hadn't the courage. Now it was here, whether she wanted it or not.

"Give me your hands." The hard authority of the order was undeniable.

"No," she said breathlessly. "What the fuck are you—"

"*Hands.*"

She knew she hadn't given them to him and yet he seemed to be holding them anyway, his grip on her wrists unbreakable. And she couldn't breathe, couldn't fight the heat that was moving up her arms, radiating through her. Heat that burned her, terrified her.

"Disobey me again," he said in a voice like cut steel, "and there will be consequences."

"Consequences?" She tried to pull her hands away only to find she couldn't move them. A burst of fear caught in her throat. "What the hell are you doing?"

He transferred both her wrists into one large, long-fingered hand while he pulled his undone tie from around his neck. Then with brisk, practiced movements, he wrapped the tie around her wrists, binding them together.

Eva stared dumbly at what he was doing. Her heart felt like it was going to burst through her chest and she wanted to struggle, to run, to get away. Only sheer force of will kept her where she was. She wouldn't give in to the fear, she just wouldn't.

She shivered, trying to stay very, very still.

When he'd finished, he sat back on his heels and looked at her.

"You bastard." She couldn't stop the words that spilled out, panicked and hoarse. "I don't know what you're trying to do but—"

Zac gripped her chin in his hand, hard and sure. Reflexively she tried to jerk away, but he only held her tighter.

"A-Asshole!" Oh, God, she was stuttering, her voice thin and thready. "Don't fucking touch me!"

He ignored her, leaning forward and taking hold of

the fabric of her T-shirt. She tried to get her arms up to stop him but by the time she moved, it was too late. With easy strength and calm force, he ripped her T-shirt open as if it was made out of tissue paper.

Shock like a bucket of ice water tipped over her head, flooding through her, freezing her to the spot.

But he didn't stop. Brushing aside the two halves of her ruined shirt, he took the practical black cotton bra in his fingers and twisted the cups apart, tearing it so that it fell away, baring her completely.

Every single one of her protection mechanisms activated.

Eva raised her bound wrists to cover herself, but he pulled them down and held them pressed to her knees. She panicked, starting to struggle, but he only leaned forward, trapping her legs with the weight of his body, holding them down against the chair. Then with his free hand he reached out and gripped her chin again.

Her heart raced, fear clawing her insides to shreds. "Get the fuck away—"

His thumb pressed down on her mouth, silencing her.

"Be quiet and listen," he said, his tone diamond-hard. "I know you're scared, Eva, but your days of using me as your scratching post are at an end. You promised me your trust and yet you still refuse to give it. I want it. Now."

She was trembling, no matter how hard she tried to keep still. Too much sensation. It was overwhelming. The smooth material of the tie binding her wrists. The astonishing heat of his body against her legs. The feel of his fingers against her jaw, her chin against his palm, and the press of his thumb on her lips. The movement of the air against her bared skin, goose bumps rising, making her teeth want to chatter.

Too much. Far, far too much.

Memory began to flicker behind her eyes. Of that first time a week after she'd been taken, when a guard had come into her bedroom one night and told her to take her clothes off. That if she didn't, he'd take them off for her.

*So terrified. Knowing and yet not knowing what was going to happen. But she was damned if she let them see how scared she was or have her choice taken from her, so she'd chosen to do as she was told. Stripping and trying to do it like she didn't care. Until they'd put the blindfold on her, taking away her sight, leaving her in darkness . . .*

"Eva." Zac's voice cracked through the flickering images, shattering them, his fingers pressing against her jaw. "Look at me."

She blinked, helplessly obeying him. Heart-stopping, those eyes. Full of heat and golden flames, burning high.

"You aren't there anymore." As if he'd read her mind and knew exactly where she'd gone. "You're here in my library. You're with me. No one else." His thumb moved on her lips, a gentle stroke that sent all her nerve endings into overload. "Nothing else exists for you, but me. You have no past, no future, only now. Only me. I am the extent of your world."

That distant, vulnerable part of her, so tired of the burden of memory, wanted to sob in relief, yet she ignored it. That way led to helplessness, to destruction.

Eva opened her mouth and sank her teeth into his thumb. Hard.

He didn't pull away. He didn't even flinch.

He smiled instead, a dark, savage kind of smile. "You'll never make this easy for me, will you? I know you're a fighter and that's good, I like a challenge. But you're fighting the wrong person, Eva. It's time to stop being blind. It's time to see."

There was blood in her mouth, sharp, metallic. His blood.

His other hand moved and a finger touched her throat before trailing down, drawing a line of fire between her breasts all the way to her stomach. It was a gentle, barely there touch. And yet it was agony.

A sound escaped her, desperate and frightened.

She hated the sound of it.

"Look at me," he ordered. "If you look away I will punish you."

There was nothing she could do but obey him, his touch still burning on her skin. Fear stole her breath, made her want to scream, and she had to close her mouth hard against it to stop it from leaking out.

"Don't be afraid of me." He said it like merely speaking words aloud could make it so. "You know me. I would never hurt you."

"I'm not afraid!" she burst out. "But you fucking ripped my T-shirt. And now you're . . . you're . . . t-touching me. And I don't . . . I don't want . . ." She couldn't say it, even now, because it was too much like admitting defeat.

"You do want it, Eva. You crave it. You crave me. But your fear is getting in the way. It's blinding you because you can't stop fighting it."

Her breathing was out of control, she could hear herself panting like a dog. The heat from his body against her legs was like a furnace, burning her. "Stop. Just fucking s-stop!"

"No." His refusal was absolute. "Here's what's going to happen. I'm going to make you face your fear. Make you admit that you feel it. You won't like it, you'll try to run from it, but I'm going to do it anyway." He didn't release her chin, the thumb she'd bitten still stroking her lip. "I need you to give me a safeword. You know what that is?"

Oh yes, she knew. "No, I'm not going to give you a fucking—"

"Say it when you get scared. When you absolutely want me to stop because 'no' and 'stop' won't work, understand?"

Eva clenched her teeth together, her whole body quaking. Not willing to give him anything.

"Very well," he said. "I'll give you a word. Your safeword is 'void.'"

"B-Bastard. You complete, fucking bastard."

"You enjoy pushing me, angel. You enjoy testing me, fighting me. You want to know why?" His palm spread suddenly on her stomach, shocking, intense heat. "Because you know I'm safe. Because deep down you understand I will never hurt you." His palm moved up higher, cupping her bare breast.

The touch blinded her, making every single nerve ending scream, a ragged, hoarse sound escaping her.

*Void . . .*

The word waited there, stuck in her throat, but she didn't say it. Because that meant admitting she was scared, and she couldn't. Fear made her vulnerable. Fear would destroy her.

Fighting, protecting herself, was what she knew how to do. That's *all* she'd been doing her whole miserable, goddamn life. She didn't even know if she *could* stop.

Her breathing came in short, hard bursts as his fingers spread out spanning her breast, her nipple against his palm. It felt like he was holding an ember against her skin, an agony of sensation too intense for her taut nerves.

*Void. Say it.*

Zac's gaze locked with hers. Watching her. Learning her. "You want to say it, don't you?" His voice was all dark heat and authority. "I can see you wanting to. But you're not going to let yourself. You're still fighting."

Eva felt her lips draw back, baring her teeth at him. Shaking and shaking and shaking.

"Little warrior." There was respect in his eyes, open admiration. "You've always been strong, haven't you? But you can't fight all the time, angel. Sometimes you have to rest. Sometimes you have to give all your burdens to someone else, let them carry the weight for you."

*Yes. God, yes. Lay them down. Let him take them away.*

"N-No, I fucking don't." That harsh scrape, oh, Christ, that was her voice.

His thumb traced her lower lip. Then the hand on her breast moved, his thumb brushing gently over her nipple.

A bolt of electricity seared through nerves already overwhelmed by sensation and a hoarse, rough scream escaped her. A wave of heat rushed over her skin, a deep, insistent ache beginning to throb between her thighs.

*You like it, see? You like me touching you . . .*

Fear howled in her head, the primal, animal need to protect herself rising inside her. *Run. Run. Run . . .*

No, fuck, she wouldn't. She would beat this. She would fight it.

"Eyes on me, Eva." That insistent voice calling her back. Calling her home.

She blinked, focusing on him again.

"You disobeyed me." Another movement of his thumb over her nipple, another charge of sensation drawing yet another sound from her. "You were supposed to be looking only at me, thinking only of me."

"B-B-But I—"

"Consequences. I told you there would be consequences." Her nipple held between his thumb and forefinger, and then a gentle squeeze.

The sensation exploded through her like agony, like a lightbulb bursting inside her.

*Void. Fucking void.*

But she bit down, and this time it was her own blood she tasted. "B-B-Bring it on, asshole," she forced out, her teeth chattering. "I c-can take it."

His face was taut, all hard planes and uncompromising angles. The face of a king or an emperor, a man used to command, who had no softness or passion in him. And yet there were those amber eyes, like molten gold. Full of hunger and want. *Desire . . .*

"Have you ever had an orgasm, angel?" he asked softly.

Scalding heat in her cheeks. She was bare to the waist and he had his hand on her breast and yet she was blushing.

*You like it. See? I told you you'd like it.*

No. No. No. "Seriously? Who hasn't?" She put as much sarcasm as she could into the words.

The look in his eyes didn't even flicker. "Did you want it?"

"Of course I did—"

He squeezed her nipple, harder this time. And she gasped, trembling with the effort it took not to scream again. "Don't lie to me. Not when I can see right through you."

Of course he could. He always had, the bastard. "N-No," she managed through gritted teeth. Because he was right to ask. She'd never wanted the few climaxes she'd been given, yet she'd been given them all the same.

"No, what?"

"No . . . I d-didn't want them."

His jaw hardened, and behind the heat in his eyes another emotion flared before it was swiftly contained again. Rage. "Then these are the consequences. When you're ready to give me the second of the things I asked for, you'll have to earn your orgasms, and I'll only give them to you if you please me. If you beg me. Otherwise I'll tease you, taunt you, make you scream with pleasure. But I'll never let you come unless you ask for it. Understand?"

She just looked at him, shivering. Trying desperately to keep still, to not let him see anything of what she was feeling. Yet she knew he could see all the same. And it was agony.

She felt torn in two. Caught between terror and a confusing, growing need that her body knew but her mind didn't want to deal with because of all the associations that came along with it. The helplessness as her body was forced to experience sensations she didn't want. The dirtiness of it, the anger that she couldn't do anything about it. Anger at herself and at the man who'd forced her. Rage at her vulnerability and powerlessness. And now, fury at another man who was forcing her again.

Forcing to face what she didn't want to face. To feel what she didn't want to feel.

But the man in front of her now had an identity. Zac. Her safety. Her haven.

Who knew her like no one had ever known her.

He must have seen her struggle because he leaned forward, keeping his grip on her chin. His other hand was firm on her breast, her nipple hard and aching between his fingers as he pressed her back in the chair.

So that he was all she could see. He filled her vision. His face hard as a statue cast in bronze. The elegant, straight sweep of his nose. Thick, soft-looking black lashes. The curve of his lower lip. His eyes. Oh, God, she couldn't look away from those eyes. Couldn't even blink. But it was like looking into the sun. Painful and bright, yet she was helplessly drawn to the heat. Wanting to bask in it, warm up the cold places in her soul.

*Get him to take it. Take it all away . . .*

And for a small, brief instant, an exhausted part of Eva

stopped fighting. Just relaxed and let the moment take her. No past and no future. Only this man and all the sensations he was opening her up to. Burning heat. An insatiable ache. Hunger for something she couldn't give a name to. Everything she'd been denying herself for years.

He knew the exact second she stopped fighting. His thumb moved on her nipple, brushing back and forth over the hard bud, turning that ache, that need, into something piercing.

It was confusing, terrifying. Because when her body started to want, her brain knew it was always going to be bad.

She began to pant, trembling with the force of her emotions, with all the physical sensations.

"Ask, Eva," Zac murmured, his voice as soft as fur over bare skin. "Ask for what you want. Or say the word and I'll stop."

A strange, foreign desire gripped her. To arch her back like a cat, press herself into his hand. Take all the heat he was throwing out like a furnace. Give in to the hunger inside her.

*Give up. Surrender.*

Alarm bells went off inside her head as the protective mechanisms he'd lulled into sleep woke up.

She couldn't do it. She couldn't surrender. Destruction lay that way.

"No," she said, making the word as steady and as hard and as cold as she could.

Zac looked at her for a long time, studying her face, his thumb still moving lazily on her breast, each pass making her tremble and shake, making her teeth clench more tightly together, making her fight the unbearable sensation that was just about killing her.

Perhaps if she did nothing, he'd keep doing that. And maybe, God, maybe she'd—

Zac took his hand away and she almost protested, almost grabbed it to put it back. Then she realized that her hands were tied. That she was helpless.

"Giving up already, huh?" she croaked.

"Not at all," he replied calmly. And began to undo the buttons of her jeans.

She tensed, every muscle locking. "Don't."

He wasn't looking at her now, concentrating on what he was doing as he flicked the buttons open. "The word, Eva. You know what to say to stop this."

Of course. That fucking word.

Her mouth was dry and she felt as if every single nerve ending was acutely sensitized. She couldn't take any more. Like a soap bubble, she'd burst at the slightest touch. And yet that stubborn, fighting spirit wouldn't let her say the word. Wouldn't let her give in or acknowledge it.

So she sat there, panting as he matter-of-factly opened her jeans and slid his fingers beneath the waistband of her plain black panties, pushing down between her thighs.

She couldn't stop the scream that came out this time as his fingers slid through the curls between her legs and over the folds of her sex. Sensation pierced her like a spear through the chest. It was even more intense than his touch on her breast, making tears start behind her eyes.

Then the weirdest thought hit her: if she lifted her hips just a little bit, she could make that feeling even more acute. She could—

Zac pulled his hand away and held it up in front of her. There was moisture on his fingertips and fire in his eyes.

And the word she wanted to say wasn't *void*. It was *again*.

"This is desire, angel." His voice wasn't smooth any longer but rougher and more uneven than she'd ever heard it. "This is your desire. For me."

She couldn't take her eyes off his fingers, off the sheen

on them. And her body wasn't shaking from fear this time or from oversensitization, but from something else. The ache that wouldn't go away, that wanted his hands to keep going, keep moving.

"Did you ever get wet like this for him, Eva? Did you ever shake like this for him?"

"I . . . I d-don't—"

"No, you didn't." And he said it like he knew, like he was certain of the fact. "That makes it different. That makes *me* different. I'm not him, angel. And when you're with me, I'll make certain you never think of him again." He leaned forward again, pressing his body against hers, and she could feel the solidity of it, the weight and heat of it. Immovable. Like a mountain. "I will block him out, Eva." His voice was soft, emphatic, like a hypnotist's. "I will obliterate him. I will scour him from your memory so that when I touch you, the only man you'll ever think about is me."

Then he lifted his fingers, still slick with the evidence of her desire. And keeping his gaze on hers, he licked them like he was licking up melting ice cream.

Eva's stuttered breathing caught. She watched him, mesmerized as his tongue curled around his fingers, tasting her, a wolf devouring its prey . . .

"Delicious," he murmured, low and deep, the vibration of it against her legs. "You know what I'd like to do right now?"

She couldn't seem to dredge up any of her usual sarcastic, snarky comments. They'd vanished from her vocabulary. All she could think of was his mouth, the sensual shape of it, how beautiful it was . . .

*How it would feel on your skin.*

"N-No," she whispered, both to the thought and to him.

He smiled, and the fingers he'd licked dipped down again. She tensed, shivering all over, dreading what he was going to do with them yet anticipating at it as well. Wanting and fearing so mixed up together she couldn't tell which was which.

But all he did was circle a finger around her belly button, the touch featherlight. Taunting.

"I'd like to have you naked in this chair," he said conversationally, his gaze holding hers. "Your hands would be tied above your head and you'd have your legs spread over each arm. Perhaps I'd even tie them there so you'd be totally restrained." His finger circled, so light yet feeling like flames licking her skin. "The restraint would be pleasurable for you, angel. Silken ropes against your skin. You'd be wide open to me and desperate for me to touch you, but I wouldn't lay a finger on you until you begged."

*Look away. Void. Something. Anything to get him to stop talking.*

But she couldn't. She felt hypnotized by his dark voice and by the touch of his finger. By the image he was conjuring up like a sorcerer weaving a spell.

"I'd kneel like I'm doing now, between your legs. And I think you'd like that too. Having me on my knees before you, angel. Ready to worship you. Because everything I do is for you and your pleasure." His finger moved slow and steady, and it felt like the most exquisite torture. Making her aware of her skin, of her body, of that nagging, desperate ache between her thighs.

"I'd just kneel there, so close you could feel my heat. But not touching. Not touching until you asked, until you wanted my touch more than you wanted your next breath. And when you ask, Eva, I'd stroke you. Your thighs. Your stomach. Run my fingers all over that beautiful pussy of yours. But not enough to make you come. Just enough to make you even wetter than you are already."

She couldn't breathe now, the air in her lungs heavy and hot, every sense she had focused on his circling finger.

God, it was like she could feel each whorl, each ridge of it against her skin.

"And then I'd lean in, run my tongue around your clit. Teasing you. Perhaps after that, I'd go lower, lick your pussy, fuck you with my tongue. Drink you up like my favorite cabernet. I'd make you burn, angel." His voice dropped lower, a caress. "I'd make you shake so hard it'd feel like you're coming apart, so that you're aware of nothing but what you want so very desperately. You'd beg me for release, but I'd keep you on the edge for as long as possible, denying you until the last minute. Prolonging the pleasure until you're sure you'd die without it. Only when you're sobbing for it would I give you release. Make you come so hard you'd see stars and scream the walls of my house down." He smiled. "And then, once you'd recovered. I'd do it all over again."

There was nothing she could say to that, no response at all. He'd taken the whole English language from her and left her with only a baser, more primitive kind of communication. Images. Sensations. Heat. Hunger.

A long silence fell, his lambent gaze fixed on her, reading her. Knowing every thought that went through her head.

Then he said softly, "But I'm not going to do that. You disobeyed me, angel. You wouldn't give me your safeword and you didn't ask for release. Which means you need to be punished."

Her throat tightened, fingers closing around it, squeezing tight. She could say it now, couldn't she? Say the word that would stop this.

*But would he stop?*

The thought was insidious, doubt winding through her brain like a snake. She didn't know what to do. Saying it would admit the fear, but if she said it and he didn't stop . . .

But all Zac did was take his hand from her, his weight

lifting as he shifted back to sit on his heels, cold rushing over her bare skin.

The loss of his warmth felt almost painful and she shivered again, helplessly.

"I'm not going to do any of those things to you, Eva," he continued calmly. "I'm going to leave you hungry and wanting and aching, with nothing but those images in your head to taunt you."

From somewhere she managed to find the ghost of her old bravado. "Seriously?" Her voice was a raw scrape of sound. "That's a punishment?"

Zac's hands rested on his thighs, the expression on his face uncompromising. "Perhaps you won't understand it now. But you will. Your body will burn for me. Ache for me. And you'll wish like hell you'd done what I told you to. Because until you do, you'll never be satisfied."

She wanted to laugh because her body had never done that in her whole life. Never burned or ached, and as for satisfaction, what the hell did that mean anyway?

*You know what he's talking about. You ache already.*

Eva tried to smile and knew it came out more of a grimace. "I don't care."

"You will, Eva," he said quietly and with such certainty she almost shivered again. "Oh believe me, you will."

# CHAPTER TEN

Zac rose to his feet, watching as Eva's wide eyes were drawn helplessly down his body to the line of his cock, pressing through the wool of his suit pants.

Yes, he was hard. So fucking hard. But physical control was easy for him and he ignored it.

What mattered now, what was balm to his dominant soul, was that he'd showed her who was in charge of what was happening between them. And who would stay in charge. Him.

That she'd needed him to be was painfully obvious the moment they'd gotten here and he'd realized, as soon as she'd tried to get into another deflecting conversation, that he'd let it go on too long as it was.

She would keep on fighting, keep on hiding behind those walls of hers, keep on protecting herself till hell froze over, and all the patience and care in the world wasn't going to make her stop. Which meant he'd have to take those walls down himself, whether she wanted it or not.

He'd thought waiting for her to step out from behind them had been the right thing to do. The gentlemanly thing. But it hadn't been. It had only let her keep running longer, harder. Prolonging her pain and entrenching her fear.

So he'd had to be cruel. Storming all her defenses, over-whelming her, forcing her to see that her fear was blinding her, trapping her. Holding her captive as surely as she'd been held captive in that house.

He hadn't left her completely unprotected though. He'd given her a safeword that she could use any time to stop what was happening. The problem was that using it meant acknowledging the fact she was scared. Which hadn't happened.

Damn, she was strong. Stronger than he'd thought. She was going to give him one hell of a fight.

*Perhaps she didn't trust you enough to use the word. Didn't trust that you'd stop.*

He didn't like that thought. Not one bit.

"Safewords are sacred," he said abruptly into the silence. "If you'd said it, I would have stopped. Always. Understand?"

Her lashes veiled her gaze as she looked away. "Sure. I understand."

No. She didn't.

Fuck.

Anger stirred inside him, heavy and slow. She should know he would stop. She shouldn't hesitate or wonder or doubt. Christ, hadn't he earned that by now? After so many bloody years?

With an effort Zac forced the anger away.

Perhaps there was no hope for her. No hope for either of them. Perhaps he'd misjudged her strength. Perhaps it was too brittle. Perhaps she'd break completely if he pushed and wouldn't be able to build herself up again. He'd thought her spirit was more resilient, but maybe he was wrong.

*You can't give up yet.*

No. Not now that he knew the pale, smooth texture of her skin, the warmth of it. The hard press of her nipple against his palm and the soft weight of her breast in his hand. The silky, damp curls between her thighs and the wet heat of her pussy. The musky sweet taste of her desire on his fingers.

She'd been worth the wait. Every day, every hour, every single fucking minute of it.

Eva didn't move, her jaw set in a familiar, stubborn line. The halves of her shirt hung open, baring her small, perfectly shaped breasts and pale pink little nipples. She made no move to cover herself even though he knew she must be desperate to. Showing him she wouldn't be cowed.

Except instead of the brittle determination she so often radiated, there was something different in it this time. She was flushed and although she'd looked away from him, her gaze kept returning to his groin as if she couldn't help herself, the silver of her eyes darkening.

His anger shifted and changed, morphing into a hard kind of satisfaction.

So. Clearly she wasn't a lost cause after all.

Because that's what he wanted. Her, thinking about him. Thinking about what he'd told her he'd do to her. Images of pleasure in her brain instead of the memories he knew lived behind her eyes whenever he touched her.

Memories he was going to obliterate if it was the last thing he did.

Zac took her bound hands and undid his tie. The silk had left faint red marks around her wrists so he chafed them gently, ignoring the way her muscles locked then relaxed, locked then relaxed.

She wanted to pull away from him, and no doubt all her nerves were at screaming point given the overload of sensations he'd piled onto her. But it seemed she wasn't going to give in to the need.

Christ, he should have started this long ago, when her barriers hadn't gotten so entrenched. Then again, given the year or so she'd spent on the streets, maybe they'd already been like that.

Releasing her wrists, he rose to his feet. Then took off his jacket, laying it down neatly on the couch, before undoing the cuffs of his shirt. Then he pulled the hem from the waistband of his pants and began to undo the buttons.

Eva blinked rapidly, watching him as a deer watches a wolf come slowly toward it. She still made no move to cover herself though he could see goose bumps rising all over her breasts and flat stomach, down to the where he could see the black waistband of her panties, the buttons of her jeans undone.

Zac shrugged out of his shirt and stood there for a moment studying her.

Her eyes had gone even wider, her gaze trailing over his chest and abs, down to his hips.

Good. He wanted her looking at him like that, wanted to fan that little ember of desire into a burning flame.

She was a sensual being, even though she wasn't aware of it herself. It was there in her need for warmth, her pleasure in soft blankets and hot tea and open fires. And now he hoped he'd stoked that need, woken it up, made it aware. Given it something to latch onto and focus on. Showing her there were other things in the world, not just fear and pain.

Certainly the way she was looking at him now wasn't that of a woman afraid. More like a woman in need.

Satisfied, Zac stepped forward and lifted the shirt. "Put your arms out."

Her gaze narrowed. "What are you doing now?"

"You need something to wear home."

A flash of surprise lit her gaze then vanished. Wordlessly she held out her arms and he got rid of the remains of her T-shirt and bra, discarding them onto the floor before dressing her with ruthless practicality in his shirt.

As he leaned forward to do up the buttons she said in a breathless voice, "You don't need to—"

"I have other ways of punishing you, Eva. Don't think that I don't. So be quiet and sit still like a good girl while I do up these buttons."

She didn't say anything more, but he could feel the tension in her. And he knew what was causing it. Him. His nearness, his bare skin. The feeling of his shirt against her sensitized skin, his scent all around her.

Good. Let it bother her. Let it maintain the level of arousal that he'd already built in her. Let it confuse and distract her. Keep her thinking about him.

He slowed his movements as he did up the buttons, allowing the tips of his fingers to brush her skin. The lightest of touches, accidental almost, yet it would keep her on the edge, heighten her awareness even further.

When he'd finished, he straightened, looking into her eyes. Gauging her reaction and, sure enough, her eyes had gone a tarnished silver color, darkening with arousal. Her lips were parted a little, and for a second he debated whether or not to kiss her. Allow himself a small taste.

As if she'd read his mind, her attention dropped to his mouth.

Oh, good girl. Very good girl indeed.

But a punishment was a punishment. There would be no kisses, no more touches until she asked for them.

He took a step back from her chair and went over to retrieve his phone from the pocket of his discarded jacket.

"What are you doing?" Eva asked, her voice thick.

"Calling your car to take you home." He dialed the number, glancing at her.

She was sitting on the edge of the armchair now, her hands on the arms, like a bird about to take flight. "I thought . . . I thought you said you didn't want me going home."

"Oh?" He arched a brow at her. "So you want to stay then?"

"No, I didn't say that. But—" She stopped, frustration and confusion clear on her face. "You . . . You're . . ."

"I'm what?" He paused as Temple answered and he issued orders for her to come and get Eva from his house. Then he ended the call and tossed the phone back down on the couch. "I'm what, angel?"

Eva's gaze once more dropped to his groin where his cock ached, still hard and ready, before she looked away. "It doesn't matter."

"If you want to get down on your knees and suck my cock, angel, I'm more than happy to let you," he said easily. "But I'm not touching you if that's what you were hoping."

"Don't." She pushed herself to her feet in a rapid, jerky movement. "I don't want you to touch me. I never wanted you to touch me."

But he was ready for her anger. He'd been expecting it. "Yes, you did. You've been craving my touch for years, Eva King." He took a couple of steps toward her, watching her gaze flare with fear, yes, but awareness too. "You've just never had the guts to ask for it."

As he'd intended, her anger leapt higher. "Well, how about you try being a sexual slave for two fucking years. Then you can talk to me about guts!"

There was pain behind the anger in her voice, all the anguish she was trying so desperately to hide. And he heard it, recognized it. He wouldn't let his protective instincts get in the way again since it was indulging those instincts that had led to this situation in the first place. But he could give her a little something of himself. She wasn't alone, no matter what she thought.

"I was kept in a Russian prison for eighteen months," he said coolly. "I know what it's like to be held captive. I know what it's like to feel helpless. Why do you think I'm still here?"

She stared at him and he stared back until her gaze dropped, wrapping her jacket around herself as if she was suddenly cold. "Well, fine. I'll go home then."

A heavy silence fell that he made no effort to break. If she was uncertain and confused, that meant change. That meant her defenses weren't as strong around him as they had been, and that was a good thing. He wanted to be there when they collapsed. And he would be the one to keep her safe as she rebuilt them.

Some things had to break in order to be put back together again. Made stronger, more durable.

"What about this . . . party thing?" she asked at last. "I thought we were going to sort it out tonight."

"Actually, I think you need a break and so do I." He reached down to where his cock was still aching like a bastard and blatantly adjusted himself, satisfied when her gaze followed his movement, lingering for a second before hurriedly glancing away. "Tomorrow, Eva. I'll come and pick you up at ten sharp."

"What for?"

"To continue your lesson in trust. And no, before you start hoping for more of what I showed you today, it won't be along those lines."

Her chin lifted, the ghost of the snarky, sarcastic Eva showing itself. "For fuck's sake. You really think I'd want anything like that again?"

"I think your fear is telling you that. But if you stop listening to it for once, I think you'll find your body is telling yourself something different."

"You arrogant son of a bitch."

"I'm not arrogant, angel. I just know you."

She had no answer to that, mainly because it was true. From the depths of her leather jacket, Eva's phone chimed. She got it out and glanced down at the screen. "That's Temple. And fucking not before time."

She turned without a word, heading toward the door.

"Eva," Zac said softly.

At the sound of her name he was gratified to see that she stopped, her back to him.

"When you're alone in your bed tonight, you'll want to give yourself some relief. But if you do I'll punish you, understand? Any orgasm you have will come from me and me only."

She said nothing, tension radiating from her.

"I'll know if you do," he added. "I can see right through you, angel. Remember that."

Eva didn't reply, heading straight for the door.

And slamming it behind her on her way out.

Eva didn't expect to sleep that night. She sat up in front of her computers, checking and rechecking her firewalls in case of any more hacking incursions, and at the same time, going over and over search results for "Evelyn Fitzgerald."

Anything to stop her thinking about Zac. About what had happened in his library. About his hands on her and his voice detailing exactly what he wanted to do to her.

About the relentless ache that sat down between her thighs, making her restless and antsy and wanting to move.

She tried her usual tactic of ignoring it, studying instead the pictures she'd pulled up of the man who, if Bryson was to be believed, had been the one to hold her captive for so long.

Nothing about him was familiar. The pictures she'd managed to find were from various social events, of him in conversation or standing around smiling for the camera. A handsome man, tall and broad, his hair still blond but now silvered with age. Blue eyes and a charismatic smile, in his mid-sixties. Looked like every other rich, powerful man she'd ever had contact with, and in the course of her company's rise she'd been in contact with quite a few.

In one photo taken a few years ago, he was standing with his family at some society function, his arms around his wife and daughter. His wife, Hilary, was an immaculate ice-blonde with a lovely smile that didn't quite reach her eyes, while his daughter Violet stood there with a sulky expression on her face, looking like she wanted to be anywhere but where she was.

Eva stared at it. Violet, who'd taken off overseas for wild times in Europe, was one of Honor's best friends. She'd had a brother once, the Fitzgeralds' oldest child, who'd committed suicide sixteen years earlier according to the media.

An innocuous picture of an innocuous family. Part of New York's elite, yes, but certainly nothing special for all that.

She focused on Evelyn's face and its bland handsomeness, its pleasant smile. According to the media, he was a veritable pillar of the community, donating big sums to charity and organizing various charitable initiatives. Respected. Loved.

Was it him? Had it been his hands that had touched her? His voice that had murmured in her ear?

A small pulse went through her, making her conscious of her aching body, as fear slid icy claws down her spine.

Eva pushed herself away from the computer, starting on the familiar pace from her desk to the windows of her apartment and New York's comforting skyline. Along the length of the windows to the opposite wall and back again.

She wasn't stupid. She knew she was aroused. But there was so much confusion around the feeling, it unnerved her. Sex had been a terrifying experience, and what had made it so terrifying was the fact that her body had apparently enjoyed it. She didn't understand that at all. Because her brain hadn't wanted it and if you didn't want it, then surely an orgasm was impossible, right?

Apparently not.

It had added to her feelings of helplessness and vulnerability. Like all she'd been was a doll that could be manipulated into whatever position was required. A blow-up sex doll.

Eva could feel her breathing start to accelerate, her heartbeat loud in her ears. She stopped by the windows and put her hands on the glass, the cool feel of it anchoring her.

She'd fought those first couple of weeks. Fought like a cornered wildcat. But the guards had easily overpowered her. Afterwards she'd decided on a different tactic: meek and mild to build up her strength, wait for a chance to escape. Then she'd had that first visit from The Man, and she'd understood what she was there for. His voice had been soft and silky, so very civilized, and he smelled like rich men did, of expensive aftershave and money. He'd told her that there would be no more fighting. That if she tried to escape, if she tried anything at all, he'd cut her throat and dump her body, and it wouldn't be a problem because she didn't have family and she didn't have friends. No one who cared she'd been captured. No one who cared should she die. No one would even know.

She had no one at all. Except him.

He'd made her so aware of her complete isolation. Of her loneliness. She'd been sixteen, living on the streets for six months by that stage, desperate for a home and a family. A safe place to live. Someone who cared about her. But there had been no one.

Those first few times, she'd tried not to let his words get to her. Tried not to care what he did, and that had insulated her for a while. But as time went on, she came to realize that in that house she had what she'd been craving for years.

Warmth. Food. Safety. Someone who wanted her. And if she had to put up with sex in order to have those things, then what was the big deal?

She'd tried to deaden herself, but sometimes The Man had wanted a response. And she'd been forced into giving it.

*But you never thought about him when he wasn't there. And you never felt this ache, this need, after he'd gone. You never wanted him like you want—*

Eva stopped the thought dead, but it refused to go away. It sat there in her head along with the memory of Zac's dark, intense face and the look in his golden eyes.

*You've been craving my touch for years, Eva King . . . You've just never had the guts to ask for it.*

God, had she? Not initially, not after she'd escaped. She'd never wanted to be touched again after that. Yet she'd needed his presence like she'd needed air to breathe, part of her wanting to replicate that intense feeling of safety she'd experienced the moment he'd stepped out of the car and introduced himself.

Except now he'd changed the rules on her and it wasn't safety she felt anymore.

*No. But he's not the only one who changed. For the first time you feel desire and of course that's not safe.*

Eva wrapped her arms around herself, and became aware that she was still wearing his shirt, his scent all around her. The cotton pressed uncomfortably against her nipples, and the awareness deepened. An awareness she'd spent most of the night trying *not* to think about. Of not only his scent but also her own body. Of her skin, soft and sensitized beneath the shirt, and how the cotton felt against it. The pressure of her arms folded across the tips of her nipples. The restless, nagging ache between her thighs.

Christ, she really needed to change then sleep. Zac wasn't kidding when he said ten a.m. sharp. He was always very punctual.

Fucking Zac. What had he done to her?

*You could have stopped it any time.*

She took a small breath. Well, okay, yes, she could have. But she hadn't wanted to admit she was scared. Also, even though he'd told her safewords were sacred, that he would stop, she hadn't been sure and hadn't wanted to test it just in case.

*How could you doubt him? He's a man of his word. You know he would have.*

A lump rose in her throat. He was right, not once in seven years had he touched her. Not once had he pushed her or forced her to do anything. He'd let her run rough-shod over him and yet she still doubted him. Still didn't trust him.

Perhaps she wasn't able to. Perhaps she was broken beyond repair. Shivering, she turned back to her computers, spending another couple of hours immersing herself in work and yet more fruitless searches about Fitzgerald, until sheer, nervous exhaustion drove her into the bedroom. She fell onto the nest of sheets and blankets she kept piled onto a mattress that sat on the floor, totally forgetting to discard Zac's shirt.

It was probably going to take her hours to get to sleep, if at all.

But unexpectedly she did, falling into unconsciousness like a stone thrown into a chasm.

Only to be woken hours later by someone saying her name.

She didn't open her eyes because she was surrounded by a faint, familiar scent that made her feel safe. Made her want to fall right back to sleep again.

Except that the voice calling her name was beautiful.

Deep and dark and smooth, all clipped aristocratic English
vowels . . .

"Eva. Wake up."

Shit. Did she really have to?

"It's ten o'clock, angel."

That voice. Somehow it had been in her dreams . . .

Consciousness began to filter through her. Hell. Wasn't
there supposed to be something she had to do at ten?

Eva cracked open an eye reluctantly, aware that she was
hot and sweaty and uncomfortable.

Only to have all of those feelings get washed away in
an abrupt surge of icy fear.

Zac was crouched beside her mattress, elbows on his
knees, looking down at her.

Jesus Christ.

She sat bolt upright, her heartbeat thundering, every
alert sense she had warning her that once again the safety
of her refuge had been breached, that there was an intruder
where he didn't belong.

"What the fuck, Zac?" she demanded, her sheets pulled
up around her in an unconscious shield. "Get the hell out
of my house!"

He ignored her. "I said ten a.m. sharp and you weren't
there. I wanted to make sure you were okay."

"I'm goddamned fine, okay? Now, get out."

But all he did was rise smoothly to his feet, towering
over her.

Today his suit wasn't black but dark charcoal, with a
black business shirt underneath and a beautiful silk tie pat-
terned in silver gray and deep gold. He looked impeccably put together as he always did, and yet somehow that
only served to make him seem even more dangerous.

*And beautiful.*

"Get up," he ordered in the kind of tone she recognized
from the day before. The one that brooked no argument.

She bristled. "And you can get fu—"

He bent and, before she could move, ripped the bedding out of her hands and off the bed. Stifling a yelp of protest, she scowled up at him, trying to resist the urge to curl in on herself.

His whisky-colored eyes swept a glance over her. "Do you always sleep fully clothed?"

"Most of the time, yeah. In case bastards like you get into my house without asking and start—"

"When you sleep with me, you'll be naked." He said it like it was already a done deal. "But I like you're still in my shirt."

All sorts of answers went through her head, ranging from "I will never be sleeping with you" to "Get fucked, asshole." But she didn't say any of them. There wasn't any point.

She got up, lifting her chin to meet his gaze head-on.

At least, she tried to meet his gaze head-on. But it was difficult for some reason. That gaze of his kept reminding her of the day before, of his weight against her, his hands on her, his heat surrounding her. The memories taunted her, making her feel confused yet again, and she hated it.

He arched a brow at the mattress. "You have something against proper beds? Or is it all furniture you don't like?"

"I like space around me. And I like sleeping on the floor," she said belligerently. "Now get out. You're trespassing and I want to get changed."

"You'll need to get used to me being in your space, angel, because I'm not going to put up with you putting distance between us like you have been doing. And as far as getting changed goes, be my guest. I brought you something I want you to wear." He turned and went over to the only other piece of furniture in the room apart from her mattress, a low chest of drawers. On top of it was a bag, the name of an incredibly expensive lingerie store emblazoned on the front of it. Picking up the bag, he brought it over to her and held it out.

She looked down at it. "What the hell is this?"

"A gift."

A gift? He'd given her many things over the years, but none of them had actually been "gifts." It made something uncomfortable twist inside her.

"I don't want—"

"No protests. No arguments. Remember? Take it."

Muttering a curse under her breath, she snatched the bag from him, making sure their fingertips didn't touch, and opened it. Inside was a mass of tissue paper. She brought it out, dropping the empty bag on the floor and digging through the tissue to find out what was inside.

A bra and panty set of silky, silver lace.

She stared at them then glanced up at him. "I don't understand."

"There's nothing to understand. You only need to put them on."

"Why?" she prevaricated, trying to resist the urge to throw the lingerie in his face.

Zac only raised an eyebrow. "Why not?"

"Screw you."

"There'll be plenty of time for that later." He glanced down at the heavy Rolex Platinum he wore. "I'm giving you five seconds."

Prick. "At least get out so I can get changed in private."

"No."

"I'm not fucking changing with—"

"Put them on," he said softly. "Or I'll do it for you."

She could feel that will of his like a palpable force. Inexorable as the tide, and there was no holding back the tide. Not with sarcasm or wit, sheer stubbornness or anything else, no matter how much she wanted to.

Furious with him for forcing her do this and with herself

for making such a stupid fuss about lingerie in the first place, Eva began wrenching her clothes off.

It didn't matter that he wanted her to wear stupid lingerie. And it didn't matter that he wanted to watch her put it on. Hell, it wasn't like she hadn't been naked in front of a man before either. But if he was hoping for a striptease, he was shit out of luck.

His expression was impassive as she tore off her clothes, which for some reason only made her even more furious with him. What was the point of him asking her to get naked when he didn't seem to care one way or the other?

Yet when she took off his shirt, baring her torso, her hands shaking as she did so, ever present fear twisting in her gut, she didn't miss the leap of heat in his eyes.

Clearly he wasn't as impassive as he looked.

"They used to get me to do this in front of them," she said, hoping her voice sounded hard and cutting, not breathy and thin like she suspected. "The guards did, before I was taken to The Man. They liked to watch before the blindfold went on." She didn't want to have say it, to go back and revisit it, but she wanted him to know what he was doing to her. What he was making her relive.

"Did they?" He folded his arms, the sleeves of his jacket pulling tight around his impressive shoulders and biceps. "And are they here now?"

"Well, I—"

"No, they are not. *I* am the only one who is here now. And you are doing it for me." The authority in his dark, beautiful voice was undeniable. "You will not think of them, angel. You are undressing for me and me alone. Is that clear?"

"Oh, sure. Like you can stop remembering something just like that."

"Really? You seem to have been very successful at it for the past seven years."

Eva stared at him, her heartbeat thumping. Wishing him in hell.

"Your jeans, angel."

Clenching her teeth, Eva ripped at the buttons on her jeans then pulled them down and stepped out of them. She shoved down her black panties and got rid of those too.

Naked, finally. Naked in front of him.

Christ, she was cold. Really, really cold.

"Look at me."

She didn't want to but she did all the same, the command irresistible.

His gaze was molten, like whiskey heated to boiling point or golden coins smelted down and turned to liquid. The cold began to dissipate, as if she was standing in front of a raging fire.

He wanted her, that much was obvious, and this time the memory that filled her head wasn't of standing in front of the guards trying to shield her teenage body from their avid gaze, but of him the day before. Standing in front of her shirtless, making no effort to hide his impressive hard-on. A strange combination of civilized gentleman in suit pants and heavily muscled, bare-chested warrior, all tattoos and bronze skin. Like a statue half unveiled.

"Put on the lingerie."

Ah, dammit. Might as well get it over and done with. Doing what he told her to was quicker than fighting him, that was for sure.

She picked up the panties from the packet of tissue she'd dropped onto the floor and stepped into them. The material was so light and gauzy she had to go slow, afraid she'd rip it. To her annoyance the panties fit perfectly and felt almost like she was wearing nothing. Not looking at him, she then picked up the bra and put it on, realizing belatedly it had a front clasp.

"Wait," Zac ordered.

Instinctively Eva stopped, her hand between her breasts ready to do up the clasp. She blinked at him, her breath catching in her throat as he stepped forward and calmly lifted his hands. "I'll do it up."

Once again he said it in that tone she knew was useless to argue with and so she just stood there, fear snaking through her as he grasped the silky fabric, pulling the cups closed. The tips of his fingers brushed her skin, a feather-light touch that sent a shockwave, and more cascades of memory, through her.

*In the chair with his weight on her legs, his finger circling her belly button over and over . . .*

She looked up at him, unable to help herself, watching his face. His expression was as calm as if he was merely tying a shoelace, thick black lashes veiling his amber gaze, his attention on his fingers.

"Why?" she asked thickly. "Why are you doing this?"

Zac didn't reply immediately, doing up the clasp then standing back, giving her a long, sweeping look that made every hair on her body stand up on end at the hunger in it.

"The lingerie because I want you to wear something soft and silky against your skin," he said. "I want you to be aware of your body with all of your senses because it'll help ground you in the here and now rather than the past." He paused. "As to everything else, you know why." The look in his eyes pinned her to the spot. "You think you're strong, Eva, you think you're tough enough not to need anyone. But your strength is thin, a brittle veneer that cracks under the slightest pressure, and one day it'll shatter. And who'll be there to help you rebuild it? Who will you trust? If Fitzgerald shatters it tomorrow night, who will you turn to?"

*He's not wrong, you know he's not.*

He wasn't. And she thought she was starting to see that now.

"I want you to turn to me, Eva," Zac went on. "I want to be the one you turn to. The one you trust. And then maybe I'll show you how to strip that veneer away and re-build it so that you're truly strong. Truly the warrior you should have been. So that you believe it, right down to your bones."

He said every word with the calm of absolute convic-tion. And though her instinct was to protest, she found she couldn't get the words out. *I am strong*, she wanted to say. *I am tough*.

*Oh sure, so tough you ran away at the thought of con-fronting Fitzgerald.*

She gritted her teeth. "Right, so lingerie is all about strength. Who knew?"

He smiled in that slow, sure way, as if he knew some-thing she didn't. "That's the first step. Next up, we're go-ing on a little day trip."

Fear twisted again like a snake. "Where?"

"Get your clothes on, angel. We're going to the Met."

# CHAPTER ELEVEN

That Eva didn't want to go was written all over her face.
But that was too bloody bad.

Zac had investigated the function Fitzgerald was giving and seen it was going to be at the Metropolitan Museum of Art, at the Temple of Dendur. And given Eva's difficulties with unfamiliar places, the most logical thing was to take her there during the day to get her familiar with it.

Because she had to go. After exchanging texts with Alex and Gabe that morning, it was clear that Eva had to attend the function. She was the only one who'd potentially had contact with Fitzgerald, and the other two couldn't go in case their appearance alerted the man to the fact that they were onto him. Gabe had also mentioned that Tremain was being brought out of his coma, but given that he wasn't likely to be in any state to answer questions—if he ever would—Eva was still their best hope.

Zac had gotten Temple to take them in Eva's limo, Eva sitting opposite him on the way there, scowling out the window.

"So I understand why the others can't go," she said, after he'd showed her the texts. "But what about you? Fitzgerald doesn't know you."

"You were the one in that house, Eva. Only you can

confirm the link between him and the Lucky Seven. I thought that was clear."

Her head was turned away, her delicate profile tense.

His night had been fairly uncomfortable as he was sure hers had been, his head full of the warmth of her body and the feel of her skin, the taste of her in his mouth. But he hadn't given himself any relief. He wanted to be in total control and that meant controlling the ferocity of his hunger for her, even under provocation.

He'd basically spent most of his sleepless night planning what he was going to do with her, how to make her beg for him.

First there was the trust issue that had to be resolved. Then there were the memories that would need the poison drained from them. He'd give her new ones in their place so the old ones didn't have any power. Yet to do that he had to awaken her sensuality. Show her what pleasures there were in such simple things as the feeling of silk against her bare skin.

Having her get changed into that lingerie in front of him had been deliberate. He'd wanted her to get used to him looking at her, to him being around her, to him being close.

As he'd suspected, the silver lace looked beautiful on her.

She didn't have a single, pretty item of clothing, as if her femininity didn't exist. But it was there, he knew it was. Buried beneath her years of captivity and before that, her time spent on the streets, yet it was there nonetheless. He wanted to show her that denying a part of herself was only making her weaker. That true strength lay with acknowledging *every* part.

*As you do, right?*

Well, of course. He knew he was selfish. That he was violent. That he had darkness inside him and he'd come to terms with it, embraced it over the years. It was where his strength came from. That and absolute control.

"The media are going to love it if I turn up," Eva said into the heavy silence, her voice curt. "That might be a problem."

She had a point. The media made a big deal of the fact that she was reclusive, that she never attended public functions, never gave interviews, never interacted with anyone apart from the people who worked for her. Her attendance at this function would be a big deal, would draw attention. But that may not be a bad thing for the purposes of the Nine Circle's investigations. It would be interesting to watch Fitzgerald's reaction to her.

A thread of anger escaped Zac's control, winding through him like a white-hot wire filament.

If Eva recognized Fitzgerald, then he and Zac could have a nice little "chat." Then once Zac had gotten all the information he needed, he'd blow the man away. Without one shred of regret.

"It could work to our advantage," he said. "It might catch Fitzgerald off guard. He won't be expecting you."

Eva flicked a glance at him, a flash of silver. "If it's him, he'll know who I am."

Again he saw fear in her eyes. "If it's him, he can hardly be unaware of who you are. Your picture has been circulating in the media for a while, and it's not as if Void Angel isn't a big name. Which means he's not interested in you anymore, otherwise he would have already done something about it."

She looked away again, saying nothing.

"I would never leave you unprotected, angel," he said quietly. "You know this."

"Yeah, I know," she muttered.

But she didn't. Or if she did, she didn't feel it. Because if she had, she would trust him more than she did.

She was still listening to her fear, letting it tell her what to do.

Not today though. Today he would silence that fear once and for all.

Zac got Temple to drop them off a little away from the Met's entrance, not wanting to cause too much in the way of attention with a long black limo drawing up to the curb. There were plenty of people around, thousands of tourists and school groups and office workers, the usual New York crowds.

Eva was tense as soon as they got out of the limo, her whole body solid with it. She didn't look around, her attention on the ground, hands in the pockets of her leather jacket.

She was always like this whenever they were outside. Her shoulders bowed, her head down. As if the entire weight of the sky was pressing on her.

Zac reached out and took her elbow, pulling her right hand out of her pocket.

That got a response. Her head came up, anger flashing across her face as she tried to pull away. "Don't —"

"You're going to let me hold your hand," he interrupted, tightening his grip. "It'll give you something to focus on. My touch is something you'll have to get used to anyway."

Her mouth firmed, but she stopped trying to pull away.

"Wise decision." He tucked her hand firmly in the crook of his arm. "Now, we're heading toward the galleries of Egyptian art since the function will be held in the Temple of Dendur."

They began to move through the crowds toward the entrance, Eva's pace fast as if she couldn't wait to get to the doors. Her hand on his arm was rigid, her body stiff.

This must be a nightmare for her with so many people around and so much unfamiliarity. The naked sky above her and nowhere to run to.

But she was going to have to deal with it because there would be crowds at Fitzgerald's party, and media too. God, he didn't want her going in there like this, with her head down, fear radiating from her. He wanted her going in there strong, showing that prick that what he'd done to her hadn't beaten her. That she was powerful despite it.

All he had to do was negate this fear of hers and he had a plan on how to do it. She wasn't going to like it however. Then again, being cruel to be kind was his modus operandi. He was good at it.

Brushing through the crowds of people outside the doors was fairly simple: people didn't tend to get in Zac's way when he wanted to get somewhere.

"What are you feeling, angel?" he murmured as they paid the entrance fee then wove through the people in the lobby, heading toward the Egyptian art galleries.

"I'm fine." Her hand was tight on his arm, her head still down.

"You're not fine. You've got a death grip on my arm."

Slowly, she raised her head. Her face was white, her jaw hard. The look on her face was like someone going to their execution. "I can do this," she said thickly. "Fuck, it's not like I haven't been here before."

"Tell me about when you were here before," he murmured, steering them around a knot of tourists all looking at their museum maps and arguing. It would give her something to think about that wasn't focusing on her fear or fighting it and, as added advantage, it would be more information about her, which he wanted very much.

"When I was on the streets," she said, surprising him, "I was small so I'd pass for an under-twelve. Meant I didn't have to pay. Sometimes I'd tell the desk staff I'd gone out by mistake and my parents were still inside, and could I go find them. They always let me in."

"Why here?"

"It was warm and safe."

That was understandable. He'd liked the cinema he used to spend all his time in as a child for exactly those reasons. "Did you like the art?"

She lifted a hunched shoulder, her fingers digging into his arm as a crowd of art students surrounded them for a moment. "Like a kid sleeping on the streets and hungry all the fucking time has any kind of opinion on the art."

More protective sarcasm. A veil she threw up to hide herself.

He wanted to stop abruptly, grip her chin and force her to meet his eyes. Rip away that veil to reveal the vulnerable woman underneath it. But there were too many people and he didn't want to draw attention.

*Later. When you have her back home.*

"I wasn't sleeping on the streets," he said instead, "but I was hungry all the fucking time. And *I* had an opinion on art." He didn't look at her, keeping his gaze on the crowds of people around them and making sure none of them got too close. But he felt the flick of her attention and heard the small silence that indicated surprise.

He hadn't shared his past with her because he didn't share it with anyone. It was full of death and violence anyway, and God knew she didn't need any more of that in her life.

Yet a mention wouldn't hurt. A small offering that might prompt more trust and less sarcasm.

"Oh," she said. "Don't tell me you were hanging around art galleries as well?"

They began to move past ancient sarcophagi and frescos, statutes of Anubis and Bast, of long dead pharaohs sitting on thrones, and urns and cases full of jewelry.

"No. The cinema."

She was still looking at him, he could feel it. "The cinema?"

But she wasn't going to get any more. Not yet anyway. He'd planned to dole it out like breadcrumbs, pieces of himself to lead her through the dark maze of her fear. Strengthening the bond between them so she'd have a lifeline to follow.

*Not to mention binding her closer to you.*

The dragon shifted inside him, heavy and hot. Wanting its treasure to keep, to hoard.

Yes, fuck, that too. He couldn't deny it. But he wouldn't keep her. The whole point of this was to set her free, not lock her in another damn cage.

"I watched a lot of movies as a kid," was all he said as they rounded a corner and walked out into the massive hall that housed the ancient Egyptian temple.

The temple itself was on a raised dais, surrounded by a pool of water. One of the gallery walls was made out of glass, letting light flood the hall and giving views out over Central Park. People moved around the exhibit, talking and taking pictures. It was majestic, atmospheric.

Eva went still beside him, clutching hard on his arm. "It's . . . big. I mean the hall is."

"You don't like that?" He began to lead her toward the stairs that led to the temple.

"I . . . not really." Her breathing had accelerated, the pulse at the base of her throat beating fast.

"Breathe slowly, Eva. Focus on your hand on my arm."

"I can't—"

"Did you touch yourself last night?"

That shocked her. She blinked, sliver blonde lashes fluttering. "What?"

"I told you not to, remember?" He kept his voice pitched low, only loud enough for her to hear. "Did you do as I said?"

They approached the steps, climbing up toward the ruined temple, floodlit and monumental on its dais.

There was color in her pale cheeks. "Yes."

He hadn't expected her to, not given her confused feelings about her sexuality, but then Eva could be unpredictable. And she did love giving him the proverbial middle finger.

"Good," he murmured. "Perhaps I won't have to punish you after all."

She turned her head away, ostensibly looking at the temple as they approached it. "As if I'd let you."

"It wouldn't be a case of 'letting,' angel. Sometimes a punishment can be exactly what you crave."

She said nothing to that as they stopped in front of the exhibit, the space around it miraculously clearing for a moment. She tilted her head back, looking up at the remains of the temple, seemingly absorbed. The tension had left her features, the stiffness dissipating from her posture.

Perhaps she was going to ignore what he'd said. Probably because she didn't know quite what to say to it. Or rather, she did know but didn't yet have the courage to say it.

*I can take any punishment you care to name.*

He'd get her to say it. Tonight he would.

But before that happened he had to put into motion the first part of his plan.

Gently, Zac uncurled her hand from his arm and put a little distance between them. Immediately Eva put her hand back in her pocket, her posture hunching. She didn't look at him, her attention wholly occupied by the temple itself.

A large group of Japanese tourists began to circulate around the exhibit, and Zac let the distance between himself and Eva widen.

She was angry, he could tell. And trying to ignore him. All excellent for his purposes.

He waited until the crowd of tourists were near. Then he turned and walked away, leaving Eva standing there.

Alone.

Punishment? Jesus, she could show him what to do with his freaking punishment.

People didn't crave it. At least, she was goddamned sure *she* didn't. She'd had enough punishment to last a lifetime.

Eva balled her fists in the pockets of her jacket and stared fixedly at the great stone pillars in front of her. Anything so she didn't have to be aware of the press of people around her and the vast open space above her head. It made her feel suffocated and dizzy, a weird, complicated kind of claustrophobia associated with wide-open spaces rather than closed-in ones. Agoraphobia technically, though she hated labels.

Fucking Zac. Yes, she could see the logic in coming here, and it did make sense to familiarize herself with the place. She just . . . hated everything about it.

*Whether you like it or not doesn't matter.*

She scowled because, unfortunately, that was true. Her feelings about it were irrelevant. She had to attend Fitzgerald's little party and she couldn't let the others down by refusing, even if the thought of confronting him left tracks of ice through her soul.

Loyalty was important to her, always had been, and hell, Alex had found the strength to confront his own personal demons in Monte Carlo. Could she do any less? Because if it was true, if Fitzgerald was behind the Lucky Seven and had a part in a human trafficking ring, she couldn't let him get away with it. Not after what she'd been through.

Eva focused on the ancient stone, breathing slowly. Her hand still felt warm from where it had been resting on Zac's arm. She shifted on her feet, the movement making her aware all of a sudden of the silk against her skin, of how it felt like she wasn't wearing any underwear at all, the fabric was so light.

She didn't like that either.

Out of the corner of her eye, she could see the edge of Zac's black overcoat as he waited beside her.

"Are we done here already?" she asked, impatient now to leave.

Zac didn't reply.

Irritated, she turned.

Only to see that it wasn't Zac beside her.

She froze. Because what she'd thought was the edge of Zac's overcoat was instead the back of one of the Japanese tourists who happened to be wearing a black jacket. Which meant . . .

She was alone.

Little crystals of ice began to form in her bloodstream. Freezing her from the inside out. The chill crept up her throat like a hand circling it, squeezing, suffocating . . .

*Breathe, damn you. Breathe.*

Eva fought to inhale, scanning frantically through the crowds of people that suddenly seemed to be all around her, swamping her. But she couldn't see his familiar figure anywhere.

He wasn't there. He'd left her.

The space above her head seemed to possess an immense weight, pushing down on her head. The people around her were a stampede, closing in on her. She turned in a circle, trying to find him, but the faces of people were all a blur as dizziness took hold.

Her knees were weak, her feet blocks of ice. She wanted to drop to the ground and curl in on herself.

*You need to get a fucking grip, idiot.*

Yeah, she did. But she couldn't. Her heart was beating so fast it felt like she was having a heart attack or something, her breathing slipping out of rhythm, becoming choppy and ragged.

*You're losing control. You need to keep yourself safe.*

Yet she couldn't seem to move. Her feet were rooted to the spot, frozen in absolute, blind terror.

She began to tremble, all her muscles locking.

For the first time in seven years, he wasn't here. And she needed him. She needed him to help her feel safe. But he'd gone. Oh Christ, why? Why had he left her here alone?

The noise from the people around her seemed to gain in volume, crashing like thunder. Too loud, too overwhelming.

"Zac?" Her voice was a whisper in the middle of a hurricane. "Zac, where the fuck are you?"

But there was no answer. There was only noise.

Nausea churned in her gut.

She was going to die, wasn't she? She was going to die right here and now, and there was absolutely nothing she could do about it.

Then just before she dropped to her knees on the floor, an arm slid around her waist, strong and sure. The heat of a solid, male body against her back.

She opened her mouth to scream, nothing but a hoarse scrape of sound coming out.

"Eva," a familiar voice murmured in her ear, cutting through all the noise, through the nausea, through the ice in her veins. Through the fear. "It's all right, angel. Be still."

Zac.

Relief swamped her, vast as an ocean. She had to close her eyes, grit her teeth to stop the little sob that threatened to escape. But there was nothing she could do to prevent her body from sagging back against him, heedless of the difficulties of touch or of her own stubborn pride, needing only to be close to him, to melt into the safety he represented.

She was shaking and she couldn't stop that either.

He didn't move, keeping one arm around her, holding her. And though she wanted desperately to move away, put some distance between them and try to recover herself on her own, she didn't think she could actually stand without his help.

"Where were you?" she croaked, her voice hoarse with fright. "You left me."

"I didn't leave." His breath was warm against her neck. "I moved away a few meters, that's all."

"That's a goddamn lie. I looked around and couldn't see you!"

"Because you panicked."

She kept her eyes closed, trying to get her breathing back under control. She wanted to tell him that she hadn't panicked, that she was fine, but there was no way she could keep denying it. No way to escape the truth that was staring her in the face.

He was right. Her fear *was* blinding her.

Yet even now, she couldn't quite bring herself to agree. "Why did you step away? Was it some kind of stupid test?"

Gently, Zac began to remove his arm, and she couldn't help herself, the words coming out before she could stop them. "Don't let me go. Please . . ."As soon as she said it she wanted to take it back, hating the pathetic catch in her voice.

But of course it was too late.

His arm around her stilled. Then firmed.

He was so warm, a wall at her back. Reassuring. Protective. Part of her wanted to keep on resting against him, while another part wanted to shove him away, angry at him for doing this to her. For making her so aware of her weakness.

"Yes," he said after a moment. There was a weird note in his voice, a strange tension in his big body behind her. "I wanted to see what would happen if I wasn't in your immediate vicinity."

"Bastard." It was all she could think of to say.

"You thought I'd gone."

"Of course I did."

A silence.

Then his voice in ear. "Did you really think I would leave you alone here?" And too late she recognized the weird note in it. Anger. "Did you honestly think I wouldn't be somewhere, making sure you were safe?" His arm tightened around her. A manacle. "Even now, even after seven fucking years, you don't trust me."

*You hurt him.*

A lump rose in her throat. "I . . . guess not."

The muscular arm around her tightened even further. "Tell me why. The real reason, not some bullshit, bloody excuse about protecting yourself."

His voice was an iron bar wrapped in velvet. Demanding the truth from her whether she wanted to give it or not. An admission she didn't want to make staring her in the face.

*You owe him.*

She swallowed. "Because I'm . . . a-afraid."

Another long silence.

Then finally he said, "Understand, I'm done with proving myself to you, angel. If you can't see past your fear enough to trust me after all this time, you never will. But I want what I want and I'm not compromising." His arm uncurled from around her waist and he let her go, stepping away.

Her back felt cold, his warmth gone. She felt bereft. Turning, she stared up into his dark face, his expression as impenetrable as the two-thousand-year-old rock of the temple behind her.

"What do you mean?" she asked, even though she already had an idea.

"Stop pretending." His voice was curt, the look in his eyes hard. "Do you want to stay safe in that prison cell you call an apartment? Crawl into Fitzgerald's party the scared, broken little girl you were just now?"

That stung. A lot.

Scared, broken little girl.

She *hated* he'd seen her like that.

Because she wasn't a scared broken little girl and she wasn't going to fucking crawl. She refused. She would go into that fucking party with her head held high and she was going to look Fitzgerald in the eye.

"I'm not a—"

"You know what I want. If you're not prepared to give yourself to me completely, to let me own you body and soul, then you'll be walking out of here alone."

And she knew, beyond a shadow of a doubt that if she refused him, he'd do exactly what he said. That he'd walk out of here and she'd never see him again.

Something inside her howled in despair at the thought.

*You can't let him walk away.*

No, she couldn't. Nor could she pretend that sex would be the price she paid to have him in her life.

Zac's hands on her body, touching her skin . . .

*Zac inside you . . .*

She had to stop lying to herself even if it terrified her. She wanted this. She wanted him. She had to trust him, otherwise what else was there for her?

*Scared, broken little girl.*

"I don't want you to go," she said thickly.

His expression didn't change. "The words, Eva. Give me the words."

She swallowed again, her throat dry. "I'll give myself to you. Body and soul, I'm yours."

# CHAPTER TWELVE

Eva didn't speak as he led her back through the museum and out into the teeming New York lunchtime crowds, her hand resting on his arm, unresisting.

He let her have the silence, granting her a bit of distance because soon enough she wouldn't have any.

A savage, possessive feeling had him in its grip, along with an anger that simmered under his skin like a fire not quite dead.

He'd stood in among the crowd not too far away from her, watching the panic creep into her eyes as she'd noticed he wasn't right next to her anymore. As she'd started searching the crowd blindly, turning in a tight little circle. A wild creature trapped in a net.

She'd gone white, terror stark in her face. And even though he'd only been a couple of feet away from her, she hadn't seen him. She'd been blind.

She really thought he'd gone, that he'd left her there all alone, her panic blatant evidence of her lack of trust in him.

He hadn't counted on just how angry it would make him.

It had been cruel to do that to her, but her denial was so extreme, he hadn't seen any other way except to confront her with it. A lesson for both of them in many ways.

He glanced at her as they moved toward where Temple had parked the limo. Eva's gaze was directly ahead, on the car. Not looking right or left, her shoulders hunched.

He didn't feel a shred of regret for the ultimatum he'd given her, not after she'd proved so blatantly how little she trusted him. But he had gotten her admission of fear. And she had agreed in the end to come with him.

It wasn't, however, exactly what he'd wanted.

Zac followed Eva into the limo and this time, instead of sitting opposite her, he sat directly beside her. She turned her head away, looking out the window.

He waited until Temple had gotten in and started the car, pulling away from the curb. Then he leaned forward and pushed the button that activated the privacy screen, before turning to the woman sitting next to him. Taking her delicate, stubborn little chin in his fingers, he pulled her around to face him.

Her skin was so soft he couldn't help but caress the line of her jaw with his thumb, watching as her eyes widened, a small silver flame leaping high in the gray depths.

Yes, that's what he wanted. Not fear but something hotter. Something more demanding. Desire.

She didn't pull away, only stared at him.

"Do you understand what I'm asking for?" He wanted to be sure because once they started down this road, there was no going back.

"Whips and chains and shit, right?"

Perhaps it was time to challenge her a little bit more. He'd already tested her boundaries back in the museum, now he needed to keep up the pressure.

This was not about keeping her comfortable.

This was about moving from the frying pan into the fucking furnace.

"Whips and chains," he echoed softly, in a voice that

many a sub would have recognized as the calm before the storm. "Is that what you think BDSM is all about?"

Maybe she sensed he was about to do something, because her eyes widened, her mouth opening as if to forestall him.

*Too late, angel.*

Zac moved, leaning forward, crowding her back against the car seat, shifting his hands so one rested on the seat beside her head, the other on the door.

He saw it again, that spark. Not fear, though fear was there. No, this was far hotter, wilder. She liked what he was doing. Liked it whether she knew it herself or not.

Her breathing was coming faster now, her gaze fixed to his. She didn't move, not to push him away or to get away herself. The pulse at the base of her throat was quick, her body rigid with tension.

"Have you ever been to a BDSM club?" he asked, deceptively mild. "Do you actually have any idea what you're talking about?"

Her throat moved as she swallowed. "Sure I do. You put women on their knees, tell them what to do. Order them around. You—"

He bent his head, nipped her bottom lip. Not hard, but enough to remind her of who she was dealing with. The soft, sharp catch of her breath was the best thing he'd heard all day.

"You want to know who has the most power during a BDSM scene?" He brushed her bottom lip with his mouth, not a kiss, only the lightest of touches, feeling the shudder that went through her. "The sub. Everything a Dom does is for them and their pleasure. The sub's pleasure is the Dom's, angel. And if the sub isn't enjoying it, then neither does the Dom." Zac lifted his head, stared into her wide eyes. "And if whips and chains is what the sub wants, then that's what the sub will get."

Two bright spots of color burned on her pale cheeks. "I'm not a fucking sub."

"You don't know what you are. You've never let yourself think about it."

"I don't want whips and chains. And I'm not having you order me around. No one gets to control me, not ever again." Defiance sparked in her eyes.

Fuck, did she know what she was doing? How irresistible a challenge that was for him?

Zac leaned in, their noses just about touching, her gaze inches from his. Letting the veil of the gentleman drop, showing her who he was. "I've been compromising what I want for seven years. That ends now. I will fucking own you, angel. And you *will* do everything I tell you. Every. Single. Thing."

Her breathing was short, hard, and she was struggling to hold his gaze.

He shifted, lifting his hand to pull her beanie off her head, tossing it down on the floor of the car. Then he reached behind her head, tugging out the tie that held her ponytail, white blonde hair falling down around her shoulders like soft, warm snow.

Her mouth opened. Then clamped shut.

Indulging himself, Zac buried his fingers in her hair, tilting her head back so she had to look up at him. So he filled her vision. Her gaze falling helplessly to his mouth then back up again.

A long silence fell, broken only by the sound of the traffic outside. The engines of cars and buses, horns and sirens. The loud purr of a motorcycle.

And the harsh sound of her breathing.

There were so many emotions in her silver eyes. So many he couldn't untangle them all. Fear. Desire. Anger. Hope. Yearning.

She smelled good too, vanilla and Eva, and she was

warm. He wanted her. Bloody, fucking hell, how badly he wanted her.

"You have questions," he said, looking down into her face. "Ask."

"What will you do?" Her voice was unsteady.

He shifted his fingers in her hair, the strands silky against his skin. "To you? Anything I fucking want."

"I don't want to be owned, Zac. I don't want to be h-helpless. Not again."

The slight stutter made something in his chest, something he'd thought long dead, tighten strangely. Of course she wouldn't. But then, she didn't understand that this would be different.

"This is where trust comes into it," he said. "You have to trust me. That's how it works. You'll have to trust me to know what you want and what you don't. And when to push even when you don't want me to."

"And how will you know that? Your amazing psychic Dom powers or something?"

Zac curled his fingers tighter in her hair, tugging hard on it, making her eyes widen and something bright spark in the gray depths. Ah. So she liked that too.

"I've spent seven years watching you, Eva King. I know everything about you. Your fears and your joys. What makes you uncomfortable and what gives you pleasure. What hurts you and what moves you." He pulled harder on her hair, tipping her head back further, exposing the long, elegant white arc of her throat, making her shudder. "And I know what arouses you, and why that makes you scared."

"Great," she said hoarsely, the word edged with fragile sarcasm even now. "Sounds fucking wonderful. For you, I mean. But what the hell do I get out of all of this?"

He smiled, slow and hungry, lowering his head so their mouths were almost but not quite touching. "Freedom, angel. Freedom from the past. From the future. From the fear and the anger, from the pain and the sadness. Give all those things to me and I'll take them away from you. And I'll give you pleasure to take their place."

She went still, staring up at him, her pupils wide and dilated. And he could see the yearning there, bright in her eyes. "I don't want to be afraid, Zac," she said suddenly, hoarsely. "I'm so tired of it. I don't want to be so fucking afraid anymore."

"Then you won't," he replied, and gently unwound his fingers from her hair, releasing her. Straightening in his seat, he pushed the intercom button. "My house, Temple," he said shortly. "Now."

Eva paced up and down in Zac's high-ceilinged hallway, her hands in the pockets of her jacket so she didn't have to see them shaking.

The minute they'd arrived, Zac had told her to wait, apparently so he could get things "ready." She didn't know what he meant by that and didn't really want to find out, though she supposed it was too late now.

She was going to do this.

Her body hummed, every sense alert. She could still feel the spot on her lip where he'd nipped her and the faint pain in her scalp from where he'd pulled her hair. She could still feel the heat of his body against hers.

She ached. This must be want, this must be desire.

Eva reached the front door, turned on her heel and walked back down the hallway once again, her footsteps soundless on the thick Middle Eastern runner that ran the length of the polished wood floor.

The walls were dark blue, with pictures in gold frames positioned at intervals. A dark wood console table with a few knickknacks on it stood near the door. The clock, also standing on it, ticked.

*I will fucking own you, angel. And you* will *do every-thing I tell you. Every. Single. Thing.*

Her fists curled in her pockets, palms sweaty.

She couldn't lie to herself, pretend it was only sex and no big deal, because what Zac wanted from her *was* a big deal. She'd be giving herself to him. She'd be letting him have power over her, and that was downright fucking ter-rifying.

*Freedom, angel. Freedom from the past.*

Impossible to go on like she was, she saw that now. After her breakdown in the museum, she could see where she was headed. To a life spent trapped in her apartment, imprisoned by her own fear.

No, she wasn't doing that. She refused. He'd promised to take away the burden of the past. Take away the fear and the pain, and she wanted to give him those things.

She didn't want to be that broken, scared little girl he'd seen in the museum. She wanted new memories.

Halfway down the hallway, in mid-pace, her phone chimed.

Eva pulled it out and looked down at the screen. A text from Alex. *We need to know what you're going to do. If you need to talk, I'm here.*

Of course it would be from Alex. He knew better than anyone else the demons she'd be facing.

Quickly she typed in a response. *Don't worry, I'll be there. And I don't need to talk.*

As Zac had so eloquently pointed out, talking was not what she needed.

"What are you doing, angel?"

The dark, seductive sound of his voice was a shock af-ter the silence in the hallway and her overstretched nerves shivered at the sound, her hands shaking as she stuffed her phone back into her pocket. "Alex wanted to know what I was going to do. I told him." She didn't want to look at him, because she really wasn't ready yet. But she forced herself.

Zac was standing at the end of the hallway, silent and still. His suit was so perfect, not a crease in it, his tie straight as an arrow. Like a wealthy stockbroker on his way to the office.

But that was his disguise, as she well knew. And quite frankly it was a shit disguise because stockbrokers generally weren't built like gladiators, nor did they have eyes that burned right into people's souls. They didn't project authority like a king holding court or the brutal charisma of an ancient god, the kind that made a person want to get down on their knees and worship them.

"Good." He lifted a hand toward the library door. "In here."

She made herself walk down the hall a few feet until she reached the door he'd indicated.

The expression on his face made her want to look away because the hunger in it was too stark. Too blatant. The intensity of his focus turned on her was . . . overwhelming. But then everything about him was, and how she'd gone for so long without ever noticing, she had no idea.

He reached for the door handle. "Once you cross this threshold Eva, you're mine. Inside that room, my word is law and you will obey it without question. Do you remember your safeword?"

The absolute authority in the words made her shiver. Made something inside her tighten and yet relax at the same time. "Yes."

"Say it now."

It was all she could do not to stutter. "Void."

He gave a short nod. "Like I told you earlier, a safeword is sacred. You may say it at any time and everything will stop." He paused, his gaze locked on hers. "Do you trust me with this?"

The fifty-six-million-dollar question. She couldn't give him empty words, not this time. This was real. This was happening. And as he'd already proved, he wouldn't go easy on her. If she gave him that trust, she'd have to go with him wherever he wanted to take her.

Wherever that was.

Eva swallowed. "Yes."

The hunger in his eyes flared. "I need you to respect the word as much as I do. Don't use it to test me or because you don't like something. I'll give you one free pass with it, but if you start using it to control me or just for kicks, I'll stop this and send you home."

The blood roared in her veins, her heartbeat deafening in her ears. "I understand."

Zac pushed open the door and stood aside. "Then go in."

She hesitated a moment, making herself look at him, not really sure what she was even looking for. Maybe some sign that the Zac she'd come to know over the past seven years was there. Protective, gentle. Kind.

But if he was, she couldn't find him.

There was no gentleness in those amber eyes, in that dark, harshly attractive face. Only hunger, iron will. A man with the soul of a predator. A predator who'd gone too long without food.

Eva looked away, took a breath and walked into the room.

Behind her the door closed, Zac moving past her over to the couch. He said nothing, taking off his suit jacket and hanging it neatly over the arm of a chair. Then he began unfastening the cuffs of his black business shirt, his movements practiced and deft.

She found herself watching him, mesmerized as he rolled up his sleeves, exposing bronze skin, muscled forearms, and the bold colors of one of his tattoos. Another reminder of what he was at heart. A warrior. A killer.

A mercenary who demanded his payment from her and yet made sure the room was warm and there was a fire leaping in the hearth.

He did always like to make sure she wasn't cold.

*You do trust him.*

A tension inside her eased.

Zac straightened and abruptly his golden eyes pinned her to the spot, bright as a solar flare. "Take your clothes off."

A perverse part of her, the part that refused to lie down and surrender, wanted to argue or refuse, yet she found her hands moving to obey the order anyway, pulling her T-shirt up and over her head then off.

He put his hand out. "Give your clothing to me."

She handed him the T-shirt, frowning as he folded it up neatly and put it on the armchair. What the hell was he doing?

"The rest," he said curtly. "I'm only going to ask you to do something once, angel. And if you don't do as you're told, there will be consequences."

It would be stupid to push him now, and yet that perverse part of her wanted to. See what kind of consequences he meant.

But she was still too uncertain, still too afraid. So instead, she bent and began undoing the laces of her Docs, taking her socks and boots off before handing them to him one by one, waiting while he arranged them neatly beside the armchair. Her jeans followed, so that soon she was standing there wearing only the lingerie he'd bought for her.

Her hands went to the front clasp of her bra, her fingers trembling.

"Wait," Zac ordered, prowling closer.

She stilled, her heart kicking insider her chest as he closed the distance, coming to stand in front of her.

He pushed her hands aside, reaching for the clasp and undoing it himself. She couldn't breathe, a wave of heat washing through her as his fingers brushed her skin and the silk cups fell away from her breasts, baring her. Goose bumps rose everywhere as Zac pushed the straps from her shoulders, taking the bra off completely. He stepped back, folding the silk carefully in his big hands, looking at her.

"Beautiful," he murmured. "You're beautiful, angel. Now stay there, exactly like that."

Turning, he went to put the bra with her other clothes before coming back to stand in front of her once more.

Ice congealed in her veins, warring with a heat that seemed to burn up from underneath it, a contradiction that made no sense to her at all.

The look on Zac's face didn't help. The sheer intensity of that focus unnerved her. Confused her. Made her afraid at what he could see in her.

*You like it too. You want to be known by him.*

The breath went out of her at that thought. Then he suddenly dropped to his knees, making her almost forget to breathe back in again. His hands rose to the waistband of those flimsy, lacy silver panties, and he began to ease them down. Slowly. So goddamned slowly.

She trembled, fixing her gaze on the wall across the room, unable to bring herself to look down at him. She could feel him drag the material down over her thighs and the backs of her knees, right down to her ankles, his hands gently urging her to step out of the fabric.

Then she was naked. Completely naked.

She wasn't used to it. She got naked only in the shower and for a few brief moments while getting dressed.

*And when you were taken to Him.*

Her throat closed. The only time she'd been naked in front of someone else had been at The House. With The Man. It had terrified her at first then and it was no less terrifying now, even though earlier Zac had watched her put on that lingerie he'd just taken off. Because now it wasn't a faceless stranger, this was someone she knew. Someone she'd known for years, and somehow that was even scarier.

What did he see when he looked at her? Did he see a scared, broken little girl? A girl who could disappear from the streets of New York without a single soul to notice she was gone?

*Of course no one noticed. Nobody cared about you. Nobody loved you.*

Like that was something she didn't know.

Eva kept her gaze fixed on the wood-paneled library wall, her vision blurring, her hands in fists at her sides. She didn't care what he saw. It didn't matter to her, she wouldn't let it.

Yet she still trembled as she felt him run his palms up the backs of her calves, her knees, her thighs. His fingers were warm, caressing as he cupped her butt, squeezing gently.

He made a deep, soft, approving sound. Then he buried his face between her thighs.

The sensation that knifed through her was like a shock from a cattle prod, a sharp, hot jolt. She froze completely, a choked gasp escaping her, all her muscles locking.

He ignored her reaction, nuzzling her, palms squeezing her, his breath warm against her sex. "Christ, you smell bloody delicious." His voice was roughened. "I knew you would."

The pressure of his hands and the press of his body against her legs put her off balance, and she reached out, grabbing onto his shoulders instinctively to keep herself upright. But that was another unexpected assault on her senses. The heat of him, the powerful flex and release of muscle beneath the cotton of his shirt. Strong, God, he was so strong. And she was so fragile and small next to him.

*Insignificant, you mean.*

She swallowed, shivering, the tremor before a major earthquake.

He must have noticed because he shifted back all of a sudden, lifting his head. And she was caught in the depths of his eyes like a dragonfly in amber. "Did I say you could touch me?"

"N-no."

Her hands slipped from his shoulders as he rose in a smooth, fluid movement. Looking down at her. "Touching me is a privilege you have to earn, angel. Now, go sit down in that armchair."

"Jesus, seriously?" She couldn't help herself, feeling cold and exposed, the way she had sometimes when she'd been on the streets. A sixteen-year-old alone and at the mercy of the city, where she'd had to keep fighting in order to merely survive.

His hand came out unexpectedly, taking her chin and gripping her hard, tilting her head back, and the full force of his dominance hit her like a slap to the face.

Nothing of the perfect British gentleman mask he wore remained. It had gone. Completely. And what was painfully clear was just how much of himself he'd been holding back.

She was almost flattened by the intensity of him. By the strength of his will bearing down on her like a freight train.

"I will not repeat myself," he said quietly, forcefully. "This once you get a pass, but next time, you *will* suffer those consequences. Now do as you're told and go and sit down."

And something inside Eva woke up. As if it had been waiting all along for him to reveal himself.

She'd caught glimpses of this man, the man he'd been hiding from her. But this was the first time she felt a part of herself rise in response. Wanting to meet that will of his, test it. Match it.

This time it wasn't fear that moved her through, but heat.

It was electric. Intense. She was transfixed.

He must have noticed too, because the corner of his mouth lifted slightly, an acknowledgment. He released her but didn't move, and she knew he was waiting for her to obey him.

As if her body was already his to command, she was turning before she was even conscious of it, going wordlessly over to the armchair and sitting down in it, the soft leather cool beneath her bare skin.

She felt strange. Hot and cold and scared and fiercely excited all at once.

Zac went over to the cabinet where he kept his wine and her tea, opening a drawer and taking something out of it. Then he turned and came back over to where she sat, standing in front of her.

Her breath caught. She didn't want to look up at him, though that humming, newly awoken part of her wanted to. Meet his burning gold eyes. Match her will to his.

Something black was dangled in front of her.

A blindfold.

And it felt as if all the air had been sucked out of the room.

No. He couldn't seriously expect her to put that on. He couldn't, not after all the shit she'd been through. Screw him and his fucking Dom crap.

Eva tipped her head back and looked up at him. There was nothing soft or tender in his expression, his face all hard planes and harsh angles.

"Put it on," he ordered.

Oh, he knew what he was doing, she could see it in his eyes. Saw the dare, the challenge. He knew *exactly* what this blindfold meant for her, and he wasn't going to protect or cajole or seduce her into putting it on. He was ordering her, expecting her to do exactly what he said.

And a realization hit her like a river of snowmelt.

All this time he'd been protecting her, insulating her, and all this time she'd let him. Helping him treat her like she was made out of glass, like she should be protected.

A broken little girl.

But not now. There was no give in him, no softness. No careful protection of her boundaries or her issues. He was treating her like she was tough. Like she could do this. As if there was nothing wrong with her. Like she was a fucking warrior.

Her chest tightened, her throat closed.

Jesus Christ, he'd been right. She didn't need to be sheltered and protected any longer. She needed the goddamned fire.

Eva held his gaze, feeling her spirit shake off the chains that had been binding it for far too long, and snatched the blindfold from his hands. Then before she could second-guess herself, she put it over her eyes and tied it on tightly.

Blackness. Suffocation.

Terror was a hand on her throat, squeezing.

She reached out, trying to find the arms of the chair to anchor herself, feeling like she was sliding down into some dark hole where there was only fear and pain. The memory of hands on her, touching her where she didn't want—

Someone caught her fingers.

Zac.

"Where are you, Eva?" His voice was close, near her ear.

"Here," she whispered, hoarse with fear. "Your library."

"And who are you with?"

She focused her attention on the feel of his fingers, how they seemed to wrap around hers entirely, their warmth sending shockwaves over her skin. "You. I'm with you."

"Damn right. And don't you think of anything but me. Concentrate on my voice, my touch. Think of my hands, my mouth, my cock. You're not his toy to play with tonight, you're mine. Body, heart, mind, and soul. Understand?"

The fierce spirit inside her leapt. "Yes. I understand." Then, because at her heart she was a warrior, she raised her blindfolded eyes to where she thought he was. "And you're mine tonight too?"

A silence fell and she could almost feel his surprise. Well, good. It was about time she did a bit of shocking herself.

The sound of movement, one of his hands tightening around hers. Strong fingers taking her chin and turning her head, the warmth of his breath near her ear.

"Angel," he said in that tone, the one that radiated authority and power. "I was never anyone else's."

His fingers tightened on her chin fractionally. And that was the only warning she got before his mouth covered hers.

The kiss was hard, sure and ruthless, giving her absolutely no quarter.

A shocked sound escaped her and instinctively she tried to pull away from the onslaught, but his hand holding her jaw made that impossible.

His tongue forced its way into her mouth, slick and sinewy and hot, taking exactly what he wanted. Ravaging. Devouring. Making no allowances for the fact that she was inexperienced. That this was, in fact, the first time she'd ever been kissed.

It felt like a bomb had gone off and she'd been knocked flat by the shockwave.

Then right when she'd got herself together enough to respond, he let her go.

Someone was breathing loudly and fast. Her.

"I," she began hoarsely, her voice stuttering, her heartbeat fast. "I haven't been kissed before."

"That wasn't a kiss." His voice came from directly in front of her. "That was a claim."

A shiver took her, going all the way down her back. Shaking something deep inside her.

His fingers tightened around her hands and she felt some kind of cool fabric beginning to be wrapped around her wrists. "I told you you were mine, angel," he said levelly. "I meant it." The fabric pulled tight as if to emphasize his point.

There was a ringing in her ears and she was suddenly acutely aware of the leather of the armchair against the bare skin of her butt, of the warmth of the fire crackling in the hearth. Of Zac's scent, cedar and woodsmoke and musk. Her nipples felt hard, a deep ache between her thighs, and her mouth was full and almost bruised from the kiss.

The physical feelings were almost overwhelming.

Fabric rustled as she heard Zac get to his feet. Then her arms were being raised above her head as she was eased against the back of the chair. He must have fastened her wrists to a hook or something embedded in the chair back, because when she pulled at them, she couldn't get free.

"What are you doing?" Fear had begun to turn inside her, but twining with it was that newly awakened excitement and curiosity. The part that was finding all of this intensely thrilling.

He didn't speak, the room silent.

One of his mind-fucks probably. Her breath caught and she stilled, her senses searching for him, the sound of him, the scent of him. The air moved a little near her cheek and she turned her head. "Zac."

A warm hand slid under one of her thighs, the opposite side from where she looked, lifting it up and over the arm of the chair. She tensed, blinking behind the blindfold. Something that felt like a thick, silky rope was wrapped around her ankle and then her ankle was pulled taut gently. She tested it. Found she couldn't move her leg.

She tried to still her breathing, but when she felt his hands on her other leg, the smooth rope wrapping around the other ankle, it started to slide out of her control.

Jesus. She was sitting naked on the chair, with her wrists bound and her legs tied apart.

"Zac?" Her voice had frayed even more, his name sounding uncertain.

"The restraints should add to your pleasure, angel." The dark heat of his voice came from in front of her. "They'll also stop you from controlling it or trying to escape it."

She pulled against the ropes that held her, testing them again, but they were tight. She couldn't move.

Helpless. She was helpless.

*No, it's okay. You're with him.*

Fear and excitement warred for supremacy. Every sense she had seemed to be attuned to the man standing in front of her and what he would do next. What he would say.

Another shiver wracked her body.

"Well, well, well," Zac murmured. "What have we here?" Her body jerked as his hands came down on her inner thighs, the touch an instant electric shock. "One beautiful, wet pussy, and all for me."

Reflexively she tried to pull her legs together but all that happened was her ankles tugging against the ropes that bound them.

He felt close. Extremely close.

"You remember your word, don't you, Eva?" His thumbs stroked over the soft, excruciatingly sensitive skin of her inner thighs. "Because I'm not going to go easy on you. I'm going to eat my fill of you, make you scream. But you're not going to get your orgasm until you beg for it. Are we clear?"

The ringing in her ears increased, her breathing rocketed out of control. She shifted in the chair, unable to help herself. Restless and afraid and full of a kind of heat she couldn't seem to contain.

"Yes," she whispered hoarsely.

"Good. Now . . . Where were we? Ah yes . . ." A hand moved from her thigh to her breast, cupping it. Then wet heat engulfed her nipple as his mouth closed over it.

It was like he'd taken a match to her, setting her on fire.

Eva arched in the chair, the fabric pulling tight around her wrists as a ragged cry escaped her, pleasure sharp as the blade of a sword cutting her in two.

He sucked hard on her nipple, increasing the intensity of the feeling. Then he bit her. The cry became a fractured scream as a fine edge of pain threaded through the pleasure, heightening it somehow. Light burst behind her eyes. His tongue licked a hot circle around her nipple before he drew it back into his mouth, increasing the suction.

She panted, unable to pull away or escape the intensity of the feeling, trembling all over.

Then his other hand covered her sex.

Another blast of sensation detonated as his thumb began to move in a tight, hard circle around her clit while he ran one finger down through her wet folds to the entrance of her body, pushing inside.

Her hips jerked and her back arched. She couldn't stop from screaming again. Her pleasures had been simple ones for so long—warmth, food, shelter—that she couldn't deal with the razor-edged physical pleasure that flooded through her now.

It was too much. It was like agony.

"No . . ." She arched again, vainly trying to move away from the ravenous mouth on her breast. "I c-can't . . ."

But he only transferred his attentions to her other breast, his thumb still moving on her clit, his finger now sliding deep inside her.

She began to shake, a blind terror overtaking her. A primal kind of fear she didn't quite understand. Her body twisted, trying to escape. "Z-Zac . . . no . . ."

He ignored her, the hand between her legs slowing down, each movement becoming a small, precise agony.

She wasn't going to be able to stand this. She couldn't. Which meant all she had to do was say the word and it would stop. He would take all these frightening sensations away and it would be over.

*No. Fucking. Way.*

She went still, shaking so hard she felt like she was going to break apart.

No. She wasn't going to say that word. She didn't need it. What she needed was this. This pleasure. Him. And her fucking orgasm.

Zac's hands fell away from her, his tongue licking a trail all the way down between her breasts, over her trembling stomach, down further still. Then she felt his fingers spreading the folds of her sex, opening her up. And his tongue was pushing deep and hard into her.

Eva screamed then screamed again as his finger circled her clit, around and around.

He was relentless. One hand slid beneath her buttocks, lifting her, his massive shoulders pressing against her inner thighs, spreading her even wider. Then he began to lick her like ice cream with the flat of his tongue, the change in sensation winding the tension inside her even tighter.

"Please . . ." Her voice was only a thin thread of sound. "Oh God, please . . ."

He pulled away, and the loss of his mouth and his hands was yet another agony. "What do you want?" The words were deep and raw, full of heat and darkness. "Tell me what you want."

She writhed in the chair, pulling against the ties on her wrist and ankles unable to help herself. But nothing was going to relieve the ache. Nothing except him. "I want . . . my f-fucking orgasm. Now. Right fucking now!"

A finger slid inside her and she gasped, her back bowing against the chair, her hips jerking. "Since when do you get to make demands?" Another finger slid deep, stretching her. "I'm the one who owns you, angel. I'm the one who gets to decide when you come. And you haven't earned it yet." A shift between her thighs, heat against her skin. His mouth brushing against her stomach. "Besides, I haven't finished playing with this perfect little pussy of yours yet. You kept it away from me for too long and now I want what's mine."

The wet heat of his tongue traced a lazy circle around her clit, his fingers sliding out of her, then in again, matching the movement.

Eva moaned helplessly, every nerve ending she had stretched to breaking point.

And he kept licking her, kept up the slow movement of his fingers, holding the release she knew was there just out of her reach.

The world began to recede, began to narrow to the agonizing brush of his tongue and the feel of his fingers. To the sharp, desperate ache that was becoming more and more unbearable by the second.

There was no future, no past. There was only this. Only this ache. Only him.

She began to sob because the immensity of her hunger

was frightening and she'd lost the capacity to pretend otherwise. Reduced to a creature governed purely by need. No fear, no pain. Only want.

It was such a relief she never wanted it to end.

But his body shifted again, his free hand reaching into her hair, his fingers twining in it, her head being pulled back. His mouth covering hers.

Then the hand between her thighs moved, his thumb brushing lightly over her clit.

And the world exploded behind her eyes.

She screamed into his mouth, lit up like a torch. Flames leaping in the darkness behind the blindfold. Burning and burning and burning, yet never consumed.

His withdrawal from her was as big a shock as his first touch had been.

One moment his mouth was on hers and she was riding out the effects of the orgasm like a surfer on a tidal wave. The next he was gone.

Tremors shook her body. She was floating in the blackness, a feather in the void. Waiting for whatever would happen next, knowing it would come and yet not being concerned. Not being afraid.

Free.

Sounds filtered through the drumming beat of her heart. Foil crackling, a zipper being undone. She knew those sounds, knew what they meant. But she wasn't afraid, or at least, the tight feeling inside her didn't feel like fear. It felt like hunger and satisfaction, tension and looseness all at the same time.

The chair dipped, Zac's palms on her butt, lifting her as his hard thighs slid beneath hers. The ties on her ankles pulled tight and she took a sharp breath.

He wasn't naked, she could feel the wool of his suit pants against her bare skin, but there was so much heat coming from him he may as well have been. It surrounded her, along with his woodsmoke-and-cedar scent, a scent that now had a darker, musky edge to it.

Her whole body shivered as she realized he must be kneeling on the chair facing her with her in his lap.

A hand stroked her stomach, then moved down between her thighs, and she gasped aloud as his fingers slipped inside her. She was still so achingly sensitive, the sensation almost excruciating. "Zac . . . God . . ."

But he didn't relent, his hand moving, sliding his fingers in and out so she began to pant and shift and moan all over again.

Then his hand was gone and he was spreading her open. She felt the blunt head of his cock against her entrance. Christ, so hot. She shivered again, her body going still, waiting.

But he didn't move. She could feel him right *there,* so close, so goddamn close.

"Beg me," he whispered, the seductive heat of his voice like the brush of flame. "Beg me to fuck you." And she shuddered as she felt his fingers curve around her throat, his palm against her frantically beating pulse. A firm, possessive, intensely erotic hold. "Beg for my cock, angel. Do it now."

Her voice wouldn't work, her mouth so dry. She had to force the sounds out. "Please . . . oh . . . please . . ."

"More, Eva." His hips moved and she felt the press of him a little firmer, a tease.

The last man who'd been inside her had been Him, and in the dark nights after she'd escaped, she'd told herself she'd never let anyone take her like that again, not blindfolded and bound and helpless, unable to do a thing to stop it.

And yet here she was. Blindfolded. Bound. Helpless.

*There's a difference.*

Of course there was. This time it was Zac, and she

wanted him. He wasn't treating her like a doll. Like a victim. He had his hand around her throat and his cock right *there.* And that voice of his that was like a caress or a whip depending on how he used it, was demanding. Making no allowances for her past.

He believed in her strength. It was time she did too.

"Fuck me, you bastard," she whispered. "And do it hard. When I remember the last man inside me, I want that man to be you."

There was a silence, and she was achingly aware of his hand, the heat of his palm on her skin. The warmth of his breath near her ear.

Then he moved, thrusting deep and hard inside of her.

Eva couldn't stop the cry that escaped her because he was big and it had been a long time. Her body struggled to adjust, sensitive flesh stretching, overloading already raw nerve endings.

"Keep still," he said harshly, his hand around her throat firm.

"I can't . . . Zac . . ." Her hips bucked as he thrust harder, deeper, fighting to do as he said. "Oh God . . ."

His hand settled on her hip, holding her down as he leaned forward, pressing her back against the chair. Slamming into her.

"I waited for you . . ." He nipped her ear. "So fucking long." His breathing was fast against her neck, each thrust of his hips winding the desperate need inside of her tighter and tighter. "Seven years, Eva. Seven fucking years you kept this pussy from me." His hand shifted from her hip, down between her thighs, stroking her hot, wet flesh. "It's mine now. Understand? Mine."

She arched against the chair again, crying out as the thrust of his cock and the relentless touch of his fingers began to shatter her. As she felt herself respond helplessly to the possessiveness in his voice.

"There will be no one else for you, Eva King. Only me." Another hard thrust, all the feelings rioting inside her making her sob. "I will be the only one you'll ever think about again."

She couldn't hold out in the end.

He overwhelmed her.

He moved faster, harder, crushing her against the chair with each powerful thrust of his hips, his fingers on her clit heightening everything so much she thought she'd shatter like a windowpane under the pressure of too much snow.

Right before the end, before she did, indeed, shatter into a thousand million pieces, he whispered, harsh and raw. "Seven years I waited for you, angel. And you were worth every second."

The orgasm took him like a club to the back of the head, and he had to wait for long moments afterwards, his face buried in her hair, just to be able to move.

She smelled musky and sweet, of sex and vanilla, the sound of her ragged breathing loud in his ear. And he could feel her shuddering, the aftershocks still going through her.

He'd taken her hard, he knew that. He'd been demanding, making absolutely no allowances for her and what she'd been through.

And she'd met him with that strength he knew had been inside her all along.

She was amazing.

He was also so angry with her he didn't know what to do. He could feel it inside him roaring up like a fire, threatening to burn everything in its path.

Even her.

*Especially her.*

He lifted his head, looked down at her.

She'd sagged back against the chair, her hair a pale, tangled silver mess. Beneath the edges of her blindfold, her cheeks were wet with tears and her mouth was open. A deep flush stained her skin, going all the way down her neck and over those lovely, perfectly round little breasts, extending even down over her stomach.

How often had he fantasized about her like this? Bound and begging. Wet for him. Wanting him. His in every single way.

Oh, he'd known that when it happened, when she finally gave herself over to him, it would be good. That it would be intense, a pleasure he'd savor for years to come.

He just hadn't thought she would break him. That when he pushed inside her, the tight, wet heat of her body would undermine his precious control quite so badly. Making him want to claim her for himself. Keep her for as long as he could. Even forever.

He'd never had that reaction to any woman before. All those beautiful subs he'd disciplined and given pleasure to. All those lovely women who'd begged him to be their Master, he'd never even felt the slightest inclination toward keeping.

But Eva was different. She always had been.

And now he was furious with her. For being different. For making him wait so bloody long. For being so strong. For being so much more than every fantasy of her he'd ever had . . .

Anger was a bad thing for a Dom. A bad thing for him.

Zac pulled out of her, making her gasp a little, which he ignored. Then he got off the chair and turned around, moving to deal with the condom and zip himself back up again.

His hands shook.

*Get. Yourself. The. Fuck. Together.*

Christ, he *had* to. He couldn't manage the rest of this night if he wasn't in perfect control of himself.

He'd intended to play with her for much longer before

he fucked her, yet he hadn't been able to stop himself from climbing into that chair and taking her like a goddamn beast.

It was just . . . the taste of her had been in his mouth, the feel of her pussy around his fingers, and he'd felt the weight of every second of those seven years descend on him like a boulder.

With her legs tied and spread and her arms above her head, she'd been a gift he hadn't been able to resist.

He turned back to the chair where she sat, still trembling, still panting, and moved automatically behind it to release her wrists from the hook in the back of the chair. Then, keeping hold of her wrists, he came around to the front of the chair again and drew them down to untie the length of silk he'd wrapped around them.

Concentrating on the small, mundane movements and not the furnace burning furiously away in his gut helped get the anger back under control.

Her fingers were cold so he chafed the skin gently, rubbing back feeling into them. When they were warmer, he laid them down on the arms of the chair and moved to untie her ankles. The silk ropes he'd used had left marks on her pale skin.

*A brand of your ownership.*

He ignored both the thought and the hot burst of desire that followed it, focusing instead on unhooking her legs from the arms of the chair and laying them back on the seat, chafing her ankles too to make sure the blood was flowing properly. She shivered as he did so, her breathing harsh.

He rose then bent, gathering her into his arms. Her bare skin burned through the cotton of his business shirt, the musky sweet scent of her wrapping around him. Making his hunger rise, the intensity of it mirroring his anger.

*She kept you at a distance all those years when you could have had this. Such a fucking waste of time.*

His jaw tightened. He was a selfish prick. It hadn't been her fault, she'd been scarred by her experience.

*She let it come to this though. And you helped her. You're to blame as much as she is.*

Zac ignored the snide voice in his head, keeping an iron grip on his emotions as he carried Eva to the couch. He laid her down on it and covered her with the soft throw she often liked to wrap around herself whenever she visited.

Then he went over to the liquor cabinet where he'd left the plate of treats he'd organized earlier, pouring a glass of wine and taking it and the plate back to the table beside the couch.

Eva lay quiet under the throw. Her breathing had normalized and the shaking had stopped.

He sat down beside her, reaching out to pull her into his lap. She didn't protest, her body loose and relaxed, her head coming to rest against his chest as if it was the most natural thing in the world.

She was so slight in his arms. She really didn't eat enough.

"Are you okay?" He brushed her hair back over her shoulders. The blindfold was still on; he wasn't ready to take it off her yet. Without her sight, her other senses would be heightened and he hadn't finished awakening those just yet.

"Yeah." Her voice had a ragged, hoarse edge to it, probably from the screams he'd brought from her. Even just hearing it made his cock start to get hard again. All those cries, ragged gasps, sobs, wild, high screams . . .

Zac shifted her a little so he could reach the plate at the side of the couch. He picked up an olive from the selection of food he'd laid out. "Open your mouth."

She let out a long breath but did as she was told.

He eased the olive into her mouth, watching her face as her lips closed around it. She grimaced then muttered, "What the hell is that?"

"An olive."

She chewed, pulling a face. "I don't like olives."

"Taste it properly, Eva."

"I am. It's . . . salty." She swallowed, her mouth twisting. "Why are you feeding me olives?"

"Because I've seen inside your fridge. All you eat are TV dinners." It had been one among many depressing discoveries when he'd used his key to come and wake her up that morning. He'd gone to try and find some food for her before he'd woken her, but there had been nothing in the freezer but ready-made meals. Bland and tasteless. Food for fuel, not for pleasure.

"I like TV dinners."

He studied her. "That's all they fed you wasn't it?" He didn't elaborate, but then he didn't need to. She knew exactly who "they" meant.

She didn't reply for a long moment, her cheek resting against his chest. "Yes," she answered finally. "That and takeout sometimes. I didn't know how to cook and they didn't want me using a stove or anything. So they bought TV dinners I could heat up myself in the microwave." She paused then added quietly. "I'd never had so much food in all my life."

Of course. She must have gone hungry when she'd been on the streets.

Ah, but this was a line of conversation he didn't want to pursue because every aspect of it made the anger inside him burn hotter. The life she'd led before she'd been captured made him want to hurt someone. Because he knew what it was like to be afraid. To go hungry. To wish someone —anyone—gave a shit about you.

That fucking refrigerator and its pathetic contents had only reminded him of the one in his parent's house back when he was growing up. A big, white thing that should have been full of food but wasn't. Only sour milk and bottles and bottles of high-end French champagne.

Luckily he'd had a nanny who had fed him out of her own purse. Eva hadn't even had that.

He picked up the next offering. A smooth, creamy piece of camembert.

"What's wrong?" Her hand was resting against his chest, the heat of her palm like a small ray of sunlight, her blindfolded face turned up toward him.

A strange shock went through him that she'd noticed. "Nothing's wrong."

"Yes, there is. I can feel it. You're all tense."

For a second it felt like there was a hot wire twisting inside him. A painful, tight, burning feeling, which only made him angrier. She shouldn't have been able to read him so easily, especially not with that blindfold over her eyes, yet she had.

*You really think after seven years she wouldn't know you like you know her?*

No. She couldn't know him like he knew her. She hadn't made him her study. He wouldn't have let her even if she had. No chinks in his armor were allowed.

"Open your mouth again," he ordered, trying to keep his tone even.

She'd gone still, like a cat sensing the movement of a bird. "Zac?"

Except he wasn't a fucking bird. And he'd already warned her once.

He twisted his fingers hard in her hair and pulled her head back across his chest, exposing her long white throat. A soft, outrush of breath escaped her. Lowering his head, he murmured, "I very much hope you're not going to make me repeat myself."

She shivered against him and he could see the goose

bumps rise all over her skin, down over her breasts, her nipples hardening into little pale pink points. "I'll eat what you give me," she said hoarsely. "But only if you tell me what's wrong."

The hot wire feeling twisted again. "Since when do you get to make demands?"

"Since you gave me a safeword that can end this right now."

Holy fucking Christ. He gripped her hair harder. "What did I say about respect?"

Her jaw had hardened, that stubborn determination he knew all too well in every line of it. "I do respect it. But you need to respect my right to ask you a goddamn question. Especially when you apparently have no qualms about forcing answers out of me."

God, she had guts. He didn't like she'd used the safeword to get what she wanted, but then she wasn't a sub he'd picked up for the night. He knew her. And whether he liked it or not, she knew him.

*Give her what she wants. What does it matter? The past can't hurt you anymore.*

Not that it ever had.

"Open," he repeated.

This time she did, letting him put the piece of cheese in her mouth. And he watched her while she ate it. No grimaces this time, and she made a humming sound in the back of her throat as she swallowed. "That was . . . different. Nice, I think. Cheese?"

"Camembert."

"Camembert," she echoed, mimicking his accent. "You're such a fucking aristocrat. Now tell me what was bugging you, otherwise this is over."

He could make it over right now too if he wanted. Crush her stubborn mouth with his, run his hands all over her body, feed her burgeoning sensuality, make her forget any question she wanted to ask. Make her forget she even wanted to ask it in the first place.

He was a selfish prick. A mercenary. A monster. And he'd been protecting himself too long. She didn't need to know anything about him, she really didn't.

Yet he found himself speaking all the same. "I was thinking your fridge looked like mine. When I was a child."

Her head shifted against his arm and he could almost feel the pressure of her gaze through her blindfold. "Oh? You had a shitty childhood too?"

"I *was* a fucking aristocrat. At least my parents were. An obscure branch related to the royal family. The title was apparently gambled away by one of my ancestors a couple of hundred years ago, but the money still remained. At least it did until my parents spent it all on heroin."

Pale and fragile and perfect in his arms, she said nothing. So he went on. "They didn't bother much with food, though they had expensive tastes in champagne. But I had a nanny who made sure I ate." He flexed his fingers in her hair, momentarily distracted by the feel of the silky strands against his skin. "So you see, I appreciate good food when I have it. And so should you."

"That's awful," she said quietly. "That's really awful. Junkies suck."

"It wasn't particularly pleasant, no, and yes, they do."

"What happened to you?"

He didn't want questions. Didn't want to talk about himself. It was a protective mechanism that had stood him in good stead for years and he couldn't see any reason to change now.

*Hasn't she earned it?*

Zac looked down into her face turned toward him, soft mouth and sharp chin. He couldn't see her eyes but he knew they'd be full of challenge. Goading him.

Typical Eva.

Then again, he was strong enough in his authority to withstand a few pushes from one small, determined young woman.

He leaned over the plate again, picked up another treat. "Open your mouth."

She obeyed without protest this time.

Yes. She'd earned it.

He put it in her mouth, feeling her body tense in surprise.

"Oh," she murmured. "Chocolate."

"Excellent ninety-percent cocoa solids dark chocolate. Bittersweet. Just like you."

She chewed. "This is better than Hershey's."

"Of course it's better than bloody Hershey's." He eased his grip in her hair, letting the silky strands sift through his fingers instead. "So what happened to me? I was brought up by a series of nannies. Some took an interest in me, some didn't. And when they weren't there, I used to go to the local cinema and watch movies." He twisted a lock of pale hair around one finger, examining it. "Surprising what values old movies can teach you. They certainly taught me more than my parents ever did about being a decent human being. Anyway, I managed to survive their parenting, and the first chance I got, I left. I joined the army, the SAS, and did rather well." He focused on the strand of hair looped around his finger, rubbed it gently with his thumb. "Then I came across an officer assaulting a woman, a new cadet." So much rage, a red cloud over his vision. He'd always hated people who took advantage of those weaker than themselves, like the dealers who used to visit his parents, preying on their addiction. He'd lost his head, overwhelmed by the emotion. "I pulled him off her. He tried to attack me, so I hit back and he hit the ground. Fractured his skull. He died in the hospital two days later."

"Oh." Her hand pressed harder against his chest. "Zac, shit, that's terrible."

It was terrible. Another example of how vigilant he had to be when it came to his baser emotions. How he had to be very controlled and very disciplined about them.

"It wasn't ideal," he agreed with supreme understatement. "In the end, to save the family name from being dragged in the mud, my grandparents had to pay off some people to stop manslaughter charges being brought against me. I had to leave England after that, which I did, gladly." In fact, he hadn't been able to leave fast enough. "There weren't any other jobs for a man with my particular skillset naturally, and I was young enough and angry enough that I couldn't see the point of working in some factory for nothing. So when an ex-military friend of mine had an opportunity come up as a gun for hire, I took it."

Eva was silent for a moment. "Why didn't your grandparents help you earlier?"

"Because they despised my father. Pretty much washed their hands of him. I was deemed to be cut from the same cloth so they didn't have much time for me either."

"So they just left you? Alone with . . . those people?"

She sounded incensed, and of course she would be. Her father had been a similar sort, hadn't he?

"I survived."

"Yeah, but still. So what happened after you got that first job? What was it?"

Now she was interested. Christ, he shouldn't have said a bloody word. He loosened her lock of hair. "Question time is over, angel."

Her mouth firmed. "Why?"

"Because that's not what we're here for."

"But I want to know. I mean, you know everything about me, Zac. Every single fucking thing. Why can't I know a bit more about you?"

The hot wire feeling began to twist again, his anger running like a hot current beneath a cold sea. She didn't understand. He couldn't afford for her to get to know him. Already his obsession with her burned like a bonfire and he couldn't feed the flames by letting her in. Sharing confidences and secrets had never been what this night was supposed to be about anyway.

It was supposed to mean freedom for both of them. Freedom from the cage of her fear for her. Freedom from his obsession with her for him—at least, that's what he hoped.

"No," he said flatly. "Rest time is over."

Her chin had a mutinous cast to it. "I could say the word."

"You could. But then you wouldn't get what you wanted either. We'd both go away hungry."

"Assuming I'm actually hungry of course."

Fuck, enough of this. It was time to reeducate her about the rules.

He wrapped an arm tightly around her, trapping her arms at her sides. Then he pushed his free hand down between her thighs, his fingers sliding over the soft folds of her pussy. She jerked, gasping as he found her clit and began to rub his thumb around and around it, sliding two fingers deeply inside her. Tight. Hot. And yes, wet.

Eva groaned, arching back, trying to pull her arms away. But he only held her tighter, trapping her against his chest. Playing with her pussy until she began to pant, her skin becoming deeply flushed. Until she was slick beneath his fingers.

Zac bent his head. "So you're not hungry hmmm?" he breathed against her ear. "In that case, perhaps you'd better say the word now."

"Bastard." She gave a soft moan. "You complete prick."

"That's not the word, Eva." He slowed the movement of his fingers inside her.

She shuddered, her mouth open, her breathing harsh. " 'Void', Zac. Fucking 'void.' "

It would have always come down to this, when he thought about it afterwards. Eva King was the one person who wouldn't follow his orders and never had done so. She had a will of her own and it was, in many ways, just as strong as his.

Which was why he couldn't let her have this victory. She would push and push and push. Challenge him, goad him in the way she'd always done. But it was different now. He wasn't safe in the way he had been before, now that he knew what it was like to be inside her, to taste her. Hear the sound of her cries when she came.

He liked all those things far too much. Craved them like that drug that had destroyed his parents. She was the weak point in his control and he couldn't allow her any more power over him than she already had.

There had once been a woman who'd had that power. He would never give it willingly again.

Zac removed his hand from between her thighs and eased her out of his arms.

Perhaps she knew what she'd done. Perhaps she didn't. Perhaps she'd only come to understand later, in her bedroom, going over and over what they'd done together, her body aching for him.

Or maybe she wouldn't think about him at all. With Eva it was impossible to tell.

He *wanted* her to think about it though. Wanted her to burn for him, the way he'd burned for her. Wanted her to regret that she'd said it. Wanted her to wish she could turn back time so she could change it.

Because one thing was for certain: it could never happen again.

He rose to his feet. "I'll give you a quarter of an hour to get yourself together. Then I'll let Temple know you're ready to go home."

She sat there for a second, still panting. Then she jerked the blindfold up, squinting at the sudden influx of light. "What?"

"You said the safeword. It's over."

She was scowling now. "What do you mean 'over'? What's 'over'?"

"Tonight. You and I."

Shock crept over her face. "I didn't mean completely. For fuck's sake!"

"I told you I take that word seriously. That if you used it when you shouldn't, I'd walk away." He turned and began heading toward the door. "I'm a man of my word. You should know that by now."

"Is this one of those 'consequences' you mentioned then?"

He paused, turned back to her. "Of course it is. You do not fuck with me, Eva. I thought you'd have learned that lesson."

The shock had gone, anger twisting her features. She was naked and flushed, and he wanted more than anything to go back over there and teach her a lesson in another way. One that would leave them both sated, not famished.

"Are you scared?" she demanded. "Did I frighten you or something?"

She was trying to goad him again, little warrior that she was. But it was too late for that.

Fuck, he'd been a fool. Even one night was one night too many.

"Fifteen minutes, angel," he said.

Then he turned and walked out the door.

# CHAPTER THIRTEEN

Eva sat on one of the purple-velvet-covered sofas in the lounge of Alex's penthouse apartment and frowned at the photo album that lay on the coffee table in front of her.

"There," Alex said, pointing to one photo in particular. He was standing beside the coffee table, Honor at the opposite end. The album was their mother's, and Honor had bought it over for Alex to look at just in case the photos might reveal anything new about the Seven Devils.

Eva had woken up that morning to find a text from him asking her to come over and look too, since there would be more pictures of Fitzgerald. She didn't particularly want to see any more pictures of him but since concentrating on something else was preferable to thinking about Zac and what had gone down between them, she went.

The picture Alex had pointed to was a group shot of seven young men, sitting on or standing around a couch and laughing at the camera. They were all holding whisky tumblers and looked like they'd had more than one.

"That's him." Alex tapped the face of one of the men standing behind the couch. Tall and blond and handsome. The quintessential, clean-cut WASP college student. He had one hand on the shoulder of the young man sitting in the middle of the couch, whose blue eyes were discernible even in the horrible flash of the camera.

Fitzgerald. And Alex and Honor's father.

"There's Guy too," Honor added softly, nodding at one of the men sitting on the arm of the couch, another blandly handsome blond.

"And fucking Conrad." Alex sighed. "I can't believe we haven't gotten anything on any of these pricks." He turned and looked down at Eva. "You haven't had any visitations from our friendly neighborhood mercenary?"

"If you're meaning this Elijah guy then no. But then I've been covering my tracks online. It'll look like I've dropped all investigations into the Devils."

"What about Zac?"

A small jolt of electricity went through her. It had been two days since she'd left his house, going home by herself in her limo, her body aching with unfulfilled sexual hunger. She'd never thought it would actually physically hurt, but it did. It also left a strange hollowness in her chest and a furious kind of anger in her blood that she didn't understand.

All she'd wanted was to know him. Was that so fucking wrong? Yeah, she'd never asked him about himself, and that had been deliberate. Mainly because she didn't want to have to reciprocate.

*Selfish much?*

Well, yes, she was beginning to understand that. But there was also another reason.

If she didn't know his past, she wouldn't know him. He would remain an enigma, hardly even a person. And that made him safe. A wall to push against when she needed to push and to support her when she needed support.

He wasn't just a wall anymore though. And as she'd lain in his arms, drifting with the aftereffects of the orgasms he'd given her, his warmth and strength around her, she'd realized she didn't want him to remain an enigma any longer either.

She wanted to know him. What had made him who he was. What tragedies he'd experienced, because she'd sensed there had been some, perhaps many.

But she hadn't expected him to distance her so completely like that.

In retrospect, she should have predicted that when she'd said the safeword, he'd stop not only what he was doing, but everything else as well. Yet she hadn't.

The thought still made her angry.

"What about him?" she asked, staring at the picture of the young Fitzgerald.

"Well, has he found anything new?"

It was tempting to say she didn't have any fucking idea since Zac hadn't been in contact with her for two days, but that would prompt questions and she wasn't ready to answer those kinds of questions yet.

"I don't think so," she replied instead.

"That's a shame," Honor said. "Especially since Guy is still too sick to tell us anything."

"Fuck," Alex muttered.

Katya was sitting on the couch opposite Eva, quiet up until now. But at Alex's soft curse, she raised a hand toward him and he went over to her, taking her hand and threading his fingers through hers. A supportive, tender touch.

Eva couldn't stop looking at them. At their linked hands. At the look on Alex's face as he met Katya's green eyes. At the look on Katya's face as she stared at him in return.

It was like she'd learned a new language, a language she'd never even noticed before and was only now realizing how many people spoke it. Only now realizing that she was beginning to understand it. The wordless communication, the touches, the looks. All the emotional cues she'd been missing.

*A burst of salty flavor in her mouth. Then something*

*richer, creamier.* "*I appreciate good food when I have it. And so should you.*"

That night hadn't only been about fear and sex and confrontation. Zac had held her, fed her. Had he been trying to teach her more of that language? And had she not understood? What more could there have been if she hadn't said the safeword?

But there was no point thinking about that, was there? She *had* said it. And he'd thrown her out.

Eva tore her gaze away from Alex and Katya, staring at the photo instead. Staring but not seeing.

She'd only wanted to push him for more and she hadn't known how else to do it but goad him. It had been her modus operandi for seven years and it had worked very well . . . until now.

*If you want more, you'll need a new strategy.*

But did she want more?

*His mouth on her, his fingers touching her. Intense pleasure. Arms around her, so warm. Saltiness against her tongue. Then a rich, dark sweetness that somehow reminded her of his voice.* "*You could. But then you wouldn't get what you wanted. We'd both go away hungry . . .*"

He'd been right. She had gone away hungry. And she'd been hungry, been cold for too goddamn long.

She *did* want more.

"Eva?"

Her head jerked up.

Alex, Katya, and Honor were all staring at her.

She could feel her cheeks heating. How stupid. "Sorry. Thinking of some . . . other stuff."

"I just wanted to know whether you need any help with preparing for the party tomorrow night?" Honor asked.

Holy shit. It was tomorrow night, wasn't it? A reflexive fear slithered uncomfortably down her back, stealing her breath.

*No. He can't touch you, not anymore.*

Something inside her shifted, firmed. Lifting her chin, she met Honor's blue eyes. "What kind of help?"

"Well . . ." Honor gave a delicate pause. "You probably don't have anything suitable to wear, do you?"

Eva snorted. "Do I look like I own a fucking gown?"

"Admittedly not," the other woman allowed. "But it is black tie. Which means turning up in Docs and jeans isn't really the done thing."

"I don't need a dress," she said reflexively. "I can wear whatever the hell I want."

"Wearing a gown doesn't have to imply a weakness." Katya's lightly accented words were quiet but firm. She'd sat forward, her blonde braid falling over her shoulder, green eyes very direct. "It can be a show of strength."

Surprised, Eva stared at the other woman. Katya was a bodyguard who customarily wore black suits and shoulder holsters. What would she know about gowns? And what did putting on a dress have to do with strength?

But it was Alex who answered, that terrible understanding in his eyes. Like he knew. "Show him you're not afraid," he said. "That he didn't take everything from you. That you're stronger than he is."

Katya and Honor remained quiet, but Eva was sure they got the subtext. Neither woman was stupid.

*Silver lace on her skin. The look in Zac's eyes as he'd stood in front of her, gazing at her . . . "Beautiful. You're beautiful, angel."*

There had been no denying that look. And now that she thought about it, she'd felt a kind of power in it too.

*Do you really want to show Fitzgerald that you're a girl to be used and discarded? That he broke you?*

Slowly, she sat back on the couch. Yet it wasn't Alex she stared at, but Katya. "What kind of strength are you talking about?"

"Being a woman is a powerful thing," the bodyguard said.

"And a woman wearing the right dress is even more powerful," Honor added. "I can help you choose something if you like."

"Oh, Christ," Alex muttered. "Shopping? Now?"

"I thought you liked shopping." Katya looked up at him slyly. "Or at least, I seem to recall one occasion that you enjoyed in particular."

He smiled at her, a very private kind of smile. Another communication in that new language. One that made her chest go tight for some reason.

She looked away from them, meeting Honor's gaze instead. "I'm not being dragged down Fifth Avenue if that's what you're thinking." At least, not without Zac at her side. Even the thought of being outside among all those crowds made her palms sweaty.

Honor tapped her chin with a meditative finger. "We don't have to go anywhere. I know a couple of people who can bring things to us." She gave Eva a smile that Eva didn't trust one inch. "Give me five minutes."

An hour or so later, Alex having left on some errand or other, or maybe just to get away from all the girly stuff that was happening, Eva was staring dubiously at the rail containing different gowns that had been couriered over and was now standing in the middle of Alex's lounge.

Honor was sorting briskly through them, shoving some down one end of the rail, the rest at the other. She'd taken charge of the whole process instantly, calling up a personal shopper she'd been using since Gabriel hadn't wanted her going out often while this stuff with the Seven Devils was still up in the air. Honor had given the woman Eva's measurements plus a description and a "money no object" brief, and sure enough, an hour or so later, the rail of dresses had turned up.

Honor pulled a floor-length strapless number from the rail. "This one." She held it up for Eva to look at. "It's simple, edgy, and yet it's feminine too. What do you think?"

It was silver, the material glittering in the light, reminding her of the lacy lingerie Zac had bought her.

Eva eyed it, an unsettled feeling sitting in her gut. Clothes had never been what she was particularly interested in. When she'd been little, her parents had been unable to afford them anyway, and once she'd escaped to the streets, the most important thing about clothes was whether they kept her warm or not.

After she'd escaped the House, she hadn't wanted to wear anything overtly feminine, and jeans and Docs projected a certain tough, fuck-off exterior that was useful. It kept people at a distance, especially men. There was also the added bonus of helping her blend into the background.

But this gown, with its glittery fabric and lack of straps, wasn't tough. Nor was it a gown that encouraged blending. It seemed to be designed for attention, for standing out in.

Gritting her teeth, Eva made herself walk over to Honor to examine the dress. "It's very nice," she said, which was the best she could come up with.

Honor held it out. "Go try it on."

"Use the bathroom down the hall." Katya, still sitting on the couch, waved in the direction of the hallway. "And if you need help with the zipper, let me know."

Eva didn't want to try it on. She didn't want to wear it at all.

And yet . . .

What would Zac think of her in the gown? He'd liked the lingerie. Would he like this?

God, she must be crazy, thinking of Zac when it was Fitzgerald she should be worrying about. A gown like this was going to draw attention and if he was indeed The

Man, then it would surely draw his attention. And he'd know exactly who she was.

Not that wearing jeans and Docs was going to hide that anyway.

She took the gown out of Honor's hand. "Fine. I'll try it."

Stalking down the hallway, she went into the bathroom and shut the door firmly. It was a surprisingly understated room, given Alex's taste. Lots of white tiles and stainless steel. A glass-walled walk-in shower stood in one corner opposite a giant floor-to-ceiling wall mirror.

Eva undressed down to her underwear, draping her clothes over the vanity. Then she took the gown off the hanger and wiggled into it.

The fabric was surprisingly heavy as she pulled it on, glittering silver sequins catching the light. It was very fitting around her breasts, hips, and thighs, a split up the side of it allowing her to walk.

She very purposefully didn't look at the mirror as she struggled with the zipper, nor did she bother with asking for Honor's and Katya's help. She wanted to first see it on herself in private.

As she managed to get the zipper up the last little bit, the fabric closing snugly around her, she took a short, hard breath. When was the last time she'd even worn a dress? She couldn't remember. Had she *ever* worn one?

Her heart was racing for some reason and she felt weird about looking at her reflection. As if it wasn't her she was going to see but someone else. A person she wasn't.

Setting her jaw, she moved slowly in front of the mirror.

A pale-looking woman in a sparkly dress looked back at her. Okay, so she looked ridiculous with the beanie still on. Pulling the black woolen hat off, Eva shook her hair out.

Better. But still . . .

She frowned in the mirror.

The silver fabric glittered, enhancing the white skin of her shoulders and arms. Drawing attention to the black strap of the bra she'd left on. Shit.

A couple more moments of struggling and Eva got her bra off, tugging the dress back up again.

This time when she looked, a fragile, ethereal creature stared back and she felt an odd sense of dislocation. As if she were truly looking at someone else, not herself.

*Zac would like the dress.*

She found herself staring, following down the shape of her figure, the swell of her small breasts, the curve of her hips, the slight roundness of her thighs. Imagining seeing herself through his eyes, and she didn't know quite how she knew, but she understood that yes, he would like the dress.

There came a tentative knock on the door.

Eva swallowed. She wasn't sure she wanted anyone seeing her like this. It made her feel exposed in the same way that the lingerie had made her feel exposed. Then again, it was only Honor and Katya.

"Come in," she said a little hoarsely.

Honor poked her head around the door, gave her a quick look, then pushed the door open more fully and stepped into the bathroom. "Good God, woman," she said, staring. "You look amazing."

Eva didn't quite know how to feel about that. Did she want to look amazing? Did she care?

Katya had followed Honor and now moved past her, blonde brows pulled together as she stalked in a circle around Eva. "You do look very good in that dress," she said slowly. "There's a split too, which will mean you can move around easily if you need to." Then the Russian woman looked up and met Eva's gaze unexpectedly. "The jeans and boots make you look tough. But the dress makes you look proud."

It was a strange thing to say, and yet something shifted in Eva's gut. "What do you mean, proud?"

Katya came to a halt. "You are afraid of being seen as a woman, I think. And I say this as a woman who was afraid of that too," she added before Eva could protest. "I don't know how or why you're linked to Fitzgerald, but I do know that if you turn up at that party in what you normally wear, it won't look like you don't care, it'll look like you're defeated. You want strength, you want pride. And you can't find that in denial, Eva. Believe me, I know."

For a second Eva stared at her, taken aback by her honesty, not to mention her perceptiveness.

*She's right. You are afraid of being seen as a woman. Because of Him. And if you go to that party wearing jeans and Docs, it means He still has a hold over you.*

Christ, was that true?

She didn't speak, looking away from Katya to the mirror again. To the woman reflected in it. Silver hair and silver sequins, slight curves . . . *Beautiful, angel . . .*

Wasn't that why she'd chosen her handle Void Angel all those years ago? Because angels could be strong. Because they could fly. Because they carried swords.

Zac had never stopped calling her angel even though after escaping the house, she hadn't wanted him to.

*Because that's how he sees you.*

An electric shock of realization shot straight through her, pinning her to the spot.

He'd always seen her as strong, had never stopped telling her. And two days ago, he'd shown her own strength to her. With a blindfold and ropes, and the heat of his body. Treating her as a woman, not the cold, sexless being she'd been trying to hide behind.

The doll The Man—no, *Fitzgerald*—had turned her into.

Fuck. That.

Eva put her shoulders back, lifted her chin. Stared into the silver eyes of the woman in the mirror, glittering as bright as the sequins on her gown. "I think I need a second opinion," she said thoughtfully. "I think Zac needs to see this."

The elevator came to a stop with a jerk, the doors opening. Zac stepped out into the cavernous floor of a half-built office building, one of a handful Woolf Construction was currently in the process of working on in Lower Manhattan.

Gabriel was standing in the middle of the massive concrete space along with a cluster of men in hardhats, all of them peering down at a set of building plans unrolled on a makeshift table—a large piece of wood sitting on a couple of trestles.

Zac's boots crunched as he approached them, the dusty floor littered with wood offcuts and pieces of metal, pipes and rolled up coils of wire. There were no walls yet, the wind blowing coldly through the space, bringing with it a few flakes of late winter snow.

Gabriel looked up from his plans all of a sudden and met Zac's gaze.

"Everyone out," he ordered, cutting off one man who'd started to speak. "We'll continue this tomorrow."

The gathered men, obviously used to their boss's authoritative ways, didn't protest, starting to make their way to the elevator, talking among themselves.

Zac waited until the elevator doors had closed on the last of them, then walked slowly over to where Gabriel stood. The other man watched him, dark eyes opaque.

"You've found something," Gabriel said flatly.

"Yes. It's not much but it's more than we had initially." Zac came to a halt on the opposite side of the table. "I've called Alex in. He'll need to hear this too."

A flash of irritation crossed Gabriel's face. "You couldn't have waited to organize a Circles meeting tonight? That meeting was fucking important."

"No," Zac said, not bothering to elaborate. Calling a Circles meeting would have involved Eva and he didn't want to be near her right now. Even after two days he could still feel the heat in his veins whenever he thought of her. The heat of anger and desire and need and hunger and all the other primitive, driving emotions he couldn't allow himself to feel.

That was the thing about an addiction. You had to starve it in order to kick it. And he hadn't starved his enough.

*At all.*

Unfortunately that was true. He'd hoped one night would end it for good, purge her completely from his system. He never thought he'd end up more addicted than ever.

Gabriel stared at him. "What about Eva?"

"Eva has other things to worry about," he said shortly.

"Yeah, she does." The doors of the elevator had opened, Alex now crossing the empty space toward the table where the other two stood. "Some kind of shopping thing with Katya and Honor. I thought discretion was the better part of valor and fucked off as soon as I could." He came to a stop at the table, looking around with some distaste. "Jesus Christ, could we not have had this in the Second Circle? It's fucking cold up here."

"I realize that," Zac answered, turning to face him. "But at least there's no chance of anyone overhearing."

Alex raised a brow. "Are you questioning the security of the Second Circle? I hope to God not."

"There were bugs in South's casino, correct? I seem to recall that mercenary you met doing a sweep for them."

Alex frowned. "Didn't you do a similar sweep of the Circle's room a week ago?"

"We're really going to have an argument about this now, Alex?" Zac had done the sweep and had found nothing. But he wasn't going to justify why he'd chosen to avoid their usual rooms, especially when that reason was Eva.

The other man rolled his eyes, sticking his hands into the pockets of his suit trousers. "Okay, okay. So tell us what news you've got that requires all this secrecy."

"I've been investigating the other players in that game of yours, as you know. And haven't found anything substantial on any of them, at least nothing that would be of interest to us." He paused. "At least until this morning. I got an email from a contact of mine who has some information about the sheikh who played."

Alex moved closer to the table. "What information? I have to say, the guy wasn't into the game at all. Now that I remember, he was *very* uncomfortable with aspects of it even."

"Unsurprising," Zac said. "His father, the previous sheikh, died three months ago so he's new to the throne. New to his father's dodgy business practices too. My contact has been in touch with someone inside the palace and apparently the previous sheikh had . . . unorthodox tastes shall we say."

Gabriel put his hands down on the table, bracing himself against the edge. "How unorthodox? Are we talking human trafficking? A similar setup to what was going down at South's?"

"Seems to be the case." At least that was what the email Zac had gotten had indicated. The contact had mentioned that there wasn't much in the way of evidence, but it was better than nothing. Or at least it was more than they'd had.

"I got the impression the guy didn't want to be there,"

Alex said. "And he left pretty abruptly during the strip-poker part of the game."

"So why was he there in the first place?" Gabriel's dark gaze flicked to Zac. "And where did he get the invite from?"

"The contact didn't say," Zac answered. "Presumably from one of the Devils. They were probably hoping to initiate the new sheikh into his father's business practices."

Alex made a disgusted sound. "Yeah, well, that sounds familiar. Poor bastard. No wonder he didn't want to be there."

"So we have some concrete evidence?" Gabriel's gaze didn't shift from Zac.

"No," Zac said flatly. "My contact said he would try to find some, but it was risky. The new sheikh is under fire from various political groups within the kingdom—possibly ones who backed his father—so the situation is fairly volatile. Information won't be easy to come by, but I've told him to give it a try."

Gabriel cursed and pushed himself away from the table. "What about that mercenary? Elijah? Did you ever find anything on him?"

"No. Nothing at all." And he'd looked. Hard. "He's a man who doesn't want to be found."

"Fuck. So what? That's it?"

Zac gave him a dispassionate glance. He knew the other man didn't do waiting well, especially when there was still that possible threat to Honor to worry about, but there really wasn't any other option. "That *is* it. We can't make a move until Eva confirms Fitzgerald is the key."

"And she's going to do that, is she?" Gabriel was scowling. "She wasn't too happy about it from what I saw."

Zac folded his arms. "I'll be with her. She knows how important this is."

"So . . . just out of interest," Alex murmured, "why did she slap your face?"

There was a tense silence, both men giving Zac assessing, not exactly friendly, looks.

"That's none of your business," Zac told them coldly.

"It's our fucking business if it's affecting this investigation," Gabriel growled. "What have you done to her, Zac?"

Anger like a bubble of magma burst in his veins. It was all he could do not to punch the other man in the face. "If you have an accusation, Gabe, at least have the decency to be up front about it."

"It's not an accusation. It's a threat. If this weird shit you and Eva have got going on is affecting our success with the Seven Devils, then it's got to fucking stop." An answering anger glittered in the other man's eyes. "Honor's at risk and I will do anything—*anything*—to keep her safe. Understand?"

Zac's jaw felt tight, tension crawling along the back of his neck and shoulders. "You think I wouldn't do the same for Eva? You think I haven't being doing exactly that for seven fucking years?"

Another tense silence fell.

Curiously, this time it was Alex who spoke. "Okay, everyone calm the hell down. No one's accusing you of anything, Zac. But Gabe's right. Eva's fragile, and if she can't handle—"

"Eve can handle anything," Zac interrupted, fixing Alex with a cold stare. "You underestimate her."

He didn't want anyone questioning her, especially those who had no idea what she'd gone through. No idea of the strength she possessed. She could handle anything. She'd handled him. Tied to a chair with a blindfold on as he'd made her revisit her deepest fears. As he'd put his mouth to her skin, tasted her, made her scream . . .

Alex gave him an impenetrable look. "You're not your usual impassive self, Zac. Anything up?"

The observation shocked him. He wasn't used to being read so easily. Repressing the anger creeping through his veins, he returned Alex's stare with one of his own. The one he used to control a wayward sub. "What makes you say that?"

Alex was unmoved by the stare. "You seem pissed about something. It's not like you."

His friend was right. He *was* pissed about something. His feelings for one small, fragile-looking white-haired woman to be exact. The way he couldn't get the taste of her, the feel of her body hot and tight around him, the sound of her cries, out of his head. Another symptom of his addiction. A siren song calling him to give in, to go back to her and take what he wanted.

He could resist that. His whole life had been about control over his physical hungers after all. No, what he struggled with was the need beneath that. The one that went deeper than physical desire, that craved something more. A more intense connection.

*That's* what he had to resist. Because a connection like that demanded a power exchange his whole soul rebelled against. He'd been there once before, and never again.

"I'm annoyed you two are looking at me like I've hurt Eva in some way," he said flatly, all either of them would get in the way of truth. "Which given the fact that I've been the one protecting her all these years, is a little difficult to swallow."

Alex lifted a shoulder, unperturbed. "Sure. But she's our friend too, man. We just want to make sure she's okay."

He shouldn't be so touchy. It only gave away more than he was willing to reveal. "She's fine."

"And that slap she gave you?" This time, it was Gabriel who asked.

He supposed he couldn't blame either man for asking the question. He'd have done the same thing in their place. Keeping his anger rigidly under control, he said, "I know what happened to her. She didn't like me referring to it in front of everyone."

Something flickered through Alex's gaze. "Fair enough."

Gabriel said nothing, just kept his flat dark eyes on Zac.

"She and I have dealt with the issue," Zac went on, making sure both men knew the subject was now closed. "It won't affect her attending Fitzgerald's party tomorrow night and it doesn't concern anyone else. Is that clear?"

Gabriel looked at Zac a moment longer, then he shot a glance at Alex, a silent kind of communication that Zac didn't much like the look of.

His phone chimed suddenly in his pocket and he pulled it out, ignoring the other two men.

There was a photo on the screen. A woman in an incredible silver dress. It seemed to be glittering in the light, the shimmer of it outlining slender curves and highlighting the pale skin of her shoulders and neck. White blonde hair fell past those alabaster shoulders, and the determined point of her chin was familiar. Her eyes . . .

Fuck. It was Eva.

He felt like he'd been punched in the face.

"Zac?" Alex, his voice sounding puzzled. "Everything okay?"

But Zac was already turning, walking away from the table and across the dusty, rubbish-strewn concrete floor, over to the edge of the building where there was no wall, nothing but air and all of Lower Manhattan spread out beneath him.

He couldn't stop looking at the photo of Eva on his screen.

All the breath had gone out of him, something burning in his blood that wasn't wholly anger or even completely desire, but something he didn't recognize. Something that he didn't want yet was there all the same.

Holy God, but she was beautiful. His angel in truth.

She was giving the camera her usual "fuck you" look, but this time there was a boldness to it that hadn't been there before. That was somehow stronger and more compelling than it had been in her usual uniform of T-shirt and jeans and boots.

A beautiful woman in a killer dress, with her chin up and her eyes challenging the camera head-on . . .

Confronting. Strong. Captivating.

The feeling inside him twisted hard, intense hunger now, making him dry-mouthed, his heart beating in his head like Big Ben thousands of miles across the Atlantic.

Why the fuck was she sending him a picture like this? What the hell did she want?

His phone chimed again, a follow-up text. *I assume I'll see you tomorrow night?*

A fair enough question when he hadn't been in contact with her since the night he'd told her to leave, and yes that had been deliberate. An asshole move considering a day hadn't gone by when he *hadn't* at least talked to her on the phone or texted her.

He'd had to do something though. Start kicking the Eva King habit somehow.

He stared at the photo on his screen, trying to crush the rough surge of emotion inside him, all of it twisted and raw and just fucking *not* what he wanted.

Jesus but he didn't want to have to be near her again, especially if she was going to look like that, yet he'd promised her. He'd accompany her tomorrow night, but that was it. After that he'd leave her alone for good.

Zac texted a curt *yes* then put his phone back in his pocket. He glanced back at the table where Alex and

Gabriel stood. They were in conversation, rather ostentatiously not looking in his direction.

A strange dislocation hit him all of a sudden. As if he were standing on the outside of the building looking in. Like he had done sometimes back in his childhood, walking from the cinema, past the lovely old homes with windows that faced the street. Where he'd been able to see the lives of people with families playing out. Families who sat around watching TV together or talking or eating.

Happy families. Normal lives.

Things he didn't have and never would.

He used to watch them. Used to want what they had. Used to imagine it was him sitting on the couch or watching that TV or eating that meal. Him receiving the hug and the kiss on the top of his head.

He'd thought perhaps he'd found something a bit like that with the Nine Circles. A sense of belonging. A kind of family. But this . . . need for Eva had ruined it.

Something in the area of his chest tightened painfully.

It never would be him.

He would always be on the outside looking in.

# CHAPTER FOURTEEN

Eva held the stupid, useless little evening purse in her lap and tried to stop herself from pulling nervously at the silver beads on it as the limo pulled up to the curb outside Zac's house.

A tall, dark figure stood there, waiting.

She let out a breath, made her fingers relax on the purse.

There was no reason to be nervous. It was only Zac. Zac, who'd been ignoring her for two days straight, apart from that short, sharp "yes" he'd texted her with the day before.

It hadn't been the response she'd been hoping for when she'd sent him the pic of her in the dress, and she was pissed about it, no point in denying that.

Pissed and nervous. It was ridiculous.

She wished suddenly that she had on her jeans and her Docs, a bit of familiarity to hold onto, because there was nothing familiar about the silver dress she wore or the little silver slippers on her feet or the feel of her hair in a straight white fall down her back or the stickiness of lipstick on her mouth.

Normally Zac would have been her piece of familiarity, her anchor point, but he wasn't now. He'd become the thing she was nervous of.

How weird to be more afraid of seeing him than of

going to the upcoming party and being face-to-face with Fitzgerald.

The car door opened and Zac got in, and all at once Eva found it difficult to breathe.

He was in an impeccably tailored tux, the austere simplicity of the snowy white shirt and deep black of the jacket only serving to enhance the rough, raw power and charisma of the man who wore it. He was dangerous and it showed.

He was also beautiful. He made her heart catch inside her chest.

As he sat down opposite her, she had the weirdest urge to run her fingers along the hard, strong line of his jaw. Or maybe trace the full curve of his lower lip, the only soft thing in his face apart from his thick, inky lashes.

She'd never wanted to spontaneously touch anyone before and she had to curl her fingers hard around her purse in order to stop herself from doing so now.

Temple shut the door behind him and there was a moment of taut silence as Eva forced herself to meet his gaze.

The gold of his eyes burned like a flame in the heart of a bonfire, and she felt a rush of answering heat. She could smell him too, the spicy, warm scent of cedar that made her want to bury her face in his neck and inhale.

God, she'd never felt such things before. Never knew it was possible to feel them and especially not about him. Nervous and hungry and aching. Afraid and desperate and wanting.

"You never told me what you thought about the dress," she said into the dense silence.

Zac had folded his hands casually in his lap. He didn't have his gloves on tonight, the black ink of the tattoos on the backs of his fingers standing out on his bronze skin. "You look beautiful," he said without inflection.

Disappointment gathered in the pit of her stomach. She

wanted more from him than that, she realized. Some kind of reaction that wasn't so . . . blank. "Not exactly what a girl wants to hear when she puts on a dress for the first time."

"I said you look beautiful. What more do you want?"

"You could look at me for a start."

"I am looking at you."

He was, that was true. But not the way he'd looked at her before she'd stepped over the threshold into his study days ago. With such focused intensity. As if she were the only thing worth looking at in the entire universe.

Now though, there was no discernible emotion behind his flat amber gaze. She could have been anyone. Just a pretty woman in a pretty dress. No one special.

It was like a door shutting firmly in her face. A door she hadn't known she'd wanted to look behind. Except she did now. She wanted to smash the lock and bust it wide open.

Eva shifted subtly in her seat, letting the split up the side of her gown ease open. It felt odd to reveal herself physically, and not entirely comfortable since the split went up to mid-thigh. But she wanted more of a reaction than the one he was giving her, and this might do the trick.

Sure enough, his eyes flickered down to where the white skin of her leg was revealed.

It was only a second, but she saw a spark of brilliant gold flare in his gaze.

Satisfaction curled like heated smoke through her, along with a strange relief.

So he did still want her. She hadn't realized how important that had been to her until now. Well, that was good. It meant she had power here, and if he thought she didn't know how to use it, he was fucking wrong. She could learn, she was quick like that.

"So," she said conversationally, leaving the split in her

dress open. "What's the deal with ignoring me for the past two days?"

He wasn't looking down now but there was a certain tension both to his jaw and to the ostensibly relaxed fingers folded in his lap. "I thought you might want distance." His voice held its usual reasonable, smooth tone. "Especially considering what happened between us."

" 'What happened between us,' " she echoed, sounding out the words. "That's very coy of you. I think you meant 'you throwing me out after tying me up and fucking me senseless.' "

The subtle tension in his jaw tightened further. "I didn't throw you out, Eva. You pushed the line and I gave you the consequences. It's not my problem if you didn't like it."

"Oh, I understand that. I just didn't know the consequences would include two days of you ignoring me completely." She eyed him, gauging his reaction. "Do you sulk like this with all your submissives or is it just me?"

A flare of warning in his eyes. She was pushing the line and she knew it. "You're not one of my submissives, Eva."

"So just tell me then."

Zac's expression hardened into granite. "I'm not explaining myself to you." The edge of authority in his voice was a hard slap.

She shivered, unable to help herself, anger and arousal arrowing straight through her. Strange to realize now how much she liked challenging him, pushing him. He'd told her that before, that she did it because he was both safe and dangerous at the same time, and she knew the truth of it now. Perhaps subconsciously she always had.

He stared at her cold and hard, every part of him locked away.

And, shit, she didn't want that. She wanted his heat, his intensity. The man who'd knelt before her and consumed her, not this perfect English gentleman with his forbidding manner and stiff upper lip.

"Don't pull the Dom shit on me here," she said flatly. "Do I look like I'm tied up in your chair waiting for a flogging?"

Another flicker of brightness in his gaze, faint but there. Like an ember fanned by a breath.

Then it died.

Zac refolded his hands in his lap. "I know you're nervous about tonight, angel, but taking it out on me won't help."

Oh crap. He would have to bring that up. And she'd been doing so well not thinking about it.

The heat in her veins began to ice over, the silver beads on her purse digging in to her fingers.

*No, idiot. He's distracting you.*

Yeah. So he was. Which meant she was getting to him.

"How is asking you a perfectly reasonable question 'taking it out on you'?" she asked.

His eyes glinted. "I gave you a perfectly reasonable answer. There's no need to push me."

Of course he'd know what she was trying to do. He wasn't stupid. Unfortunately.

"Sure, a perfectly reasonable answer that happens to be a fucking lie."

He tilted his head. "Because I don't want to be questioned as to my motives, it means I'm lying? Let me ask you this then. Have I ever lied to you, Eva? Even once?"

Bastard. She had no answer to that because he was right, he'd never lied to her. Yet . . . he hadn't liked her questioning him, that was obvious. Admittedly he'd never liked that, but she was sure this time there was more to it than merely 'I was giving you space.'

He'd never ignored her before.

*You've never slept together before either. Perhaps this*

*is what he always does. Perhaps you really* are *just another of his subs.*

She swallowed, her chest going tight and sore. She'd never felt possessive over anyone before but she felt a wave of it now. At the thought of him with other women, him treating her as if she was just another of the subs he picked up wherever it was he picked subs up from.

She didn't fully understand why but she didn't want to be that to him. Their friendship might have been strange and twisted, but it had been friendship nevertheless, and now that seemed to be under threat by the night they'd shared. A night that he'd initiated.

Wasn't she more important to him than that? Or was it a case of now he'd gotten what he wanted, she didn't matter? He'd been quite prepared to leave her completely if she hadn't given what he'd wanted after all.

*I'm a mercenary, Eva. Everything has a price.*

And now she'd paid it, she was expendable?

Zac was watching her, the look on his face impenetrable. Waiting for her answer presumably. The one she didn't have.

"No," she said softly. "You've never lied before. Which makes it strange that you're lying to me now."

An expression crossed his face then, one she couldn't read, the burning ember in his eyes flaring into life, into heat. She didn't look away.

Maybe hours later, maybe minutes, she became aware that the car had stopped. That there were was a crowd outside and media pushing and shoving, all vying for a good shot of the line of beautifully dressed people going up the stairs of the Met.

They'd arrived.

Zac broke her gaze, turning to glance outside. "So the plan for tonight will be you getting close to Fitzgerald," he said as if the tension inside the car didn't exist. "Meet him face-to-face. If there's nothing immediately recognizable about him, we draw him off somewhere private." Zac paused, still studying the crowd outside. "And then I will ask him a few questions of my own."

There was no doubt as to what this meant.

Foreboding deepened inside her, along with fear. A fear that wasn't about her for once, but was wholly centered on him. On the things he'd done in his past. The damage it had done to his soul. Because he was damaged, there was no doubt about that. And whatever happened with Fitzgerald would only damage him further.

*You don't want that to happen.*

Eva made herself look at him, at the strong, aristocratic lines of his face. He was so hard, like he was carved from the side of a mountain. Like he could withstand anything, even the power of nuclear blast.

But what if his strength was a façade like hers had been? What if inside he was fragile too, like she was?

Did he have anyone to hold him the way he'd held her?

*Of course he doesn't. For the last seven years he's had no one but you.*

It hit her suddenly, in a blaze of terrible insight, what a lonely, arid existence that must have been for him. Tied to a woman who didn't want anyone to touch her. A woman he'd wanted to touch.

There was a thick feeling in her throat, emotion choking her.

"Promise me something, Zac," she said abruptly.

He turned, giving her a quick, sharp look. "Promise you what?"

"That you won't do anything without coming to me first."

He didn't answer. Because he knew what she meant, oh yes, he knew.

"I want your word." She put all the conviction she had

into her voice, her meager authority. "Or I don't even get out of this car."

His expression became even harder than it already was. "If you're trying to protect me, angel, you've got the wrong man."

"Your word, Zac."

A long moment passed and she thought that he might not give it to her, in which case she'd no idea what to do. Because this was the only thing she could think of. The only way she could show him that he wasn't alone.

Then he said shortly, "You have my word."

"Say it."

His tone was utterly blank. "I'll come to you before I do anything."

It wasn't much, but it was something.

"In that case," she said quietly. "Let's go."

Temple had gotten out of the car and had come around to the door. She pulled it open, and the outside noise flooded in. Shouts and cries and the echoes of music, the sound of car engines and horns, sirens, and the grind of buses and trucks. A wall of sound that rushed in like a wave, and she had to take a deep, sharp breath to stop it from drowning her.

Zac got out then turned back, holding out his hand to her.

This was it. Showtime.

Eva took his hand, felt his fingers close around hers. Warm, strong, protective. So familiar.

*Loved.*

She blinked, allowing herself to be drawn out of the car and into the glare of the assembled media.

*Loved.*

The thought echoed through her. Love. What did that even mean? Love had been absent from her life almost completely. Maybe her mother had once loved her, but that was only a maybe since the woman had left her when Eva was eight. Her father definitely not. He wouldn't have kept spending money on meth if he'd loved her. Money they'd needed for food. And certainly no one had come after her when she'd disappeared to the streets. No one had reported her as missing. No one had cared she was gone.

What the hell did she even know of love? So why did she keep thinking of the word when she thought of Zac? Maybe it wasn't love. Maybe it was just a twisted kind of Stockholm Syndrome, the way she'd felt about The Man—*Fitzgerald*—toward the end.

*He didn't love you. He wanted to get rid of you.*

That was true and yet toward the end, she'd felt . . . cared for at least. In that she'd been given food to eat and a place to sleep. Clothes to wear and books to read. That was a kind of love, wasn't it?

Flashes went off. Someone screamed "Miss King! This way!"

Zac's hand firmed on hers, tucking it into the crook of his elbow the way he had when he'd taken her to the museum the first time around. She couldn't take her eyes off him, and since that was easier than focusing on the screams of the crowds and the dizzying open space above her head, she stayed staring at him.

The light threw the powerful bone structure of his face into stark relief. The slight crook in his nose where it looked like it had been broken once. High cheekbones that gave him a predatory, hawkish look. A beautifully carved mouth, sensual and warm, hungry and demanding. Then there was that tall, massively built frame. So much contained strength and leashed violence. Yet he moved with such athletic grace, as fully in command of his body as he was of everything else.

She remembered that feel of him close to her, burning like a furnace. Him inside her.

"Miss King! Over here! Can you give me a smile!"

"Tell us what's special about tonight, Miss King!"

She'd never gotten to see him because of that blindfold. Never gotten to touch him because he hadn't let her. She'd never thought she'd want to.

But there were a lot of things she'd never thought she'd do that she was doing now, so what was one more?

She didn't look around as they moved toward the stairs. Kept her attention on Zac.

He didn't look at her, his gaze firmly ahead, but that was fine. That allowed her to drink him in and not have to be aware of the crowds, of the media jockeying for position for a shot of the reclusive Void Angel CEO.

She felt calm. The fear was there, but it wasn't paralyzing. Not if she kept focused on Zac. Her hand on his arm, on the feel of his body close to hers.

Inside the building, they joined a queue where invitations were being vetted and guest lists checked. She'd gotten one of her Void Angel staff to make sure she was on the list and that Zac's name wasn't given, that he was only listed as 'partner.' He always did like to maintain a low profile.

The man checking the lists gave them a smile and waved them through into the party proper, the huge gallery where the Egyptian Temple she'd visited a few days ago stood.

It had been transformed into a major party area, with magnificent colored lighting, tables and chairs clustered into groups everywhere, and a bar at one end. Up on the dais where the Temple itself was—up-lights casting the pillars of the ancient monument into stark relief—a string quartet played.

The whole area itself was packed with the upper echelons of New York's high society, mostly old-money families with connections to America's biggest corporations and financial institutions, as well as Capitol Hill itself. In amongst all of those were a few movie stars and New York personalities, probably invited for a bit of local color.

Eva found it overwhelming.

She clutched on tight to Zac's arm, her heartbeat accelerating, doing her best to act calm and together when all she felt like doing was running and hiding like a cornered animal.

He seemed to be aware of it, drawing her to a quieter spot up one end of the room behind a huge potted palm where they could get a good view of the gallery without being seen themselves.

He didn't ask her whether she was okay or not, which she was grateful for. "Can you see Fitzgerald anywhere?"

The task focused her, and she scanned the glittering crowd, trying to get a handle on the stupid fear that kept closing its fingers around her throat. "No," she muttered. "I don't see him . . . Wait. Down there, near the bar. Is that him?"

The crowd moved and surged, waitstaff circulating like a school of black fish in a glittering sea. Through the heaving mass of people, a tall, broadly built man could be seen surrounded by a crowd of important-looking business types. Fair hair, bland, handsome features creased in a smile.

She recognized him from the pictures on the net she'd poured over. Evelyn Fitzgerald.

"Yes," Zac answered slowly. "That's him."

As they watched, a man moved out of the crowd and approached Fitzgerald. A flunky of some type, Eva guessed. The flunky spoke to Fitzgerald for a couple of minutes then disappeared back into the crowd again.

Fitzgerald's head turned.

And Eva's heart climbed into her throat as he looked in her direction.

She was too far away to make out his features distinctly and surely that meant he couldn't see her either. Nevertheless, she felt his attention like a spear pinning her to the spot.

It lasted only a moment before he turned away to talk to someone else.

Warmth at her elbow, a firm pressure on her arm. The scent of home around her. "Looks like someone told him you're here," Zac said softly in her ear. "I wonder if he wanted to be kept informed of your arrival?"

"H-He might." Goddamn that stupid stutter. "It doesn't mean he recognizes me. I've never actually attended any functions before, so that could be reason enough for someone to tell him I'm here."

"Or because he knows who you are anyway."

"That's true." She took a deep, slow breath. "Shall I go introduce myself, or shall I wait to see if he comes to me?"

"Let's take it to him." Zac answered without hesitation. "No point dragging this out any longer than it needs to."

His arm slid around her waist, his hand sitting on her hip, the warmth of his body up against hers. Letting her know he was there.

She wasn't used to leaning against people for support, but now she let herself, just for a moment. Absorbing his heat and his sheer physical strength. Taking a little bit of it for herself.

Then she said, "Come on, then. I'm ready."

They moved into the crowds and even with Zac standing beside her, Eva found it almost too much. There were more people here than when she and Zac had come a few days ago and it was much noisier. Everyone was packed tighter, laughing and talking loudly above the civilized sound of the music.

It was like moving through a field of tall, exotic flowers

planted too close together and looming over her. Suffocating her.

The crowd swirled. Someone brushed against her and she felt the fear turn over in her gut, mindless and blind.

God, she didn't want to hold onto Zac like a drowning woman clutching a life preserver. She wanted to be strong, to lift her chin and be able to walk through all these people without fear. Confront Fitzgerald while standing tall and proud.

But she knew if she let go of Zac's arm, she'd freeze. Or throw up. Or humiliate herself in some other way.

This was not how she wanted it to go.

"Miss King?" A man appeared suddenly out of the crowd, standing in front of them. He was smiling. "Mr. Fitzgerald would like to have a word with you in private if you're willing. He's very honored to have you join us this evening."

A word in private?

She felt Zac tense beside her, but she didn't look at him. She knew he'd think it was a bad idea. Then again, she had to meet Fitzgerald sometime and perhaps this presented her with the opportunity they'd been looking for.

"Of course," she said before she could change her mind. "I'd be happy to."

The man's smile widened. He looked at Zac and then back at Eva. "If you'd like to follow me." He turned and began to make his way through the partying crowds, heading for the gallery exit.

"I know," she muttered as she and Zac began to follow. "It's not a good idea. But then we'll have him in private and that could be useful."

"True," Zac began, and then stopped abruptly as a young woman reeled back from the little group she was talking to and just about collapsed on top of him.

Eva heard him curse and let go of her, catching the falling woman in his arms before she could hit the floor. Instantly he was surrounded by her friends, all of them talking and exclaiming.

"Miss King."

Eva, her heart thudding with foreboding, turned around.

The man she'd been following, Fitzgerald's flunkey, was at her elbow, still smiling. "If you could come with me, please?"

"But my friend—"

"He can catch up. Mr. Fitzgerald hasn't got much time, as I'm sure you'll appreciate."

She swallowed, glancing back to where Zac was still on the floor bent over the fallen woman and now surrounded by a large crowd of people.

"Miss King?"

She didn't want to leave without him. Already she could feel the walls rushing in on her, the vast space above her head pressing down. The noise of the crowd and the crush of people threatening to drown her.

*Broken little girl.*

No. She was not. And if she couldn't do without him for even a couple of minutes, then she was in worse shape than she thought.

Determinedly, Eva turned away from Zac and started to follow the other man.

It wouldn't be for long. Zac would indeed catch up and everything would be fine.

She kept her gaze on the flunky's back, focused hard on it and not on the crowds pressing on her. Crushing her. Suffocating her.

Her heartbeat was loud in her head, her jaw tight with the effort it took to not give in and run and hide. Find somewhere safe to curl up.

Much to her relief, they soon left the gallery and the crowd behind, moving into a much quieter, echoing corridor. Which would have been fine if not for the fact that Zac still hadn't caught up with them.

"Can we stop, please?" she said after a moment, trying to make it sound like less of a hoarse question and more of an order. "My friend is still back in the main gallery and—"

"Miss King?" The voice was hard and icy. And then the massive shape of a tall man stepped out of the shadows of a nearby intersecting corridor. He was about the same height as Zac, with a scarred face and the coldest black eyes she'd ever seen.

Eva's heart froze in her chest, fear beginning to sink sharp claws into her.

"You need to come with me," he said.

The flunkey had disappeared. There was only her and this terrifying, scarred man.

From somewhere she managed to dredge up her voice. "I want to wait for my—"

"Mr. Rutherford has been detained," the man interrupted. "Mr. Fitzgerald wanted to see you alone."

Mr. Rutherford. They knew who Zac was.

*Run. Run now.*

Eva clutched her purse, dug her fingers into it. The beads were sharp, and the slight pain helped focus her. No, she was not going to run. She couldn't. She had to confirm Fitzgerald was the man who'd taken her. And she had to do this for the others who were counting on her.

She had to do this for Zac, who believed she was strong.

"Okay," she said, pleased that her voice didn't shake. "Lead on."

There was no expression at all on the man's face as he turned and began to walk back down the smaller corridor. He didn't even glance behind to see if she'd followed.

Perhaps he didn't need to. Perhaps he knew she wouldn't run.

She didn't know whether that was significant or not, and pretty soon, she'd ceased to worry about it. Because she had more important things to be concerned about.

The man led her down a few more corridors, turning a few times, screwing with her sense of direction, which had always been fairly shitty, so she soon lost track of where they were. She couldn't hear the noise of the party. She couldn't hear anything but the beating of her own heart, racing with the fear that was growing and growing with every second that passed.

There were pictures on the walls, statues here and there. The lighting was dim, the corridors echoing with the sounds of her footsteps.

*He could kill you right here and no one would know. No one would care.*

Eva kept her gaze fixed on the back of the man in front of her again, ignored the stupid thoughts that went around in her head.

She could do this. She could.

Eventually the man led her around a corner and into a small gallery hung with black-and-white photos.

Standing in the middle with his back to them, apparently staring at one of the pictures, was Fitzgerald's tall figure.

The scarred man said nothing, but Fitzgerald must have heard them approach.

He was silent a long moment, contemplating the picture on front of him. Then he slowly turned around.

Eva waited for recognition to hit, but there was none. He looked like his pictures, handsome and smiling in a beautifully tailored tux. Blue-eyed and unthreatening despite his height and broad build. A friendly, charming older man, the kind who could have been a well-loved teacher, a respected family doctor, the father of a best friend.

And then he spoke. "Good evening, Miss King."

And Eva fell into the dark.

It took Zac five minutes to extricate himself from the crowd of concerned people all clustered around the woman he'd saved from falling into a heap on the floor.

He'd thought at first she was drunk, but then was assured by her friends that she suffered from low blood pressure and often experienced fainting fits. These didn't last long and once she'd sat down for a couple of minutes, she was usually fine.

Irritated by the fact the woman had the temerity to faint on him, he finally got away from her attentive and grateful friends to discover that Eva had disappeared.

Completely.

Somewhere in him something howled like a wolf, clawing at him to smash through these crowds to find her.

But he didn't allow himself to give into the feeling. He was a soldier. Fear and panic were not permitted.

Instead he stood still for a long moment, assessing the crowd, gauging it. Scanning around to see if he could spot the glitter of her gown.

Then he spotted the flunkey who had approached them earlier, coming out of one of the doorways that led to the other museum galleries and then disappearing in the crowd.

Zac debated for a second whether to go after him, then discarded the idea. Going after the man and interrogating him would take up precious time. Quicker to just go through the door the man had exited from.

Slipping into soldier mode, he headed straight for the doorway, reaching into the inner pocket of his tux where he'd put his weapon. He had no reason to take it out since he had no reason to believe that Eva was in danger. But that didn't stop him.

Eva wasn't here. Which meant she was alone somewhere. Alone with Fitzgerald.

Christ, why hadn't she waited for him? She'd either thought she could do this herself or someone had taken her.

Another thought occurred to him.

Perhaps the woman and the fainting had been intentional. Staged in order to get Eva by herself.

Zac's hand tightened on his Glock.

If Fitzgerald touched her, Zac would kill him. No, fuck that. Fitzgerald was going to die anyway.

It would only be sooner rather than later.

There was no mistaking that voice. Smooth yet cold. The sound of her nightmares.

Eva would have known that voice anywhere.

She felt cold. So cold she might as well have been carved out of ice. She couldn't take her eyes from his face. His pleasant features, the smile that curved his mouth. A rich, powerful man. A pillar of his community.

A drug dealer. A pimp. A murderer. A rapist.

"It's good of you to come tonight," Fitzgerald said affably. "Though I confess, I'm surprised. I didn't think you got out much."

She couldn't speak. Fuck, where was her voice? It was frozen solid, just like everything else about her.

He tilted his head a little, studying her. It made her skin crawl. "It's probably a bit of a shock, isn't it? I suppose it has been . . . what? Seven years?" He smiled, though it didn't reach those icy blue eyes. "I keep forgetting you didn't know who I was."

He confessed it so easily. Like it was nothing.

*Say something you fool.*

"Why?" was the only thing that came out. A sad, broken little sound. A sad, broken little question.

Fitzgerald's eyes widened momentarily. "Why what?

Why did I take you? Why did I keep you? Stupid questions, Miss King. I took you and kept you because I could. It's that simple."

She'd begun to shake, her vision tunneling. No. Fuck, no. She wasn't going to faint. She was stronger than that, hadn't Zac shown her how?

*He can't touch you ever again.*

Eva tried to slow her breathing, tried to stop herself from shaking apart at the seams. "No," she forced out. "I mean why did you want to speak to me?"

"Tonight?" Fitzgerald lifted a shoulder. "I was curious to see what brought you out of your little mouse hole. And I suspect, given the investigations that you and your guard dog have been conducting, that it was to confirm my identity as your abductor, am I right?"

He knew. Holy Christ, he knew.

Her expression of shock must have been plain on her face because he gave a soft laugh. "What? You think I wasn't aware exactly of what your little group have been doing? Poking their noses into my private business affairs?" The amusement vanished as quickly as it had come. "Of course I know. Just like I know all about you, Miss King. About how you stay in that little apartment of yours and never go out. Unless of course, Mr. Rutherford is with you. How you manage to run your little company I have no idea."

Fear turned over and over inside her, wild and blind. While a distant part of her stood back and merely nodded. Because of course he knew all about her. A man like him would.

"You can't escape," she said ridiculously, dredging up the ghost of her old courage. "We know all about you too."

A crease appeared between his brows. "I suspect you think you know. But the sad fact is you don't have any solid evidence nor will you find any. I'm many things, Miss

King, but stupid I am not." He began to walk forward toward her, and she found herself rooted to the spot, unable to move. A deer in the headlights.

"Sir?" The cold voice of the scarred man behind her. "I suspect Rutherford will be trying to find her. Shall I make sure you're undisturbed?"

Fitzgerald waved a casual hand. "Well, it's not as if I'm in danger from this child here. Another few minutes should do it, Elijah."

The name shot through the maze of fear clouding Eva's brain. Elijah. The mercenary Alex had met in Monte Carlo. Was Fitzgerald his employer? It certainly looked that way.

The sound of Elijah's retreating footsteps faded behind her.

It was now just her and The Man who'd taken her. Raped her. Kept her his prisoner for two years.

He continued to come toward her, and every part of her wanted to shrink into a ball. Curl up at his feet and pretend he didn't exist. The urge was so strong it was only the sharp press of the beads on her purse that kept her on her feet.

And Zac's voice in her head.

*"I will be the only one you ever think about."*

If she thought hard, she could conjure up the feeling of his hands on her skin, not the crawling sensation that was creeping through her now as Fitzgerald got closer. Zac's hands on her body. Zac's mouth on hers. Zac's cock inside her.

Zac owning her completely, utterly.

She'd been wrong when she thought no one cared if she was killed right here and now. Zac would care. And Christ, he'd be pissed.

Eva lifted her chin and met Fitzgerald's cold blue eyes. "You can't touch me, you know," she said, her voice surprisingly calm. "I'm not invisible anymore."

Fitzgerald stopped, inches away from her. He put his hands behind his back, his expression considering. "Yes," he allowed. "That's true. But you know, I've thought about killing you a few times over the years. And I didn't, not because you weren't invisible, but because . . ." He stopped, looking almost rueful. "Well, what would be the point? All that effort for nothing. The truth is that your life, Miss King, doesn't matter. You were insignificant then and you're insignificant now."

She didn't want them to, but his words found the vulnerable places inside her, hitting their targets with unerring accuracy. Hurting.

"You're simply not a threat," he went on. "You don't have it in you to go to the authorities anyway, not that there is any evidence to convict me. You just want to pretend it didn't happen, don't you, Eva?"

She shivered as he said her name. The one thing she'd never given him. "Don't," she said hoarsely. "I'm Miss King to you."

He stared at her for a long moment, frowning. Then he began to walk around her in a slow circle. "You were my favorite, did you know that? I was extremely angry when you escaped. Several of my men had to be taught a hard lesson. God knows why they thought giving you access to a computer was a good idea." He came to a stop in front of her again. "I was surprised you got away so cleanly, that they couldn't find you no matter how hard they looked. And then a few years later you turned up again, this time as the owner of a promising computer company." The lines of his face softened. "I have to say I was almost proud of you and what you'd become. I thought you'd disappeared into some crack house like all the other street rats, but no, you didn't. I even congratulated myself that the whole reason you were so good with computers had to do with the time you spent with me. Because how else would you have learned to hack like that if you hadn't been in my house?"

She wanted to protest, to say it wasn't true. That it wasn't anything to do with him. But . . . she couldn't say that for certain. Being in that house *had* taught her all about hacking. And if she hadn't been captured in the first place, would she have done all the things she had after she had escaped?

"Ah, yes," he said. "I see you agree with me. Funny how life turns out isn't it? In many ways, you've achieved all you have *because* of me. When you look at it like that, you even owe me."

"Fuck you," she forced out. "I don't owe you anything. I am where I am today *in spite* of you, you asshole."

"And where exactly is that, child?" His voice was mild. "Cowering in your little tower? Unable to go out unless you have Mr. Rutherford by your side? Afraid of all the world?" He raised a hand then, and to her horror ran a finger along her jaw. "That's where you are, Eva. And that's why I'm letting you live. You're simply not worth the bother of killing."

Unable to help herself, she jerked away, her whole body recoiling in shock and fear.

Fitzgerald only gave a slight smile. His hand dropped. "Be glad of your insignificance, child. It saved your life. "

Then he stepped around her and simply walked away.

# CHAPTER FIFTEEN

Zac stalked down the corridors, all emotion kept ruthlessly locked away. Every sense he had expanded outward, checking shadows, listening for sounds, alert to anything and everything that could give a hint as to where Eva had gone.

The place was silent apart from the faint echoes of the party going on behind him.

Where the fuck was she?

He paused at the entrance to a corridor off to his left and glanced down it, listening.

Nothing.

And then, faintly, the sound of—

Zac turned suddenly, lifting his arm and pointing his Glock at the shadowy figure who'd been approaching behind him.

The man stopped instantly, his scarred face absolutely without expression.

Zac kept the muzzle of his Glock exactly where it was. "Where is she?"

"He won't kill her."

"Please don't make me ask again."

"If he wanted to kill her he would have done so years ago." The man didn't seem to be at all anxious about the fact that there was a gun pointed at his head. Then again, he'd probably been in this situation many times before.

Zac knew a mercenary when he saw one.

"Last chance."

"If you kill me, you won't find out where she is."

It was a reasonable point. The prick.

Still, Zac didn't lower his gun. "Say what you have to say then."

The man's cold eyes were as black as space and just as empty. "You can't win, Mr. Rutherford. I tried to tell Mr. St. James back in Monte Carlo, but he wouldn't listen."

Christ. He should have known. "You're Elijah."

"Who I am is irrelevant. You and your people need to back off before you do something stupid. " Elijah smiled. In the dark his teeth were white, the smile as sharp and hungry as a tiger's. "He's mine to deal with, understand? I'm the only one who can take him down."

Zac didn't bother to ask who the other man was talking about. He knew. "You think rather a lot of yourself if that's the case. We have evidence—"

"You have nothing. He has half the city in his back pocket." That white smile was almost taunting. "Like I said, you can't win."

Zac gritted his teeth. "So is that it? That's all you wanted to say?"

"If you want to make sure your woman lives, you'll do what I tell you."

She wasn't his woman, but Zac didn't bother to correct him. "You just said he wouldn't kill her."

"He won't kill her tonight. That's not to say she'll ever be safe. None of you will. Not unless you leave him alone and let me do what I came here to do."

Zac stared at him, trying to read the look on his face,

trying to determine whether he was telling the truth or what his angle was. An impossible task. Elijah's expression gave absolutely nothing away.

"Down that corridor, second gallery to the right."

Zac kept his gun trained on him for a long moment. Letting Elijah leave wasn't the logical thing to do, but short of killing him, Zac didn't have many other options. Not when he needed to find Eva too.

He lifted his Glock. Pocketed it.

Elijah's smile was white in the dim light before he turned and walked away.

Zac didn't waste another moment on him, instead turning down the corridor Elijah had indicated, walking swiftly until he came to the second gallery.

Eva was standing in the middle of it, her back to the doorway, motionless.

A great wash of relief swept through him, so intense he could only stand there looking at the straight white fall of hair down her back, as motionless as she was.

And he realized then that he'd been afraid. An emotion so foreign to him these days that he hadn't even recognized it. Bloody hell, was this what she carried with her wherever she went? This paralyzing, cold fist that closed around your heart?

The respect he already had for her deepened.

She felt such fear, and she'd come here anyway. She was even braver than he'd guessed.

"It was him," she said without turning around, her voice so brittle and fragile it was like spun glass. "I didn't need to say a thing. He basically admitted it all before I spoke a word." She was so still. Holding herself as if she was afraid to move or else she'd shatter.

Fear began to dissipate inside him, a thick and vicious anger taking its place.

Fitzgerald was dead. He'd hunt that fucker down like

prey, make him wish he'd never set eyes on Eva King. Make him wish he'd never been born.

He stepped forward, put his hands on Eva's pale shoulders and turned her gently around.

Her face was the color of ashes. And the expression on it . . . like she'd seen her own death.

Something inside him cracked all the way through. He gripped her shoulders tight, staring down at her. She looked okay physically, but harm had been done. He could see it in the darkness of her eyes.

"What did he do to you?" he demanded harshly, unable to temper his tone. "What did he say?"

"He let me live. He said I wasn't worth the bother of killing." She looked up at him, the bright silver of her gaze now darkened into charcoal. "He said I was insignificant. That I didn't matter. He knew me, Zac. He knew I never go outside without you. He knew that I'm . . . afraid."

Her skin felt cold against his palms. She looked like she was in shock.

Rage was a living thing inside him. Like the night he'd found that officer forcing that young woman against the wall in an alley beside the pub. No one had gone to help her, everyone ignoring her screams. He'd never felt so angry. That a man in a position of power could take advantage like that, that no one was there to save her.

He hadn't cared when he'd punched the officer in the face and the man had hit his head on the pavement. Scum like that deserved the death they got.

And so did Fitzgerald.

He let Eva go. "Wait here. I'll only be a minute."

"Where are you going?"

But he was already turning around, reaching again into his pocket for his gun.

A hand gripped his arm, slight strength pulling at him. "Stop."

He shook her hand off. This was going to end. Tonight.

She moved in a rustle of skirts and a glitter of sequins, putting herself in front of him. "Zac."

"Get out of my way, angel."

"No." A hand came up, hitting him square in the chest. The spontaneous touch was enough to halt him in his tracks, and he looked down at her.

Her eyes weren't so dark anymore, a bright silver spark glittering in them. "You said you'd come to me before you did anything."

"I have."

"No, Zac." There was an expression in her face he didn't quite understand, but it wasn't quite so shocked-looking now. In fact, she looked about as furious as he was. "Don't you dare take another step."

Her hand was warm, he could feel it right through the cotton of his shirt, his body starting to wake into life at her touch. Fuck, he wanted that hand on his bare skin.

Ah, but he couldn't. He'd promised himself it wasn't going to happen. He'd take out his fury on the bastard who deserved it instead.

Gently, he took her wrist and removed her hand.

Or at least he tried to. Her arm had gone rigid, her hand pressing down. There was a familiar look in her eyes. Stubborn, bloody-minded determination. "You go after him and you're making me as helpless and as insignificant as he said I was. That I need to be protected. Coddled." She pushed suddenly against him. Hard. "I'm not his fucking victim, Zac. I'm not anyone's fucking victim. So stop acting like I am!" There was no darkness in her eyes now at all. Only the pure quicksilver of rage. It caught at his own anger like a fishhook on the end of a line.

"Is that what you think I've been doing all this time?" He couldn't make his voice sound calm. "Keeping you a victim?"

Her mouth was a firm, hard line. "I don't think you did it purposefully but that's what I've become. And if I let you keep protecting me, that's all I'll ever be." She removed her hand all of a sudden. "You were right. You should have left me years ago. It would have been the best thing for both of us."

He could feel the imprint of her palm on his chest like a brand. Her mark on him. It made him want to put his mark on her in return. "The best thing for *you*," he repeated for emphasis, to remind himself.

But Eva shook her head, white hair falling in among the sequins of her gown. "Not just for me. I understand now, Zac. What it was like. How it must have hurt to tie yourself for seven years to a woman who hated to be touched. Who needed protection but couldn't give you what you needed. Friendship is a two-way street, but that's not the street we've been on. It's all been one way." She took a breath. "My way."

Now, after all this time, she understood. It hurt and he didn't know why. "It was my choice," he said curtly. "No one forced me to stay with you."

She stared at him, the force of her silver gaze almost palpable. "Well. Now you're free. You don't have to stay and protect me anymore, Zac. I have to learn how to do that myself."

Perhaps it was the thing she'd cracked inside him with the earlier devastation on her face. Or perhaps it was the culmination of fear and anger overwhelming all his restraints. Or perhaps he just wanted to touch her and couldn't stop himself from doing so any longer.

But one minute she was setting him free, the next he had his hand on her throat and she was backed up against the wall of the little gallery, his other hand on the wall beside her head.

She'd gone very still, her eyes wide, the rise and fall of

her breasts quick and hard with her accelerated breathing. She didn't speak, but he could feel her pulse against his palm, a precious sign of life.

"I will do whatever the *fuck* I like," he growled. "And if that means protecting you, if that means being there for you, if that means fucking you here up against this wall then I will. Understand? You don't get to tell me what to do anymore."

Her lashes came down for a moment, veiling her gaze. He could scent her, the familiar vanilla of her skin and the soft musk of something else. Arousal. It slid through him like a drug, setting fire to him and all his good intentions, burning them to ash.

Then her lashes came up, her clear, gray eyes looking into his. "You want to be there for me? Then prove to me I'm not a victim. Prove to me that I'm as strong as you keep saying I am."

He didn't pretend to misunderstand her. He knew a sensual challenge when he heard one. "I've already done that once."

She didn't even blink. "Don't you want to do it again?"

This time he couldn't say to himself she didn't know what she was getting into. That she didn't understand what he wanted from her. She knew.

He wanted it more than he wanted life itself.

*Weren't you not going to have her again?*

Sex. It was only sex. It didn't have to mean anything beyond the physical. He could control that other hunger, that hunger for more. He would never give her anything more. God knew, she already had enough power over him as it was.

He stroked his thumb almost absently across the soft, vulnerable skin of her throat. It felt like silk. There was so much he wanted from her, so much he wanted to do . . .

"Yes," he said, reduced to nothing but painful honesty now. "I want to do it again."

She swallowed, and he could feel her throat press against his palm. "So do it."

"I swore I wouldn't."

Frustration sparked in her eyes. "Why not? Was it really so bad the first time?"

"No. Fuck, no." He paused, still stroking her, unable to help himself. "It was too good. And that's why. You test my control, Eva. I can't have that."

"Why? Because of your parents? That officer you hurt? That's bullshit, Zac, and you know it." The sequins of her dress glittered in time with her accelerated breathing, her breasts pressing against the fabric.

"Addiction is hereditary. Violence stains your soul."

"You spent seven years with me, wanting me, and yet you didn't touch me, not even once. Addicts can't do that. They take eventually and damn the consequences. And as for the violence part . . ." Her jaw firmed. "That was an accident. You didn't go in there trying to kill him, only to protect the woman he was hurting. Shit, I would have done the same thing myself if I'd been in your shoes."

Of course she would. Little warrior that she was.

He stilled his thumb over her pulse.

Yet he hadn't given her the whole truth. There was another memory, another truth he hadn't given her. But that was his, a private pain he wouldn't share with anyone.

Her complex, bright heartbeat thumped against the tip of his thumb. The smell of her was intoxicating, the heat of her skin a seduction all by itself.

Relief and anger echoed through him, weakening all his usual restraints.

"I need this, Zac," she whispered into the silence. "And I think you do, too."

Such a simple statement. It shattered him completely.

Zac slid his hand higher up her neck, his palm cupping her fragile jaw. He firmed his fingers along the delicate line of it, tilting her head back. Holding her in place.

Then he covered her mouth with his.

She quivered, her lips parting beneath his without hesitation. As if she'd been waiting centuries for him to kiss her. And she tasted exactly as he remembered from two nights ago, so fucking sweet. She was hungry for it too, he could taste it, her desire delicious on his tongue.

He kissed her harder, deeper, keeping his hand on her jaw. Demanding everything. Taking everything.

But before it consumed them both, he lifted his head. Stared down into her darkening eyes. Keeping his hand exactly where it was on her throat, he reached with the other into his pocket to get his phone. Dialed a number.

"Temple?" he murmured when it was answered, not taking his gaze from Eva's. "Make sure the car is outside. Miss King and I will be leaving in five minutes."

He put his phone away and slowly, very slowly, let Eva go.

She stayed where she was, the wall at her back. A flush had crept over her pale skin, her mouth full and pink from his kiss.

"Fitzgerald can wait tonight," he said roughly. "Right now we're going home."

"What about Gabe and Alex?"

"They can wait too. We'll call a Circles meeting in the morning." One more night. That's all he wanted and that's what he was going to have.

Zac stepped back to give her some space. "Angel. You're going to walk out of here with your chin up, your head held high like you're the queen of the fucking universe. And you'll do it alone. Show him you won't be beaten. That you're not insignificant."

She blinked, but there was determination in her expression, her usual courage coming to the fore. "What about you?"

"I'll follow you." He allowed the dragon to flicker through his eyes. "So I can watch your delectable arse."

She flushed, but didn't say a word. Instead she lifted her chin and swept past him as if she was, indeed, a queen.

He followed her back through the corridors to the crowded gallery where the party was still going on. Watching the graceful way she walked, the sway of hips and arse.

She kept her head high and her chin lifted, not looking either right or left, keeping her gaze squarely in front of her. Moving without hesitation.

People stood by to let her go past, some of them staring, some of the whispering, but she didn't stop or falter as she headed toward the exit. The flush had faded from her skin and she was pale, but apart from that she betrayed no sign of fear.

Not even as she passed the cluster of people surrounding Fitzgerald.

The man continued talking but his gaze followed Eva all the way to the door.

Prick.

As Eva vanished through it, Zac paused. Sure enough, the other man's attention soon focused on him. Zac smiled politely. Then showed his teeth.

Fitzgerald didn't know it yet, but he was already dead.

The car journey back to Zac's house was silent, but Eva didn't feel the need to speak. She felt silenced by the memory of Zac's mouth on hers and his hand on her throat.

There had been possession in the way he'd touched her. Like he was claiming her back from the man who'd made her feel so small, so ashamed. Humiliated.

She wanted him to keep going, no matter that they were in a public place. Wanted to bask in the feeling of his possession like a cat in the sun, absorbing the heat of it. The strength of it. Because she'd never felt insignificant with Zac. Never felt like she didn't matter. Not when he'd made her feel like she was the center of the universe.

But then this wasn't entirely about herself any longer. There was him now.

She'd told him she'd needed this, to test her strength against him, to feel like she mattered, that she wasn't as insignificant as Fitzgerald had told her she was. Yet she'd known when she'd looked up into his face and seen the conflict in his eyes, that he needed it too.

He had demons he hadn't told her about. Demons he was afraid of. And if they could make a man like Zac Rutherford afraid, then they were formidable indeed.

She wished he'd let her help him fight them.

Eva stared at him in the deep, heavy silence of the car. He was sitting opposite her as he usually did, his hands folded with their normal elegant simplicity in his lap. Every aspect of him was neat. His suit tailored to perfection, his bowtie centered, his white shirt crisp. His black hair had gotten a little long, the ends curling over the collar of his shirt, but that was the only aspect of him that hadn't been ruthlessly contained.

He was *so* controlled. Polite and correct.

And yet it was a façade, hiding the heart of a man who was anything but.

A memory flashed in her head, of the sound of his voice and the heat of his body as she'd been tied to that chair and blindfolded. He'd been rough and raw then, she'd bet her life on it. Yet it still felt like he'd been holding back.

Only one explanation made sense. He was protecting himself because he was afraid of something. Was it simply the idea of being out of control? Yes, there were passions in him, intense desires, yet he didn't act on them without thought or disregard the consequences.

He wasn't his parents. He wasn't an addict, surely he knew that? Or was it something more? Something he hadn't shared with her?

The car was slowing, coming to a halt outside his house. A moment later, Temple had opened the door, letting the cold of the late winter air into the warm interior of the car.

Eva got out, waiting until Zac had followed her before they both went up the stairs to his front door. He unlocked it, pushed it open, and gestured for her to go inside.

It was warm in his house and she couldn't stop herself from shivering in reaction, the door shutting heavily behind them.

"Angel," he said, and she heard the hard edge of the Dom in his voice.

She turned.

He was standing by the front door, tall and dark in his tux, golden eyes glinting in the dim light of the hall. "Stay there. Don't move." Then he began to stalk toward her.

Her heart kicked against her ribs, but she did what she was told, watching him approach. "I'm . . . I'm not afraid," she said shakily, wanting him to know. "You don't have to hold back like you did before."

He circled around her like a wolf circling its prey, coming to a stop behind her. "Oh, I don't intend to. Believe me." His fingertips brushed her bare back, finding the tab of the zipper on her gown. "You remember your safeword?"

Another shiver whispered over her skin. "V-Void."

"Good girl." Slowly he began to draw the zipper down, the material loosening around her.

Eva swallowed as the fabric fell from her. She hadn't worn a bra because the gown was strapless, which meant that now she was standing in his hallway in only the silver lace panties he'd bought for her days before and the little silver slippers Honor had ordered for her so she didn't have to negotiate a party in unfamiliar heels.

Fear made a reflexive appearance, but along with it, running through it like a vein of gold through a seam of coal, was desire. Pure and glittering, molten with heat.

Desire for him.

She waited, shaking a little with anticipation, staring at the wall in front of her while every sense she had was focused behind her on where he stood. Her skin felt strangely tight and she was half scared of what would happen if he touched her, half desperate for it anyway.

Yet he did nothing.

"Zac?"

"Keep still," he murmured, his voice taking on that deep, dark, sensual quality she remembered from days ago. "I don't want to hear a sound from you unless it's your safeword."

Why? What the hell was he doing?

She took a breath.

"You can obey me, can't you, angel?" His voice was near her ear, freezing her in place. "You can do it? For me?"

Her chest constricted painfully, her throat tight with emotion.

Such simple questions and yet she could hear the need in each word, a rough, frayed edge running beneath the smooth sensuality of his tone.

She'd never wanted to give anything of herself to him or to anyone else. She'd been too afraid. But she wasn't afraid any longer. And he deserved everything she had.

So she let go the questions and didn't speak, only nodded. And when she felt his lips brush the sensitive skin beneath her ear, she knew he'd understood. But then he

stepped back and she had to bite down on her instant protest, determined to prove herself to him.

His hands moved to her hips, fingers sliding underneath
the waistband of her panties. "You like my gift I see." He
began to tug them down. "I'll have to get you some more."

She didn't move as she felt him slide them down her legs
till they were around her ankles. Then he helped her step
out of her slippers, taking her panties off as she did so,
leaving her completely naked.

Staring at the wall, goose bumps rising all over her skin,
Eva felt his hands close around her ankles then slide up-
ward, caressing. "Or maybe not," he said softly, stroking
her thighs. "Maybe I'll just keep you naked twenty-four
hours a day. Accessible whenever I want."

She took a ragged, shaken breath as his fingers grazed
her upper thighs, a subtle, insistent ache beginning to grip
her tight. The light touch was only making her hungrier,
more desperate in a way she'd never experienced before.
How strange to actually be hungry for more touch. To ache
for it.

His hands fell away and she felt the absence like a loss.
But not for long. The rustle of fabric came from behind
her as he rose to his feet. And when his fingers came to
rest lightly on the bare skin of her hips, she almost gasped
aloud at the shock.

"You're being so very good," he murmured, his breath
against the bare skin of her shoulder. "So very obedient. I
like it, angel. I like it very much indeed."

Then sudden heat pressed against her spine, her buttocks, the backs of her thighs and she had to bite her
lip this time in order to stop the sound that almost escaped her.

His grip on her hips had firmed, the hard length of his
body against her. Even through his clothes she could feel
the heat of him, burning like a summer bonfire.

She trembled, pushing back against him almost instinctively, feeling the ridge of his hardening cock pressing into the curve of one buttock. Oh, he wanted her, he really did. And she liked it.

"Hmmm . . . Getting demanding, I see." He slid an arm around her waist, holding her against him. "Unfortunately for you, I'm the one who's in charge. And tonight I'll be the one getting what I want." The hand on her hip moved, curving down over her butt, caressing, before pushing between her thighs, cupping her sex, making her shudder. "If you're good, though. You might get a reward. I'm feeling generous tonight."

Eva swallowed, her mouth dry, her pulse getting faster and faster. He moved a finger, pressing the tip of it lightly against her clit, igniting a shock of pleasure. Another shudder ripped through her.

Zac circled her clit, hard enough to provide friction, light enough to prove maddening.

Her jaw went tight, her teeth clenched together. She wouldn't make a sound, just like he'd ordered. She would give him this, she would.

He pressed harder, more insistently, his touch knowing and skilled, and she had to take a ragged breath against the intensity of the sensation. It was still new to her, still overwhelming, and she didn't know how to fight it.

But he'd know that of course. Which meant he was doing this deliberately, the bastard.

At that thought, his finger pushed suddenly inside her with no warning at all, sliding deep. Her teeth sunk into her lip, biting down hard to stop the cry that threatened to break free.

His thumb stroked over her clit, while his finger withdrew then pushed back in again, the fierce arc of pleasure making her knees tremble.

But she wasn't going to make a sound. She would stay quiet. She would prove to him she could do this. Nothing was going to stop her. Nothing.

"You're so wet already," he murmured. "Almost ready to come, aren't you?" His thumb moved in a slick circle, a little faster, a little harder. "But I'm afraid you haven't earned it quite yet, angel." His voice deepened. "There are quite a few punishments I want to take out on your beautiful body tonight. Seven of them to be exact. One for each year you made me wait." Another finger joined the first inside her, stretching her enough to feel a burn. "If you can handle them, if you can prove what a good girl you are, I'll give you a reward. But if you can't . . ." His fingers slid deeper still and she tasted blood in her mouth as she bit down harder to stop the moan that threatened to escape. "Then you won't get what you want." His thumb moved, another tight circle. "Are you ready for your first punishment? Nod if you are."

She could barely think, the tremble in her knees beginning to shake her entire body. But she managed to make herself give a short, sharp nod.

The bastard only stroked deeper, slowing his movements, the pleasure becoming a low moan inside her, one that pushed hard against her throat, wanting out.

"Your first punishment is that you may not make a sound and you may not come. Not until I say. Do you understand?"

Eva managed another sharp nod, fighting against the wave of sensation that was threatening to drown her.

God, the asshole knew what he was doing. The movement of his fingers increased the pleasure by subtle increments, drawing her to the edge of climax and holding her there with brutal insistence. Allowing her no time to rest or recover.

Pleasure drawn to the point of almost exquisite pain.

But she wanted her reward. And more than that, she wanted to prove herself, wanted to be strong for him.

So she bit down harder, the metallic taste of blood in her mouth, her knees almost unable to keep her upright as his fingers taunted and teased. And she thought about code, about firewalls, about viruses, about Black Hats and hackers, about anything to fight off the climax that he was building with relentless, inexorable care.

Until her body began to scream, until she didn't think she could bear it any longer.

"Now, angel." The dark sound of his voice in her ear was the sweetest thing she'd ever heard. "Come for me, scream for me, now."

Her body arched in his hold as she came almost instantly, pleasure a flare of white-hot magnesium lighting her up from the inside, tearing her wide open. Her head pressed back against his shoulder as the scream that had been building for so long demanded to be let out.

But his lips covered hers, taking her scream of release into his mouth, his arms tight and strong around her as she convulsed and shook with the aftershocks, collapsing completely against him.

As the intensity began to fade, she felt weightless, light as a feather. She kept her eyes closed, reveling in the warmth of Zac's mouth still on hers and the feel of his arms around her, holding her up. Her body felt loose and relaxed, and she didn't want to move. Not ever.

She'd done it though, hadn't she? She done what he wanted. Hadn't made a sound.

Zac shifted her, and suddenly she really was weightless, lifted and held against his chest.

She opened her eyes to see that he was carrying her up the stairs.

"Can I talk now?" she asked, her voice gone husky.

He glanced down at her, his amber gaze glittering in a way that told her that though she might feel safe now, she was actually very far from safe. "For the moment."

"Not the library tonight?"

"No. We need a bedroom. My bedroom in particular."

"I guess I can't sleep now."

Another sharp glance from those dangerous, predatory eyes. "There will be no sleeping, Eva. Not tonight."

She wanted to protest at that, but knew it wouldn't go down very well. So she stayed silent, allowing herself to simply rest in his arms as he carried her down a long hallway and into a bedroom. His bedroom.

He kicked the door shut behind him, carrying her over to the bed and setting her down on it.

She'd never seen this room before, but then she'd never had any reason to.

It was big —it had to be to contain the massive four-poster bed she was currently sitting on.

The walls of the room were a rich, dark blue, the floor polished wood with Eastern-looking rugs of brilliant reds and golds. There were a few bookshelves, a couple of Renaissance-style paintings in gilt frames. A comfortable-looking couch down one end of the room, covered in well-worn black leather.

The bed itself was of dark wood and covered in a midnight blue velvet quilt. It was very cozy, the velvet against her bare skin so soft she wanted to roll herself up in it and go to sleep.

Zac had gone over to one end of the room, pulling open a couple of doors to what must be a walk-in closet. He disappeared for a moment and she heard the sound of drawers being opened.

Okay, so he was probably getting . . . equipment.

Seven punishments he said. Holy shit, she hoped she could handle it.

"Can I ask what my reward will be?" she asked, with a touch of her usual bravado. "I mean, I think I need some incentive here."

Zac reappeared from the closet. He was holding a few things in his hands. She couldn't stop looking at them. Long black straps. Cuffs. Jesus . . .

"I mean," she went on, knowing she was starting to babble, "considering I have to receive seven punishments, it had better be something good."

"Good point." He came back over to the bed. "What would you like your reward to be?" He'd begun to unravel the straps in his hands, laying them on the bed.

Fear gave another little kick to her gut and her mouth went dry. "I . . . well . . . I think I'd like to . . ." She could feel herself going hot. "Touch you, maybe. Touch you how I want."

Zac smoothed out one of the straps as she watched his movement, his fingers long, the tips blunt. There was a tat-tooed cross on his middle finger, between the knuckle and the first joint. From that Siberian prison probably. What did it mean?

"That's a pretty major reward," he said softly. "You'll have to be extra good if you want to earn that."

She looked up from the straps arranged neatly on the bed, met his gaze determinedly. "I can do that."

His mouth curved, his smile sharp and hungry, taking all the breath from her. "I hope so. Because now it's time to show me." He tossed the cuffs down on the bed beside the straps. "Your second punishment, angel. I want you to undress me, but you're not allowed to touch me, under-stand?"

She swallowed, frowning, not sure what he meant. "How can I do that?"

"You can touch my clothing. But you can't touch my skin."

"That's going to be . . . difficult."

"Yet not impossible." He stepped back from the bed, his arms at his sides. "Come, Eva."

She slipped off the bed, coming closer to him. He waited, motionless. Watching her with those hot, golden eyes. How was she supposed to do this?

Her mouth was a fucking desert and she'd started to shake again. She had no idea why getting close to him made her feel this way, and it was going to make this even more difficult.

Then again maybe that was why it was a punishment.

She stopped in front of him, deciding not to look up into his face since that stare of his only made the shaking worse.

He still wore his jacket so she decided to tackle that first, reaching up to slide it from his shoulders. He helped her, shifting so she could get it off. Afterwards she held it in her hands, unsure of what to do with it. Then, remembering how he'd neatly folded up all her clothes after he'd undressed her, she awkwardly tried to fold it before moving to the couch and laying it down on the black leather.

She'd never folded a man's clothes before and didn't do a good job. Hell, she'd never folded her own either, but she tried to keep the creases out of it at least.

When she came back to face him, there was a curious, faint smile on his face as he looked down at her. "You folded my jacket."

"Well, yeah. It's expensive." She reached up to his bow-tie, trying not to brush his skin. "And you were careful with my clothes so . . ."

He didn't reply to that, but she could feel the pressure of his gaze anyway. Watching her still.

It made her task even harder and she wanted to tell him to stop it, but that would come close to admitting she couldn't do this and fuck that. She wanted her damn reward and she was going to get it.

She managed to get the bowtie undone, pulling it out from underneath his collar and placing it on the bed. Then she put her fingers on the top button of his crisp, white shirt, beginning to undo them one by one. It was hard to keep the tips of her fingers from brushing against him, and soon, as the white material parted, it became even harder still.

His skin was bronzed, definitely no pale English skin here. The legacy of a Mediterranean ancestor maybe? She undid another button, strangely hypnotized by the slow reveal of tawny skin stretched over powerful muscle.

She'd never wanted to look at a man like that before. With desire. Wondering what it would feel like to touch him, trace all that sharply defined muscularity with her fingers, with her tongue. But as she pulled the tail of Zac's shirt out from the waistband of his trousers and undid the final few buttons, she found herself wanting to do just that. Desperate for it in fact.

Of course, she couldn't. Not yet.

To stop herself from staring at him, she moved around behind, pulling his shirt from his shoulders before realizing she couldn't actually get them over his hands.

She frowned, tugging. Trying to ignore the broad sweep of his shoulders and the elegant musculature of his back.

There was a tattoo there too. A brightly colored red and gold dragon with outspread wings that reached up to his shoulders. She wanted to touch that as well, trace the lines of it with her fingers.

He gave a soft laugh at her tug, the sound almost a caress as it washed over her. "You forgot the cufflinks."

"Shit," she muttered, feeling like an idiot. Cufflinks had never even occurred to her. "I didn't . . . I mean don't . . ."

"Don't sweat it." Zac began to take them off himself

and she indulged herself by watching the movements of his broad shoulders, the shift and release of those sleek, powerful muscles. Throwing the cufflinks onto the bed, he held out his arms, ready for her to take the shirt off. And she did, pulling it from him, her fingers feeling stupidly clumsy as she turned away to fold it and put it on the couch, not wanting to see him shirtless quite yet.

But there was no putting it off. And no bracing herself for it either.

The impact of him was like a blow.

He was a predator. A wolf or a tiger, or the dragon on his back. A beautiful, lethal animal, radiating strength and danger and an intense sexual charisma that made her breathless. That compelled her and yet made her afraid all at once.

Her breathing was fast. She couldn't seem to get enough air.

To give herself something to focus on, she stared at the tattoo sleeve that ran up his right arm. Another dragon, a beautifully drawn blue Chinese dragon in amongst koi carp, the coils of the beast wrapping around his biceps, the neck snaking over his shoulder, the head on his right pectoral. On the opposite side of his chest, over his heart, was a small winged creature.

She didn't look at that one, disturbed by it for some reason she didn't understand.

Well, okay, so she'd managed the top half of him. Now the bottom.

Slowly, she sank down onto her knees, remembering her effort with the cufflinks and dealing with his shoes and socks first, setting them neatly aside. Then she got to her feet again and took a deep, silent breath. Reached for the button on his trousers.

The heat of his hard, flat stomach was right there, she could feel it nearly touching the backs of her fingers. For some reason the button was next to impossible to undo and she fumbled.

Zac closed his fist around her hair and she froze, breathing hard, shivering as his fingers brushed the back of her neck.

Of course he wouldn't play fair. She should have expected it.

"You're doing very well." The fist in her hair tightened. "Too well. I did warn you I wouldn't make it easy for you."

She moistened her dry mouth, focused hard on the button and not on the feel of his hand in her hair. It came undone at last and she was able to grab the tab of his zipper, drawing it slowly down. Her knuckles brushed the hardening length of his cock through the fabric, his hand tugging hard on her hair as she did so.

"You're pushing," he murmured. "Be careful of doing that, sweetheart. You've already got seven punishments. You don't want any more."

A thrill went through her, though she couldn't understand why. She wanted to pull against his hold. Make him tug harder for some reason.

Well, there wasn't any reason not to. As long as she didn't touch his skin. And God, if he was going to tease her like this, then she'd pay him back in kind.

As the fabric loosened on his hips, she drew down on the material, accidentally on purpose brushing her fingers down the length of his cock again. There was only the thin black cotton of his boxers separating her from his bare skin, but given the heat coming off him, he may as well have been wearing nothing at all.

"Oh, angel," he breathed as she sank down on her knees again, pulling his pants down his powerful thighs. "You do like to test the boundaries."

Abruptly she gasped as she felt him wind her hair around his wrist, drawing it tight. Little prickles of pain bloomed over her scalp, making the ache between her thighs more intense. How strange that pain could do that to her. To make her want more.

"I did what you s-said," she forced out, her voice all breathless and stuttery. "I didn't touch your skin."

He laughed, soft and dark, and she wanted to touch him again, turn that laugh into a gasp the way he kept doing to her. "You should have been a lawyer. Just for that, I'll take my boxers off myself."

A surge of anger went through her. No, he couldn't take that away from her, not when she'd so nearly managed to do what he'd asked and successfully too.

"No," she said before she could stop herself. "I mean . . . I've nearly finished. Let me do it. Please."

He was silent, the hand in her hair still tight.

She kept her gaze to the floor. If he wanted her fucking submissive, then she'd damn well be submissive. There was power in it, as she was beginning to discover.

"Apologize," he said, his voice hard. "Tell me how sorry you are for not doing what you're told." And he pulled her hair again. Hard.

Pleasure and pain twined around her, forcing another strangled gasp from her. "I'm sorry," she managed raggedly. "I'm sorry I didn't do what you said. I'll . . . be better next time."

"Don't touch my cock." His tone was absolute. "You can't have that yet. You have to earn it, remember?"

"I r-remember. And I won't t-touch it. I promise."

The tension in her hair released as Zac let her go. "All right. Now finish undressing me."

She swallowed. How the hell did he do that? Make her desperate to finish the simple task of taking off his boxers? Make her want to be equal to it? Show him she could do it?

Eva lifted her hands, taking the soft cotton between her

fingers and drawing it down. She didn't look as she uncovered him, knowing she wouldn't be able to concentrate
if she did. Her face heated as she pulled the black fabric
down to his ankles, waiting as he stepped out of it.

He was naked now and she'd never seen a naked man
in the flesh before.

*Not even The Man.*

And yes, he would stay "The Man," not "Fitzgerald."
She wouldn't dignify him with his name.

That small decision eased the flick of memory and when
Zac's fingers slid back into her hair, not hard this time, the
tips massaging her aching scalp, she nearly groaned.

"Have you ever sucked a man's cock, angel?" he asked
softly.

She kept her gaze on the floor, the slight pain dissipating under the aching pleasure of his fingers. "I did at the
house—"

"I said 'a man.' Not that pathetic excuse for one."

Only a few words, yet they eased the memory of what
had gone on in that house even further. How did he do
that? Was he magic?

"No," she whispered, silently letting go of those particular memories. "I never have."

"You will tonight. But it's a privilege so you'll have to
beg for it." The tips of his fingers pressed a little harder,
soothing all the knots and painful places on her scalp. She
moaned softly at the pleasure of it. "I'm sure you can do
that as prettily as you've done everything else so far."

She nearly forgot herself then. Nearly leaned against his
legs, relaxing against him. Only catching herself at the last
minute.

He was right. This was a punishment. The fucking
bastard.

He tugged her hair gently. "Up."

She rose reluctantly and this time couldn't help herself, glancing down his naked body.

Her cheeks heated.

Jesus Christ, she never thought a man's cock could be beautiful, but his was. Long and thick and hard, brushing against the flat plane of his abdomen.

And she was glad, all of a sudden, that she'd been blindfolded before with Fitzgerald. That Zac was the first man she'd seen naked in the flesh.

*He'll be the only one.*

The realization was as certain and inevitable as night falling.

She wouldn't ever be able to be naked like this with anyone else. Wouldn't want anyone else touching her or being inside her. Wouldn't be able to stand anyone else's kiss or even bear to have their arms around her.

There would only and forever be Zac.

He was the only one she trusted enough. The only one she wanted enough.

She looked up at him reflexively and felt the impact of that amber gaze go through her like a sword thrust to the heart.

"I can't do this with anyone but you," she said, the words coming out before she could stop them. "Only ever you, Zac."

Molten gold leapt in his gaze for a second, a flickering passionate response, then it was gone. But the embers remained, glowing hot.

"Get on the bed," he said.

# CHAPTER SIXTEEN

Zac watched as Eva turned around and got up on the bed behind her, moving with that innate grace that was part of her. She was so small, seemingly so fragile.

Yet, just now, she'd been strong enough to open up his chest and pull out his heart.

*Only ever you, Zac.*

He hadn't realized how badly he'd wanted to hear those words until right now. Until she'd said them, her voice husky and cracked.

Ah, but he couldn't let himself think about those words or ascribe meaning to them. Give them weight. He knew the dangers of wanting too much. He'd spent his childhood wanting what he couldn't have and his adulthood trying to get rid of those wants. Only to fall back into the trap the moment Eva King had stepped out from under a street-light wearing only a man's overcoat to cover herself.

Small and pale. With eyes the color of cold steel.

His Void Angel. The hacker he'd been chasing for months.

He'd known in that moment that he was in for the fight of his life. A battle against the dragon inside him that wanted her for its hoard. But the dragon couldn't have her, not with those bruises on her neck, the shards of agony in her gaze.

*Things are different now. She's strong enough.*

Yes, she was. But he was starting to think that perhaps he wasn't. That he was the one who was weak.

That ever-present anger turned over inside him, howling at her and the hunger she'd ignited inside him. A hunger she'd stoked even higher over the past seven years by denying him until it was all he could think of.

It wasn't her fault. It was his. He should have left years ago.

She laid herself back on the blue quilt, her white hair across the pillows.

"Put your arms out and spread your legs," he ordered, moving over to the bed and picking up a couple of the cuffs. They were lined with soft fabric so they wouldn't chafe, the leather nice and soft too.

She obeyed him, her cheeks pink, flickers of trepidation in her eyes as he approached with one of the cuffs, lifting her hand and fastening it around her wrist. "Another punishment, huh?"

"How did you guess?" He pulled the buckle tight then moved down the bed to put one around her slender ankle.

"Oh, just a wild stab in the dark."

He could hear the bravado in her voice and along with it came the impulse to reassure her. But he wouldn't give it to her. Not tonight. She didn't want to be a victim? Well, he wouldn't treat her like one. Not that she ever had been one in the first place.

Silently he moved around the bed, fastening the cuffs on her wrist and ankle on the other side, then grabbing the straps he'd put on the bed earlier.

She watched him. Her breathing had heightened, her breasts rising and falling fast and hard. The pink tips of her nipples were tight. He would start there, he decided. And there would be no blindfold this time, so she could see everything.

See how utterly at his mercy she was.

There were D-rings in the cuffs, to attach to the straps, and from there he could attach the straps to the hooks he'd put into the posts of his bed.

He hadn't ever had a woman in here, preferring to use the club dungeons. He'd thought maybe he'd find someone at some point, someone he wouldn't mind bringing into his home. But he never had. And when he'd put those hooks into his bed, he hadn't been thinking of some vague 'someone.' He'd been thinking of Eva.

Once he'd clicked the straps into place, leaving her spread-eagled and bound, he stepped back from the foot of the bed purely so he could look at her.

Satisfaction wound through him, his deep, heavy anger, loosening its grip.

*She's made for you. She's made to be here, tied to your bed. Yours.*

She looked unearthly, like she was made out of mother-of-pearl and fine silver. A snow maiden from the book of fairy tales his nanny had once read to him from. The only color to her were the pink of her nipples, the deep rose of her lips, and the pale coral of her pussy revealed by her spread legs.

Possessiveness swept through him and he let it fill him completely.

After Fitzgerald had hurt her, had cast his hungry eyes over her, tonight he would stake his claim on her once and for all. He would do whatever the fuck he wanted to her. Because tonight she was his.

She was shaking a little but that was okay. The cuffs wouldn't hurt her physically, they were only there to heighten her feeling of being bound. To allow her to let go and submit to him and to the pleasure he would give her.

That was his real punishment for her. To overwhelm her with pleasure. Make her aware of everything she'd been denying them both for so long. Make her understand what they could have had. It wasn't fair and it wasn't right, but he'd be fucked if he wasn't going to do it anyway.

She wanted to see what he was capable of? Well, he'd show her.

He didn't keep a lot of equipment at home, because he liked to keep things simple. But in the drawer in his closet, along with the straps and cuffs, he kept a paddle and a flogger.

Maybe not those yet. Not while being bound was still new to her. Besides, he could get a lot of play out of simple bondage. Using her mind to start with.

He came around the side of the bed and her gaze followed him. Her throat moving, her lips parting. Not knowing what he was going to do must be driving her crazy.

Gently he ran his fingers down her outstretched arm, watching the goose bumps rise on her skin in response. A quiver went through her.

Christ, but she was responsive.

"W-What punishment are you going to give me now?" she asked shakily.

"That's for me to know and you to find out." He curved his hand lower, down over her breast, cupping the soft weight of it in his palm.

The straps pulled tight as she jerked, her breath a hiss in the silence of the room.

He brushed her tight little nipple with his thumb and she shivered again. "Do you like your cuffs, angel?"

"N-Not really."

"Good." He pinched her nipple hard between his fingers, watching her delicate features twist as she gasped in response. There was pain there, but the flush to her cheeks told him there was pleasure too.

He leaned over, licked her nipple, the salty sweet taste of her skin on his tongue. Another rattle of her restraints as she tried to pull away, so he sucked her into his mouth, drawing hard on her, the sharp cry she made hardening his cock painfully.

"Zac . . ." She was breathing hard, her voice hoarse.

He released her nipple, circling it lazily with his tongue, bracing his hands on either side of her bound body. Then he lifted his head, looked into her eyes. They'd gone dark with arousal and anticipation. And a healthy dose of fear. But not that cold, sick terror he'd seen in her face earlier tonight after she'd faced Fitzgerald.

This was a delicious kind of fear, the kind that heightened arousal.

"You've denied me your body for a long time, angel," he said softly, leaning over her. "You've kept me helpless, wanting you and unable to have you. Do you know what that does to a man like me?"

She looked up at him. A flicker of anguish crossed her face. "I know, Zac. God, I know."

Perhaps she did. But he was going to make certain of it. "No, I don't think you do. Which is why I've bound you, made you as helpless as you made me." He bent further, so his mouth was almost touching hers, her breath warm and sweet between them. "And I'll make you want like I wanted, Eva. I'll make you so desperate it'll become a physical pain. So you'll do anything, anything at all to end it. What you had downstairs was just a taste of what I can make your body do. The desperation I can make it feel."

She was shaking now as well she should. But there was nothing but challenge in her eyes despite the tremble of her body. "Do it then. I can take it. I can take anything you give me."

He loved it that. A glimpse of her brave, reckless spirit. It made him want to test it in so many ways. "We'll see, angel." He put his hand on her stomach, spread his fingers out. Then slid it down between her thighs, wetness and heat coating his fingers, feeling her body jerk again at the touch. "We'll see."

He was angry, that much was obvious.

Eva took a long, shaken breath as Zac's hand fell away and he moved away from the bed, going over to the closet again and disappearing inside.

She wasn't afraid—or at least, it was a different kind of fear that sat inside her this time. Fear of not being able to take what he wanted to give her. Fear of disappointing him in some way. And along with that was her own anger.

She knew she'd kept him on a leash even though she hadn't understood at the time. Knew that he realized it and didn't blame her. But shit, it had been his choice to stay. It wasn't like he'd said anything to her about what he wanted.

Of course if he had, she would have run for the hills, but still.

*You want this punishment though. You're curious about it. You want to see if you can take it.*

She flexed her wrists in the restraints, the soft fabric moving against her skin.

Yeah, it was true. She did want it. For her own curiosity's sake and yes, for pleasure, because it would be a sensual torment—of that she had no doubt.

But she could sense he also needed this. And she wanted to give it to him because, shit, after seven years, he deserved something from her, didn't he?

She shifted again, the feeling of being restrained, of being held open, exposing and strangely arousing at the same time. The bastard sure knew what he was doing.

Zac came out of the closet, carrying yet more items in his hands. A blindfold and some headphones. How weird.

Eva eyed the blindfold warily, not exactly thrilled to see it. "I thought we weren't going to use that."

"I changed my mind." He moved to the head of the bed

and laid the black material over her eyes, tying it securely behind her head. "It's a punishment, Eva. You're not supposed to like it."

"But . . . I want to see you." The darkness didn't feel so intimidating this time, yet she still didn't want it. Looking at him was a pleasure she hadn't realized she wanted until he took it away from her.

"Too bad." His voice was near her ear now. "I'm also going to take away your ability to hear. So you'll be blind and deaf."

Trepidation whispered through her. "Why?"

"It'll heighten your sense of touch. Also . . ." There was a pause and she shuddered as she felt his finger trace a line down her throat. "You're blind because you refused to see me as anything but a crutch you needed when you couldn't walk. And forgot about when you could. I'm going to take away your hearing so you'll have no choice but to trust what I give you. Seven years and you didn't trust me, angel. You need to suffer for that."

She wasn't given a chance to reply, the headphones covering her ears. Music started to play, and it was so very Zac that despite her trepidation she almost smiled. Violins and piano, refined and classical.

The bed moved and the warmth beside her was gone.

She was alone in the dark and she couldn't hear through the music in her ears. Couldn't move because of the restraints.

What had she gotten herself into?

Fear slithered through her and she let it go. Him. She was doing this for him.

She waited, her arms beginning to shake again. Was time passing? How long had she been lying here? It felt like a long time and yet it was probably only a minute.

Where was he? What was he doing? What was he *going* to do?

The music played and, although she strained to hear, she couldn't detect any movement anywhere.

Then something brushed over her nipple, something that felt white hot, scalding her tender flesh, yet at the same time sending an intense pulse of pleasure straight between her thighs.

Eva cried out, her brain struggling to make sense of the sensation as she arched helplessly against her restraints.

It happened again, a burning pain around her nipple. But at the same time not exactly pain either. She couldn't work out which it was. Then she felt something hot close around the same nipple and pressure, and realized that it was cold she'd been feeling. Cold that he'd just replaced with the heat of his mouth.

Sensation was a rip in reality, making her gasp and shudder. He alternated the icy cold with the heat of his mouth and the pressure of suction, heightening the feeling until it became acute. Until her body writhed. Until the darkness around her was full of jagged flashes of lightning, the music adding an agonizing classical soundtrack to the pleasure/pain.

And suddenly he was gone.

Eva panted, trembling. Every sense heightened and sensitized. Desperate to figure out where he was and whether he'd do it again. Her other nipple throbbed, hardened into a painful point. God, if he started there next, she'd scream.

But he didn't.

He ran the ice cube over the exquisitely sensitive flesh inside her elbow then the backs of her knees. Her spread inner thighs, making her jerk her ankles desperately to either close them or to urge his fingers higher, to where she was aching and hungry for more contact.

His tongue left trails of fire behind the cold burn of the ice, both sensations so intense she began to lose track of which was cold and which was hot. There was only this one feeling. Pleasure and pain so entwined together she couldn't tell one from the other.

It was heaven and hell. She wanted to it to stop and to never end.

The ice found her neglected breast at last and she did scream, another flash of lightning lighting up the dark behind her blindfold.

*Void. Void. Say it.*

No, fuck, she wouldn't. She'd had this battle with herself the first night he'd taken her and she'd won then. She'd win this now.

She had a damn reward to claim.

Eva screamed again as his mouth closed over her nipple and sucked hard. She was barely aware of the soft velvet beneath her or the material of the cuffs around her wrists and ankles. Her whole world was centered on her left breast and the movement of his mouth.

The unbelievable agony of the sensation. The incredible pleasure of it.

Then the heat around her nipple was gone. Her blindfold was ripped away, the headphones jerked off.

Light flooded her eyes and she blinked. After the music, the silence of the room was as loud as a crashing ocean. She could even hear the echoes of her own scream. Certainly someone was breathing harshly and fast. It was probably her.

Squinting against the sudden assault of light, her vision swam. And then came into focus on the man kneeling on the bed between her spread thighs like a conquering god.

His gaze was like the sun, too hot to bear, his jaw hard, his expression set. His whole posture was rigid, and sudden understanding struck her with the force of a blow.

He was rigid because he was struggling to maintain control and was probably finding this as difficult as she did. In punishing her, he was punishing himself too.

Good fucking job. Even though she wanted to give him this, she also didn't want to be the only one suffering.

"I didn't say it," she said in a cracked voice. "You can't stop yet because I didn't say the safeword."

His smile was feral. "Who said I was stopping? You have to see in order to fully experience this particular punishment."

Oh, God. What was he going to do now?

His hands fell to her stomach, trailing his fingers over it then down to lightly brush inner thighs. She groaned, her hips lifting reflexively off the bed. She could feel the heat of his skin next to hers. It was like a fire on a cold winter's day and she was freezing to death.

"Zac . . ." His name was a helpless whisper. "Please . . ."

That sharp, hungry smile became even sharper as slowly he leaned over her, one hand coming down beside her head. "Are you begging me, angel? Is that what you're doing?"

His other hand reached down to take hold of the hard length of his cock.

She stared, mesmerized by the sight, her breath coming faster and faster.

His hips flexed and she gave a little stuttered gasp as the head of his cock brushed through the folds of her sex, pushing lightly at the entrance of her body.

She arched up, desperate.

"You want this don't you?" he murmured. "You want my cock."

"Yes, yes, yes . . . God . . ."

"Well, you can't have it, Eva." He teased her again, circling her sex with the slick head, rubbing it against her clit. "You denied me your hot little pussy. Why should I give you my cock?"

Frustration clawed at her, a growl escaping as he drew his hips back, denying her.

God, she ached. The pulse between her thighs unbearable. Every part of her felt pushed and stretched. Like she was teetering on the brink of something yet not allowed to fall.

She stared up at him, into his amber eyes. Watched the flames leap there. Saw the anger and the desire and the pain, and a thousand other emotions she couldn't hope to untangle.

A complicated man. A man she didn't realize the worth of until this past week.

Until he'd opened her eyes.

"Do you want me to beg?" she whispered. "Because I will. I'll give you anything you want, Zac. Anything." And she meant every word of it. "Just take me. Please."

His expression tightened, the flames in his eyes burning even higher. He leaned down, his mouth inches from hers, so all she could see was his golden eyes, the heat in them like the corona of the sun. "No."

Before she could speak, he shoved himself away from her and got up off the bed.

Shaking, she watched as he began to undo the restraints, unhooking the straps from the hooks in the bedposts, then taking them off the cuffs.

The release of the tension made her arms ache, the blood rushing back into her fingers and toes. With a certain matter-of-factness, Zac examined her extremities, chafing them to make sure the circulation had returned.

Even that light touch made her groan. Made her desperate for more. Her thighs felt slick, her sex throbbing.

She had no idea what he was going to do next and was afraid of it. Yet at the same time, she was also afraid that he would stop. That he would think she couldn't deal and give up.

"Please don't tell me that's it," she forced out, her voice

barely sounding like her own. "If my count is right, that's only four punishments."

Finishing coiling up the straps, he put them on the bedside nightstand, then stood back to survey her. "Perhaps I should stop. Perhaps you're liking this too much."

She pushed herself up on her elbows, absurdly angry with him. "No, fuck that. I want my reward. And shit, if ice cubes and blindfolds are all you've got, then you'd better give it to me now."

Zac stared at her for a long moment. Then he turned and stalked down the side to the foot of the bed, graceful as a panther. "That," he said, "is not all I've got."

He got onto the bed, kneeling on the quilt. Then before she could move, he'd pulled her into his lap in one easy, fluid motion, turning her over so she was spread over his knees, her face turned toward the quilt, her butt in the air.

Oh fuck. She had an idea where this was going.

One arm pressed down hard on her back, keeping her in place.

"Zac." His name was a frightened breath of sound, fear curling tight in her gut. Was he going to . . . hit her?

The palm of his other hand came to rest on her buttocks, the heat of it making her swallow. "Punishment five. You caused me pain, Eva." He didn't add any other explanation, but her brain had no problem filling in.

*You caused me pain. Now it's your turn to feel it.*

Eva stared at the dark blue quilt, trying to calm herself the hell down.

"Seven strikes for seven years," he said, his voice rolling over her in a dark wave. "You count them out. And ask me for more after each one. I'll pause to allow you to use your safeword if you need to."

No, damn him. She wouldn't need the safeword. She

would handle it like she'd handled everything else. Even this, being spanked like a naughty child.

She clenched her teeth. "I won't need to."

Seven strikes. Easy.

But she knew, as soon as the first blow fell, that anything involving Zac Rutherford was never going to be easy.

It hurt. The shock of his hand striking her sensitive flesh, the sound it made in the room. Because he didn't hold back, she felt the strength behind the blow, the sharp sting it left behind. Yet that wasn't the worst part. The worst part was when that same hand dipped between her thighs, his long, blunt fingers stroking the folds of her sex, brushing her clit, circling the entrance to her body, probing gently yet not pushing in.

"One," she gasped, unable to help herself from pushing into his hand.

"What else, Eva?" He pressed against her clit. "Don't make me ask again."

"More . . . please."

His hand fell again. And again it hurt. And again he somehow turned the pain into astonishing pleasure.

She counted out each blow, panting, and when she said "more," it wasn't only a repeat of the word he wanted her to say. She began to mean it. As if she wanted more of his hand cracking sharply against her flesh, more of the burn that came afterwards. And especially more of the heel of his hand bearing down on her clit, making her shift and grind against it, trying to find relief.

But there was none.

He was merciless. Holding her on the brink of climax like he had downstairs. So close and yet so far. Every blow seemed designed to inch her closer, the movement of his hand another push toward it. Then he'd take his hand away so she was left trembling and aching with a hunger he wouldn't feed.

She tried to shift and rub against his knee, desperate for some friction, but all he said was, "If you move again, I'll stop."

So she stilled, her fists clenched in the soft velvet of the quilt, her lip sore from where she hadn't been able to stop herself from biting it.

She would endure. She had to.

As the seventh blow fell, she pressed her face into the quilt. Her butt felt like it was on fire, her skin tight and sore and sensitive. It also felt as if the slightest touch would send her over the edge into orgasm. The heat of his bare thighs against hers was almost an agony.

Zac's hand touched her, caressing her sore behind, and a pathetic, needy little sound escaped her.

"I know," he said. "But now you have punishment number six."

A full-body shiver shook her. She turned her head on the quilt, the material damp beneath her. Shit, were those tears? Had he made her cry? Perhaps they were because it felt like there was a vast lump of emotion sitting in her chest and throat. As if the pleasure/pain had coalesced inside her and was trying to find a way out somehow.

"I'm going to fuck you, Eva." Zac ran a hand along her spine to the back of her neck, curling his fingers around it in a possessive hold. "But you're not allowed to come on my cock. You have to wait until I've finished before you can come."

She swallowed, squeezing her eyes shut. Impossible. That was going to be impossible. "I . . . can't . . ." she whispered. "I'm too close . . ."

"That's too bad. You left me with only my hand for pleasure when I could have been balls deep inside that sweet little pussy of yours. So now it's your turn to feel the loss."

He shifted, easing her off him and onto her hands and knees, facing away from him. She heard foil being unwrapped, a second's pause, and then his arm coming around her waist, holding her in an iron grip.

Heat against her spine, against the backs of her thighs, against the tender flesh of her butt. The shift and flex of a big, hard, muscular body.

She gripped the quilt tightly, trying to breathe, trying to think of anything other than what he was about to do and about how she was going to fall at this final hurdle. Because all he'd have to do is slide into her and she'd come . . .

Eva bit down hard on her already bitten lower lip, the pain holding the climax at bay as he thrust into her in one deep, hard motion. Without waiting to give her time to adjust, he withdrew and thrust again. Deeper. Harder.

He slid a hand around to her stomach and down, his fingers finding her swollen, aching clit, and brushed over it, around it.

Unfair. So unfair.

The climax ripped her in two and she had to bury her face against the softness of the quilt, sobbing and shaking as it crashed through her. She'd failed. She'd fucking failed.

Now she'd never get to touch him.

She cried, but Zac didn't stop. He reached for her hair, wound it around his wrist and jerked her head back while continuing to thrust deep and hard, his other hand on her clit driving her back up toward another climax.

Against that assault, her grip on reality began to loosen. Her grip on herself.

What did it matter now, anyway? Fighting wasn't going to help, if it ever had, and besides, she didn't have the energy for it anymore. He hadn't wanted her to hold out anyway. He'd wanted her surrender.

So she gave it.

This time, when the orgasm came for her, when Zac pulled hard on her hair, tugging her head back, she didn't resist or struggle. Only opened herself up to the intensity of the pleasure, let it sweep her away.

Let it become her whole world.

Walking willingly into the flames and letting herself burn.

# CHAPTER SEVENTEEN

He felt like he was drowning. In slick heat and sweet, feminine musk. In the broken little sounds she made as he slammed himself into her. In the tight clasp of her pussy around his cock.

Everything he'd ever wanted.

Zac tightened his arm around her waist as she convulsed around him, her desperate cry echoing around the room. Yes, he'd been a deliberate bastard, ensuring there was no way she'd be able to obey his order, but she'd told him not to hold back and so he hadn't.

He knew she wouldn't be able to withstand too much more. But then there had been many impossible tasks that she'd doled out to him and this was all about returning the favor.

Impossible tasks such as not touching her. Not wanting her. Not caring for her.

*Not falling for her.*

No, not that. Never that.

He growled low in his throat, pulling her hips hard against his, burying himself so deeply inside of her she'd never be able to forget the feel of him, the heat of him. Then he tugged against the hair around his wrist, tightening the tension so her long, pale throat was exposed. He stroked faster in and out of her, building the pleasure for himself this time. Watching her back bow and her neck arch, listening to her soft cries.

He could feel the climax start coiling at the base of his spine, ready to explode. Christ, it would kill him. He'd held back too long.

As it built, Zac let go of her hair, leaning over her. Putting his hands down on either side of her head, covering her. He wanted suddenly to be all around her, keeping her safe with his body.

*Never let her go.*

He thrust one more time, feeling it start to explode inside him, and he turned his face against the side of her neck and bit her, the salt of her skin a delicious counterpoint to the pleasure crashing through him.

It felt like the end of the world, the end of his entire existence. And what's more, he was glad about it. He had Eva beneath him, naked and panting and hot. That's all he needed.

There was a peace to that thought. A peace it felt like he'd been searching his whole life to find and for a second he let himself just exist in the moment.

Of course it couldn't last. Because this had only ever been about sating a desire.

Sating it then moving on, the last of his seven punishments. Giving her the absence she'd so often given him.

He opened his eyes on pale hair and white skin. She was still on her hands and knees, her head hanging down, her body trembling under his. His arm was around her waist, her butt pressed to his groin, fitting him perfectly.

Everything about her fitted him perfectly.

Too perfectly. He didn't want to leave.

Her shoulders shook, her breathing hitched.

She was crying.

Zac eased out of her, stroking down the curve of her spine, then turning her over onto her back on the bed. She flung an arm over her face, her cheeks pink and shiny with tears.

Quickly, he got off the bed and dealt with the condom in the ensuite bathroom, then came back, wrapped her up in the blue velvet quilt, pulled her into his arms, and carried her over to the black leather couch and sat down on it.

"I don't know why I'm crying," she said thickly. "It didn't hurt or anything."

"Pain and intense pleasure can release certain emotions," he answered, smoothing her hair over the quilt. "It can be an emotional release as well as a physical one."

There was a box of tissues on the table near the couch and he leaned forward, taking out a few and handing them to her.

She glared at him as she took the tissues. "You're not crying."

"I'm not the sub." Yet his heart was beating fast and for some reason he was finding it difficult to look at her. Her tears . . . they made his chest feel like someone had wrapped barbed wire around it.

Well, it wouldn't matter soon enough. He was going to make sure she was okay then he was going to leave. That had always been his intention.

*You don't want to.*

No. He wouldn't grant her that power. The power to make him stay.

"So it's a sub thing then?" She blew her nose almost defiantly.

"It's a sub thing," he agreed.

She lowered the tissue. "I don't want to be just another sub to you, Zac."

"You're not." He'd never lied to her before. He wasn't about to start now. "You're actually the first woman I've ever bought into this bedroom."

She blinked, tears caught on her lashes glittering in the light. "But you've got those . . . hooks in the bedpost. Surely . . ."

"No." It was hard to meet her bright silver gaze, though he didn't really understand why. "I've never used them. When I want a woman I go to Limbo, the club I used to belong to."

"Used to?" She'd settled against him the way she had that night he'd held her in his arms and fed her treats. Her pale hair was silky and soft, spread over his bare skin, the warm weight of her in the quilt making him not want to let her go.

*You really don't want to.*

He ignored the voice in his head because he would let her go eventually. Inflict his last punishment. Just . . . not quite yet.

"I stopped going a year or so ago."

Her head turned against his chest, looking up at him. "Why?"

"I didn't want any of the women there." This time he didn't flinch from her gaze. Because this was all part of it, the anger inside of him wanting her to know what she'd done to him. "They didn't do anything for me."

Puzzlement flickered over her tear-stained face. "So . . . where did you go instead? I mean, if you didn't bring women back here, did you go . . . I don't know, somewhere else?"

"I didn't go anywhere."

"Why . . ." She trailed off all of a sudden, her eyes widening. "Please don't tell me you haven't been with anyone in over a year."

He didn't reply, only lifted a strand of her hair, winding it casually around his finger.

"Zac," she said, stricken. "That . . . that can't possibly be because of me."

"Why can't it?"

"Because . . . Because I . . ." She stopped, and he saw anger glittering in her eyes. "No," she said flatly. "No, I won't take that blame. That's all on you. That's your choice—"

He stopped her words dead, reaching down to grip her jaw tightly. Because there was anger inside of him too, and it felt like it had been there for centuries. Lifetimes. Because the harder he forced it down, the more it escaped his grasp. Because she called it from him so easily. She was the firestone that made the dragon breathe flame.

*And you know why.*

He forced that thought away, locked it away in the box where he kept all such thoughts. Where they could never escape.

"You made me want you, Eva. You made me burn like a fucking virgin. You made—"

Unexpectedly, Eva jerked herself from his grip and pushed herself up. Already, like a reflex he was reaching for her, keeping her with him, but she didn't actually get off his lap.

Instead she twisted around so she was straddling him, facing him, her palms hard against the bare skin of his chest, her face inches from his.

"No more fucking Dom shit," she said fiercely. "I want to know why the hell you're so angry. And it's not with me."

Shock broke over him in a wave. Of course he was angry, it didn't take a genius to work that one out. But it was directed at her. Wasn't it? After all, she was the one who denied him. Who kept him waiting for so long, burning for so long.

*She's not the first woman to hurt you.*

The shock turned to ice, sliding down his spine, more memories threatening to escape. Memories he'd deliberately cut from his life. In anger. In grief. Memories of another woman he hadn't been able to save.

He took Eva's wrists in an iron grip, pulled them away from his chest. "I didn't give you permission to touch me."

That fierce anger flicked over her face as she pulled her wrists free. "I don't care. I didn't do what you told me anyway, remember? I came when you didn't want me to. Because you're a prick and you made sure I couldn't stop it."

"It's not a punishment if I can't make it difficult for you."

"Why are you punishing me at all?" Her sharp, gray eyes searched his face. "Or maybe it's not me you're punishing."

He could feel it, the defenses he'd placed around all those memories, starting to kick in. Warning him to attack, fight off the threat.

*Keep her safe. Protect her.*

He put his hands on Eva's warm, silky skin, preparing to push her off. The last punishment. It was time.

But before he could, she leaned forward, taking his face between her small hands, holding him fast. Her breasts grazed his chest, sending fire through him, and he could feel himself getting hard again. Will burned in her gaze, as hard and as strong as his.

"I gave you myself, Zac Rutherford. I took your punishments. I fucking surrendered." Her gaze was molten, like quicksilver. "Don't you think I've earned the right to ask you a few questions, goddammit?"

Inside his chest, something twisted. A hollow, yearning kind of ache. Like there was a part of him that was tired of being nothing but a façade, who wanted to be seen. The part of him that seemed entirely composed of guilt and grief and anger. The part that wanted more than sex, more than domination. That wanted a connection.

He went still. Unable to push her off him, unable to let her go.

A crease appeared between her fair brows and gently her thumbs began to trace the line of his jaw in the kind of caress he used to dream about at night. A nonsexual touch. One that was about comfort, about care. One that told him he was precious. That he mattered.

He hadn't mattered to anyone in a long time, if he ever had.

"Don't," he said thickly. By which he meant "don't ever stop."

She seemed to understand because she didn't stop, her thumbs caressing his face, tracing his jaw, his cheekbones, his mouth.

"No one's ever pushed you, have they?" she said quietly. "I bet no one was ever brave enough."

Bloody hell, she was going to undo him.

Too late. He was already undone.

"It's not me, is it?" The tip of one finger traced his lower lip. "What happened, Zac? You can trust me. Was it the prison?" A pause. "Your parents?"

He'd been protecting her a long time. Her story. Her memory. The girl he couldn't save, no matter how hard he tried. The girl who wouldn't let him save her.

Theresa.

He met Eva's perceptive gaze. Out of all the people he could have told, she was possibly the only one who would understand. Perhaps she might even know why it had happened, because even now, some twenty years later, he sure as hell fucking didn't.

One thing he was sure of though. He'd pushed too hard. Pushed when he shouldn't have.

"Don't shut me out, Zac," Eva whispered. "Please."

*"Don't shut me out, Theresa. Tell me what's wrong. Tell me what I can do to help you."*

"I had a little sister," he said, not even knowing he was going to say it until it came out. "Her name was Theresa."

The crease between Eva's brows deepened. "You never mentioned her."

"No, I didn't." He never did. He kept Theresa's memory locked up safe in the box in his mind. Where no one could get to her, harm her, ever again.

Eva's caressing thumbs paused. "What happened to her?"

The filthy squat he'd found her in was still there in his head. An abandoned building in Brixton she and her junkie friends had taken over. Peeling wallpaper and dirty mattresses on the floor. Blocked toilets and moldy showers. The smell of vomit and cigarettes, and spilled alcohol heavy in the air.

And Theresa, splayed on one of those mattresses like a broken doll, without dignity or care. Her mouth open, her eyes glassy, stringy black hair everywhere. So pale.

Dead at eighteen.

"She died," he said. "It was my fault."

Eva stared into Zac's dark face, her heart going tight and small in her chest. The expression in his amber eyes had gone flat, but she could see the barely concealed pain in them. It leaked out like blood in a pool of water, staining everything. His features were stone, his jaw tight with control—she could feel the muscle go hard beneath the tips of her fingers.

She wanted to comfort him in some way but she didn't know how. No one had ever comforted her when she'd been in pain, and she wasn't sure what was involved. Hugs and such probably, but hugging, any kind of touch, wasn't exactly something she'd had experience in either. Then again, he hadn't pulled away from her fingers on his face. Perhaps he liked it. Certainly she did, the feeling of his warm skin and the roughness of stubble along his jaw a sensual pleasure she'd never imagined.

So she kept her fingers where they were, stroking him lightly, hoping it helped the pain she saw in his eyes. "Tell me what happened," she said and she didn't make it a request.

"There's not much to tell. Theresa was three years younger than me and I tried to protect her from what went on with my parents. Tried to give her the attention they didn't, make her childhood as normal as I could. Which wasn't very normal all things considered, but I did what I could." He paused, the look on his face going distant. "I told her all about addiction. How it could leave you an empty shell. How it destroyed you. How it destroyed our parents." His gaze met hers. "They usually took their drugs in their bedroom, and once I let her see them passed out on their bed. They never cleaned, would never let any of the maids inside, and the room was filthy. It stank and there was rubbish everywhere. I wanted her to see all of that though. I wanted her to see the squalor of it so she'd know what addiction led to."

Foreboding twisted inside Eva's chest. Fear for the boy he must have been, trying to do the right thing for his baby sister.

She shifted in his lap, letting her fingers trail down the sides of his strong neck then back up again. Again, he didn't pull away so she kept doing it. "I take it . . ." she broke off.

"No," he confirmed. "It didn't work. She fell in with a bad crowd when she was fifteen. Started smoking pot, dropped out of school, then got hooked onto other things. I tried to help her. Got her into another school, did some tough love with her friends, imposed a curfew. And that helped for a little while." There was stark pain in his eyes, a brief flash of it, bright as a freshly sharpened blade. "She was good for a year, at a boarding school that helped kids who went off the rails. I'd joined the army by that stage and visited her as often as I could. But somewhere along the line, she slipped away from me. I don't know why. I don't know what she was looking for or what she got out of the drugs she kept injecting. All I know was that the more I tried to hold onto her, the more she escaped." His hands came up all of a sudden, gripping her wrists and pulling her fingers away from him. "She ran away from school and disappeared. It took me weeks to find her. For some reason she'd fallen back into her old crowd and they'd found a squat in a shady part of London, an abandoned building they started living in basically."

She tried to pull her hands away from his imprisoning grip, but his fingers around her wrists were like iron.

"Theresa had started injecting. Heroin. I tried to stop her. I argued. I cajoled. I bribed. I even called the police to raid the building. She wouldn't talk to me in the end, wouldn't even see me. Whenever I came to visit, she'd turn her face to the wall and ignore me. And then, just after her eighteenth birthday, I got a call from one of her so-called friends. She'd OD'd." Zac's voice had gone hard and flat, though she could hear the despair and hopelessness running through it, undermining everything like a stream of water undermines a bank of loose earth.

She swallowed. "How could you think it was your fault though? You didn't hold the needle. You didn't push it into her arm."

"I pushed her, Eva. I pushed and pushed and pushed. Right from when she was little, I told her the dangers. I showed her the evidence."

His fingers pressed against the fragile bones in her wrists. There would be bruises later, but she didn't pull away. She didn't want to do anything that might cause him to stop talking, to shut her out again. A few bruises were nothing. "You did what you thought was right, Zac. You were trying to prevent her from falling into the same trap."

"But what if I hadn't shown her Mum drooling on her pillow. Dad lying in a puddle of his own piss? What if I hadn't talked to her about drugs and what they did to your body? I planted the seeds. I put the idea in her head. And then later, I pushed her too hard. Perhaps if I'd walked away, she might have come to it in her own time. She might have done better. But I couldn't leave it alone. I couldn't—" He broke off all of a sudden. Then he dropped her wrists, shifting her off his lap, and rose from the couch in a restless, fluid movement. Striding toward the ensuite, he disappeared inside, shutting the door firmly behind him.

The sound of it closing echoed through the room, heavy with finality.

Eva stared at the door, clutching the velvet quilt more firmly around her as the cold began to creep over her skin. Her chest hurt. She felt like she'd been taken from a cozy place in front of the fire and dropped into a snowdrift.

He was an intensely private man, she knew this about him. All those years and they'd never shared themselves with each other, and with good reason. Both of them had scars and clearly his were still bloody and raw.

The need to comfort him, do something for him, bloomed inside her, pressing insistently against her skin.

It would be easy to let him shut her out, to let him have the space he wanted, to not push him. Because after all, what did she know about helping someone with their pain? What did she know about comfort? About protecting someone, shielding them. Healing them.

Nothing. She knew nothing at all.

She swallowed, her throat thick.

The need to go to him pressed harder. Shoving at her insides. He had no one else, she knew that now. He was as alone as she was. Locked safe in the armor he'd protected himself with. The suit, the calm manner, the image of the perfect English gentleman.

But she'd seen underneath. Seen the heat and passion of the man inside that armor, a man full of anger and pain, with tattoos on his skin and scars on his heart.

She couldn't let him shut that man away. She had to let him know he wasn't alone. After all, he'd always been there for her. Why shouldn't she be there for him? He wasn't the only one who could push.

Eva gathered the quilt around herself and slipped off the couch, going over to the door of the ensuite.

"Zac." She put her hand on the door. "Can I come in?"

There was no answer.

"Zac. Come on. You can't just tell me all that stuff then walk away."

Again. Nothing.

The pain in her chest constricted. No, he couldn't do this to her, the prick. He couldn't lay her bare the way he had and then walk away when it was his turn. It didn't work that way.

She tried the door handle, but it was locked. Anger blossomed. She hit the wood hard with her palm. "Open the damn door, asshole! You think I'm going to let you walk away from me? You didn't let me do it so why should I let you?"

More silence.

Eva pulled her hand back to hit the door again, when suddenly the lock clicked and it opened a crack. Zac's face was like iron, his amber eyes cold. "Get dressed. I'll get Temple to take you home."

"Fuck that." Propelled by anger and a fear she couldn't name, Eva dropped the quilt from around her shoulders, then shoved the door open with as much strength as she could.

Taken by surprise, Zac shifted back and she took the

opening, stepping into the bathroom before he could close the door again.

She didn't stop, moving forward, sliding her arms around his waist, pressing her naked body up against all that bare, bronze skin. She didn't know what to say to him to show him he wasn't alone, but she could show him. Like he'd shown her. Touch had a language all its own and she was only just now discovering how powerful that could be.

"Eva, stop." His fingers were tight around her upper arms and the cold look in his eyes had given way to anger. "It's best if you go."

She ignored him, locking her arms around him, tilting her head back to meet his furious gaze. "Why? Because you don't want to talk about it? Because you don't want to remember? Well back at you, asshole. You can't take all my secrets from me, make me remember all the most agonizing things in my life, and then refuse to do it yourself. I won't let you."

His hands tightened painfully. "I told you pushing me was a bad idea."

"So you keep saying. And I still don't know why."

Gold flashed in his eyes. And suddenly she was being lifted in his arms without any ceremony at all and shoved onto the white marble vanity behind him. Then he held her there, his fingers pressing into her hips. "I don't want you poking and prodding at my fucking life," he said fiercely. "And if I don't want you to talk about it, I don't want you to fucking talk about it!"

She ignored him and the painful grip he had on her hips. "I get it. You're still protecting her. And, God, I'm not trying to take that away from you, understand?" She reached out, took his face in her hands again, held him as tight as he was holding her. "I only want to show you you're not alone. That I'm here if you need me." The tight feeling was back in her chest again, the hurt that wasn't hers, but his. How strange to take someone's pain like that, to feel it like it was yours too. "You helped me, Zac. You were there for me. Please let me be there for you."

The look in his eyes burned into her, no longer cold. Fierce and hot as a lake of fire. "You want to be there for me?" He released her quite suddenly, stepping back in a quick, sharp movement. "Then get on your knees."

Eva's eyes widened and for a moment she only stared at him. Then her jaw firmed and she pushed herself off the vanity, dropping gracefully to her knees on the floor.

This wouldn't be what she wanted but he didn't care.

She'd gotten too close. Too close to memories he didn't want to dredge up again. Of a failure he couldn't quite put behind him no matter how hard he tried. And he was pissed, that anger that was always there, that wouldn't leave him alone, boiling up inside him like all his blood had been superheated.

He couldn't lock it down. Not with her. She seemed to get underneath all the walls he'd put in place to protect both her and himself. No, not get underneath. She fucking kicked them down, smashed them. With only the touch of her hand and the soft heat of her body. The look in her eyes that told him she knew. That she understood.

But he didn't want that look or that understanding. Didn't want any of it focused on him. Because he needed those walls. Or else the pain and the anger of his failure to protect the only person in the world who meant anything to him would destroy him.

He had to protect himself, protect Theresa's memory. And there was only one way he knew of to do that.

Distance Eva. Take control.

Eva looked up at him, a beautiful flush staining her cheeks and neck, reaching further down. She must know what was coming, what to expect.

He wasn't going to disappoint her. Already he was hard, the press of her body and touch of her skin enough for his dick to get the message and declare an interest.

"Open your mouth," he ordered, a harsh edge entering his voice. The anger starting to bleed through.

She did, without hesitation.

He reached for her jaw, holding it with one hand. "Suck me."

Her throat moved, uncertainty in her eyes. But she reached for him, the soft touch of her hand on his cock making him ache. Then she leaned forward and swirled her tongue around the head.

It was not what he was expecting, the slick warmth sending his heartbeat racing and his mouth dry, ripples of electricity arcing through his body. She licked him again, her tongue running down the length of his dick then back up.

Then she opened her mouth and swallowed him whole.

Heat engulfed him, a sharp growl escaping from his throat. The pleasure was indescribable, becoming even more acute when she ran her hands up the backs of his thighs, holding on to him as she increased the suction.

Her inexperience was obvious but somehow that only made it even better. Hotter. More erotic. Her nails dug into the backs of his thighs, and he found he was cupping her face in his hands, watching her suck him, her pale lips wrapped around his cock.

It was the most erotic thing he'd ever seen in his life.

There were some commands he should be saying, words to control what she was doing to him but he couldn't remember what they were. She'd somehow taken the power away from him and he realized, with a shock, that this was a scene in which he didn't have control. She did.

He'd had plenty of subs who tried to direct a scene with

a bit of subtle Dom manipulation. Topping from the bottom. He'd always been wise to their tricks.

But this was Eva and she had no tricks. No manipulations.

All she had was honesty and determination, and the power to crack him apart like an egg. Power he'd given her from the moment he'd met her.

Why hadn't he seen that? Why hadn't he realized? He'd never wanted anyone to have the power over his emotions that Theresa had. The power to destroy him like Theresa had.

He should be shoving her away, walking out that door, and yet pleasure began to overwhelm him in a way he hadn't experienced in years, not since he'd first walked into a BDSM club and an experienced sub had taken one look at him and handed him a whip.

Eva's hands cupped his butt, digging her fingers into the tight muscles, her head moving as she sucked hard on him.

His knees were weak and he had to lean back against the vanity to stop himself from dropping to the floor. "Angel," he said raggedly. "Oh, fuck . . . angel . . ."

*She will break you.*

No. She'd broken him already. All she was doing now was picking up the pieces.

He tipped his head back as pleasure gripped tight, drowning even his anger, leaving him with nothing but this feeling. Eva's mouth around him and her hands on him. Holding him up.

He groaned as the climax threatened. "Stop. Christ . . . Eva . . . stop." But she didn't, so he pushed his fingers into her hair and pulled her away. She made a soft sound of protest, which he ignored as he bent to scoop her up from the floor. Turning, he lifted her up onto the vanity again, pushing her back against the white marble, easing her thighs apart.

He wanted to be inside her so badly. And he'd thought he could hold her back, keep her at a distance. But she wouldn't be distanced.

As he pulled a condom from the vanity drawer and protected himself with it, she leaned forward, winding one arm around his neck, reaching for his cock with the other. Then she gripped him and lifted her hips, sheathing him in slick silk and hot velvet.

He stilled, all the breath taken from him, as the astonishing heat of her pussy clenched tightly around him. Her legs circled his hips, her naked body pressing up against him, the softness of her breasts against his chest, her mouth finding the hollow of his throat.

He felt the lick of her tongue on his skin, then the sharp bite of her teeth.

Warrior. Angel. Seductress.

"Eva," he whispered, his hands full of her hair, pulling her back so he could take back the control.

She didn't let him.

Her mouth found his, her wicked little tongue flicking inside, exploring hesitantly at first then with more confidence. Seducing him with her sweetness and inexperience, her hunger. She moved against him, her hips undulating, the feel of her body around his aching cock so exquisite, he knew it wouldn't take long for him to come.

A voice in his head was shouting at him to take back the control, dominate her, distance her, but he couldn't bring himself to do it.

He'd never had gentleness. He'd never had sweetness. He'd never had a woman run her hands up the back of his neck, cradling his head in her small palms, her fingers twining his hair as she kissed him to ecstasy.

And he let her because he couldn't help himself. Because that hunger inside him, the dragon, was desperate for tenderness, for connection.

Because Eva King had always had the power to break him. He'd given it to her long ago.

The orgasm, when it came, almost crushed him. He called her name as it pulled him under, turned him over and over, and nearly drowned him. Then it receded, leaving him gasping, leaning forward against the vanity and shaking, the warmth of her body wrapped around him.

He felt her head rest against his shoulder, her breath soft against his skin. And for a long, long time, they remained like that, neither of them ready to move or break the silence.

After a while, he touched her hair, sifting the silky strands through his fingers. "You didn't stop when I told you." His voice sounded rough, not like his at all.

"Yeah, I know." Her hand drifted down his back, stroking. "Perhaps you'll have to punish me. You still have one left, remember?"

It was odd but right now, he seemed to have lost his taste for punishment. "I don't want to punish you anymore tonight."

She let out a breath, the warmth of it chasing over her skin. "I'm good with that."

He let his fingers tighten in her hair. "But I don't want to talk either."

"Then we won't. But don't . . . go off and shut the door on me again."

Zac raised his head and looked down.

Brilliant silver eyes met his.

"We have the rest of the night." He touched her mouth, traced her lower lip with one finger, feeling the softness of it. "So get back into bed. I have a favor to return."

# CHAPTER EIGHTEEN

Honor watched her mother flutter around her husband's wheelchair, adjusting the blanket covering him and making sure he was comfortable. The orderlies had come to transport him to another hospital, a private one where he could convalesce from the gunshot wound that had nearly taken his life a month earlier.

His speech was slurred and he had difficulty walking, so he needed care that her mother couldn't provide. He also had difficulties with his memory, and that didn't make things any easier. But he was alive and that was all that mattered.

As the orderlies wheeled Guy from the room, Honor began to gather up the last of his belongings. There were only a few, a couple of books her mother had brought in hoping he'd be able to read (he hadn't), some spare items of clothing, a toothbrush in the adjacent bathroom.

She'd almost finished packing them all away in the bag she'd brought, when she spotted Guy's overcoat hanging from a coat stand near the windows. The nursing staff must have hung it up when he'd been brought in, and clearly Elizabeth had forgotten to pack it up with his other clothes.

Honor crossed the room and lifted his coat off the hook, taking a reflexive look out the window as she did so. There was a view of the street below and she could see Guy being loaded into the ambulance that was going to take him to the new hospital, her mother following him in.

A discreet distance away were the two bodyguards Zac had hired after Guy had gotten shot. In case whoever it was who'd shot him decided to come and finish the job.

The two guards moved toward a car, ready to follow the ambulance.

As the car pulled out into the traffic, Honor's attention was caught by another movement. The tall, arresting figure of a man. Initially she thought it was Zac since he was about the same height and build, wore an overcoat against the March chill, late winter snowflakes settling in his black hair.

But no, it wasn't Zac. This man had rough, blunt features and scars twisting his mouth.

He was standing on the sidewalk staring after the retreating ambulance, his hands thrust into the pockets of his overcoat. Menace radiated from him though she couldn't have said exactly why.

Abruptly he looked up, and eyes as black as ink met hers.

A chill entered her blood.

Instinct had her backing sharply away from the window, her heart beating fast, only to come to a complete stop in the middle of the room.

God, what the hell was wrong with her? The man was a complete stranger, so why was she getting all wound up?

Irritated, she eased closer to the window again, checking to see if he was still there.

The sidewalk was empty.

Oddly shaken and annoyed with herself, Honor threw the overcoat over her arm, turning on her heel to leave the room.

A piece of paper fluttered to the ground.

Frowning, she bent to pick it up, unfolding it to see what it was.

Her heart froze solid in her chest.

Slowly, she took a couple of steps back to the empty hospital bed and sat down on it, reading over the piece of paper once more to make sure she hadn't misinterpreted what she'd seen.

She hadn't.

Shit. Shit. Shit.

Folding it up, she stowed it carefully away inside her purse. Then she grabbed her phone.

"Hey, baby." Gabriel's deep, rough voice eased the cold feeling in her heart. "What's up?"

"Are you at home?"

"Yeah." There was a pause. Then, sharper, "Are you okay?"

She wasn't. Not really. But it wasn't anything she could tell him over the phone. "I need to show you something."

As soon as Gabriel saw Honor's face, he knew that whatever she was going to show him was going to be bad.

She tossed a man's overcoat over the back of his big leather sofa as she came into the lounge area, but held onto her purse. The weak, cold light of the afternoon shone through the massive windows of his apartment, making her pale face look even paler, her blue eyes darker.

"Tell me," he said brusquely.

"Actually, I think it's better if I show you." She opened up her purse, took the small folded piece of paper out, and crossed the room to where he stood by the windows, her heels tapping on the polished wood floorboards.

He'd remember that sound afterwards. And the darkness of her eyes.

Foreboding clenched tight inside him as he moved, meeting her in the middle of the room, taking her face in his hands and tilting her head back. "Are you all right?" he demanded, suddenly cold with fear. "Is there any-thing—"

"It's not me, Gabe," she interrupted. "I'm fine, okay? I promise."

The fist in his chest loosened and he bent his head, claiming her mouth in a hungry kiss, his hands sliding over her hips and down over the curve of her butt, pulling her hard against him, suddenly needing the taste of her and the reassurance of her warm body.

She returned the kiss for a long moment, just as hun-gry as he was. Then she pulled away, shoving the piece of paper at him again. "You need to read this."

"I'd rather fuck you on the couch."

"Gabriel. It's important."

"So is my cock."

But she only looked at him. Of course he was stalling and they both knew it.

Reluctantly, he reached for the paper, unfolding it and looking down.

It took him a moment to figure out exactly what he was looking at. "This . . . is a paternity test."

"Yes." Her voice sounded strained. "It fell out of Dad's overcoat when I was at the hospital packing up his things."

There were two sets of results from the looks of it. The one for Guy Tremain was negative, but the other . . . was not.

The fist in his chest was back, locking tight fingers around his heart.

Somehow Tremain had gotten hold of Gabriel's DNA, matching it against his own. And someone else's.

A warm hand rested on his back, a slender figure at his side.

The world settled back into familiar lines.

Once, this piece of paper would have changed his life.

Would have made him so angry he'd have committed all manner of violence in the name of revenge. In the name of filling up the void inside of him.

But that void was now filled. He wasn't empty anymore. He had Honor.

Knowing Evelyn Fitzgerald was his father changed nothing.

He glanced up and found the blue eyes of the woman he loved looking anxiously at him. "Gabe?" she asked uncertainly. "I know, this is a horrible shock but—"

"It doesn't matter." Gabriel let the paper fall to the ground. Then he pulled her into his arms. "At least, he doesn't matter to me."

She relaxed against him, her arms winding around his neck, but her gaze was still anxious and searching. "You'll tell the others though?"

"Yeah. Though this won't make any difference to what we decide to do."

"What if Eva tells us it's not him? That he didn't do those things?"

"Then nothing." His arms tightened around her. "I don't want anything from him. Like I said, he doesn't matter. The only thing that matters to me is you."

The tense look on her face eased a fraction. "But what if he's behind whatever happened to Eva? And . . . Daniel . . ."

Gabriel gathered her closer to him. "We'll cross that bridge when we come to it."

She searched his face a long moment. "If he's the one who hurt Eva, Zac won't sit by twiddling his thumbs, even if he knows Fitzgerald is your father."

Gabriel smiled and it wasn't a pleasant one. "Like I said, I don't care. If Zac wants to take the law into his own hands, that's up to him. I won't stop him."

Honor let out a breath, a small blue spark of pain flaring in her eyes. "What about Violet? God, Gabriel. She's your half sister."

Fuck, so she was. After years of being an only child, he now had a sibling.

Not quite sure how to deal with that, he bent, brushing Honor's mouth with his instead. Soothing her. "We can't do anything until we hear from Eva. Violet will have to wait."

"You're right." Honor leaned her head against his shoulder. "You're taking this very well, I have to say."

"Hey, I always knew my father was going to be a prick. Knowing he's an even bigger prick than I first thought isn't too much of a stretch." He caressed the long, elegant arch of her spine. "If he's the one who ordered your father killed and threatened you though, I might be forced to take action."

She looked up at him and a ghost of a smile turned her mouth. "Little boy, you might just have to get in line."

At that moment, Gabriel's phone went off. A text.

Keeping a firm arm around Honor, he hauled it out of his pocket and glanced down at the screen. It was from Eva and consisted of two words.

*It's him.*

Eva finished sending her text then dropped her phone back down on the bed and went over to the only other piece of furniture in the room—her chest of drawers. Pulling out some jeans, she rummaged around in her T-shirt drawer trying to find something she wanted to wear but ending up feeling vaguely disgruntled.

Black. That's all there was. Black T-shirt after black T-shirt. It had never bothered her before because she'd never consciously thought about her clothing, but now . . .

*You want to wear something nice for him.*

Eva grimaced. Jesus, if she was getting into primping

and preening over Zac, she was a lost cause. Not to mention an idiot. Especially when she'd woken up that morning, extremely late, to find the bed empty and Zac gone.

She'd been angry about that. And hurt, no denying it. He'd left her a note telling her he had a few things to do at his office in the Meatpacking District and asking her to organize a Circles meeting as quickly as she could. They needed to formulate a plan on what to do about Fitzgerald ASAP.

There was no mention of what would happen between them now or about what the night before had meant. She assumed nothing. He'd told her it was one night and one night only, so there was no reason to expect anything else.

She'd made her way back to her apartment alone, trying to ignore the pain in her chest and the sense that she'd made a mistake somewhere along the line. She couldn't figure out what that mistake might be though.

Last night she'd given him everything she could. Without reservation. Let him do whatever he wanted, over and over again. They hadn't talked again and Zac hadn't let her sleep until the early hours of the morning.

So now she was tired and hurt and furious, none of which was going to be very helpful when it came to dealing with Fitzgerald.

Pulling out her favorite black Ramones T-shirt, she began to dress.

Time to stop thinking about Zac and the mess they'd created between them anyway. There were more important things to deal with.

As she was putting her hair into a ponytail, her phone rang. Crossing back to the mattress on the floor that was her bed, she bent to pick it up.

Alex.

"I've talked to Gabe," he said without preamble the moment she answered. "We'll meet at the club in half an hour."

"I'll be there."

There was a slight pause. "You okay?"

Eva stared out the window at the day beyond. For once it was beautiful, the sun shining, glinting off metal and glass and the puddles in the street below.

She knew what Alex meant, that he was thinking of her confronting Fitzgerald the night before. It felt like a lifetime ago. An age.

"Yes," she said and then, for reasons she couldn't have explained even to herself, she added, "Remember that girl you rescued from Conrad's casino? Who you sent back here to Zac?"

"What about her?"

Eva paused. "Well, what happened to her, happened to me."

Alex said nothing for what seemed a very long time. "Fitzgerald is your Conrad, isn't he?"

"Yeah." She held the phone very tightly.

There was another long silence.

It was time the others knew. Alex had been right, she couldn't run from what had happened to her forever.

"We will take him down," Alex said at last. "I promise you this, Eva. He will pay for what he did."

"As long as he doesn't hurt another girl, I don't care what happens to him."

"Are you sure about that?"

She frowned, staring out at the blue sky above the rooftops, trying to sort through the emotions that roiled around inside her. Yes, she was angry. And yes, she was afraid. But both those feelings had strangely nothing to do with Fitzgerald.

It was like he'd receded in her mind, becoming an

insubstantial figure. A ghost from the past who'd ceased to haunt her because another man had taken his place. A man who wasn't a ghost, who wasn't insubstantial in the slightest. A man who was real and vital and whose touch still burned on her skin from the night before.

Zac. He was the only thing that mattered to her. He was the only thing that counted.

She didn't give a shit what happened to Fitzgerald. As long as Zac was there, that's all that mattered.

"Yes," she said, her voice steady. "You guys can take him down if you want. I only want to make sure any trafficking rings he's got going are taken apart. And if there are any other operations like the Lucky Seven and Conrad's casino, they need to be burned to the ground."

"Hey, I'll hand you the match myself." There was nothing but approval in Alex's voice. "We'll make plans. See you in half an hour."

After Alex had disconnected the call, Eva punched in a text to Zac, telling him they'd be meeting at the Second Circle in thirty minutes.

There was no response.

Her anger clenched tight. Shit, don't say he was giving her the silent treatment again, the bastard. Then again, surely he wouldn't let what was happening between them affect what was going down with Fitzgerald. That wouldn't be like Zac at all.

She gave him five minutes, bending to grab her leather jacket and beanie as she made her way out of her bedroom and into the lounge. When he still hadn't responded, she dialed his number. It went straight to voicemail.

Distinctly pissed now, Eva left him a curt message then ended the call.

Perhaps he was busy, though she'd thought that after what they'd discovered last night, he'd make himself unbusy.

*Perhaps he's avoiding you?*

Yeah, but avoidance wasn't Zac's style. At least it wasn't usually.

She grimaced as she put the phone in her pocket and went downstairs to the front door. Now wasn't the time for Zac to be playing games, that was for sure.

Stepping outside, Eva barely thought about the wide-open space around her as she headed toward the car. Her head was too full of Zac.

Temple waited on the sidewalk, holding the car door out for her. "Good morning, Ms. King."

"Hey, Temple. We're going to the Second Circle. And make it quick, okay?"

"Certainly."

Eva got in, the door shutting behind her. She checked her phone again to see if Zac had somehow miraculously gotten back to her in the course of the minute it had taken to get from her front door and into the car.

He hadn't.

Then she noticed something weird. Her phone didn't have a signal. Strange.

She fiddled with it for a couple of moments, turning it off and on, trying various other tricks she knew of, but the "no service" message stayed stubbornly at the top of her screen.

The car began to pull away from the curb, sliding into the midmorning traffic.

Frustrated, Eva leaned forward, reaching for the intercom button and pressing it. "Are you able to get a signal on your phone, Temple?"

There was no response.

Puzzled, Eva pushed the button again. "Temple?"

Again, no answer.

What the fuck was going on?

She reached for the button that slid the partition down

between the backseat and the front, but that didn't work either. As if it was locked.

Little threads of unease began to wind through her. She pressed the button a couple more times and again there was no response.

Shit.

She looked around the car's interior, and the unease began to solidify into pure ice.

The doors were locked. And they were never locked. To be sure, she reached out and tested the handle. The door remained closed.

Eva took a breath, trying to calm her suddenly racing heartbeat. Then she tried to unlock the doors.

Nothing happened.

Now she was cold. She was ice all the way through.

Eva stared out through the glass partition, to where Temple sat in the driver's seat, her attention apparently on the road.

They weren't going to the Second Circle either.

They were heading in the opposite direction.

Zac stood on the Park Avenue sidewalk, ignoring the stream of people passing by him and the heavy traffic in the street ahead of him. All that mattered was the building across the street. An elegant, white limestone building that housed some of Manhattan's exclusive apartments. And was owned by one Evelyn Fitzgerald.

Zac checked his watch. Another five minutes.

Ever since he'd gotten Fitzgerald's name from the pathetic bodyguard the week before, he'd begun putting together a plan of action. One he hadn't told anyone else since it wasn't anyone else's business. Calling in favors from various people and going over the information his security staff had managed to glean, he'd figured out what he was going to do if Eva positively identified the bastard.

Now that she had, all that remained was to put the plan into motion.

He knew this wouldn't be what she wanted and that the others would no doubt be extremely pissed off with him too, but that didn't matter.

There was only one thing of paramount importance to him and that was Eva's safety.

*Sure it is. Keeping telling yourself it's about that.*

Zac waited, motionless, as cars and buses lumbered past.

Of course it was about Eva. Who else? He'd failed Theresa, and whether he'd done too much or too little in the end didn't matter. What mattered was that she was dead and some part of him had always felt responsible.

He wasn't going to let that happen with Eva.

Naturally there was also a certain amount of pleasure to be had in the thought of putting a bullet through Fitzgerald's brain. A simple action that would solve many of the problems they were having now. After, of course, Zac had gotten a few pieces of relevant information, such as how big his trafficking operation was, who else was involved, etcetera.

His phone vibrated in his pocket, but he didn't look at it. He knew already that it would be Eva, no doubt trying to get hold of him. They'd be meeting at the Second Circle, armed with Eva's confirmation, pretty soon.

Well, that wouldn't matter either. By the time they'd sorted out what they were going to do, Fitzgerald would already be dead. Zac was going to make sure of it.

The phone vibrated again so he reached into his pocket and turned it off.

There could be no more distractions, not now.

Another couple of minutes passed.

Outside Fitzgerald's apartment a woman paused to adjust the beanie she was wearing, revealing a flash of blonde hair.

Zac's entire being froze. But it wasn't her. No, he'd left Eva in the early hours of the morning, making sure she was still asleep and curled up in his bed like a pearl in a seashell. She was safe. With Fitzgerald out of the way, soon she would be safer still.

After that . . . Well, he'd had his night with her. That's all it would be.

*You could keep her. She could be yours.*

An ache filled him. A familiar yearning for what he shouldn't want, for what he couldn't let himself have. But he ignored it the way he'd been ignoring it for seven years.

He couldn't keep Eva. Even though he could give her everything she'd been missing in her life, he couldn't give her the one thing she needed most. Love.

*Couldn't give her? Unwilling to give her, you mean.*

Couldn't. Wouldn't. They amounted to the same thing: love was something he wanted no part of. But Eva deserved it and she should be free to have it, find it with someone else who could return it, unlike him.

The hungry possessive part of him howled at the thought of her with another man, but he ignored that.

*Only you, Zac . . .*

He ignored that too.

Zac glanced down at his watch. It was time.

Right on cue, the front door to the building opened, the doorman letting out a small woman wrapped up in a fur. Fitzgerald's wife, Hilary. She'd be on her way to meet with the charity following the no-doubt successful function the night before. A familiar figure followed her. The mercenary, Elijah. Both of them got into the limo that waited at the curb.

Good. According to the intel he'd received, Fitzgerald didn't like too much personal security when he was at home and only had at most two security staff on deck at any one time. Which was going to make it easy for Zac. Two men were nothing.

Once the limo containing Fitzgerald's wife had pulled away, Zac crossed the avenue and approached the building. Through the big glass doors he saw the doorman's eyes narrow briefly as he strode closer. Obviously the man had been warned to look out for him.

It wasn't anything Zac hadn't expected, but he'd need to move fast.

The man's hand went into the pocket of his jacket. Metal gleamed as he began to withdraw it.

Zac pulled open the door, bringing out his silenced Glock at the same time, aiming and firing in one smooth movement before the other man could even get his weapon out. Then almost in the same movement, Zac turned his gun on the concierge who'd risen from his desk and was in the process of pointing his own gun in Zac's direction.

Zac fired and the concierge fell without a sound.

Silence reigned.

Looking quickly around to make sure there was no one else in the lobby, Zac then dragged the fallen doorman around behind the desk to join the concierge. After making sure both bodies were out of sight, he retrieved a couple of the keys he knew would be behind the concierge's desk, then glanced up at the lobby security camera. There were no red lights blinking, which meant the camera was off.

Excellent. The guy he'd called in a favor from had obviously done his job and made sure the cameras would be down.

Zac wouldn't have long though. The guards upstairs would soon spot the camera fail and start to investigate.

He headed for the elevator, using one of the keys from the desk to operate it, punching in the button for the penthouse floor, his Glock held at his side.

They'd probably be waiting for him by the time he got to the top, and sure enough, as the doors opened, he spotted a flash of movement. He didn't hesitate, firing immediately. The movement stopped. As the elevator chimed and the doors opened fully, one of the guards lay face down on the floor of the hall right in front of him.

Zac stepped over the body, checking the hall.

It was empty. Silent.

The hallway was white. White walls, white carpet, a white console table with a spray of white orchids sitting perfectly in the center. Expensive. Tasteful. Yet also lifeless. Passionless.

Perhaps like Fitzgerald himself?

Zac moved noiselessly down to the end of the hall, where a corridor branched in two directions. He knew, because he'd studied the plans to the apartment, that one way led to the lounge area. The other to Fitzgerald's private office.

Another flash of movement coming from the lounge.

Zac ducked back behind the corner of the hall, waited a beat, then stepped out and fired. The other guard who'd been coming for him dropped to the floor.

Zac kept still, listening.

No sound from anywhere else.

Two guards down which, if his intel was good, meant Fitzgerald was here by himself.

Zac turned and headed down the hall toward Fitzgerald office. The door was closed.

He kicked it open.

The room beyond was white, like the hall, a huge picture window framing the tops of the Manhattan skyscrapers and the beautiful blue day that was shining outside. Sunlight fell on the big white desk that sat in front of the windows, gleaming on the sleek silver computer screen that was pretty much the only thing on it.

Illuminating the man sitting behind it.

"Good morning, Mr. Rutherford," Fitzgerald said, smiling. "I wondered when you'd get here."

Zac raised his Glock. He hadn't planned on killing Fitzgerald right away since there was a good deal of information he wanted first. But a little in the way of an inducement wouldn't hurt. At least it wouldn't hurt him. It might hurt Fitzgerald quite a bit.

"I'd wait before pulling that trigger if I were you," Fitzgerald said calmly. He didn't look the slightest bit worried, though he must have known Zac had just killed four of his henchmen.

It was his calm that made Zac check his desire to pull that trigger. "Give me one good reason."

Fitzgerald leaned forward, putting his elbows on his desk, clasping his hands together. "You're very clever, Mr. Rutherford. But don't say I didn't warn you. If you pull that trigger, kill me or harm me in any way, the person you care about most in the world will suffer the same fate."

Zac went still as the other man's calm words began to penetrate.

Because there was only one person in the world he cared about.

Eva.

"Where the fuck are they?" Alex checked his watch for the fifth time in as many minutes. "It's not like them to be this late. Especially not Zac." Worry sat in his gut like a stone.

Katya was sitting on the couch, and he could see the same worry reflected in her green eyes. Honor stood near him by the empty fireplace, her arms folded. She was looking anxious too.

"Twenty minutes," Gabriel said from his place behind one of the armchairs, his elbows on the back of it. "How long are we going to wait?"

"Something is wrong," Katya said softly. "I can feel it."

Alex glanced over at her, the worry becoming heavier and heavier. He trusted his bodyguard's instinct implicitly and if she felt something was wrong, then it definitely was.

Fuck.

He stopped pacing and thrust his hands in his pockets. "I hope to Christ you're wrong, Katya mine, but I don't think you are. I mean, they're never this late. I spoke to Eva an hour ago and she told me she'd be here."

A heavy silence fell.

Gabriel abruptly pushed himself away from the armchair. "Fuck this. I'm not sitting around here wringing my hands. We need to go find out where they've got to."

"How?" Alex demanded. "I've called Eva but it just goes straight through to voicemail. Zac's the same. Either their phones are out of juice or they've turned them off."

"Both at the same time?" Honor looked from him to Gabriel, then flicked a glance at Katya. "Maybe there's a more innocuous explanation."

Alex knew what his sister was getting at. Sex. But then, she didn't know either Eva or Zac as well as she knew Alex or Gabriel, and she wasn't aware of what Eva had revealed to him over the phone earlier that day. Sex was probably the last thing Eva wanted, especially with a guy like Zac. And most especially after what she'd been through.

"No," he said flatly. "They're not sleeping together."

Honor raised a brow. "How do you know?"

It wasn't his secret to tell, it was Eva's. But if something was wrong, the rest of them needed to hear it, especially if it had something to do with Fitzgerald. "Let's just say that Eva has personal experience with the kind of traffic-
ing Fitzgerald could be associated with."

er silence fell.

the fuck did you find that out?" Gabriel's voice
sh, a black kind of anger in his dark eyes.

Honor moved suddenly, crossing the space to where her lover stood, laying her fingers on his shoulder while covering his hand where it rested on the back of the armchair with her own. Gabriel glanced down at her, the two of them sharing one loaded, intimate look.

What the hell was going on there?

"She told me this morning," Alex said, staring at them. "You guys need to share anything?"

Gabriel let out a short breath, meeting Alex's gaze. "Honor found papers in Tremain's overcoat when she was collecting his things from the hospital. The overcoat he wore when he was shot. It was a paternity test."

"Fuck," Alex breathed. "Not—"

"Fitzgerald is my father."

The flat, uninflected words fell into the room like boulders.

Alex blinked, studying his friend's blunt features. "Shit, Gabe . . ." He stopped, not knowing what to say.

Gabriel lifted a shoulder, but his hand turned over, his fingers wrapping around Honor's. "It doesn't matter. I always knew my father was a prick. That he's turned out to be a fucking major prick isn't much of a surprise."

"Why was Tremain carrying a paternity test?" Katya asked coolly.

Gabriel glanced over at her. "He was coming to meet me to tell me who my father was. But he was shot before he could. I guess that was proof. There were actually two tests. One proving he wasn't my father, and one proving Fitzgerald was."

"Tremain must have had access to your DNA somehow," Alex muttered, thinking it over. "I suppose getting Fitzgerald's was easy enough, considering they were buddies once."

" 'I had to take the fall if anyone asked . . .' " Honor's voice was soft. " 'You can't say no. No one can say no.' "

Alex frowned at her. "What?"

"Tremain was forced into covering up for Fitzgerald," Gabriel said. "That's what he told us the night I met him outside the Lucky Seven. He wrote the check that was supposed to pay my mother off."

Honor's blue gaze turned from Gabriel and met Alex's. "Guy told us 'they' also forced Dad into running the casino. That 'they' were furious at him for running up debts."

Ice water slid down Alex's spine as he stared at his sister. "Shit. 'They' being Fitzgerald." It made sense. It made a fuck load of sense. And it also meant that in all likelihood, Evelyn Fitzgerald had been the one to order his father's death.

"He's behind all of this." Gabriel's dark voice promised retribution. "And I bet you anything you like that when Eva turned up at that fucking party, he decided to do something about it once and for all."

"Elijah," Katya said from the couch.

They all turned to look at her.

"The mercenary from Monte Carlo who warned us off," she explained. "He must be working for Fitzgerald. I mean, why else would he want to destroy the evidence on Conrad's computer? He didn't want us to find anything that would link Conrad with Fitzgerald, that would identify Fitzgerald as being the ringleader. But Eva recognized the guard on the tape."

Alex moved over toward her. "So what are you saying? We need to find this guy somehow?"

She stared up at him. "He warned us off. Told us that Eva and Zac's investigations had been discovered. Do you think that was his warning or Fitzgerald's?"

"You think he's on our side you mean?" Honor asked.

"Nothing is certain. But . . . he could be. And if he's working for Fitzgerald, then maybe he knows if Zac and Eva are in trouble."

"Good enough for me," Gabriel growled. "I say we track this prick down. Now."

Zac kept himself very still. Did not lower his gun one inch. "I think," he said carefully, "that you had better explain."

Irritation crossed Fitzgerald's features and he sighed. "And here I was thinking you were intelligent. Explaining is clumsy, much better if I just show you instead." His attention went to the screen of his computer. "Everything ready, Elijah?"

"Yes." A cold, familiar voice sounded through the speakers. "We've just arrived."

"Good." Fitzgerald put a hand to the screen and turned it around to face Zac. "Say hello, Miss King."

There was a window on the screen open, showing the interior of a car. Zac knew that car. It was Eva's limo. The camera was focused on a man sitting in one of the seats. Scarred face, emotionless black eyes. Zac met those eyes for one long second before the camera turned around to show the other person sitting in the car.

Eva. She was sitting there with her arms folded around herself, her expression tight, her mouth in a hard line. Yet as the camera turned and she saw him, her chin lifted, a small, determined tilt. "Hey asshole," she said in what sounded like her normal voice. "Thanks for not answering your phone."

But of course, it wasn't her normal voice. He could hear the fear in it. Could see terror in the depths of her gray eyes.

A clawed and taloned hand squeezed around his heart.

He opened his mouth to tell her it was going to be okay, but Fitzgerald turned the screen around before he could speak.

"Thank you, Elijah," the older man said. "I think I've illustrated my point nicely." He hit a button on the keyboard, then leaned back in his chair, his hands clasped on the desktop. In his beautifully tailored, dark blue Hart Brothers suit, he looked like a wealthy and prosperous banker, not what in actual fact he was. A murderer. A rapist. A human trafficker.

"The gun, Mr. Rutherford," he reminded mildly. "I'm sure you won't want anything to happen to your lovely girl should it go off accidentally."

Inside Zac, his rage howled. It beat at the walls of its cage, wanting to get out. Pull the trigger. Spray the bastard's brains all over his spotless window.

Instead Zac lowered the gun. He could, of course, have pretended that Eva meant nothing to him, but he didn't think Fitzgerald would believe him. The man was too cold and calculating to leave anything like that to chance. "You don't mind if I keep it?" Zac made sure he betrayed no sign of the fury that burned as hot as lava. "It has sentimental value."

Fitzgerald, supremely arrogant, lifted a shoulder. "Be my guest. Just don't point it at me."

Zac put his gun away in his overcoat pocket.

Christ. They'd got to Eva. He hadn't had her as well protected as he'd thought. How the fuck had Fitzgerald managed to do that?

Fear had joined the anger, a current of cold running through the heat, but Zac shoved the emotion away.

As if the man knew exactly what he was thinking, Fitzgerald gave a slight smile. It didn't reach his eyes, which remained chips of blue ice. "You should be more careful with your employees in the future. In case you were wondering."

His employees . . . The hand in his pocket still close to his gun clenched. Eva had been in her own limo. Which could only mean one thing. "Temple."

Fitzgerald inclined his head. "Indeed. Everyone has a price, as you should know."

Zac had vetted Eva's driver thoroughly. Had hired her himself based on a number of excellent references. So how had Fitzgerald gotten to her? What had he promised?

With an effort, Zac unclenched his fingers. Made himself relax. He couldn't afford any distracting emotions, not now. Not if he wanted to get them both out of this alive.

"Well," he said flatly. "Now we've got the drama out of the way, I suppose we're at the point of the proceedings where I ask you what the fuck you want?"

Fitzgerald gave another slight smile, his brow creasing. "You know, I haven't quite decided yet." He paused. "I have to admit, I was moderately annoyed with you and your little group of friends. Poking your noses in where they weren't wanted, interfering with my business. In fact, I've had to close down a number of lucrative operations because of you. The Lucky Seven, my friend Conrad's casino in Monte Carlo. Both of them good businesses." Fitzgerald let out a breath. "I don't like people messing with businesses, Mr. Rutherford. I don't like it at all. It makes me very angry."

Zac said nothing, watching him as he rose slowly out of his chair and came around the desk to lean back against it, his arms folded.

"I also had to order the deaths of several good friends because of you and your interference," Fitzgerald went on conversationally. "That also makes me angry."

"Tremain?" Zac asked.

"Yes, indeed. Poor Guy. Who was going to go to Mr. Woolf with his information. I wasn't happy with Elijah for missing his target, but then we discovered he has no memory due to the head injury so that turned out for the best. He's an old friend after all so I thought his life worth sparing." He frowned. "I'm not pleased about Conrad, though. Mr. St. James will have to pay for that at some point."

"He's paid enough already." If the man was in the mood to talk, then Zac wasn't going to stop him. It was all information that could be used later.

*If you manage to get out of this alive.*

No, there was no "if" about it. He would. And if he didn't, then he'd make sure Eva would.

"You mean being made to be Conrad's catamite?" Another one of those smiles. "That was purely business. As was having to make sure Daniel stayed quiet." He let out a soft breath. "Honestly, if people only did what they were told, we wouldn't have all these problems."

"What do you want?" Zac snapped, losing patience.

"I'm sure you can imagine. I'd like you and your friends to do as they're told and stop interfering in things that don't concern them." He shifted against the desk, his cold eyes meeting Zac's. "And since you've seen fit to ignore my warnings, I've had to take action. I told Miss King last night that she was irrelevant. That she didn't matter, and to some extent it's true. But then again, she's quite high profile and that could potentially be useful to me." Another icy little smile turned his mouth. "As leverage."

Zac found his hands wanting to clench into fists again. He kept them straight. "I see."

"Do you, Mr. Rutherford? I think perhaps you don't. Because if you had, maybe you would have taken better care of her."

So. Fitzgerald had found the one chink in his armor. And was exploiting it. Ruthlessly.

Of course he should have expected it. Of course, he should have foreseen it. The bastard was right. He should have taken better care of her. But he'd thought . . .

*You were as arrogant as this prick here, thinking that*

*because you'd protected her, she'd be safe. But she's not. Like Theresa wasn't.*

A red haze had begun to cloud Zac's vision. He blinked hard to clear it, forcing aside the rage. "Stop posturing," he said coldly. "I'm assuming you're now going to use Eva as hostage for our good behavior?"

Fitzgerald lifted a shoulder. "Naturally. Killing Mr. Woolf and Mr. St. James is problematic. You, on the other hand, are not as high profile as they are. I should imagine I could kill you with impunity and no one would notice." Another small smile turned his mouth. "I'm quite adept at finding people whom the world doesn't care about, you see. Anyway, I'm sure you'll be pleased to know, I decided against it. Killing you makes no business sense whatsoever. You're a highly skilled man, Mr. Rutherford, and I could use some of those skills of yours."

The man clearly meant it as a compliment. But all Zac felt was rage. "What makes you think I would ever let you use them."

"Oh, I'm sure I can get you to do any number of things for me with sufficient inducement. Take Miss King, for example. Did you know she was my favorite? The homeless girls were always the best because all they needed was food and a nice bed, and they'd do anything you wanted. Eva particularly. A quiet, biddable girl and not without talent."

The urge was there to shut the man up with his fists. To smash that blandly handsome face into oblivion. He imagined it in his head, imagined how satisfying it would be.

But he didn't move. Kept his hands in his pockets. The more the man kept talking, the longer it gave Zac to come up with another plan. And he would come up with a plan. All he had to do was wait.

"You're failing to make your point, Mr. Fitzgerald," Zac said with exaggerated patience. "Yet again."

Fitzgerald gave an icy little laugh. "My apologies. I'm only reliving happy memories. I'm actually quite proud of Eva, did you know that? I've been watching her and her company rise for several years now, and it's fascinating how she did it. I even like to think I had a hand in it—I mean, if I'd left her on the streets, she certainly wouldn't be where she is now, would she?"

The bastard was trying to push him, no doubt. Make him angry, perhaps angry enough to use his fists.

Zac stared into the other man's cold, cold eyes. And knew that Fitzgerald was waiting, looking for an excuse, a reason to hurt Eva.

"Eva is where she is now because she's intelligent and driven, not for any other reason," Zac said with equal coldness. "Now, I presume you're going to get to the point sometime this century?"

Something sparked in the other man's eyes. A ripple of emotion that hadn't been there before.

About fucking time.

"A man in your position might like to be a little more polite," Fitzgerald said, his voice mild, though the look on his face was anything but. "I was merely expressing my admiration of Miss King's ambition. And maybe of her, herself. She looked beautiful last night, truly a woman, not the skinny little girl I fucked seven years ago."

Both the word and the image it conjured up were designed to shock, to anger, of that Zac had no doubt. And they did both.

Christ, he had to have a plan. He had to *think*. He'd never been in a situation he couldn't get out of, not once in his long career, and he was *not* going to be in one now.

He said nothing, staring back at Fitzgerald. Giving him no reaction at all.

"I want your skills, Mr. Rutherford. They would be useful in my business, very useful indeed. I also want your friends off my back." His cold smile vanished utterly. "And if I don't get those things, I'll turn Miss King back into my own personal fuck-toy until you change your mind."

Rage swept through Zac, deep and hot, and it was only long experience of repressing his emotions that kept him from lashing out.

All it would take was a bullet. One tiny little bullet right between the eyes. And all of this would go away. Problem solved.

*You can't. You have to protect her.*

Fitzgerald tilted his head at Zac's continued silence. "You don't believe me? Perhaps you'd care for a demonstration." He turned and went back around the desk, sitting down in front of the computer screen again and hitting a button. "Bring her in Elijah."

Zac stiffened. Fuck, no. Not here. Surely not—

The door behind him opened and he turned sharply to see it admit Eva and Elijah. The mercenary was following behind her closely, a gun pointed at her back.

Despite his best intentions, Zac found his fingers had closed around the butt of his Glock and he had to fight the urge to pull it out and blow the mercenary away. Perhaps he could. He'd been in situations like this before and had managed it. He'd always been fast.

Elijah, clearly taking no chances, pulled Eva abruptly closer, the muzzle of his gun pressed firmly to her spine. The look on her face was blank, nevertheless Zac saw fear lurking beneath like a shadow.

Shit. He couldn't take action now. No matter how fast he was, he wouldn't be fast enough to stop Elijah from pulling that trigger. Eva would be dead before she hit the floor.

"Welcome, Miss King," Fitzgerald said, as if he was inviting her into his home for tea. "I'm so glad you could join us."

She said nothing. Her gaze flickered toward Zac then away again.

"Take her out," Zac ordered, putting every ounce of authority he possessed into the words. "She doesn't need to be here."

But Fitzgerald only raised an eyebrow. "Au contraire, Mr. Rutherford. She'll need to hear about our little agreement, don't you think? Women like to know what men sacrifice for them, or at least that's my experience."

"You know nothing about women," Eva said unexpectedly, her tone dripping with loathing. "Or sacrifice."

Fitzgerald only shrugged. "You got me. I don't. Nor am I interested. The only thing that concerns me is my business. And speaking of which, as much fun as this little drama has been, I suggest we move on to why we're here. Or at least, why both of you are here."

"You've made yourself clear," Zac said. "It's a ridiculous overreaction, but never mind, I'll let it pass. Certainly, I'll get the others off your back. My only stipulation is that you leave her alone." Better to agree quickly, get her out of here. He had people he could contact who'd help him get her away from Fitzgerald. Then he'd take her to his island where she'd be safe, where he could protect her better.

She'd turned her head toward him. "What are you doing, Zac? What are you talking about?"

He ignored her. Didn't even look at her. He couldn't allow distractions. The only thing that had any meaning was that she be put out of Fitzgerald's reach forever.

Fitzgerald's mouth twitched. "I think you've misinterpreted who has the power here, Mr. Rutherford."

"Really? I don't think so. You assume my friends and I have no evidence against you, a patent error on your part." Perhaps he should have taken up poker. Seemed bluffing was his forte after all. "If anything happens to Miss King,

I will get them to release what we have on you, and I guarantee it will destroy you."

The older man studied him for a long moment. Then he shrugged. "I guess it depends on how badly you want my destruction and whether Miss King's life is worth it."

"Oh shit, no," Eva murmured. "He's using me to get to you, isn't he? God, are you insane, Zac Rutherford? Don't do it."

Fitzgerald smiled that cold little smile. "And if he doesn't, you and I go back to our . . . old arrangement."

Zac kept his attention on the older man, but he could almost feel Eva's shock radiating through the room.

"I see," she said, her voice fraying. "Well, what do I care? It's only sex. And not very good sex at that."

Fitzgerald laughed. "That we can fix, Miss King." Then his gaze flicked to Zac, the amusement in his face abruptly wiping clean. "No, I'm not striking any bargains with you, Mr. Rutherford. You will go where I tell you to go. Do what I tell you to do. That's if you want to keep your pretty angel whole and healthy. And if you perform well, I may just decide not to revisit old memories with her. Then again, that's entirely up to you."

Powerless. He was fucking powerless and the prick knew it. Trapped by his feelings for the small woman standing next to him. Helpless, impotent rage welled up, pushing against the restraints he'd laid on it, a rage that seemed somehow as familiar to him as his own name.

"I'll do it," he said through clenched teeth, trying to force the emotion back into his cage. "I give you my word. Only leave her out of it."

The lack of emotion on Fitzgerald's face was chilling. "Your word, Mr. Rutherford?" He said the words as if they were poison. "You really think I'd let a man like you off the leash with only your word to back it up? This is business, not fucking Eton. Your word means nothing.

Collateral, assets, money. Those are the only things that mean anything and those I already have. Miss King is collateral. That's all."

All Zac's frustrated anger boiled up, threatening to choke him. And he was reaching into his coat, pulling out his Glock, and aiming at Fitzgerald before he could think straight. "Let her fucking go," he said, coldly. Clearly.

"Oh, come now," the older man said with mild irritation. "Haven't we already been through that tedious drama? If you hurt me, etcetera."

"You'll still be dead."

Fitzgerald looked bored. "And so will Miss King."

But the rage inside him didn't seem to care. It wanted blood. It wanted release. *Kill him*, it said. *Think of all the people he's hurt. All the people he's trapped. Think of all the people you'd save.*

Yes. Men like him deserved to die. Men who preyed on others, who took advantage of the weak. It was men like him who'd killed his parents. Who'd killed Theresa.

*Bullshit,* his rage whispered. *The only person who killed Theresa was herself. And she made you watch.*

If only he hadn't loved her, it wouldn't have hurt. He wouldn't have felt so helpless, so fucking angry. But he did love her. And now here he was again, in the very same position with another woman under threat. A woman he couldn't save because he cared too much.

Emotions. They were the problem, they were the weakness. They made you helpless. If you didn't care, then no one had power over you. It was that simple.

His hand had started to shake. He steadied it.

*Killing this man is the only way. It will make the world a better place, save a lot of people. You can't let him have the power.*

He took at step forward, keeping the Glock pointed firmly at Fitzgerald.

Something flickered through the older man's cold blue eyes. The first glimpse of a reaction. "Careful, Mr. Rutherford. Be very careful indeed."

Behind him he could hear Eva's fast, ragged breathing and something inside him hurt, but he ignored it. The red haze had descended again and he couldn't clear it. What was the point anyway? Rage like this was power. It was strong. It could save, like he'd used it to save that woman all those years ago. And if he'd killed a man, then what of it?

Zac took another step. He was right in front of Fitzgerald now, the muzzle of the Glock inches from the man's forehead.

He hadn't been able to stop Theresa. He'd had to watch her die, unable to do anything. But he could do something now. He had his rage and a gun. He wasn't helpless and he could make it stop.

One bullet and he could save everyone.

*But not Eva.*

The expressionless mask on the other man's face had begun to crack, fear leaking out. "She will die, Mr. Rutherford. Are you prepared for that?"

*One death. It's worth it.*

"Let her die," Zac heard himself say, his voice echoing as if from a long way off. "God will find his own."

A heavy silence fell, a flash of genuine puzzlement crossing Fitzgerald's face.

There was movement behind him. The sounds of something happening. Fitzgerald's gaze flickered and this time there was no mistaking the shock in his face. "Elijah?" he said in tones of complete disbelief.

A voice beside him, so calm, soothing the red rage like ice on a burn. "Give me the gun, Zac." And her hand reaching up to his, slender white fingers against his skin, loosening his hold. Taking the Glock away from him.

He couldn't move. Couldn't speak.

Realization, clean and sharp as an arrow, sliced through him. Through the years of anger that had build up, layer upon layer like pearl around a particle of sand. Hit with precise and devastating accuracy, a body blow.

He'd been going to kill Fitzgerald. He'd been going to sacrifice Eva.

"It's okay," she said softly. "Let me take care of you."

Then she raised the gun, pointed it at Fitzgerald.

And shot him in the head.

# CHAPTER NINETEEN

Alex had a limo organized and waiting outside the Second Circle within minutes.

Since the only link they had with Elijah was through Fitzgerald, they'd decided a little visit to Fitzgerald's Park Avenue apartment wouldn't go amiss.

He'd paused only to take a quick dash up to the penthouse to grab his own handgun before following the rest of them out onto the sidewalk.

Only to find a small redhead in a driver's uniform standing next to the limo.

She was familiar.

"That's Eva's driver," he muttered as they walked toward the limo. "What the hell is she doing here?"

"Trying to find Eva as well," Honor offered.

"I don't think so," Katya said in that decisive way she had. "She's not looking worried in the slightest."

She didn't. Then again, her face was expressionless so she wasn't looking much of anything.

"Temple, isn't it?" Gabriel said as they approached her. "Miss King isn't here, if that's who you're after."

That's when Alex saw it, something like fear in the woman's light amber eyes. Just a glimpse, like a shadow crossing the sun. And felt it touch his own heart.

No. He wouldn't let anything happen to either Zac or

Eva. They were part of the family he'd created years ago. A family he'd protect no matter what. They were important. They were *all* important.

"Where is she?" he demanded coldly. "You know something."

The woman's gaze flickered, and he knew nervousness when he saw it. "That's why I'm here. Miss King is with Mr. Fitzgerald.

Gabriel stilled, the air around him suddenly dropping ten degrees. "How the fuck did that happen?"

Honor quickly put a hand on his shoulder, but she didn't say anything, her gaze fixed on Eva's driver.

But that didn't stop Katya. She moved past Alex, slamming her hand into the center of the other woman's chest and shoving her hard against the car. "Tell us what you know," she ordered. "Now."

Temple didn't struggle. She took a gasping breath, her features twisting. "I took her there."

"You what?" Gabriel took a step forward, the look on his face frightening.

Katya kept one hand on Temple's chest as she reached into her jacket for her Springfield, heedless of the people on the footpath passing around them.

"I had to!" Temple said quickly before Katya could get her gun out. "I had no choice. Anyway, the why doesn't matter. Miss King is with Fitzgerald and probably by now so is Mr. Rutherford."

Alex moved forward, trying to figure out the play of emotion on the woman's face. It was difficult. She was obviously used to guarding her feelings. "If you're the one who took her, then why are you now telling us?"

Temple's pale eyes caught his. "My reasons are my own. All that matters is that you know where she is and that she isn't alone. Mr. Hunt is with her."

"Who the fuck is Mr. Hunt?" Gabriel demanded.

But it was Honor who answered. "Elijah."

"Yes," Temple said. "Elijah."

Alex stared at her. She seemed to be telling the truth, at least, he didn't see any little tells that usually meant someone was lying. Then again, some people were very proficient at lying. "Why should we believe you?"

"I have no reason to lie."

"And yet you fucking took her to Fitzgerald." Gabriel reached behind him, grabbing something from the waist-band of his jeans. A handgun. He didn't aim it, merely clicked off the safety. "Seems to me you've got some ex-plaining to do."

Temple didn't look at him, her gaze on Katya instead. "I'll explain all you want later. Mr. Hunt wanted me to pass on that Miss King needs your help and that you should come now."

Alex closed his fingers around his own gun. "I'm good with that."

"Excellent," Gabriel said. "Then we'll blow my fuck-ing father away."

Fitzgerald slumped to the floor, a hole punched clean through his head.

"What the fuck are you doing?" a hoarse voice de-manded.

Before Eva could react, strong fingers wrapped around her upper arm, jerking her around. Black eyes burned into hers, almost incandescent with fury. "He was mine, you bitch! You'll fucking pay for that."

"No, she won't."

The fingers around her arm were ripped away as Zac shoved the other man away from her, stepping in front to shield her. "Leave her the fuck alone." His voice was raw with anger, pain sharp as glass running through it.

There was a dead body inches away from her, the body

of the man she'd killed, and maybe she should have felt regret about that. She didn't give a shit about him.

Only one person mattered.

Watching Zac point his gun at Fitzgerald's head, seeing the struggle in his beloved face turn into something cold and frightening, should have terrified her. Knowing he was going to pull that trigger, that he'd doom her in doing so, should have terrified her.

But, strangely, it wasn't her impending death she'd cared about.

All she could think about was that he didn't deserve it. Didn't deserve to have his care for her used like that. His protective nature twisted into something it should never have been.

That if she'd been stronger earlier, she could have looked after herself. She could have fought and maybe if she had, they wouldn't be here. He wouldn't be forced to make this choice.

It wasn't fair.

He'd protected her so long and this was how it ended.

Her heart had ached for him, even though it was herself he was going to sacrifice to kill Fitzgerald. She couldn't blame him. What was her life compared with the lives of their friends? Compared with all the lives of the people Fitzgerald had hurt?

And then Elijah had whispered unexpectedly in her ear. "You need to stop this." And let her go.

She hadn't stopped to wonder why Elijah suddenly seemed to be on their side. She only knew that it was her chance now. Her chance to take care of Zac the way he'd taken care of her.

So she'd gone to him and taken the gun from his fingers. And she'd shot Fitzgerald. Not for herself and what he'd done to her, but for what he'd done to Zac. What he'd done to her friends.

For that alone he had to die.

And she wasn't sorry. She wasn't sorry about that at all.

Elijah was now staring at Zac like he wanted to kill him. "I told you," he said in that horrifyingly cold voice of his. "I told you Fitzgerald was mine."

"Yes, well, he's not anyone's anymore," Zac replied, just as cold. Just as hard.

The mercenary spat on the floor. Then without any warning at all, he lifted the gun he was holding and pointed it at Zac. "Five years I've wanted revenge on that fucker. And in one second she took it all away. She's going to have to pay for that and if you don't get out of the way, you will too."

But Zac was already moving. His hand came up with blinding speed, gripping Elijah's wrist and twisting to get rid of the gun. But the mercenary moved too, his body following the twist to get Zac off balance.

Shit.

Eva was still holding the Glock but if she pulled the trigger, she'd probably end up hitting the wrong man, if she managed to hit anything at all.

As the two men began to fight in earnest, she backed around the desk to where Fitzgerald's phone sat. Calling the police was probably the right option but then how to explain the dead body of one of New York's most respected citizens?

Fuck, she needed someone else. She needed Alex and Gabriel. Who were probably wondering where in the hell she and Zac were.

A small coffee table exploded in a shower of wood chips as Elijah fell through it, thrown there by Zac. There was such savage fury on Zac's face, Eva had no doubt his next move would probably be to kill Elijah.

But before Zac could pounce, the mercenary rolled,

recovering and managing to block the punch Zac threw at him. He'd lost his gun from the looks of things.

Eva frantically dialed Alex's number.

A bookcase against the wall shuddered, several photographs and a small glass vase smashing onto the floor as Zac was slammed against it.

No fucking answer.

Elijah's hands wound around Zac's throat, crushing.

Eva ditched the phone, picked up the gun again, circled her way around the desk so she was behind the black-eyed mercenary. He didn't pay any attention to her, all his focus on crushing the life out of Zac while Zac reached for the other man's face, his thumbs going for his eyes, his body twisting to get Elijah off him.

She wrapped both hands around the gun to steady herself. Perhaps Zac could beat the other man. Perhaps he couldn't. Whatever, she wasn't wasting time hanging around like a scared little girly to find out.

At that moment, Zac roared in fury and gave a sudden surge, shaking off Elijah's crushing hands. He planted one booted foot squarely in the man's chest sending him flying backward, only narrowing missing Eva.

With barely a pause and without looking, he reached down. To come up with Elijah's own weapon held firmly in his fist.

Eva felt her knees go weak, but she couldn't seem to loosen her own grip on Zac's Glock. So she kept holding it, pointing at Elijah's massive figure on the ground as he struggled to his feet.

"I want to kill you." Zac's voice was thick and twisted with rage. "Except you let Eva go and that earns you a pass. But if you don't sit down and shut the fuck up right now, you're dead. Understand?"

Elijah bared his teeth. His mouth was bloody, his eyebrow split. "Fuck you."

Then he made for the door.

Zac fired.

The mercenary faltered, grunting as the bullet hit home, but he didn't stop, disappearing fast through the door. Zac pulled the trigger again, the bullet embedding itself into the doorframe.

He cursed, making for the doorway.

"Zac, wait," Eva said. Her calm was beginning to seep away, reaction setting in. Still, she was pleased at how steady her voice sounded.

He halted, one hand on the doorframe as he turned sharply around. His amber eyes were furious, his mouth bleeding. "What? We can't let him go. He's got information we need."

"I know." She finally lowered her gun. "But I need you more."

The expression on his face twisted. "Fitzgerald is dead. Elijah worked for him. Which means we have to get Elijah back if we want to know anything about what Fitzgerald's been up to."

He was right. Of course he was right. But there was something in his eyes that made her afraid, and it wasn't the anger. It was the way he looked at her. Like she was a stranger . . .

She shook off the feeling, waved the gun. "Go then."

Zac didn't wait, was out the door before she'd finished speaking.

For a long time she stood there, staring blankly at the space where he'd been. Then she pulled herself together, moving over to the desk and putting Zac's gun back down on it. She didn't look at the man slumped on the flood, his blood making a red pool on the white carpet. He was meaningless to her. He only mattered in that he would never hurt anyone else ever again.

She stared at the desk, frowning slightly.

Well, well. Perhaps Elijah wasn't the only source of information.

Moving around the desk, Eva sat down in the chair. Then she pulled the keyboard of Fitzgerald's computer toward her and began to type.

By the time Zac got downstairs and out the front door of the building, Elijah had vanished.

After standing on the sidewalk for long minutes, scanning the crowds of people moving to and fro, and the traffic building up in the street ahead without success, Zac was forced to admit he'd lost the man.

Fuck. *Fuck.*

Rage sang inside him, blind and savage, the dragon roaring at the loss of its prey.

He'd never been so desperate for a target, anything to focus that rage on.

*Why not on yourself? You're the one who nearly killed Eva.*

The dragon sunk its claws into his heart and he didn't fight the pain. He welcomed it. Because yes, if she hadn't taken the gun from his hands, he would have pulled that trigger. And it didn't matter that Elijah had seemingly let her go—how else could she have gotten away?— that maybe she hadn't even been in any danger to start with.

What mattered was that he'd been willing to sacrifice her on the altar of his rage.

A woman passing by threw him a frightened glance, making him aware that he was standing on the sidewalk in public with a weapon in his hand and no doubt bruises on his face.

Jesus fucking Christ.

With a ruthlessness borne of long experience, he forced the rage away, trying to compose himself. Tucking away

Elijah's gun and reaching for his phone, he pivoted on his heel and went back into the building.

He didn't let himself think about Eva or the look in her eyes as she'd told him she needed him. Or about how she'd been the one to turn the gun on Fitzgerald and save herself.

The fight with Elijah had been just the outlet he'd needed right then, but that prick getting away was not what he'd planned.

He punched in a number he'd had to use on occasion and gave the man who answered the required code and the address. Then he ended the call.

The cleanup crew who would deal with the bodies would be here in ten minutes. Which meant it was time to get Eva and get out of here as soon as possible.

"Zac? What the fuck?"

Zac spun around, reaching for the weapon in his pocket. Then stilled.

Alex, Gabriel, Honor, and Katya had come through the doors and were now standing in the lobby.

He couldn't deny it was good to see them. Relaxing his hand, he removed it from his pocket. "You're too late," he said, unable to quite get rid of the rough thread in his voice. "It's over."

Gabriel moved toward him, his arm held low by his side, a battered but very serviceable automatic pressing against his leg. "What's over? Where's Eva?"

"She's safe. She'll be coming downstairs shortly I imagine." He glanced at his watch. "We can't stay here for too much longer."

"I can see why." This from Alex who'd circled around behind the concierge's desk and was now looking down at where the concierge and the doorman were lying.

"Fitzgerald?" There was a strange note in Gabriel's voice.

Zac glanced at him. "Dead."

Something glittered in the other man's eyes. "You killed him?"

"No. I did."

They all turned to look as Eva came toward them from the elevator area. She had her hands in her pockets, her expression hard and sure.

Small, prickly, and fragile. Yet so, so strong.

Savage heat turned over inside him, wanting her. Needing her.

*Never again.*

He'd been right to keep himself distant all this time. Right not to give anything of himself to her. He was far, far too dangerous. He'd nearly gotten her killed.

"You did?" A smile crossed Alex's features, brilliant and brief. "You're one hell of a badass, Eva King."

"Gabriel?" Honor had started forward, moving after her lover as he headed purposefully toward the elevators.

Where the hell was he going? "We can't stay," Zac warned harshly. "My team will be here soon and we can't be around when they get to work."

"I need to see him," Gabriel said shortly without turning. "I won't be long. Stay with the others, Honor."

Honor halted next to Zac. There was a taut expression on her face.

Zac forced himself to pay attention. "What's going on?" he asked, frowning in Gabriel's direction as the elevator doors closed on him.

"We found out who Gabe's father is," Honor said quietly. "It's Fitzgerald."

Shock moved through him. Well, that explained the look on Gabriel's face.

"Shit," Eva muttered. "I didn't know."

A faint smile turned Honor's mouth. "I don't think he'll

be too concerned, Eva. Don't worry about that. I'm glad to see you're okay."

Eva shrugged as if it hadn't been a big deal. "Yeah, well, it was touch and go there for a moment."

"How did you know where we were?" Zac asked.

"Temple," Katya said from her position near the front door. She looked as if she was guarding it. Which she probably was. "When you both didn't turn up for the meeting, we decided to come and find you. Temple was waiting outside and she told us where you were."

Ah, yes, Eva's driver. Another of his failures. There would have to be consequences.

"That's fortuitous," he said. "But I don't take kindly to employees betraying my trust. I'll have to make sure that doesn't happen again."

"She told us where you were," Honor pointed out in a cool voice. "Which she didn't have to. I don't know why she took Eva, but I'd bet anything on the fact she meant Eva no harm. Knowing Fitzgerald, she may not even have had a choice."

"No one gets second chances with me, Honor," he said, not bothering to temper himself this time. "Especially not when Eva's involved."

"Eva is right here," Eva murmured. "And since Temple is my employee, I'll deal with her."

There was a certainty in her voice he'd never heard before, and when he glanced at her, that same certainty gleamed in her gray eyes as they stared back.

He remembered her hand on his, her touch cool as she'd taken the gun from him.

*It's okay. Let me take care of you.*

"What happened to Elijah?" she asked.

"I lost him." Frustration bled into his tone no matter how hard he tried to keep it steady.

"Don't worry. We may not need him anyway." A smile turned her mouth. "I just downloaded the contents of Fitzgerald's computer to one of my cloud drives. It's encrypted, but I'm sure that won't be a problem. I'm quite good with code."

"Holy shit, Eva," Alex muttered. "You're not wearing superhero tights underneath those jeans are you? Christ, I feel superfluous. We may as well pack up and go home right now."

Alex wasn't the only one. Then again, was it any surprise how Eva had handled herself upstairs? She'd saved herself and in all likelihood him too.

She'd always been a warrior.

"Yes, you might as well," she said bluntly. "Give me a couple of hours to break the encryption and we'll go over what's there. Second Circle, tonight. Okay?"

"Zac?" Katya from the door again. "I think I see your crew."

He wrenched his gaze from Eva's. "Let's go."

Outside, the others headed toward the SUV they'd arrived in to wait for Gabriel.

"You go with them," Zac said to Eva as they followed.

Her gaze flicked over him. "You're not coming?"

"No. I need to handle the cleanup, plus I want to let some of my contacts know about Elijah. See if they can keep an eye out for him."

She slowed, then stopped, glancing in the direction the others had gone in then back at him. "I'll come with you."

Zac stared down at her. Was she expecting things to go on as normal? As if he'd never told Fitzgerald to let her die?

*It wasn't her you meant. It was Theresa.*

Like it was important who he meant.

He'd put Eva's life on the line because he couldn't stand to be helpless. Because he'd wanted to take control more than he'd wanted to save her life. And maybe his despair at watching Theresa slip away from him was at the root of it, and maybe it wasn't. But knowing that wouldn't change what he'd done.

The important thing was what he did now. If he really cared about Eva, he'd let her go. Keep her as far away from him as it was possible to get.

And as for him, well, he had his anger. That's all he'd ever had.

"I'll be taking the subway," he said. Which was pretty much Eva's idea of hell. Or at least, it used to be.

"Oh." Her shoulders were hunched, yet the old fear that used to tighten her delicate features wasn't there. She looked pale though, shadows under her eyes. "But hey, I just killed a man so I'm sure I can handle a few crowds."

"No." He made it hard. Made it certain.

"Okay, so why don't you come to my apartment after you've done that? We could look at this code together."

"I think," he said flatly, "that I'll be busy until this evening."

She searched his face. "Why do I get the feeling this is about more than just being busy?"

He didn't want to have this discussion now, in the middle of the street, with the crowds around them. "You should go with the others."

A crease appeared between her brows. "No. I want to go with you."

"Go, Eva." He put all his authority in it, all the weight of his dominance.

People streamed past them like the currents of the ocean around a pair of islands, ebbing, flowing.

"You're leaving, aren't you?" she said quietly. "For good."

Ah Christ, she was too sharp, too perceptive. "I'll see

you tonight, angel." He tried to moderate his voice. "We can discuss it then."

"Why? Is it because I shot Fitzgerald?" Her gaze searched his. "No . . . it's not that."

"Eva—"

"It's about you nearly pulling that trigger, isn't it?"

He couldn't talk about this in the middle of the street, with the sun shining and people all around. With Fitzgerald dead and a massive cleanup on their hands, not to mention figuring out just what the hell Fitzgerald had been doing, what kind of empire he'd been building.

Authorities would have to be advised—if they could find the evidence, that was. Hell, perhaps Eva had already found it in the contents of Fitzgerald's computer.

Yet despite all of that, he didn't move.

"I would have done it, Eva," he said at last. "I would have killed him. I would have killed you."

"But you didn't."

"Because you stopped me."

"It doesn't matter. Elijah let me go. It didn't happen."

"It does matter. I was angry and I wanted to kill him. Angry enough that your life wasn't important."

He expected to see pain in her eyes, but there wasn't any. Only her direct, silver gaze staring back at him. "So? I wasn't scared, Zac. All I could think about was that it wasn't fair. That you shouldn't have had to be put in that position. That he used me to get to you. But . . . I wasn't scared for myself, not once."

His heart twisted. "You should have been."

"No and you know why?" She lifted her chin in that way she had. "Because I trusted you. Because deep down, I think I always have. You wouldn't have pulled that trigger, Zac. You would have found a way. You would have found a way to save both of us."

She spoke with the certainty of absolute conviction,

saying the words he'd wanted to hear for so many years. He believed her, that she had indeed trusted him.

The problem was that she shouldn't. Her trust was the last thing he deserved. Because in the end, his anger had been more important than she was.

"That doesn't change anything," he said, trying to be gentle when the pain in his chest felt anything but. "I can't give you what you want, Eva."

Her jaw tightened, a glitter of pain in her eyes. "Because of what happened—"

"Because I never could."

"So what? That's it? For seven years I've been your closest friend and now you're just going to throw that away because of some stupid anger management issues?"

His fingers were clenched. He tried to relax them. Tried to breathe past the weight that felt like it was crushing his chest. "I can't be friends with you, angel. Not anymore. Not after last night."

She tilted her head back. Mutinous and stubborn to the last. "What if I don't want friends? What if I want more than that?"

The weight grew impossibly heavy. "What more?"

"I want what Honor and Gabriel have." She was looking at him as if he held all the answers to the universe. And she was demanding he give them to her. "What Alex and Katya have. I think we could have that. You and me. I think we deserve that."

The weight on his chest turned into a mountain." We can't have that, Eva. That's what I'm trying to tell you."

"Why not?" She didn't seem to care that people were glancing at them. That they were out in the open, in the middle of a public street. "Why can't we? Shit, if it's the Dom-sub stuff you're worried about, I don't care. I got off on what you did to me, you know that."

"It's not the Dom stuff."

"Then what?" Something glittered in her eyes. It wasn't pain, though that was there. It was something far more tangible. Something he'd never seen from her before. A tear. "I'm alone, Zac. I've always been alone, my whole goddamned life. My mother abandoned me, my father may well have done so, and then I was taken and I spent two years in that house alone." The tear slid down her cheek and she made no effort to brush it away. "And I'm tired of it. I don't want to be alone anymore. And . . . and I think you're tired of it too. So what I'm saying . . . what I'm trying to say is . . . We don't have to be alone anymore. Neither of us do. Not when we can have each other."

The mountain broke his ribs. Crushed him flat.

She didn't understand. Being alone was the ultimate in control, the ultimate in power. He was master of himself and he answered to no one. Cared for no one. And that was the best part of all because then there was no vulnerability, no helplessness.

He couldn't give that up, especially after what had happened in front of Fitzgerald. Emotions were a weakness he couldn't afford.

Not even for her.

It hurt. But then punishments weren't supposed to be easy.

He made sure none of the agony he told himself he didn't feel showed on his face, kept his voice level. Calm. The Dom in charge. "Yes, you're right. We could have that. But you're missing one thing, angel."

"What thing?"

"I don't want what you want." He said it gently. Clearly. "I've come to terms with being alone. I like it. It's easier. And I'm afraid that's the way it has to be."

Another tear slid down her cheek. "I don't know what's worse. The fact that you're lying to yourself or you're lying to me."

"I'm not lying. It's the truth."

"Zac—"

"This is your seventh punishment, angel. "

She blinked. "What? What do you mean?"

"You had one more, remember?"

"But—"

"Absence, Eva. I get to leave you alone. The way you left me alone."

Her cheeks were wet, the tears in her eyes painting them bright silver. Like mirrors. Reflecting his own agony back at him.

*Unnecessary, you bastard.*

Perhaps. But it was better to be sure she knew there was no hope. Cruel to be kind. One day, she'd understand that.

She looked away, brushing one hand across her face, wiping away her tears. And he had to clench his fists tighter in order to stop from wiping them away himself.

"Okay," she said thickly. "If that's the way you want it. But just remember this, Zac Rutherford." She turned back and took a step toward him, the look on her face suddenly fierce. "I'm not Theresa. I will never leave you. I will never leave because I love you."

The words vibrated in the air as if they had power. Magic.

*I love you.*

He found he couldn't move. She'd turned him to stone. If only he hadn't cared, it wouldn't have hurt . . .

"You should trust me," Eva said quietly. "You should."

He didn't understand. Trust her? With what? And what the hell did that have to do with love? With Theresa?

For one long, intense minute she stared at him and as if she was expecting a response.

But he couldn't speak. There was nothing he could say.

Abruptly Eva turned on her heel and left him standing there.

* * *

Eva approached the door to the usual Second Circle rooms and stopped. It was open a crack and she could see that Gabriel and Honor were already there. They were standing close together in front of the fire—which had been lit. Gabriel was cupping Honor's face in his large hands, looking down at her, an impossibly tender look on his face.

It was obviously a deeply private moment and it rooted Eva to the spot. She couldn't drag her gaze away from them. From the look on Gabriel's face. From the way Honor's fingers had risen to cover his. From the aura of closeness and intimacy that surrounded them.

Something she would never have.

She jerked herself away as Gabriel bent to kiss Honor, turning to lean against the wall beside the door, giving them some space.

Her eyes felt scratchy and sore, her throat thick, chest aching.

Fuck that. She wasn't going to cry. She'd already done so once today and once was enough. Zac had been very clear.

The asshole.

She swallowed, trying to force away the emotion clogging her throat and weighing heavy on her chest.

After she'd left Zac standing in the street, she'd gone back to her apartment and thrown herself into decoding the information she'd downloaded from Fitzgerald's computer. That was certainly easier than thinking about what Zac had said to her, how she'd laid herself bare for him and he'd thrown it back in her face.

Love was still a new concept for her and no, she hadn't seen much evidence of it in her life. But over the past week it had been her friends who'd given her an inkling about what it could mean. Gabriel and Honor. Alex and Katya.

Love was in the way they touched each other. The way they looked at each other. The way they spoke to each other. There was just an extra quality to those interactions she'd never noticed before. A tenderness in their voices and a private, knowing look in the glances they exchanged. As if each of them knew a secret that only the other person knew and were sharing the knowledge together.

It had taken her a long time to figure out that secret for herself. But she knew what it was now. Had realized it for certain the moment Zac had pointed that gun at Fitzgerald.

She'd wondered why she hadn't been afraid when by rights, she should have been terrified. Why in that instant what fear she'd had, had been for him.

The lack of fear for herself was her trust in him, that he would get them out of this no matter what. But the fear for him . . . that was love. As was the sorrow she'd felt when he'd told her about his sister. As was the safety as she'd lain in his arms.

And the pain as he'd told her he didn't want what she wanted. That he had another punishment for her. Absence.

That was love too.

Love was for stupid people, clearly.

He'd said he'd liked being alone, that it was easier. What bullshit. He *was* lying to her and to himself as well. She knew fear, knew it intimately, and that's what she'd seen in his eyes, lurking there so far down he probably didn't even realize it.

Zac was afraid. What had happened with Fitzgerald had scared him. And she didn't know quite what it was that had made him push her away, but she was certain it had something to do with losing his sister in the way he had. Maybe he was afraid that she'd leave him like Theresa. It was why she'd told him to trust her. Because she never would leave him.

Fuck, how weird that in the end, she'd come to understand how much she'd trusted him and yet he was the one who wouldn't trust her.

Eva let out a breath, staring at the wall opposite, blinking back the tears in her eyes that had risen no matter how hard she'd tried to get rid of them.

No, she wasn't going to cry. She may not have Zac, but she wasn't alone these days. She had Alex and Gabriel, and Honor and Katya. She had them, and that was more than enough to be thankful for.

Pulling herself together, Eva turned to the door again, peering through the crack. Mercifully Honor was now sitting on the couch while Gabriel stood in front of the fire, smiling at something she'd said.

Eva pushed open the door and walked in.

Gabriel lifted his head, dark eyes catching hers, and Eva paused a moment.

"I'm sorry, Gabe," she said. "I mean, I'm not sorry for killing him, don't get me wrong. But I am sorry that he was your father."

"So am I." He pushed his hands into his pockets. "And just so we're clear, I'm glad you killed him. Saves me the bother."

A flush of pleasure went through her. A strange and wrong emotion when it involved having killed a man, but that didn't stop her from feeling pleased about it.

Fitzgerald had hurt too many people she cared about for her to feel even the slightest shred of remorse for him.

"Any time." She lifted a shoulder. "And anyone else you need killed, you just let me know."

A smile tugged the end of Gabriel's mouth. "I think you might be the baddest of us all, Eva King."

"Oh come on, I'm pretty badass." Honor had picked up a cracker from the plate on the table, having loaded it up with a piece of soft brie, and now waved it for emphasis.

"I rode on that bike of yours. Followed you into a dark alley at night. Etcetera."

Gabriel grinned. "Sure, baby."

"Hmmm. Why do I get the feeling you're humoring me?"

"You're both wrong," Alex commented as he pushed the door wide, coming into the room. "Katya is the most badass of us."

Katya, following on his heels, rolled her eyes. "Thank you, but computers are my fatal weakness. I think Eva beats me on that front."

"True." Alex reached out, winding a casual arm around Katya's waist and holding her close. "But I don't think Eva could beat me in a fight."

Eva, who'd settled herself in her usual armchair, gave the two of them an incredulous look. "You beat him in a fight?" she asked Katya.

The Russian woman was blushing, which was rather sweet. "I would have. If he hadn't used a couple of dirty tricks."

Alex smiled at her. "Emphasis on the dirty."

Gabriel cleared his throat ostentatiously. "Okay, enough with the romantic bullshit. We need to hear what Eva found on that computer."

"As I recall," Honor murmured, "you were the one who started it, but by all means . . ."

"Well hell," Alex said as he rounded the couch to sit down next to Honor. "People are actually eating my goddamned food. Finally."

Katya came to lean against the arm near where Alex sat, while Gabriel seated himself in the armchair on the other side of the fire from Eva. As he did so, Honor rose, dusting cracker crumbs from her skirt then moved over to his chair, calmly seating herself in his lap like she was sitting on a throne.

Another little barb of anguish slid through Eva, spoiling her enjoyment of the relaxed atmosphere. Probably for the best anyway. It wasn't as if the information she'd discovered was particularly pleasant.

"Where's Zac?" Alex asked, glancing around before looking directly at Eva.

Naturally. Because everyone expected she and Zac to be together. Because they always were. Unfortunately that wouldn't be for much longer.

The barb of anguish settled deeper inside her.

"He'll be here," she said shortly. "But I can start without him."

"You don't have to." Zac's deep voice came as a shock to her system. "I'm here now."

He strode into the room, tall and forbidding in his black suit and charcoal tie. The chiseled lines of his face were impenetrable as rock, the expression in his amber eyes completely opaque. How he usually was in other words.

But Eva could see the tightness in his jaw and the tension in his shoulders. A stiffness in the way he carried himself.

It didn't give her any satisfaction that he was in pain too.

Zac came over to stand behind the couch. He wasn't wearing his overcoat or gloves today, the ink on the backs of his hands dark against his skin. "Go on, angel," he said in his usual calm tone, the look he gave her one of measured interest. Treating her as he normally did and not as if she'd told him she loved him not a few hours earlier.

Not as if they'd shared the deepest parts of themselves the night before.

She looked away from him, determined to be as calm and emotionless as he was. "Okay, well, I spent the afternoon decrypting the info on Fitzgerald's computer. It wasn't easy." At least, it wouldn't have been if she hadn't been so determined not to think about Zac. "Some of the info had various fail-safes embedded in it, which meant quite a few of the files were wiped unfortunately. But I did find evidence that Fitzgerald was building quite the empire." She paused, looking around the room at her friends. "The Lucky Seven was one of a number of different establishments around the world that operated as Fitzgerald's shop front. The drugs and money laundering seem to be a sideline to the main operation. Which is basically people. Women, mainly."

"Fuck," Gabriel muttered. "Dear old Dad."

"I could say the same thing," Alex said, his voice stripped of the sarcastic amusement that had been in it before. "My Dad was one of his fucking cohorts. Not that he was happy about it from what we've been able to figure out."

"Yes, Fitzgerald mentioned Daniel," Zac said without inflection. "He ordered his death."

Honor and Alex shared a glance at that. Katya slipped off the arm of the couch and went around to sit next to her lover, putting one hand on his thigh.

Eva wished she didn't have to see that. Wished she wasn't quite so aware of it.

"I figured as much," Alex said, covering Katya's hand with his own. "I suppose the consolation is that he didn't want to be part of it anymore."

"Neither did Guy," Honor murmured. "He wanted out too."

Eva folded her hands in her lap. But it wasn't like touching someone else for comfort. It really wasn't. "I found quite a few emails and various other files, with names and things. A few financial details, money transfers and receipts. But . . ." She hesitated, glancing at them all. "Fitzgerald was very careful. Even on his private computer, everything was very vague. There's actually nothing concrete to tie him personally to this. Everything I found on his computer could be explained away easily enough I'm afraid."

There was a silence as the others digested this.

"What about your crew, Zac?" Gabriel said at last. "What's the angle on the cleanup they did?"

Zac put his hands on the back of the couch and leaned forward. "They got rid of the henchmen in the lobby. As for the guards upstairs and Fitzgerald himself, they planted enough evidence to point to a professional hit. With any luck the police will start investigating and perhaps they'll turn up the evidence we haven't been able to." He glanced at Eva. "You made certain no one would be able to tell you accessed his computer?"

Eva straightened in her chair. "Of course I did. I'm not an idiot."

"So we can't take this to the CIA?" Alex asked. "Seriously? There was nothing at all we can use to pin anything on him?"

Eva shook her head. "No and believe me, I looked."

Another silence fell.

She didn't look at Zac. His presence felt like a pressure, like someone was squeezing her. Squeezing all the air out of her lungs.

"What about Elijah?" Katya said, glancing up at Zac. "Did you find anything on him?"

"I have some contacts keeping an eye out for him, but, and I may have mentioned to the others, he's not in any databases I have access to, not even on the ones I don't. But it seems he was working for Fitzgerald."

"Not entirely," Eva murmured. "He let me go, remember?"

Zac's golden eyes met hers, the look in them entirely impersonal. "And he was not happy you killed Fitzgerald either. He wanted to do it himself."

"A man out for revenge," Alex said quietly.

"Well, that sounds fucking familiar," Gabriel commented. "He must have been pissed with you, Eva."

Her arm ached at the memory of Elijah's fingers wrapped around her arm, the cold fury in his black eyes as Fitzgerald lay dead on the floor.

*"He was mine, you bitch."*

"Kind of an understatement," she said. "But . . . he saved me."

Honor shifted on Gabriel's lap, frowning in Eva's direction. "What exactly happened up there? How did he save you? I mean, I think we need to work out what his intentions are, don't you think? The problem when a man like Fitzgerald dies is that there's—"

"A power vacuum," Gabriel murmured, interrupting. "And that motherfucker is gonna leave one hell of a power vacuum."

The expression on Zac's face was tight and hard. Cold. "What happened," he said, his mild tone completely at odd with the look on his face, "was that Fitzgerald was using Eva as leverage to get to me. To us. He wanted us off his back and wanted my skills personally. He told me Eva would be the leverage he'd use to get us to back off and me to work for him."

The rest of them were quiet, all staring at Zac.

But Zac only looked at her. There was almost accusation in his eyes, as if it was her fault she'd been used the way Fitzgerald had used her.

She seen him look that way before: when he'd told her about Theresa.

He was a man for whom being in control was everything, and yet nothing he could do had saved his sister. He must have hated that. No wonder he'd been so angry up in Fitzgerald's office. He'd been helpless yet again while the life of yet another woman hung in the balance.

*Let her die. God will find his own.*

She'd hadn't let herself think about what he'd said, because surely he couldn't have meant her. He'd been protecting her for too long for him to think that.

But maybe it hadn't been her. Maybe he'd meant Theresa. Maybe that's who he was angry with. The sister he couldn't save.

Eva's heart clenched tight. "Zac couldn't kill Fitzgerald," she said quietly.

"I was going to—"

"No, you weren't," she cut him off, meeting his cold, golden stare. Willing him to believe it. "You wouldn't have done it. You would have lowered your gun and we both would have suffered in the end. But Elijah let me go and I still don't know why. All I know is that it was enough for me to grab your gun and kill Fitzgerald. So that's it. That's what happened."

The others were silent, watching the pair of them. And what they thought she had no idea, but she didn't want to do this anymore. Didn't want any more secrets. Didn't want "don't ask, don't tell."

She was tired of being alone. Of being isolated. Of holding herself at a distance.

Zac didn't want her, but there were the others. The only family she'd ever had.

She slipped off the chair, standing in front of the fire, pulling off her beanie and letting it drop on the floor. Her hair fell down around her shoulders, her hands falling loose at her sides. Open, without her usual defenses.

"I killed Fitzgerald because he took me from the streets when I was sixteen. Held me for two years as his personal sexual slave. Because he raped Gabriel's mother. Because he hurt Honor's stepfather. Because he had Alex's father murdered." She took a breath. "Because he hurt Zac. And it was my turn to protect him."

The silence deepened.

She didn't look at anyone else. She looked across the room at the still figure of the man she loved. A man carved from stone. The only sign of life, the golden flames in his eyes.

A man who'd always been alone.

And it struck her then, a realization she knew down deep in her bones.

He'd been at her side for seven years. He'd pulled her out of hell and stopped her from returning to it.

It wasn't only her turn to protect him. It was her turn to show him he wasn't alone.

It was her turn to show him he could trust her.

"Zac, I was going to tell you to go," Eva said, her voice only a little unsteady. "That I've paid your price. Taken your punishment. That I won't hold you here anymore. That you're free." She braced herself, looked into those cold amber eyes. "But I'm not going to. Because the fact is you'll never be free of me. No matter where you go, no matter how far you run, I'll always be there. I love you and I'm not letting you go. Not ever."

Everyone was looking at him, shock on their faces, and yet he was barely conscious of them. Barely conscious of the room around him. All his attention focused on the woman standing in front of the fire.

His whole world had taken on the shape of her. White hair and gray eyes. Slight, fragile curves. Pale skin. Delicate as an alabaster vase, yet with a backbone of pure titanium.

He felt brittle in comparison. A hollowed-out façade of a man. All he was, eaten away by the fire inside him, the anger he couldn't get rid of. The memory of a sister he couldn't let go.

He'd been strong coming in here. Resolute in his intentions. He'd listen to what she had to say, then he'd let them know, one by one, that he was leaving New York. And never coming back.

He'd expected her to set him free. He'd never expected her to fight.

She was all he'd thought about for so many years, been close to her for so long, and yet it was only now, right this single, incandescent instant, that he truly saw.

Standing in front of the fire, the flames behind her, she looked . . . strong. Resolute. And not the brittle, breakable kind of strength that came from denial, but the true lasting kind that came from acceptance.

She was a warrior. She always had been.

*And now she's fighting for you.*

Something inside him expanded like the sudden gasp of a long-denied breath.

The silence was complete and yet still he didn't move. Didn't look away from her.

*You should trust me,* she'd told him. *I'm not Theresa.*

Only now did he understand what she'd meant. He had to trust her not to leave him. Trust her not to destroy him.

*I'm not letting you go. Not ever.*

Theresa had never fought for him. She'd turned her head to the wall and died.

"No," he said in a voice that didn't sound like his. "No. No. No."

Shock fell across the room.

Eva's mouth opened, pain flashing in her eyes.

"No," Zac repeated, in case they hadn't heard it the first four times. "Fucking no."

He shoved himself away from the couch, his footing unsteady. He was shaking.

Eva stood there, staring at him. Her chin coming up. Resolute.

"*No!*" he roared.

And then he was rounding the couch, heedless of everyone else in the room. Kicking aside the coffee table with all the food on it, everything smashing on the ground.

He didn't care. There was only one thing in the world that mattered. Only one thing that would ever matter.

"Zac?" someone demanded. "What the fuck are you doing?"

"Hey—" someone else said.

"Everyone get out!" Eva shouted, her face white.

Zac didn't bother to see if they obeyed because by then he'd reached her and she was in his arms, where she'd always belonged. Where she'd always been meant to be.

Her hands pushed against his chest. "Zac, wait—"

But he didn't wait. He cupped her face in his hands, cutting her words with his mouth. Kissing her as if all the air in the world was contained in her. As if she were his one hope of survival.

She was still for a moment, but he didn't stop. Gently coaxing her mouth to open, stroking the fragile bones of her jaw with his thumbs, letting her taste his desperation. His need.

Eva shivered and then she melted, her lips parting under his, the delicate touch of her tongue. Nothing then but sweetness and heat. Everything he'd ever wanted right here in his hands.

He kissed her because he couldn't speak. Because he didn't have the words to tell her all he felt. So he just kept on kissing her until language returned to him. Until he could breathe again.

It could have been years but probably was only minutes when he at last lifted his head. Because no matter how much he wanted to keep on kissing her, he knew he'd have to speak eventually.

Her face was flushed, her eyes dark. She leaned against him, her hands pressed flat to his chest as if she wanted to dig her nails into him and pull him even closer. A fierce light burned in her eyes. "Is this a case of no meaning yes?" Her voice was thick, a thread of her usual snark in the words.

"No, you shouldn't want to stay." His own voice didn't sound much better. "No, I don't want you to set me free. No, you can't leave me."

She was breathing fast now. Challenge flickered in the tarnished silver of her eyes. "I thought you'd come to terms with being alone. At least that's what you said."

"Turns out I was wrong," he said hoarsely. "Turns out I was wrong about a lot of things. I was wrong to push you away. I was wrong not to trust you. " He stared down into her beautiful face. "I was wrong to pretend I didn't love you."

Eva blinked. "I don't understand. You said—"

"I know what I said. I'm a liar. A fucking coward. I've been so angry with Theresa for so many years. Angry at her for not fighting for me. For leaving me. She was all I had, the only family left. And she wouldn't stay. She destroyed herself. She left me alone and I've never, ever forgiven her for that." He tightened his arms around Eva, staring fiercely at her. "I didn't want anyone to make me hurt like that again. I didn't want anyone to have that power over me. But I'm willing to let you have it. I trust you, angel, I do."

She stared at him, searching his face for what, he didn't know. It made him suddenly conscious of the silence behind him. But if the others were there, he didn't care. The only person of any significance was right here in front of him.

"You're an idiot, you know," Eva said huskily. "Yes, love can make you hurt. But it can make you strong too. You think I would have been able to stand up to Fitzgerald without you? Why do you think I wasn't afraid? Because I loved you. Because you made me strong, Zac."

She was warm in his arms, her body melting into his. And yet the core of her was pure titanium. How had he ever thought her fragile? "You'll have to teach me how it works, angel. I don't have any practice with love."

Eva's hand slid up his chest, curving up to his shoulder then further up to his jaw, stroking lightly. "Of course you do. You loved your sister. You just need to look past your anger and remember that."

How did she know that? How could she see so clearly? "I don't know if I can. All my memories of her are . . . angry ones."

She caressed his jawline, sending a tendril of fire through him. "It might take time, but you'll remember. It'll still be there. Some things are like that. I mean, it took me a long time to see who you were and figure out what you meant to me. Seven years to be exact."

Zac turned his head, brushing his mouth against her stroking finger. "I knew from the minute I saw you waiting for me under that streetlight."

"Knew what?"

"That you were mine. It just took me a long time to admit it to myself." There was a burning in his heart but it wasn't anger this time. It was almost painful and yet there was a sweetness to it. The very best kind of pain. "I'm sorry, I said those things in the street to you. I'm sorry I hurt you. I just . . . I've been angry so long and this is so new. I'm not sure how to do it."

And finally, finally, her mouth curved. A smile that had been a long time in coming. "You're doing pretty well so far. How about you just keep going? I mean, practice makes perfect, right?"

The pain and pleasure deepened in his heart. He turned his head to check the room—it was empty. The others must have gone and left them to it. Good fucking choice.

He turned back to her and before she could say anything,

he gathered her up in his arms and carried her over the mess on the floor to the couch, laying her down on it.

"If you go in there, I will personally hurt you." Katya put a hand on Alex's chest. "And you know I can, Alexei."

Alex glared at her then at the closed door of their club-rooms at her back. "You've met Zac. He's a mean fucker. If he hurts her, I'll—"

"I don't think he wants to hurt her," Katya said calmly. "Do you?"

Gabriel, dragged out by Honor and who was still holding onto his arm, was scowling at the door too. "Katya, I respect you, you know that. But I don't think you know what the fuck you're talking about. Eva is vulnerable and—"

"Actually," Katya cut across him coolly, "Eva is stronger than Zac. Stronger than either of you two as well. I know a soldier when I see one, Gabriel. Eva King is a soldier and she's more than a match for Zac."

Honor said nothing, but Katya saw the other woman smile then roll her eyes in Gabriel's direction.

Alex was shaking his head. "No. That bastard needs—"

Calmly Katya reached into her jacket and pulled out her Springfield. "Take a step toward that door and I'll shoot you myself."

Alex's eyes widened. "You wouldn't."

"Try me."

"Fuck's sake," Gabriel said with some disgust. "We're just looking out for Eva, okay?"

Honor slid an arm around Gabriel's waist. "Katya's right, Gabe. Eva can look out for herself. In fact . . ." She smiled. "I'll lay money on the fact that Zac is on his knees right at this very moment."

"A thousand bucks and you have a bet," Alex said instantly, then raised an eyebrow at Katya. "Though maybe

Zac'll have her on *her* knees. I've heard some things about him that'll—"

"Right. That does it," Gabriel interrupted. "Half an hour, then we're going in."

From behind the door, came the sound of a gasp. It didn't sound like pain.

Satisfied, Katya stared at the two men and raised a brow. "Are you sure about that?"

Gabriel glanced at Alex. "Maybe we could leave it a bit longer."

"An hour," Alex agreed. "At least." He paused, then frowned. "They'd better not be getting any wine on my fucking rug."

She reached up and pulled him down onto the couch with her, opening her mouth beneath his, kissing him hot and demanding. This time there were no punishments or consequences or orders. Only the frantic need to get rid of the barriers between them, warm skin against warm skin, mouth to mouth, hands reaching, touching, caressing.

There was a minor frustration when both of them realized neither one of them had any protection, but then Zac remembered where they were and that Alex, always the gracious host, usually had a stash of condoms somewhere. Finding some in the drawer in one of the side tables, he brought it back to the couch and let her roll it on him.

Then he lay back and lifted her, sliding her down onto him, sheathing himself in the slick, wet heat of her body.

Fuck, she felt so good. The rightness of it made him want to be still, savor the feeling of connection with her.

Her fingers moved over his chest and he let them, craving the touch. Then they paused over the angel he'd had tattooed over his heart, the one he'd gotten the night he'd first met her.

"An angel," she said softly, tracing the outline of the figure.

He reached up and covered her hand, pressing her palm against the tattoo, feeling the heat of it brand him.

She met his gaze, her eyes as bright as stars. "Is . . . that me?"

"Yes."

"I have a sword."

He smiled. "How else are you supposed to protect me?"

"Zac . . ."

He reached up, slid his hand through her hair, cupping the back of her head, drawing her head down for a kiss. "Not now," he murmured against her mouth. "Tell me you love me again. I want to hear it."

"I love you," she whispered. "I love you so much."

"Show me."

And this time when the dragon began to rise, he let it. Because this time the dragon was love.

# EPILOGUE

Violet Fitzgerald hated the subway, but she took it precisely because she knew how much it annoyed both her parents. They seemed to think that a Fitzgerald should be above riding in such common things as buses and subway cars. Even taxis were, to some extent, verboten.

Which meant Violet took great pleasure in riding *only* the subway. In New York's traffic, it was silly not to anyway.

Across the subway car from her, a man sat slumped against the windows. He looked drunk and was muttering under his breath. Several people had already given him a wide berth, and Violet was debating the merits of changing carriages at the next stop.

There were too many weirdoes; that was the problem.

The subway rattled around a corner and the lights flickered, the darkness on the outside pressing in.

Not long now.

The train began to slow and Violet got to her feet, moving to the doors, her heart thumping, impatient to get off.

She'd spent all day in a café, painstakingly doing the usual internet searches, trying to find something, anything, that could shed light on her brother's death. Sixteen years since he'd supposedly died and she'd discovered nothing.

Until she'd gotten that call today.

God, she couldn't wait to get off. She needed to discuss this with Honor.

Footsteps shuffled behind her as other people began to get to their feet in preparation for their stop.

Something hard pressed up against her side, making her stiffen in shock.

"If you scream, I'll kill you," a dark, deep male voice said in her ear.

Ice ran down her spine, the marrow in her bones freezing solid. She turned her head.

Cold black eyes. Scarred face.

He smiled. "You don't want to die, do you, Violet?"

Read on for an excerpt from the next book by
JACKIE ASHENDEN

# KIDNAPPED BY THE BILLIONAIRE

Coming soon from St. Martin's Paperbacks

Elijah waited by the store counter, his hands in the pockets of his leather bike jacket. One hand curling around his gun, because shit, he had to hold onto something that reminded him of his goddamn purpose. Especially when he was also trying to quell the intense hard-on in his jeans.

He couldn't get the sight of Violet out of his head. The way she'd pulled off his shirt and dropped it on the ground, then staring at him, her eyes full of challenge as she'd stood there completely naked.

Of course he'd known what he was in for when he'd joined her in the fitting room. And he'd known she wouldn't be happy about it. But he hadn't wanted to leave her there by herself, because who knew what she'd manage to get up to if he couldn't keep an eye on her? He couldn't afford any surprises like the one she'd sprung on him in the bathtub the day before.

He'd thought he could handle her. He'd thought he had himself under control enough that her taking off her clothes wouldn't affect him in the slightest.

But he'd been wrong.

She'd walked towards him, her body smooth and golden and lushly curved, and he'd felt the weight of every single day of the past seven years of abstinence pressing down on him. Crushing him. Those small, high breasts he'd touched, stroked. The graceful indent of her waist and the swell of her hips. The soft thatch of golden curls between her thighs.

He'd gotten hard, so hard, almost instantly. And then she'd walked towards him, all determination, showing him she wasn't afraid, getting right up close. He'd seen the triumph in those beautiful turquoise eyes of hers, had known he hadn't hidden his desire from her as well as he'd thought.

So he'd had to assert himself somehow, show her he was still in control.

*That didn't work out so well, did it?*

He could feel the heat of her skin against his palm even now. Smell the scent of her body, musk and sandalwood. He'd frightened her, and yet it hadn't only been fear in her eyes; there had been heat there too.

All he'd been able to think about then was the way she'd been in his lap the day before, the way she'd arched into his hand, wanting more. A little cat wanting to be stroked.

Fuck, he'd wanted her. And that had made him so goddamned angry, because he knew that she was also playing him. That she was using the strange chemistry between them to get to him, probably using sex to change his mind about giving her to Jericho.

*You should have just taken her.*

His fingers curled on the gun, the metal warming beneath his palm. The fucking sales assistant was still talking on the phone, oblivious.

Perhaps he should have. He could have lifted her up against the door of the fitting room and unzipped his jeans, let her sink down on his cock, holding her there while he emptied himself of this ridiculous craving.

*"I wouldn't mind . . ."*

Christ, that husky voice, the spark of pure blue in her eyes as she'd stared at him. . . . She'd wanted him too. But he'd known in that instant he couldn't do it. It was hard enough managing his own hunger let alone hers, and bringing them together would be madness.

It would negate the whole of the last seven years.

Movement near the fitting rooms caught his attention and he turned to see Violet coming towards him, holding the empty hangers in her hands.

She wore a pair of tight fitting black leather pants, a silky looking green top, and a black leather bike jacket. It was such a change from her normal hippy looking outfits that he couldn't help staring at her. Gone was the free-spirit in the chiming jewelry and brightly colored silk skirts. In her place was a tough biker chick with a guarded, wary expression.

He wasn't sure if that was an improvement or not.

Stopping by the counter, she handed him the hangers and the tags she'd obviously removed from the clothes. "Here. You'll need these."

He took them from her and pulled out his wallet, adding up the prices then extracting some cash and dumping it on the counter. The sales assistant clearly had the phone attached to her ear because she didn't stop talking, but he wasn't waiting. He didn't need the change anyway.

Grabbing Violet's arm again, he tucked her in close as they headed out of the store.

The walk back to the apartment was far more tense this time and she made no effort to talk to him, which he appreciated. It was hard enough trying to keep his mind on what he was supposed to be doing and not on the way the smell of the leather of her jacket combined with her scent to make something new and utterly sensual.

Fuck, this was ridiculous. With any luck Jericho would

be getting in contact real soon and then she wouldn't be his problem anymore.

They came to a stop by a street crossing, waiting for the signal. His building was just up ahead and he was running over in his head his plans for when Jericho got in contact, where he was going to get the man to meet him and how that was all going to play out.

Then Violet suddenly jerked away from him.

Because he was a little distracted, his reaction wasn't quite what it should have been, his fingers closing around her arm just a fraction too late.

He cursed viciously, but she was already running, flinging herself across the street heedless of the traffic, ignoring the sounds of car horns as she dodged them. And for a second he found himself watching in amazement, because shit, the gall of the woman. She just never gave up, did she?

Then he was running himself, plunging into the crowded mass of vehicles after her. Tires squealed, more horns sounding, the shouts of drivers echoing as he slid over the hood of one car then dodged a motorcycle. He ignored all of them, his attention fixed on a small figure in black running for her life down the sidewalk.

She hadn't a chance of course. He was stronger and faster, and although fear must have given her wings, his anger was rocket fuel. She was his only chance to get to Jericho and he was not letting her get away.

The distance between them decreased by the second and when she turned her head to look behind her, it decreased even more as she slowed. She whipped her head back around and tried to put on a burst of speed, but even that wasn't going to save her.

He wasn't even near to being winded.

There weren't a lot of people around, but even so he had to catch her and catch her quickly in case someone decided to take action and call the cops. Which would be the last fucking thing he needed.

He ran faster, closing the distance.

Violet was heading towards a group of people standing on the sidewalk up ahead and chatting, but she must have realized she wasn't going to reach them in time, because she suddenly changed direction, darting down what must have been an alley way between two buildings.

Bad idea.

He reached the alley seconds later, racing after the dark figure in black fleeing down it.

Catching her at the halfway point, Elijah reached out and grabbed her, hauling her around then pushing her up against the rough brick of one of the buildings bordering the alley.

She struggled at first, pushing against him, and then, when he didn't move, she went still, lifting her chin and staring up at him. She was panting, her skin flushed pink with exertion, her blue-green eyes glittering. Fear flickered there, unmistakable. Yet not as much as he'd thought. In fact, she looked more angry than anything else.

Christ. This woman.

"What the fuck was that?" He put a hand on her shoulder and pinned her against the wall. "You do that again and I'll make you wish you'd never been born."

She stared at him, the fear disappearing, replaced by a kind of determined defiance. Then, shockingly, her mouth curved and she gave a breathless laugh. "Oh, come on. I had to try, right?"

And for some reason he couldn't possibly fathom, her laughter made a surge of intense rage go through him. He was sick of her bravado. Sick of her defiance. This determination to push him, test him. This complete refusal to be cowed.

She had to stop. She had to learn he was something to be feared. Not some weak little fuck in a suit that could be manipulated into doing whatever she wanted.

She wanted to push him? Consider him pushed.

"You think this is a game?" He leaned in, so close they were almost nose to nose. "Well, do you, Violet? You think that when I catch you, it's your turn to chase me?"

Her smile became twisted and he could see the rage begin to flicker again in the turquoise depths of her eyes. Rage and fear, they always went hand in hand. So she was scared and she hated it, and she didn't want him to see it. Well, fuck, he could work with that.

"Of course this is a game," she said, a sneer in her voice. "It's called outwit the big, dumb criminal." Her breath was coming in rushing bursts, he could hear it despite the noise of the traffic coming from the street. "Am I winning yet?"

"No." He stepped closer, forcing her harder against the wall with his body, physically intimidating her. "You don't get to win. You don't get to do anything but shut the fuck up and do as you're told."

Even now, even when he was looming over her and his anger had to be scaring her, she had that little chin of hers lifted. And there was something other than anger gleaming in her eyes. A spark of . . . Jesus. Was that excitement?

"Or what?" Violet demanded. "You keep telling me about all this stuff you're going to do—"

He reached out with his other hand, took her jaw in a hard grip, cutting off the stream of words. "I keep telling you that you should be afraid," he said, coating each word with ice. "But you don't listen. Perhaps you'll listen now."

Her eyes had gone wide and for some reason her gaze had dropped to his mouth. And unwanted physical awareness began to seep through him. Of how soft her skin felt against his fingers and how red her lips were. How she'd trembled when he'd put a hand to her throat back in the store . . . She'd wanted him. Except she had no idea what she was asking for.

*So? Show her. Scare the shit out of her.*

Elijah tightened his grip on her jaw just a little, tilting her head back.

Then he covered her mouth with his.